USA TODAY bestsell[...] he loved books and writ[...]ld. But it took multiple re[...]re she sold her first three[...]nd second grade for a number of years, Janice turned in her lesson plan book and began writing full-time. Since then she has sold over thirty-five books and novellas. Janice lives in east Tennessee with her husband, Charles. They love hiking, traveling and spending time with family.

Hearing from readers is one of the best perks of the job!

You can connect with Janice at twitter.com/janicemaynard, facebook.com/janicemaynardreaderpage, wattpad.com/user/janicemaynard, and instagram.com/janicemaynard.

A typical Piscean, *USA TODAY* bestselling author **Yvonne Lindsay** has always preferred her imagination to the real world. Married to her blind date hero and with two adult children, she spends her days crafting the stories of her heart, and in her spare time she can be found with her nose in a book reliving the power of love, or knitting socks and daydreaming. Contact her via her website www.yvonnelindsay.com.

Cat Schield has been reading and writing romance since high school. Although she graduated from college with a BA in business, her idea of a perfect career was writing books for Mills & Boon. And now, after winning the Romance Writers of America 2010 Golden Heart® Award for series contemporary romance, that dream has come true. Cat lives in Minnesota with her daughter, Emily and their Burmese cat. When she's not writing sexy, romantic stories for Mills & Boon Desire, she can be found sailing with friends on the St. Croix River, or in more exotic locales, like the Caribbean and Europe. She loves to hear from readers. Find her at www.catschield.com. Follow her on Twitter @catschield.

Lies and Lullabies

JANICE MAYNARD
YVONNE LINDSAY
CAT SCHIELD

MILLS & BOON

First Published in Great Britain 2019
by Mills & Boon, an imprint of HarperCollins*Publishers*
1 London Bridge Street, London, SE1 9GF

LIES AND LULLABIES © 2019 Harlequin Books S. A.

Courting the Cowboy Boss © 2015 Harlequin Books S.A.
Lone Star Holiday Proposal © 2015 Harlequin Books
Nanny Makes Three © 2016 Harlequin Books

Special thanks and acknowledgement are given to Janice Maynard, Yvonne Lindsay and Cat Schield for their contribution to the Texas Cattleman's Club: Lullabies and Lies series.

ISBN: 978-0-263-27477-6

0219

MIX
Paper from
responsible sources
FSC www.fsc.org   FSC™ C007454

Printed and bound in Spain
by CPI, Barcelona

COURTING THE
COWBOY BOSS

JANICE MAYNARD

For Jamie and Daniel,
who have made Texas their home…
we miss you in Tennessee!

One

"To our new president!"

Three of the four men at the table lifted their glasses in a semicongratulatory toast. Case Baxter, the object of their wry tribute, shook his head and grinned. "Thanks, guys. You're all heart."

Mac McCallum finished off the last bite of his Angus burger and wiped his mouth with a linen napkin. "Seriously, man. What were you thinking? You're like all the rest of us…up to your ears in work. Adding president of the Texas Cattleman's Club to your résumé means more headaches."

Mac was CEO of McCallum Energy…and understood as much as anybody that success was a double-edged sword. Even so, with his big laugh and extrovert ways, he always seemed laid-back and easygoing.

Though the formal dining room at the Texas Cattleman's Club was an elegant venue, the majority of the diners were men like Mac and Case. Tough, honed by physical labor, perpetually tanned by the hot Texas sun. And wealthy... wealthy enough to think they had the world on a string.

Case shrugged. "I know what you're saying. And you're right. But when the committee asked to put my name on the ballot, I could hear my great-grandfather cheering from the grave. It's an honor. And a privilege."

His companions hooted with laughter. Jeff Hartley wiped his eyes. "Of course it is. No denying that. But unless you have some magic formula for adding an extra eight or ten hours to every day, I'm not exactly sure how you're going to manage." Jeff owned and operated the Hartley Cattle Ranch. He knew more than a little about hard work and long days.

Case had an ominous feeling in his gut that said his buddies were right. The truth was, though, Case's family had lived in Royal for generations. They believed in tradition, honor and service. He hadn't been able to bring himself to say no to the nomination. Then again, he hadn't expected to be elected. The other two candidates were older and, as far as Case was concerned, more suited for the position.

But now it was too late for second thoughts. "I'm counting on the three of you to be my unofficial advisors."

Parker Reese leaned back in his chair. "Don't look at me. I'm a doctor, not a rancher. I can get your baby through colic, but all I know about cattle is not to wave a red flag in front of a bull."

In the general laughter that followed, Case spared a moment to marvel at how things had changed. Not long ago, women had finally been admitted into the hallowed halls of the club as full members.

Times, they were a-changin'...

Case looked at Mac with a lifted brow. "I thought Logan was joining us for lunch." Logan Wade was Mac's best friend and one of his key investors.

"He bought three new horses last week," Mac said, "and they're being delivered today. You know how he is."

They all nodded. Horses and women. Logan's two favorite things.

Mac pinned Case with a knowing gaze. "Quit changing the subject. We were talking about you and your soon-to-be-impossible schedule."

"Gil Addison has a son and a wife," Case pointed out. "And he's been a great president. I'm blissfully single."

"True," Mac said. "You're forgetting, however, that Gil is Superman. No offense, buddy, but those are big shoes to fill."

"Your support is duly noted."

Parker, arguably the smartest man in the room, added his two cents' worth. "You've always liked a challenge, Case. Don't let them mess with your head. You've got this."

"Thanks." Case had enormous respect for the dedicated though reserved neonatal specialist. Royal's hospital was lucky to have a doctor of Parker's caliber on staff.

Jeff chimed in, mischief written all over his face. "Parker has more faith in you than I do. I've been in your house, Case. It's such a mess you can't even find the TV remote half the time. I'd suggest burning your place to the ground if we weren't in the middle of a drought."

Case's neck heated. Organization was not his strong suit. Another fact that called his ability to perform his newly acquired duties into question.

"I've already thought about that," he said. "And I have a plan."

Mac gave their waitress a smile as she brought their desserts. "Do tell."

Case stuck a fork in his apple cobbler. "I'm going to hire a housekeeper."

The other three men stared at him.

Mac lifted his spoonful of ice cream and waved it in

the air. "You do know she would have to come inside your house for that to work?"

"Very funny." Case squared his shoulders. "I have the Texas Cattleman's Club to run now. I have to make compromises."

Jeff still seemed shocked. "But what about your rule number one? *Never allow a female into the man cave.*"

"Unless she's a relative." Parker supplied the exception. "Is this new housekeeper a relative?"

Case deserved the inquisition. He was known for his only-half-joking rules for dealing with the female sex. When he was involved in intimate relationships, he preferred to spend the night at the woman's home. So he could leave when he wanted to. "I made the rules," he said, his chin thrust out. "And I can change them. This woman will be a stranger…an employee. She won't be a relative, but she might as well be. I'm not hiring a woman—I'm hiring a housekeeper."

He gave them a warning scowl. "I've learned from my mistakes, believe me." The men at the table knew the unsavory details of Case's not-so-happy marriage. He'd had a fling with his family's accountant, married her and soon found out she was more interested in spending Case's money than in being a loving wife. It was a salutary lesson.

Jeff turned down a second beer but took a long swig of his water. "Hey, man. A guy's gotta do what a guy's gotta do. And besides, up until the tornado last year, this club-president gig wasn't all that onerous. You'll be fine."

Everyone nodded, but Case saw his own reservations reflected on their faces. Ever since the F4 tornado that had decimated Maverick County and the town of Royal barely over a year ago, the Texas Cattleman's Club had become one of the anchors that held things together.

Coordinating rescue efforts, keeping up morale, apply-

ing for grants, planning reconstruction and renovation—
the club and its president had served the people of Royal
well. Life was mostly back to normal, but there was still
work to be done. So Case couldn't kid himself into thinking that his new job title was ceremonial only.

Jeff interrupted the momentary silence. "If we're finished raking Case over the coals, I have a serious subject to
bring up. Shouldn't we be worried about all the ranches and
other parcels of land that have been sold in Royal lately?
And almost all of it to a single buyer? Does anybody but
me think it's a little odd?"

Mac shrugged. "I'm not really concerned. A number of
people were demoralized by the storm or too strapped for
cash to rebuild. It sounds like they're getting good offers
and the chance to start over somewhere else."

Parker's brow furrowed. "I hadn't heard about this."

Case nodded. "Nolan Dane is back in town and is rep-
resenting a company called Samson Oil in these acquisitions. It doesn't make sense to me, though. Why would
an oil company be interested in the land? The tracts he's
buying up were checked for oil decades ago." Nolan was
raised in Royal, but had been gone for a long time.

"Maybe they're planning to use some of the newer technology and hoping to get lucky," Mac said.

Jeff shook his head. "Nolan seems like a decent guy, but
I'm not a big fan of lawyers, particularly when someone
else is hiding behind that lawyer's legal speak."

"We should give him the benefit of the doubt," Parker
said. "At least as long as the people selling are getting a
fair shake. It seems to me that Case will be in a perfect
position to keep tabs on this kind of thing."

Case glanced at his watch. "Speaking of my upcoming
lifestyle change, I have an appointment in forty-five minutes to interview my new domestic assistant."

"Is that the politically correct term these days?" Jeff seemed dubious.

Parker scrawled his name on the check, charging it to his club account as was their custom. "I think Case is trying to convince himself that a woman won't ruin his carefully preserved chaos."

Mac nodded, his grin broad. "I never met a woman yet who didn't want to domesticate a man. No matter how old she is."

Case lifted an eyebrow. "I am the newly elected president of a venerable organization whose members have run this town for over a century. I think I can handle a housekeeper." He stood, and his friends followed suit.

Mac shook his hand. "You can count on me in the days ahead, sir."

Case grinned. "Bite me."

Parker saluted. "Happy to serve under your command."

Jeff bowed. "*Mi casa es su casa* if you need a place to hide out."

"Everybody's a comedian." As Case said his goodbyes and headed out to the parking lot, he reminded himself what a lucky man he was. He had a ranch and land he loved, a wide circle of friends, and now the respect and a nod of confidence from his peers who had voted for him.

If he could iron out this housekeeper thing, no pun intended, his life would be under control.

Mellie Winslow took in the sights as she made her way down the long driveway leading to the B Hive Ranch. Case Baxter's fields and fences were immaculate, several varieties of placid cattle grazing peacefully as far as the eye could see. She envied him the order and success of his thriving operation.

Though her own small business, the Keep N Clean, was

doing well, it couldn't compare to the prosperity of this massive endeavor. Case must be an extraordinarily busy man—hence his request for a housekeeper.

Mellie knew that a good word from Case Baxter could be a boon to her business. What she didn't know was whether or not Case would accept her proposition.

When at last she pulled up in front of the charming ranch house that had housed generations of Baxter men and their families, she noticed something odd. Apparently, Case's cattle received more attention than did his aging home.

It would be an exaggeration to say the place looked run-down. That wasn't it at all. But the two-story white ranch house with blue shutters seemed tired. Although the wraparound porch was large and appealing, no flowers were planted at its base. No colorful cushions bedecked the porch swing. No toddler bicycles or teen sports equipment lay scattered about the yard.

Although the B Hive Ranch had been in the family for decades, everyone in Royal knew that Case's parents had both died young, and Case was an only child. It would be sad to see the place end up in other hands if Case had no heirs.

It was a possibility, though. Case was in his midthirties and apart from—or perhaps because of—his youthful marriage, which had ended badly, he showed no signs of settling down.

Taking a deep breath to steady her nerves, Mellie reminded herself that this was not her first rodeo. Keep N Clean had just celebrated its eighth anniversary. Mellie herself was a seasoned businesswoman. There was no need to feel intimidated by the power and stature of Case Baxter.

She didn't know him well. Really only in passing.

Hopefully, that was about to change.

Along with her stylish tote that served as purse and catchall, she picked up a navy-and-lime-green folder that she now handed out to all prospective clients. Though the expense of producing the upscale advertising materials had been wince-worthy, she hoped the professional presentation would take her expanding company to the next level.

For some reason, she'd expected someone other than the owner to answer her knock. But only seconds passed before the tall blue-eyed man with dark brown hair opened the door and swung it wide.

He greeted her with a polite smile. "I'm Case Baxter. I'm assuming you're here for the interview?" He filled the doorway, lean and long and wildly handsome.

Mellie shook his hand, feeling his large, warm fingers momentarily squeeze hers. *Wow.* His photograph in the newspaper didn't do him justice. His short hair was neatly cut, though an unshaven chin gave him a rakish air. His clasp was not a second too long. Nothing out of the ordinary.

But her heart beat faster.

He was the perfect specimen of a Texas male. He wore faded jeans that molded to his body in interesting ways… scuffed hand-tooled cowboy boots, a cotton shirt with the sleeves rolled up and an expensive watch that looked as if it could pick up cable channels on Mars.

She found her voice at last. "I'm Mellie Winslow. I own Keep N Clean."

Case frowned slightly. He didn't invite her in. "I thought I was interviewing a prospective housekeeper."

"Well, you are," she said, squirming inwardly. "The truth is, Mr. Baxter, I've been expanding my business. Things are going very well. But when you called asking for help, I decided I wanted to take this job myself."

"Why?"

It was a valid question. She decided that honesty was the way to go. "May I come in so we can talk about it?"

"I supposed so." He led her into the adjoining dining room, where a large formal table groaned beneath the weight of stacks of mail. In the few places not covered by papers, a layer of dust coated the wood.

"Have a seat," he said. "As you can see, I didn't exaggerate my need for assistance."

Mellie sat down, and when he did the same, she slid a Keep N Clean folder across the table. "My rates and services are all listed here. The reason I'd like to do this job myself, Mr. Baxter, is because all of my current staff have taken on as much as they can handle. But I don't want to turn you away. Having the newly elected president of the Texas Cattleman's Club as a client would be invaluable advertising."

"Always assuming you're as good as you say..." He opened the folder and scanned testimonials she'd included from satisfied clients.

Mellie frowned. "I'm a hard worker. I'm meticulous. Also, I don't need anyone to hold my hand every moment. Once you tell me what you require and give me detailed instructions about what I should and should not muck with in your home, I'll be invisible."

Case leaned back in his chair, folded his arms across his chest and stared at her.

She refused to fidget. If this silent showdown was part of his interview strategy, she would pass muster or die trying.

At last he shrugged. "Your rates seem fair. But how do you propose to run your business and at the same time keep my house in order?"

"How do you propose to run *your* business and still keep the TCC in order?"

Sarcasm was one of her failings. Having a smart mouth was not the way to win over prospective clients. Fortunately for her, Case Baxter laughed.

His eyes went from glacial blue to sunshiny skies when he was amused. "Touché." He tapped the fingers of one hand on the table, the small restless gesture indicating some level of dissatisfaction or concern.

Mellie leaned forward, giving him her best reassuring smile. "Have you used another service that wasn't up to par? We could talk about where they fell short."

"No." His jaw tensed for a moment as if some distasteful memory had unsettled him. "I don't tolerate strangers in my home very well. I like my privacy."

"That's understandable. If you prefer, we can arrange for me to clean when you're gone. Or maybe that's the idea you don't like. I could make sure to work while you're here. Whatever it takes, Mr. Baxter. How about a month's trial run? At the end of that time, if you're unhappy with the quality of my work, or if having someone come in to clean bothers you too much, I'll cancel the contract with no penalty."

"I can see why your business is doing well. It's hard to say no to you."

Mellie saw a definite twinkle in his eyes. She flushed. "I'm ambitious. But I think a man like you understands that. You won't regret having me here, Mr. Baxter, I promise. In fact, I swear you'll wonder why you didn't hire Keep N Clean a lot sooner."

"Perhaps I should be absolutely clear. It's more than cleaning. If you come to work for me, I'll want you to take a shot at organizing my home life."

His request wasn't out of the ordinary. Structuring a client's daily environment to maximize family time and personal efficiency was something Mellie enjoyed. But it was hard to imagine Case Baxter allowing anyone, much less Mellie, access to something so personal.

When she hesitated, his eyes narrowed. "Is that a problem?"

"No. Not at all. But you mentioned protecting your privacy, so I would want to be perfectly clear about boundaries."

"Such as?"

She floundered mentally, oddly put off her game by a conversation that shouldn't have seemed the slightest bit provocative and yet drew her thoughts to sex-tossed sheets and whether Case Baxter favored boxers or briefs.

"There are many levels of organization, Mr. Baxter. Everything from creating a well-aligned sock drawer to alphabetizing kitchen spices."

He chuckled, ratcheting up his masculine appeal at least a hundredfold. "I'm sure we can settle somewhere between the two."

"So that's a yes?" She cocked her head, her stomach a swirl of anticipation and feminine interest. Mixing business with pleasure had never been an issue, but with this man, she might have to be on her guard. He had neither said nor done anything to acknowledge the fact that she was a woman and he was a man. But it was kind of a hard thing to miss.

He nodded. "I think it's a workable compromise. We'll see how we get along together. And in the meantime, if you find that one of your other staff members is free to take over here, I'll certainly understand."

"Does that mean you don't want me?"

Sweet holy Hannah. Where had that come from?

Two

His body tightened, on high alert. Though he was almost certain Mellie Winslow hadn't intended anything suggestive by her question, there was enough of a spark in the air to make him react with a man's natural response to a beautiful available woman.

Case hadn't expected the punch of sexual interest. Truth be told, it reinforced his reservations about hiring any housekeeper, much less one who looked like Mellie. He was a sucker for redheads, especially the kind with skin the color of cream and wide emerald eyes reflecting a certain wariness...as if she had been disappointed one too many times in life.

Though she was clearly accustomed to hard physical labor, she was thin but not skinny. The shade of her red curls, spilling from a ponytail that fell past her shoulders, was a combination of fire and sunshine.

He should tell her to go. Right now.

"Are you saying I make you nervous, Ms. Winslow?"

She wrinkled her nose, as if smelling a refrigerator full of rotten eggs. "A little. I suppose. But I'll get over it."

That last sentence was served with a side of feminine defiance designed to put him in his place. She reminded him of a fluffy chicken warning the rooster away from the henhouse.

"Duly noted." He tapped a stack of envelopes. "The trial period works both ways. You may find me such a slob that you'll run screaming for the hills."

Mellie's smile was open and natural. "I doubt that. I've reformed worse offenders than you, believe me."

At that precise moment, he knew he wasn't imagining the sizzle of physical awareness between them. Maybe Mellie didn't notice, but he did. At thirty-six, he surely had more experience than this young woman, who was on the dewy-skinned right side of thirty.

"Don't say I didn't warn you." He glanced at his watch, ruefully aware that he had to put an end to this provocative interview. "I'm afraid I have another appointment in town. So we'll have to wrap this up. Why don't you plan to start Thursday morning? I'll put some thoughts on paper in regard to what I want you to tackle and we can go from there. Does that work for you?"

Mellie stood, smiling. "Absolutely. Thank you, Mr. Baxter. I'll see you soon."

"Call me Case," he said.

"And I'm Mellie."

Case stood at the window, his hand on the lace curtain as he watched his new housekeeper drive away. He knew the time had come to put his house in order—literally— but he had a sinking feeling that he might be making a bad mistake.

The fact that he found Mellie Winslow so appealing

should have put an end to things. He'd fallen for an employee once before and ended up with a broken marriage
and a bank account that had taken a severe hit. His track
record with long-term relationships was virtually nonexistent.

He'd never had sisters. With his mother gone, the only
female relatives he had were two cousins in California
whom he saw maybe once a decade. He wasn't a good
judge of what made women tick. He enjoyed their company in bed. He was even willing to concede that women
and men could be friends under certain circumstances.

But as one of the wealthiest ranchers in Maverick
County, he'd learned the hard way that a man was not always judged on his own merits. He might marry again
one day...maybe. But only if he was damn sure that his
prospective bride cared more about his character than his
financial bottom line.

As he drove into town, he noted, almost unconsciously,
the signs that Royal was flourishing after last fall's F4 tornado. He took in the new storefronts, fresh landscaping
and a few empty lots where damaged buildings had been
razed in preparation for upcoming construction.

The town had rebounded well, despite tragedy and hardship. Case knew there were still problems to be addressed.
Insurance woes remained an issue. Slow payments. Court
battles over settlements. The Texas Cattleman's Club had a
history of benevolence and community service. Case was
determined to use his new position to keep the organization headed in the right direction, particularly in regard
to the ongoing tornado cleanup.

For Royal to rebound from tragedy and prosper in the
twenty-first century, it would be important to keep all sec-
tors of the local economy alive. Which meant looking out
for small businesses. Like the Keep N Clean.

When he pulled up on the side street adjoining the Royal Diner, he saw that the sheriff's squad car was already there. He found Nathan Battle inside, sipping a cup of coffee and flirting with his wife, Amanda, who owned and operated the diner.

Case took off his cowboy hat and tucked it under his left arm. "Sheriff. Amanda. Good to see you both." He shook Nathan's hand and slid into the booth opposite the tall uniformed man he'd come to meet.

Amanda smiled at him. "Congratulations on the election. I just heard the news."

"Thanks." Nathan and Amanda had been high school sweethearts. After a tough breakup as kids, they'd eventually reconnected, fallen in love all over again and married. Case envied the almost palpable intimacy between them. Two people who had known each other for so long didn't have to worry about secrets or betrayals.

Amanda kissed her husband on the cheek. "You boys have fun. I've got to go track down a missing shipment of flour, so Helen will be your waitress today. I'll catch you later."

The server took their order for coffee and dessert, and Case sat back with a sigh. He worked long hours. His daddy had taught him the ranching business from the ground up and drilled into him the notion that in order to be the boss, a man required more than money in the bank. He needed the respect and loyalty of his employees.

Nathan drained his coffee cup and raised a hand for more.

Case shook his head. "Do you live on that stuff?" Nathan was tall and lean and beloved by most of the town. But he rarely had time for leisure.

The sheriff shrugged. "There are worse vices." He smiled at Helen as she gave him a refill, and then he eyed

Case with curiosity. "What's up, Case? You sounded mysterious on the phone."

Case leaned forward. "No mystery. I'm hoping you'll be available to look over the club's security procedures and disaster plans. Last year's tornado taught us all we need to stay on top of emergency preparedness."

"Not a bad idea. I'd be happy to…just email me some dates and times, and I'll block it off on my calendar."

"Thanks. I appreciate it."

They chatted for half an hour, and then almost as an afterthought, Case asked Nathan the question that had been on his mind. "What do you know about Keep N Clean?"

"Mellie Winslow's business?"

"Yes."

"They're a solid outfit. Amanda has used them here at the diner, and I know a lot of people around town who sing their praises. Why?"

"My housekeeper retired eight months ago. Took her pension and headed to Florida. I need help around the house. Especially now that I'm taking on leadership at the club. But I'm out on the ranch a lot of the time, and I don't like the idea of having strangers invade my personal space."

"I'm sure Mellie vets her employees thoroughly. I've never heard a single complaint about anyone on her staff, and I would know if there had been a problem."

"And Mellie herself? She says her staffing situation is stretched to the max, so she would be the one working for me."

The other man obviously knew about Case's short-lived marriage. It was no secret. But it was humiliating nevertheless. Back then, Case had been thinking with a part of his anatomy other than his brain. The resultant debacle had been a tough lesson for a twentysomething.

Nathan raised an eyebrow. "Are you asking as a boss or as a man?"

"What does that mean?" Case hadn't expected to be grilled.

"Well, Melinda Winslow is not only a savvy business-woman, she's a gorgeous unattached redhead who's smart and funny and would be a great companion for any guy."

"Hell, Nathan." Case took a swig of coffee and nearly choked to death when the hot liquid singed his throat. "Why do all of my married friends feel the need to play matchmaker?"

Nathan grinned. "How many times have *you* gotten laid in the last month?"

"Not all marriages are like yours," Case muttered, re-fusing to be jealous of his buddy's good fortune. "Amanda is a peach."

"So is Mellie. Don't let your prejudices get in the way. And to be clear, *now* I'm talking about business again. She can be trusted, Case…if that's what you're asking. You can relax on that score. She's not going to steal the silver or run off with a Picasso."

Case's parents had been art collectors. The ranch house was filled with priceless paintings and sculptures. "Good to know. I liked her during the interview, but it never hurts to get a second opinion. Anything else you want to add to your glowing recommendation?"

Something flickered across Nathan's face…something that gave Case a moment's pause. "What?" Case asked, mildly alarmed.

"Nothing bad about Mellie. But be on your guard if her dad comes around. He's a drunk and a scoundrel. As far as I can tell, fathering Mellie is the only good thing he ever did. I arrest the guy for public intoxication at least several times a year."

"And Mellie supports him?"

"No. He lives off the rents from a handful of properties around town that have been in the Winslow family for generations. In fact, the Texas Cattleman's Club sits on Winslow's land. Mellie helps out with the leasing company now and then, but I think she started her own business in order to keep as far away from him as possible."

"No mother in the picture?"

"She died a long time ago. I imagine she left her daughter some kind of nest egg that allowed Mellie to start her business. The family used to be financially solvent, but Mellie's dad has almost destroyed everything. Booze mostly, but gambling, too."

"Thanks for the heads-up." After taking a bite of pie, Case moved on to another subject. "What do you know about Samson Oil and their connection to Nolan Dane? I hear he's handling a lot of land sales for them."

Nathan nodded. "I've heard it, too. Dane seems a decent sort. And his roots are here. So I assume he's trustworthy. Still, Samson Oil is not a household name. No one seems to know much about them."

"Do me a favor and keep an eye on Dane and the Samson Oil situation. Something about that whole thing seems a little off to me…"

Thursday morning Case found himself pacing the halls of his way-too-big-for-one-man house. At least half a dozen times he'd pulled out his phone to call Mellie Winslow and cancel her services. But he couldn't think of a single explanation that wouldn't make him sound like a paranoid idiot, so he'd resisted the impulse to wave her off.

Relishing his privacy was one thing. But if he continued to keep women out of his house, he'd wind up a withered, curmudgeonly octogenarian with a fortune in the bank and a cold, lonely existence. Still…old habits were hard to break.

Mellie arrived five minutes before their arranged appointment time. He'd have to give her points right off the bat for promptness. When he opened the door at her knock, he blinked momentarily.

It could have been a reaction to the blinding midmorning sun. But more probably, it was the sight of a slender, smiling woman in knee-length navy shorts and a navy knit top piped with lime green. On her feet she wore navy Keds with emerald laces.

The name of her business was embroidered above one breast. A breast that he didn't notice. Not at all.

He cleared his throat. "Come on in. I fixed us some iced tea." Though it was November, the day was extremely hot and muggy.

"Thank you." Mellie carried a large plastic tote loaded with various cleaning supplies.

"Leave that, why don't you? We'll sit down in the kitchen. I hope that's not too informal."

"Of course not."

Mellie seemed at ease when she took a seat. Thankfully, she tucked those long, tanned legs out of sight beneath the table. The back of his neck started to sweat. He wanted to get this over with as quickly as possible and get to work.

He sat down on the opposite side of the table and held out a piece of paper. "Here's a rundown of my priorities. Feel free to add things as you see anything that needs attention."

His newest employee glanced over the list. With her gaze cast downward, he could see how long her lashes were. "This looks good," she said. "I'll start out working full days for a couple of weeks until I get everything deep-cleaned and organized. After that we can talk about how often you'd like me to come."

Case caught himself before his mind raced down a totally inappropriate path. Perhaps Nathan was right. Maybe Case *had* gone too long without sex. Because everything that came out of Mellie Winslow's mouth sounded like an invitation.

Case cleared his throat. "I was at the diner and saw Nathan the other day. The sheriff had good things to say about you and your business…that you were completely trustworthy."

"How did that come up in conversation? Were you investigating me?"

"No, no, no," he said, backpedaling rapidly. "But you can't fault me for asking what he knew about you."

She stood up, her expression going from affronted to glacial in seconds. "In the folder I gave you several days ago there were half a dozen references. Any one of those people could have vouched for me. It wasn't really a *police* matter, Mr. Baxter."

"I've offended you," he said, surprised at her reaction.

She tossed his list at him. "If you're going to constantly keep tabs to make sure I haven't cleaned out your safe or absconded with a priceless painting, then I don't think this is going to work out. Good day, Mr. Baxter."

Before he could react, she spun on her heel and headed for the front door, her ponytail bouncing with each angry step.

"Wait." Belatedly, he sprang to his feet and strode after her, whacking his hip on the corner of the kitchen table. "Wait, Mellie."

He caught up with her in the foyer as she picked up her supplies. "Don't leave," he said. "We agreed to a trial period."

"Shortest one on record," she snapped.

He really had no choice but to grab her arm in a gentle grip. "I'm *sorry*," he said…as forcefully as he knew how. "If you leave, I'll sue for breach of contract." He said it with a smile to let her know he was joking. But Mellie Winslow didn't look the least bit amused.

Wiggling free of his hold, she faced him, her expression turbulent. "I'm proud of my business. It's been built on word of mouth and the quality of the employees I hire. Keep N Clean has never had a single complaint of anything going missing…or of anything being damaged, for that matter."

Case rarely made a misstep, but he knew this was a bad one. "I am sincerely sorry. I shouldn't have asked the sheriff about you."

"Amanda Battle is a friend of mine. Do you understand that I'm embarrassed?"

He did. For the first time, he looked at his actions from Mellie's perspective. To a Texan, honor was everything. She had a right to be upset.

"Let's start over," he said.

She stared at him. "Under one condition. No trial period. You sign the contract today."

The negotiator in him was impressed. But more importantly, as a man, he found her bold confidence arousing. Everything about her was appealing. In other circumstances, he would have made an effort to get to know her more intimately.

Mellie Winslow, however, was here to put his house in order, not warm his bed. "I begin to see why your business is so successful. Very well, Ms. Winslow." He held out his hand. "You've got a deal."

Touching her was his next mistake. Awareness sizzled between them. Her skin was smooth and warm, her hand small and feminine in his grasp. He maintained the contact a few seconds longer than necessary.

When he released her and she stepped back, for the first time, he saw uncertainty in her eyes. "I probably overreacted," she muttered. "I have a temper."

A grin tugged the corners of his mouth. "So the red hair is the real deal?"

"It is. I'm sorry, too. I shouldn't have been so touchy."

They stood there staring at each other, the air rife with things best left unspoken. "I should go," he said. "And let you get started."

She nodded. "If I have any questions, is it okay to text you?"

"Of course."

Her green eyes with a hint of gray warmed slightly. "I'll try not to bother you."

Too late for that. He picked up his keys from the table beside the front door. "See you later, Mellie Winslow. Good luck with my house."

Three

Mellie watched him go with mixed feelings. On the one hand, it was much easier to familiarize herself with a new house if the owner was not underfoot. Still, she wouldn't have minded if her new boss had lingered. She was curious about Case Baxter. Even though he was an arrogant, know-it-all male.

He was an intriguing combination of down-to-earth cowboy and high-powered businessman. It was no secret he was worth millions.

From what she'd heard around town, in addition to running his massive and wildly successful cattle operation, Case liked investing, particularly in small businesses. He believed in supporting the local economy. After the tornado—when the banks were stretched thin giving out loans—Case had floated some cash around the community, as well.

People in Royal liked and respected Case Baxter. Which explained his recent election as president of the Texas

Cattleman's Club. The newspaper had run a bio along with the article announcing the results. Mellie knew that Case was thirty-six, which made him seven years her senior.

The age gap wasn't significant, except for the fact that she still felt as though she was starting out, while Case was a man in his prime…in every way that counted.

Shrugging off her absorption with the sexy cowboy, she made herself focus on the job at hand. Case's home was a stunning example of what could happen when the past was carefully preserved even amidst modern improvements. Unfortunately, the beauty of the old house was obscured by clutter.

Judging by the kitchen, Case apparently grabbed only breakfast and lunch at home. Presumably, he ate dinner out most nights. She found orange juice and milk in the fridge and a couple of boxes of cereal in the cabinet. Lunch items were similarly sparse. Aside from pizzas and a couple of steaks in the freezer, his larder was woefully bare.

There was no reason in the world for her to feel sorry for Case Baxter. The man had everything he wanted or needed. He could hire a full-time chef if he liked. But the thought of him rattling around this big old house on his own gave her a twinge.

Not many men had the gift of making a home cozy and warm. Case was a Texas bachelor. Macho. Authoritative. Accustomed to giving orders and running his ranch. He wasn't the kind to bake cookies or pick flowers.

That mental image made her chuckle. Time to get to work.

She started with the dining room, since it seemed the most straightforward. Case had instructed her to pitch all the junk mail into the recycle bin and to keep only the things that looked personal or otherwise important. Though the stacks of envelopes, catalogs and circulars were high, anybody with half a brain could sort through this kind of stuff in no time.

When she was done, there were maybe a dozen pieces of *real* mail remaining. She carried them down the hall and put them on Case's desk, a beautiful antique rolltop. His office was curiously impersonal. No knickknacks. No photographs, not even of his parents.

That was the thing about cleaning someone's house. It was an oddly intimate activity. She understood suddenly why a man like Case had been hesitant about hiring help. If the state of his home was any indication, he was a guarded man, one who didn't easily reveal his secrets.

By the time she made it to his bedroom, she had spent most of the day in only three rooms. That was no surprise, really. Decluttering was a slow process, especially when it involved someone else's belongings. But she had been successful. The living room and dining room were now spotless, as was Case's study.

It was past time for her to leave, so his bedroom would have to wait. But she did take a moment to gather discarded clothing and carry the items to the laundry room. Tomorrow that would be her first priority.

She paused in the doorway, lingering a moment, unable to help herself. The man's bed was hedonistic. An enormous carved four-poster that looked Spanish in origin dominated the room. No expense had been spared in the bed linens. The ecru sheets and thick, fluffy coffee-brown comforter were both masculine and luxurious.

The covers were tangled, as if their owner had passed a restless night. In the jumble of clothing she'd picked up off the floor and from a chair and in the bathroom, there were no pajamas. Maybe Case Baxter slept in the nude.

With her face hot and her stomach jumpy, Mellie went back and made the bed quickly before retreating, content to leave this battlefield for another day. Never before had she taken such an intense interest in a client's sleeping arrangements. Her imagination ran rampant, imagining Case's big, tanned body sprawled against those whisper-soft sheets.

She swallowed hard, feeling the unmistakable rush of sexual arousal. This was bad. Very bad. Not only was she too busy for any kind of relationship, sexual or otherwise... but Case was one of Royal's most eligible bachelors. He wasn't likely to be interested in the hired help.

Mellie's family went way back in Royal, maybe as far back as Case's did. Despite that, when she eventually married and started a family, she wanted an ordinary man, one who would have time to be a daddy...a man who was interested in home and hearth.

As far as she could tell, Case had tried marriage and found it lacking. He'd be unlikely to dip his toes into that water again anytime soon, if ever. And since she wasn't the kind of woman who was comfortable having casual sex, there was no point in seeing Case Baxter as anything other than a paycheck and a valuable advertisement for Keep N Clean.

Feeling unaccountably morose, she told herself she was just tired after a long day's work. She gathered her things, let herself out and carefully locked the front door.

After the short drive back to town and a forty-five-minute stop at her office to check mail and phone messages that hadn't been routed to her personal cell, she headed for home. She had a date tonight with a favorite TV show, some leftover spaghetti and her comfy sofa.

But the plan changed when she found her father camped out on her doorstep. It looked as if he had been sitting there for a while, because he had an empty beer bottle at either hip. His eyes were bloodshot. Though he stood when she walked up the path to the small duplex she called home, he was unsteady on his feet.

"You changed your locks," he said, a look of bafflement on his florid face. Harold Winslow was short and round with salt-and-pepper hair and skin weathered by the Texas sun. Once upon a time he had been a successful business-man. But when his beloved wife died, his alcoholic ten-dencies had taken over.

Hugging him briefly, she sighed. "I'm a grown woman, Daddy. I like my privacy. You don't seem to understand that." She had tried her best not to fall into a codependent relationship with her only living parent. But that was eas-ier said than done.

The trouble was, Mellie felt his pain. Ila Winslow had been the center of their lives. When cancer took her away from her husband and sixteen-year-old daughter, their world had caved in. Harold found solace in whiskey. Mel-lie had been forced to grow up far too quickly.

Harold followed her into the house. "Any chance you might fix dinner for your dear old dad?"

She counted to ten beneath her breath, keeping her back to him. "We can order a pizza. I'm beat. I was planning to eat leftovers."

"Pizza works. You got any cash? I left my billfold at home."

It was an old game they played. Harold could live com-fortably off the rents from the properties he still owned. But money slipped through his fingers like water through a sieve. When he ended up broke again and again, he came knocking at Mellie's door…sometimes figuratively, but more often than not, literally…like tonight.

Swallowing her disappointment at having her hopes for a peaceful evening shattered, she managed an even tone. "Go ahead and order what you want. I'm going to change clothes."

By the time she returned to the living room, her father was sprawled in a recliner, the television remote in his hand. He gave her a smile, but behind it she thought she saw despair. His existence was aimless. No matter how hard Mellie tried, she couldn't get him to understand that his life wasn't over. She loved her dad, but once in a while, it would have been nice to lean on him instead of always having to be the grown-up.

Dinner arrived soon after. She paid for the two small, fragrant pizzas and tipped the young man, wondering if the fact that she and her father couldn't even agree on toppings was proof that she would never convince him to see things her way.

They ate in silence, the television filling the void. Finally, she finished her meal and decided it was now or never...a conversation that was long overdue. But she would come at it indirectly.

"I started a new job today, Daddy. I'm going to be cleaning and organizing for Case Baxter."

Harold raised an eyebrow. "The new Texas Cattleman's Club president?"

"Yes. Having him as a client will be a coup, I think."

"I'm proud of you, baby girl."

For once, she thought he meant it. "Thank you." She paused and said a prayer. "I'm doing well, Daddy. Keep N Clean is solvent and growing."

He nodded. "Good for you."

An awkward silence descended, but she forged ahead. "We need to talk about last week."

Immediately, his face closed up. "I'm fine," he muttered. "Quit worrying. I don't drink as much as you think I do."

"Sheriff Battle found you passed out in the street." She

hesitated, dreading his reaction. "I'd like to pay for you to go to rehab before it's too late."

"I hadn't eaten breakfast. My blood sugar was too low. I fainted, that's all."

"Daddy, please. I know you miss Mom. So do I. Every day. But at the rate you're going, I'm likely to lose you, too."

Harold lumbered to his feet and stood with what dignity he could. "There's nothing wrong with me. Surely a man can enjoy a couple of beers without getting a lecture."

It was more than beer. A lot more. And the alcohol abuse was aging him rapidly. "Just think about it," she pleaded. "It won't be so bad. I've read about some beautiful places right here in Texas. I want you to be healthy and strong so you can play with your grandchildren one day."

Her father snorted. "You don't even date. That cleaning company of yours won't keep you warm at night. Maybe you'd better quit worrying about me and find yourself a man."

It was exactly like Harold to go on the attack when she tried to talk to him about his drinking. "I've got plenty of time for that."

For a split second the naked pain in her father's heart was written on his face. "We all think we have plenty of time, Mellie. But love isn't a permanent gift. Losing it hurts. I'm pretty sure that's why you don't let any man get too close. I'll make you a deal, darlin'... When you get your life in order, I'll let you muck around with mine."

She stood at the door and watched him go...his gait slow but relatively steady. He'd had his driver's license revoked time and again. Fortunately, the home where Mellie had grown up and where Harold still lived was centrally located in Royal, making it possible for her father to walk to his destinations for the most part.

As she showered and got ready for bed, she pondered her father's words. It was true that she rarely went out on a date. She'd told herself that getting a business off the ground required determination and hard work. But did it demand the sacrifice of any kind of personal life?

Her pride stung a bit to know that her father had pegged her so well. In her desperate need to get him to admit his failings and seek help, had she overlooked her own response to grief?

Over the years, she hadn't cared enough for any of the men who populated her modest social life to let them get too close. Channeling her energy into Keep N Clean kept her focused. Romance would only get in the way of her life plan.

Ordinarily after a hard day, she was out by the time her head hit the pillow. Tonight, though, she couldn't get settled. Her father seemed increasingly out of control, and she didn't know what to do to help him. He was an adult…with resources. So why did she feel responsible for his actions?

Reaching for a more pleasant subject, she reminded herself that tomorrow she would have the opportunity to spend more time in Case Baxter's beautiful home. It had personality…and history. Bringing it to its full potential would be a pleasure. Not to mention the outside chance she might run into the man himself.

He'd given her a set of keys along with his permission to come and go as she liked during the day. According to Case, he was going to be very busy at the club and also with the ranch. She got the distinct impression he planned to make himself scarce as long as she was working in his house.

Something about that notion made her feel weird and discouraged. Case was exactly the kind of man she found appealing. It hurt that he wanted to avoid her.

Thumping her pillow with her fist, she rearranged the light blanket. The cold would come, but for now, her bedroom was stuffy.

She was finally almost asleep when her phone dinged quietly, signaling a text. Groaning, she reached for her cell and squinted at it in the dark.

Mellie—I hope I'm not disturbing you. I know it's late, but I wanted to tell you thanks. You're a miracle worker. I almost thought I was in the wrong house when I got home tonight. Kudos to Keep N Clean…

Case Baxter. The last person on earth she expected to be texting her at this hour, or any hour, for that matter. Was she supposed to answer? Or simply let him think she was asleep? She hesitated for a moment and then put down the phone.

It was nice of him to take the time to acknowledge her work. Perhaps the message was a peace offering after the argument that had started their day.

With a smile on her face, she snuggled back into the covers, unable to squelch the hope that she would run into Case tomorrow and maybe even see him in her dreams.

Four

Case jammed his Stetson as far down on his head as it would go and hunched his shoulders, trying to bury his chin in the collar of his rain jacket. The weather gods had finally sent Maverick County some moisture, but it wasn't the days-long, soaking rain they needed.

Instead, the precipitation was a miserable, icy-cold drizzle that chilled a man right down to the bone, a dramatic shift from the previous day. Since seven this morning, he'd been out riding the fence line with his foreman, looking for problems. They'd lost two dozen head of cattle in the past few weeks. Everyone suspected rustlers, but before Case involved the authorities, he wanted to make sure the animals hadn't simply wandered away through a hole in the fence.

Now, though he was wet and weary, at least he had the satisfaction of knowing that his fencing was not compromised. Giving the foreman a wave, Case turned his horse and galloped back toward the house. Already this new housekeeper thing was getting in his way.

Ordinarily in a situation like this, he would strip down in the mudroom, walk through his house naked and climb into the hot tub on the sheltered back porch. Unfortunately, that wasn't going to happen today, with Mellie around.

Muttering beneath his breath, he handed off his horse to one of the stable guys in the barn and then strode toward the house. He was grumpy and wet and hungry, and he wanted his castle to himself. His bad mood lasted all the way up until the moment he found Mellie Winslow bending over the side of his bed dusting the base of one of the posts. She was wearing Spandex pants, the navy fabric curved snugly against a firm, shapely butt.

His heart lodged in his throat at about the same time his gut tightened with swift and wicked arousal that swept through his veins. He actually took half a step backward, because he was stunned.

Mellie straightened and smiled, her expression cautious. "Mr. Baxter. Case. I'm sorry. I didn't think you'd be home in the middle of the day. I can move on to another room for now."

He shrugged. "I need a hot shower. Won't be long." Unless maybe he got distracted imagining Mellie in there with him…

"I put fresh towels in your bathroom a few minutes ago. They're probably still warm from the dryer." She paused and seemed hesitant. "Have you had lunch?"

Come to think of it, he hadn't. Which might account for his surly attitude. "No. I'll grab something in a minute."

"Would you like me to fix soup and a sandwich? It's no problem."

His fingers were cold, his skin damp. But inside, he was

burning up. He should have hired a seventy-plus grand-motherly type with a bun and absolutely no sex appeal.

But he hadn't. Oh, no…not at all. He'd brought tempta-tion into his house. Hell, into his bedroom, to be exact. He cleared his throat. "That would be nice. Thanks."

Mellie nodded and walked away.

Case slumped against the wall, his heart thundering in his chest. There was far too much going on in his life right now to get sidetracked by a very inconvenient attrac-tion. He was a grown man. Not a boy. He could control his physical impulses.

In the shower he turned the water hot enough to sting his skin. Maybe the discomfort would take his mind off the fact that he had an erection…a big one. Damn. What was it about Mellie that caught him off guard and made him hungry to strip her naked and take her to bed?

She was beautiful in a girl-next-door kind of way, but Royal had more than its share of attractive women. Case didn't find himself panting after every one of them. Maybe it was the fact that Mellie was in his house.

That was *his* mistake.

He dried off and changed into clean clothes. His others, wet and muddy, lay in a pile on the bathroom floor. Pre-sumably, his new housekeeper would take care of wash-ing them.

Standing in the middle of his bedroom, he acknowl-edged the truth. He didn't *want* Mellie Winslow washing his clothes. He had far better plans for activities the two of them could enjoy.

It was bad enough that she was cleaning up after him. Maybe he was weird, or maybe his first marriage had ru-ined him, but he liked relating to women on an even foot-ing. Mellie was talented and capable and she was doing exactly what he had hired her to do. So why was he getting freaked out about everything?

He found her in the kitchen. She hummed as she moved around the room. His oak table, situated in the breakfast nook, was set with a single place mat, a lone plate and glass and a set of silverware.

Mellie waved a hand. "It's all ready, if you want to sit down."

He leaned against the doorframe. "Aren't you joining me?"

Her eyes widened momentarily and a faint pink crept up her neck. "I had a big breakfast. I usually work through lunch."

"At least a cup of coffee, then. You're on the clock, and it's my clock." He smiled to put her at ease, since she was eyeing him dubiously.

"Okay."

He refused to sit at the table and be served as if he were in a restaurant. Instead, he waited until she placed the bowl of tomato soup and the grilled cheese sandwich at his place. "This looks great," he said. "Thank you."

"Coffee to drink?"

"Yes, please. Black."

Mellie poured two cups, added milk and sugar to hers, and then joined him as they both sat down. He hadn't realized how hungry he was until the aroma of freshly prepared food reached him and his stomach growled loudly.

It was Mellie's turn to grin.

They sat in companionable silence for a few moments, Mellie sipping her coffee and Case wolfing down the food she had prepared for him. Though soup and a sandwich wasn't exactly haute cuisine, the comfort food was filling and delicious.

"So tell me, Mellie…what are your ambitions for Keep N Clean?"

If she was surprised by his interest, she didn't show it. "When I'm dreaming big," she said, "I think about franchising and moving into medium-size towns all over Texas."

He raised an eyebrow. "I'm impressed. You must have a knack for numbers."

"I have an associate business degree. But most of the hands-on stuff is self-taught. It's important to discern what a client wants and then be able to provide it. Especially in a service industry like mine. You have to stand out from the pack."

"Very true, I'm sure." He finished his meal and stood to get more coffee. He held out the coffeepot. "More for you?"

Mellie shook her head. "No, thanks. I'd better get back to work."

"Not so fast," he said. The urge to detain her was unsettling. He had plenty to keep him busy. But he didn't want to walk away from Mellie. "Tell me about yourself."

Mellie smiled wryly. "Is that really necessary?"

"Humor me."

"Well…"

He watched her search for words and wondered if she was going to avoid any mention of her father. Fortunately, he was a patient man…so he waited.

She shrugged. "It's not very exciting. I grew up in Royal. My mom died of cancer when I was sixteen. My dad went into a tailspin of grief, meaning I ended up being the parent in our relationship. I knew I wanted to start my own business, so I looked around and tried to find something that filled a niche. Royal had an industrial cleaning company but nothing smaller, other than individuals who worked for themselves."

"And here you are."

She wrinkled her nose. "Working for the brand-new president of the Texas Cattleman's Club."

"Are all your employees as eye-catching in that uniform as you are?"

Her jaw dropped a centimeter. "Um…"

"Sorry. Was that out of line?"

"More like unexpected." She stared at him, gaze narrowed, clearly trying to get inside his head. "Someone told me that you don't like women invading your house."

He winced. Royal's gossipy grapevine was alive and well. "That's not exactly accurate."

"No?" She cocked her head as if to say she knew he was skirting the truth.

"I like my privacy. But since I have neither the time nor the inclination to round up dust bunnies or clean out the fridge, I have to make compromises."

"Ah."

"What does that mean?"

"It means I'm accustomed to wealthy people who barely even acknowledge the presence of a service worker. We're invisible to them. Nonentities."

He frowned. "I can't speak for all the comfortably well-to-do families in Royal, but my friends aren't like that."

"If you say so. And for the record, Case, no one would describe you as only 'comfortably well-to-do.'"

Mellie Winslow had a bit of a chip on her shoulder. He hadn't noticed it before, but she wasn't trying to hide it now. "Does my lifestyle offend you, Mellie?" he asked gently, wondering if she would rise to the bait.

She sat back in her chair, pushing a few stray wisps of hair from her forehead. The set of her jaw was mutinous. "Let's just say that I don't have a single Modigliani hanging in my hallway."

"My parents were art collectors. They traveled the world. But believe me when I tell you I would trade every sculpture and painting in this house to have Mom and Dad back with me for just one day."

Mellie knew she had stepped in it…big-time. She felt hot color roll from her throat to her forehead. The taste of shame was unpleasant. "I am *so* sorry, Case. You're right, of course. Relationships matter more than things. Money doesn't buy happiness."

He grinned at her, his scruffy chin making him dangerously attractive. His hair was still damp from his shower. "Don't get carried away. Money is good for a lot of things."

"Such as?"

He leaned his chair back on two legs, defying gravity, and crossed his arms over his chest. "Flying to Paris for the weekend. Buying a yacht. Scoring Super Bowl tickets. Supporting a charity. Spoiling a woman."

She had a feeling he threw that last one in to get a reaction.

There *was* a reaction. But it happened someplace he couldn't actually see. She cleared her throat. "Being spoiled is nice, but most women I know want to take care of themselves."

For the first time, she saw a shadow of cynicism on his face. "Maybe you know the wrong rich people and I know the wrong women."

Mellie stood abruptly, feeling out of her depth and alarmingly sympathetic toward the man who'd been born and reared with every possible advantage. "There's more soup on the stove, if you're still hungry. I really do have to get busy."

Case unfolded that long, lean body of his from the chair and joined her at the dishwasher, his hands brushing hers as he put his plate alongside her cup. She felt his breath on her cheek when he spoke. "Is your boss such a slave driver?" he muttered.

She turned around to face him. They were almost in an embrace, the counter at her back and one big contrary cowboy planted in front of her. She lifted her chin and propped her hands behind her. "*I'm* the boss, Case. And I don't need to be spoiled. If I want to fly to Paris this weekend, I'll buy my own ticket."

His gaze settled on her lips. For one heart-thumping second, she knew he was going to kiss her. "Don't be so touchy, Mellie. There's nothing wrong with a man doing nice things for a woman."

Things? Oh, Lordy. "Um, no… I guess not." She stopped and looked him straight in the eyes. "Are you flirting with me, Case Baxter?"

He shrugged, a half smile doing interesting things to that enticing mouth. "What happens if I say yes?" His thick eyelashes settled at half-mast. She could smell the soap from his shower and his warm skin.

Her inclination was to tell him. The truth. The shivery, weak-in-the-knees truth. She wanted hot, sweaty, no-holds-barred sex with Case Baxter on his newly made bed.

But sadly, she was known for being smart and responsible. "I suppose if you say yes, I'll have to point out unpleasant things like sexual harassment in the workplace."

"You just told me I'm not your boss. We're here as equals, Mellie. So I guess whatever happens, happens."

Before she could react, he brushed his lips against her forehead, turned on his heel and strode out of the kitchen.

Mellie put her fingers to her lips like a schoolgirl who had just been kissed by the captain of the football team. Case's chaste kiss had not made contact with her mouth at all. But she felt the imprint of his personality all the way to her toes.

Moving cautiously toward the window, she peeked out and saw him striding toward the barn. She hadn't expected him to actually *work* on his ranch. Which made no sense, because if Case had been an entitled, supercilious rich jerk, he'd never have been elected president of the Texas Cattleman's Club. People liked him.

She might like him, too, if she could get past the huge neon sign in her brain that said Off-Limits.

In the meantime, she had things to do and places to be.

The master suite had occupied most of her time today, and not only because she was fascinated with its owner. The bathroom and bedroom were huge. By the time three o'clock rolled around, she had deep-cleaned everything from the grout between the tiles to the wooden slatted venetian blinds.

In addition to an enormous teak armoire, the quarters boasted a roomy walk-in closet. Her fingers itched to tackle the chaos there, but that chore would require a chunk of time, so she would postpone it until tomorrow. No sense in starting something she couldn't finish.

She left earlier than the day before and told herself it wasn't because she was avoiding Case. He was an important client, true, but she still had to run her business.

Back at her office, she popped the top off a bottle of Coke and downed it with a sigh of pleasure. Sure, the sugar and caffeine weren't good for her, but as addictions went, the soda was fairly harmless.

Which was more than could be said for her inability to erase Case from her thoughts. If he was seriously testing the waters with her, she would have more to worry about than a sugar rush. Allowing herself to be lured into a multimillionaire's bed would be the height of folly.

She knew herself pretty well. Guarded. Suspicious. Independent.

On the flip side, she was hardworking, generous and ambitious. The one thing that she was *not* was a good judge of men's motives. Perhaps because her mother had not been around to share advice, Mellie's father had gone overboard in warning her about guys and sex.

He'd told her sex was all boys wanted from a girl…that it was up to her to make good decisions. Well, here she was. Almost thirty. A modest financial success. A dutiful daughter. And only steps away from missing out on things like romance and motherhood and the chance to meet a man who could make her toes curl with his kisses.

Case might not be her idea of the perfect man for the long haul, but he might be exactly the right guy for the here and now.

Five

Case returned to the house at four thirty, anticipating another round of verbal sparring with the delightfully prickly Mellie. But her car was gone. Was she avoiding him? And didn't she know that the male of the species enjoyed a chase?

He had dinner plans with Nathan Battle tonight. Amanda was out for the evening with her book club. So Case and the sheriff were looking forward to medium-rare steaks, a couple of games of pool and a sampling of sports on Nathan's brand-new big-screen TV.

Nathan had offered to do the cooking. Case brought a case of imported beer and an apple pie he'd picked up at the bakery. The rain had ended several hours ago, so the two men sat outside in the gathering gloom and enjoyed the crisp air.

The scent of beef cooking made Case's stomach growl. Which made him think of the last meal he'd eaten. The one a certain redhead with kind eyes and a stubborn chin had made for him.

Nathan kicked the leg of Case's chair. "I'm the quiet one. You're supposed to entertain me with tales of the rich and famous."

Case slunk farther down in his chair. "I'm not famous."

Nathan laughed out loud. "What's eating you, Baxter? I've had livelier conversations at a morgue. Is the new job title weighing you down?"

"I'm not official for ten more days, so no."

"Then what?"

Case drained his beer and popped the top on a second. "You're imagining things."

Nathan stood, flipped the steaks and sat back down with a sigh. "Then it must be the new housekeeper. Is she making you take off your shoes at the door? Or forbidding you to eat popcorn in the den?"

"Very funny. It's my house. I can do whatever the hell I please. Mellie doesn't run my life."

"Mellie? Wow. First names already?"

"I wasn't going to make her call me Mr. Baxter."

"Fair enough." The other man paused. "Here's the thing, buddy. I have to pass along a warning."

"A warning?"

"Yes. From Amanda. But to be honest, I agree with her."

"Should I be worried?"

"It's not a joke, Case. If you screw around with Mellie Winslow either literally or figuratively, Amanda will come after you. And my wife can be pretty scary when she's on her high horse."

"I don't understand."

"Mellie hasn't had an easy life. You're way out of her league."

"Now, wait a minute." Case felt his temper rise.

"I'm not insulting Mellie. She's great. But you're older than she is, more experienced, and your financial position puts you at an advantage. I'm merely suggesting you not do something you'll regret. I know you, Case. You're not interested in a serious commitment. Admit it."

Case dropped his head against the back of his chair, scowling at the crescent moon above. "You know what it's like to have a failed relationship in your past." Nathan and Amanda had spent years apart. They had been high school sweethearts, but malicious lies had destroyed that bond, and it had been a very long time before they'd reconnected.

"I do. It makes you second-guess yourself. Especially when the reason it happened was that you were young and stupid."

"Are we talking about me or you?"

"Both of us."

Fortunately, Nathan dropped the subject. The steaks were ready, and neither man was the type to spill his guts, even to a friend.

The rest of the evening was lighthearted and comfortable. Sports talk. Good food. But as Case drove back to the ranch later that night, disappointment filled his chest. Mostly because he knew the sheriff was right about Mellie.

She was not the type of woman to indulge in casual sex. And Case wasn't interested in anything else.

Mellie sat at her desk and groaned as she hung up the phone. Two of her employees had called in because their kids had the flu. Which meant a major juggling act on the boss's end. Several houses couldn't be postponed for one reason or another. She called a few clients who weren't tied to a certain schedule and changed their cleaning days, offering a credit toward next month's bill for the kerfuffle.

In half an hour, she had reassigned her workforce and

come to the inescapable realization that she was going to have to put Case off for a couple of days. It wasn't a problem in the grand scheme of things. He didn't have any big social events at his home coming up. He merely wanted her to deep-clean and organize his house.

Postponing the job for forty-eight or even seventy-two hours was not a crisis. But what made her squirm was the fact that Case Baxter would think she was running scared.

She was not completely inexperienced. There had been two serious relationships in her life, both of which she'd thought might turn out to be the real deal. But in the end, the first one had been puppy love, and the second a crush on a man fifteen years her senior.

When she'd finally realized that the older guy was more of a parental figure than a soul mate, she'd broken things off. That was four years ago. She'd been alone ever since. By choice.

She knew when a man wanted her. And she had the confidence to turn a guy down without apology. Her body was hers to give. She was old enough now to understand that true love was rare. Even so, she would not allow herself to be physically intimate with a man on a whim.

Case Baxter tempted her. Her own yearning was what scared her. She liked him and respected him. Even worse, no woman under eighty and in her right mind could be immune to his bold sex appeal.

He was at the height of his physical maturity. Tough, seasoned, completely capable of protecting a woman or giving her pleasure. He was wealthy, classy and intelligent.

Damn it. She was vulnerable around him, and the feeling, although stimulating, was not one she welcomed.

She didn't believe in postponing unpleasant tasks. Pulling out her smartphone, she rapidly composed a text…

Case—I have a couple of employees out today, so I have to cover some shifts. I'll be back at your place in a few days. Will give U a heads-up beforehand. Sorry for the inconvenience. Mellie Winslow

She added her name at the end because she wasn't sure he had entered her contact info into his phone. Before she hit Send, she stared at the words. She was shooting for businesslike and professional.

Would he read her message in that vein, or was her genuine need to postpone the Baxter house going to be seen as a ploy to snag his attention? Oh, good grief. The man probably didn't give a flip about whether or not his cleaning lady showed up. He probably flirted automatically.

She was making a mountain out of a molehill.

The next three days were long and physically taxing. Mellie worked hard, much as she had in the beginning. In her early twenties, by the sweat of her brow, she had turned Keep N Clean into a viable operation. Clearly, she needed to rethink her staffing situation, though. She couldn't continue to work on a shoestring.

She needed enough flexibility to handle unexpected illness on the part of her employees as well as the occasional new customer like Case. The past two weeks were a wake-up call. If she really had dreams for expansion, she would have to take her game up a notch.

The one thing that needled her now was Case's total lack of communication. Given his past behavior, she'd expected some kind of cheeky text from him in return. All she'd gotten was No problem, and that was it. Even this morning when she had messaged him to say she was returning to the B Hive Ranch, there had been no response.

Was she miffed with her for putting him off? Did he

think a man in his position deserved to be kept at the top of the list? Maybe it wasn't egalitarian, but the truth was, he did. The significant fee he was paying her, combined with the cachet of having him on her client list, made keeping Case happy a priority.

It was barely nine when she arrived at the ranch. She saw some activity out in the fields and down at the barn, but the house looked much as it always did. Case had probably been up at first light doing whatever he did when he wasn't tormenting unsuspecting housekeepers.

Though she would have died before admitting it, her heart beat faster than normal as she ascended the front steps. Another weather front had moved in. The morning air was damp and cold, reminding her that Thanksgiving was not far off on the horizon. The date fell early this year.

Hesitating at the front door, she held her key in her hand. Case still hadn't replied to her text saying she was on the way. But he hadn't said *not* to come.

What if he was in bed with a woman? What if he hadn't seen or heard her text? To stumble upon her client in a very personal moment would be humiliating in the extreme.

Muttering beneath her breath, she closed her eyes and wrinkled her nose, berating herself silently for having such a ridiculously over-the-top imagination.

At last, she knocked firmly, listened and finally opened the door. The house seemed empty. Besides, she'd heard the rumors about Case's famous rules. He didn't entertain females at his place.

After hovering in the foyer for several moments, she told herself she was being foolish. Today she was going to tackle Case's kitchen. The sooner she started, the sooner she could escape, and maybe she wouldn't have to deal with the aggravating rancher.

The house was cold, but she didn't adjust the heat. By

the time she'd been working for an hour she would be plenty warm. The windows in the yellow-toned kitchen were designed to let in lots of light, creating a cheery center to the house. But today the skies over Royal were gray and sullen.

November could go either way in Maverick County. At the moment, the weather was depressing and chilly to the bone.

Mellie left her jacket on, shivering in spite of herself. Her usual routine was to clean from the top down. Which meant unloading all the cabinets above the beautiful amber-toned granite countertop. In the utility cabinet she found a stepladder that was just tall enough to give her access all the way to the ceiling.

Cleaning the tops and outer surfaces of the cabinets was not so hard. But when she opened the first one, she grimaced. Dishes and other items were crammed in with no regard for maximizing space. There wasn't even the barest nod toward order.

The best thing would be to empty everything and then come up with a system for replacing items in a manner that would make them easy for anyone to find. The contents of the first couple of cabinets were puzzling. On the very top shelves she found exquisite antique china…lots of it, cream-colored with an intricate pattern of yellow and gold. Farther down were ultramodern dishes in black and white.

She frowned. She was no designer, but the monochrome set looked as if it belonged in a high-end loft in SoHo, not a historic ranch house in Texas. Maybe Case thought the old stuff was not masculine enough for his taste. That was a shame, because there was a good possibility that the stacks of delicate porcelain were something that had been handed down through his family for generations.

Glassware was heavy. By the time she had emptied three

cabinets—three shelves each—her back was aching. The little bottle of ibuprofen she kept in her purse was empty, but she remembered seeing some in Case's bathroom.

In the elegant hallway with its hardwood floor and celadon walls, she stopped dead when she heard a sound. A groan. Not the house creaking as old houses often did, but something human.

She hurried her steps. "Mr. Baxter... Case?"

Another sound, this one muffled.

By the time she reached the open doorway to Case's bedroom, she half expected to find him passed out on the floor, felled by a blow from a burglar. Her imagination ran rampant.

But the truth was equally distressing. Case lay facedown on his bed, wearing nothing except a white buttondown shirt and gray boxer briefs.

Thank goodness he was facedown. Her first response was honest and self-revelatory but not pertinent to the situation.

Was he drunk? Surely not on a weekday before noon. She said his name again, approaching the bed with all the caution of a zookeeper entering the cage of a sleeping lion.

When she was close enough to touch him, her brain processed the available info. His head was turned toward her, his face flushed with color. Thick eyelashes lay against his cheeks. His lips were parted, his breathing harsh.

Ever so gently, she laid her hand against his forehead. The man was burning up with fever. Case Baxter had the flu. Or at least something equally serious.

He moaned again as she touched him. When he turned on his side toward her, she stroked his hair before she realized what she was doing. It was the same caress she would have used with a hurting child.

But Case was no child. His big masculine body shook

uncontrollably, though his tanned chest was sheened with sweat. She probably shouldn't have noticed his chest, but with his shirt completely unbuttoned, his flat belly and the dusting of dark hair at his midriff were hard to miss.

Her knees were less than steady, and she felt a bit woozy. Even passed out cold, Case did something to her. Something not entirely comfortable.

Ignoring her inappropriate reactions to the half-naked man, she pushed and pulled at him until she had him covered all the way to the neck. Case's limbs were deadweight. The rest of him was equally heavy.

She sat down at the edge of the bed. On top of the covers. "Case?" she said. "Can you hear me?"

He muttered and stirred restlessly.

"Case." She put a hand on his shoulder, injecting a note of authority, hoping to pierce the layers of illness that shrouded him.

His eyelids fluttered. "What?" The word was slurred.

How long had he been like this? People *died* from the flu. Not that Case was elderly or an infant, but still. "You need a doctor," she said firmly. "Who can I call?"

The patient scrunched up his face. "Head hurts."

Those two words destroyed her defenses entirely. Her newest client might be handsome and rich and arrogant as heck, but right now he was just a man in need of help. "I'll get you some medicine," she said. "But I need to check with your doctor."

"Call Parker." The command was almost inaudible.

She knew who he meant. Parker Reese was a gifted doctor who had saved more than one newborn at Royal Memorial Hospital. Parker and Case were friends. But for the flu?

"Don't you have a regular doctor?"

"Call Parker…"

This time she could barely hear the words. "Sure," she

groused. "I'll call a very busy specialist in the middle of the day to talk about a case of the flu." But she didn't really have much choice. Picking up Case's phone from the bedside table, she sighed when she realized she couldn't access his contacts.

She shook his shoulder again. "I need your code, Case."

"2…2…2…2."

Was he delirious, or did he really have such a ridiculously easy password? Apparently the latter, because it worked. Seconds later she located Parker Reese's info and hit the green button.

She fully expected to get an answering machine, but on the third ring, a deep masculine voice answered. "Hey, Case. I'm about to go into surgery. What's up?"

Mellie flushed. Luckily, the highly educated doctor couldn't see her face. "Dr. Reese, this is Mellie Winslow. I showed up at Case Baxter's house this morning to clean and found him passed out on the bed. I think it's the flu, but I have no idea how long he's been like this."

"Several of us played poker last night. Case left early. Must have been feeling bad. I have a full schedule today, but I'll pop by this evening."

"And in the meantime?"

"Push fluids. Alternate acetaminophen and ibuprofen every two hours. Chicken soup and anything else bland."

"I don't think he's going to be eating anytime soon, but I'll try."

Parker's voice changed. "Do you want me to send out a nurse?"

Mellie hesitated. Two seconds. Three at the most. "Thank you, but no. I can do my work and look in on him from time to time. I don't think he would be happy if we brought a stranger in to look after him."

"Good point."

"I'm sorry I bothered you."

"No worries. I'm glad you did. I'll be by later to check on you both."

Mellie ended the call and stared at the man in the bed. Somehow she had gone from being a paid housekeeper to a volunteer nurse.

What would Case Baxter think of this new development?

Six

Mellie located both medicines and fetched orange juice from the kitchen, as well as a notepad to record the time. She didn't want to be responsible for overmedicating her patient. With a little prayer for patience, she returned to the bedroom.

It was a relief to know that Case hadn't been lying sick and alone in this big house for three days. But that also meant he still had tough hours ahead of him. The flu had hit early this year and with a vengeance. Many people had been caught off guard, thinking they still had time to get a flu shot. Fortunately, Mellie had already gotten hers.

Now she knew why Case hadn't answered her text this morning. He'd been out cold, maybe since he'd stumbled home last night. Poor man. She sat on the edge of the bed again, choosing to ignore the fact that the *poor* man was worth seven or eight figures. Even so, he was human. And at the moment he needed her.

She put a straw in the juice since she wasn't sure she

could coax him into sitting up. "Case…" She spoke in a loud voice, hoping to rouse him. He stirred but didn't open his eyes.

"Case." She touched his arm. While she'd been in the kitchen, he had tossed back the covers. His body was still hidden from the waist down, but a broad masculine chest was on display.

His skin was hot. Too hot. She said his name a third time. Finally, he lifted one eyelid. "Leave me alone."

Grumpy and sick was better than semiconscious. "Dr. Reese—Parker—said you need to drink some juice and take something for your fever."

Case rolled to his side, taking the covers with him. He started shivering again. Big, visible tremors that shook the bed. "Parker c-c-can kiss my a-a-ass."

Exasperated, she glared at the lump of truculent male. "You told me to call him."

"Did not."

"Oh, for goodness' sake." She moved around to the other side of the bed and crouched so she could reach his mouth with the straw. "Drink this. Now." She was only slightly astonished when he opened his lips and sucked down a good portion of the OJ.

The muscles in his throat worked. "Tastes good."

"Of course it does. Now open up one more time. You have to swallow these pills."

She tapped his chin. He cooperated, downing the medicine without protest, but afterward he blinked and focused his fever-glazed eyes on Mellie. "Did you just poison me?" he asked.

"Don't tempt me." She glanced at the clock. Hopefully, his temperature would improve in half an hour or so. She grabbed the extra blanket from the foot of the bed and spread it over Case. "Better?"

His nod was barely perceptible. "Thank you."

Those two words went a long way. He might be sick and ornery, but at least he had enough sense not to alienate the only person helping him. "I'll check on you again in a bit. Sleep, Case. That's all you need to do."

Unexpectedly, he reared up in the bed. "Gotta go to the bathroom." He lurched to his feet before she could stop him. And promptly fell over like a giant redwood. His head caught the edge of the bedside table as he went down. A trickle of blood oozed from the small wound.

Dear God in heaven. Save me from stubborn men. She got down on her knees beside him. "Are you okay?"

He rolled to his back, his face ashen. "I never get sick," he said, a look of puzzlement creasing his brow.

His bafflement would have been funny in another situation. But their predicament erased any humor she felt. How in the heck was she going to put him back in bed?

"Can you get on your hands and knees?" she asked. "I'll help you up."

"Of course I can." Five seconds passed. Then ten. Case didn't move. His eyes were half-open, his attention focused upward. "Please tell me there aren't really snakes on my ceiling."

"Your fever is very high. Those are swirly lines in the paint."

"Thank God." He closed his eyes, and his breathing became heavy.

Mellie rubbed his arm. "You said you needed to visit the bathroom. Let's go." Her heart contracted in sympathy, but she kept the drill-sergeant tone in her voice.

She pushed on his hip, hoping to give him a nudge in the right direction. Finally, muttering and coughing, he rolled over and struggled onto his knees.

"Good," she said. All men responded to praise, right?

Putting her arm around his shoulders, she urged him upward, her back screaming in protest. Fortunately, his brain got the message, and he finally stood all the way upright, albeit with a little stagger.

Slowly, carefully, she maneuvered him toward the open bathroom door. She had cleaned every inch of this luxurious space. It was now as familiar to her as her own. But somehow, with the master of the house sharing it with her, the area shrank.

Case noticed himself in the mirror. His mouth gaped. "I look like hell."

"No argument there." She steered him toward the commode.

Her patient locked his knees suddenly, nearly toppling both of them. "I don't need your help."

She counted to ten. "If you fall in here, you could kill yourself on the ceramic tile."

"I'll hold on to the counter."

"Fine." It wasn't as if she wanted to be privy to a personal moment, no pun intended.

Case leaned on the vanity. Mellie retreated and closed the door. She hovered in the middle of the bedroom, half expecting any minute to hear a crash. Instead, nothing but silence.

At last the commode flushed and water ran in the sink. Finally, she heard something she hadn't expected at all. "Mellie? I could use a hand."

She opened the door cautiously and found him sitting on a bench underneath the window. His face was pasty white. He looked miserable. The fact that he had actually asked for help spoke volumes.

Without comment, she leaned into him and looped her arm beneath his armpit and around his back. "You ready?"

He nodded. It was hard to keep a professional distance

from a guy when pressed hip to hip with his big, muscular body. Fortunately, the brief trip across the bedroom rug passed without incident. She managed with Case's help to get him underneath the covers and settled with his head on a pillow.

Without thinking, she put a palm to his forehead to gauge whether or not his temperature was improving. Though Case was clearly befuddled, he raised one eyelid. "You should go home."

His voice was hoarse and thready. She could barely make out the words. "I marked off my book today to work on your house. I'm cleaning the kitchen. It's no trouble to check on you now and then." It was possible he didn't even hear her response. Already his chest rose and fell with steady, harsh breathing.

There was nothing she could do for him now. Instead, she returned to the kitchen and tackled the mess she had made. She had learned a long time ago that to completely overhaul a closet or a cabinet meant creating chaos in the beginning.

The rest of the day crawled by. Dr. Reese's reference to bland foods was a moot point. It was all she could do to coax Case into drinking water and juice from time to time—that and keep him medicated.

At five o'clock she had a decision to make. She didn't have a child at home or a husband waiting. If she'd been in the middle of something jobwise, she would have stayed an extra half hour to complete the task.

But the kitchen was mostly finished, no mess in sight. And Case's request to put his house in order came with no timeline, no urgency. So there was no reason for her to hang around except for the fact that Case Baxter was sick and alone.

They barely knew each other…at least if you overlooked

the not-so-subtle physical attraction and the way he had almost kissed her earlier in the week. Still, this wasn't about flirting or finding a possible love interest or even indulging in some carnal hanky-panky.

Her current situation was dictated by the need of one human to help another.

Wow, even in her head that sounded like pretentious rationalization.

Finally, she worked out a compromise between her conscience and her sense of self-preservation. She would wait for Dr. Parker Reese to arrive, and then she would head home.

Seven o'clock came and went. Then eight. Then nine. The sun had long since set. Outside, the world was cold and gray. Case's house echoed with silence.

Mellie lived alone, and she was perfectly happy. Why was she so worried about a man who chose to be a bachelor? He liked his freedom and his privacy. It was only because he was sick that she felt sorry for him. Surely that was it.

At nine thirty Case's cell rang, with Parker Reese's number appearing on the caller ID. Mellie had kept Case's phone with hers, not wanting him to be disturbed.

She hit the button. "Hello? Mellie Winslow here."

Parker sounded harried and distracted. "I am so sorry, Ms. Winslow, but we've had two moms check into the hospital in early labor and they're having problems. I'll likely be here most of the night. How is Case?"

"He's sleeping. The fever is down some, but it hasn't broken." She'd found a thermometer in Case's bathroom and had kept tabs on the worrisome numbers.

"You're doing the right things. Don't hesitate to call or text if he seems dramatically worse."

"Oh, but I—"

Parker said something to someone in the background, unwittingly interrupting Mellie's response. "I've got to go," he said, his tone urgent. "Keep me posted."

Mellie hung up and stared at the phone. How had she gotten herself into such a predicament?

She wandered down the hallway and stood in the doorway of Case's bedroom, watching him sleep. Today was Friday. The only things she had planned for the weekend were laundry, paying bills and a movie with a girlfriend on Sunday afternoon. Nothing that couldn't be postponed.

But what would happen if she stayed here? Case might be furious.

Then again, could she live with herself if she went home and something happened to him? He was wretchedly sick, certainly not in any shape to prepare food or even to remember when he had taken his doses of medicine. As long as the fever remained high, he might even pass out again.

Her shoulders lifted and fell on a long sigh. She didn't really have much choice. Only a coldhearted person could walk out of this house and not look back. Even if Case hadn't been handsome and charming and sexier than a man had a right to be, she would have felt the same way.

It was no fun to be ill. Even less so for people who weren't married or otherwise attached. Fate and timing had placed her under the man's roof. She would play Clara Barton until he was back on his feet. When that happened, if he tossed her out on her ear, at least her conscience would be clear.

Her bones ached with exhaustion. Not only had she worked extremely hard today, she'd spent a lot of time and energy on her patient. Suddenly, a hot shower seemed like the most appealing thing in the world. Fortunately, she kept spare clothes in the car for times when she needed to change out of her uniform.

Though it seemed like the worst kind of trespassing, she made use of one of the guest bathrooms and prepared for bed. She found a hair dryer under the sink and a new toothbrush in the drawer. In less than twenty minutes, she had showered and changed into comfy yoga pants and a soft much-washed T-shirt.

Case's king bed was large and roomy, and he was passed out cold. She would get more rest there than if she slept in the guest room and had to be up and down all night checking on him.

That reasoning seemed entirely logical right up until the moment she walked into his bedroom and saw that he had, once again, thrown off the covers. The man might have the flu, but looking at him still made her pulse race.

She would have to set the alarm on her phone for regular intervals, because Case was still racked with fever. When she managed to get the thermometer under his tongue and keep it there for long enough to record a reading, it said 101.2 degrees. And that was with medication.

No telling how high it would go if left untreated.

She gave him one last dose of acetaminophen, coaxed him into drinking half a glass of water and straightened his covers. After turning on a light in the bathroom and leaving the door cracked, she stood by the bed.

When this was all over, he would be back to his bossy, impossible self. But for now, he was helpless as a baby.

Refusing to dwell on how unusual the situation was, she walked around to the other side of the bed and sat down carefully. Case was using two of the pillows, but she snagged the third one for herself. There was no way she was going to climb underneath the covers, so she had brought a light blanket from the other bedroom.

Curling into a comfortable position, she reached out and turned off the light.

* * *

Case frowned in his sleep. He'd been dreaming. A lot. Closer to nightmares, really. His head hurt like hell and every bone in his body ached. Not only that, but his mouth felt like sandpaper.

He had a vague memory of someone talking to him, but even those moments seemed unreal.

Suddenly, the shaking started again. He remembered this feeling…remembered fighting it and losing. Aw, hell…

He huddled and gritted his teeth.

Above his head, a voice—maybe an angel—muttered something.

He listened, focused on the soft, soothing sound. "Oh, damn. I didn't hear the alarm. Case, can you hear me? Hold on, Case."

Even in the midst of his semihallucinatory state, the feminine voice comforted him. "S'kay," he mumbled. "I'm fine."

Vaguely, he was aware of someone sticking something under his tongue, cursing quietly and making him drink and swallow. "You are definitely *not* fine."

The angel was upset. And it was his fault. "Hold me," he said. "I can't get warm. And close the windows, please."

The voice didn't respond. Too bad. He was probably going to die and he'd never know what she looked like. Angels were girls, weren't they? All pink and pretty with fluffy wings and red lips and curvy bodies…

Belatedly, he realized that if he survived whatever living hell had invaded his body, he might get struck dead for his sacrilegious imagination.

Suddenly, his whole world shifted from unmitigated suffering to *if this is a dream, I don't want to wake up*. A body—feminine, judging by the soft breasts pressed up against his back—radiated warmth. He would have whimpered if it hadn't been unmanly. *Thank you, God.*

One slender arm curved around his waist. "You'll feel better in the morning, Case."

The angel said it, so it must be true. Doggedly, he concentrated on the feel of his bedmate. It helped keep the pain away. Soft fingers stroked his brow. Soft arms held him tight.

Maybe he would live after all.

Seven

Case opened one eyelid and groaned when a shard of sunlight pierced his skull. *Dear Jesus.* If this was a hangover, he was never going to drink again. And if this was hell, he was going to beg for another chance to relive his thirty-six years and hope for a better outcome.

He moved restlessly. Even his hair follicles hurt. His chest felt as if someone had deflated his lungs. But his brain was clearer than it had been. Though he didn't want to, he made himself open both eyes at the same time. Sitting in an armchair beside his bed was Parker Reese.

Parker hadn't yet noticed that Case was awake. The other man was checking emails and/or texts, frowning occasionally and clicking his responses.

Case cleared his throat. "Am I at death's door? Have you come to show me the error of my ways?"

His doctor friend sat up straight, his gaze sharpening as he turned toward the bed. "You should be so lucky. No…you're going to be fine." Even so, Parker's expression held enough concern to tell Case that something serious was afoot.

"I didn't know you made house calls." Turned out, it even hurt to talk.

"I don't. Here. Drink something." Parker picked up a glass of ice water and held the straw to Case's lips.

Case lifted his head and downed the liquid slowly, trying not to move more than necessary. "Seriously. Why are you here?"

Parker's eyes widened, expressing incredulity. "Maybe because you're half-dead with the flu?"

"Only half?" Case tried to joke, but it fell flat.

Parker pulled out his stethoscope, ignoring Case's wince when the cold metal touched his skin. Listening intently as he moved the disc from side to side, Parker frowned. "We have to watch out for secondary infections, pneumonia in particular."

"How did you know I was sick? Did I look that bad when I left the poker game last night?"

Parker sat back, his head cocked with a clinician's focus. "Today is Saturday. The poker game was Thursday night."

Case gaped at him. "What happened to Friday?"

This time Parker's grin held a note of mischief that rattled Case. "You tell me. I've only been here twenty minutes."

Case subsided into the warm nest of covers and searched his brain for an explanation. He remembered someone in the bed with him, but that someone definitely hadn't been male. He'd been far too sick for any fooling around, so the woman he remembered must have been a dream.

He wet his chapped lips with his tongue. "No more jokes, Parker. Did I really lose an entire day? Surely you didn't wait on me hand and foot. You're a good friend, but not that good."

Parker chuckled. "I'll take pity on you. Yes, you lost a day. You've been out of it for thirty-six hours. And no. I wasn't here to help, though I'm damned sorry about that. You picked the worst possible time to get sick. We've had baby after baby born at the hospital, some of them in worse shape than you, unfortunately. I haven't even been to bed yet, but I wanted to see how you were doing."

"Then who—?"

Parker held up his hand. "Mellie Winslow showed up to work yesterday morning and found you semiconscious, burning up with fever. She stayed with you all day and all night. To be honest, you might have ended up in the hospital if it weren't for her. You've had it rough."

"Damn." It was the best response Case could summon, and the most articulate. With a sinking feeling in his stomach, he remembered someone helping him into and out of the bathroom. Mellie Winslow? Good Lord. "Where is she now?" he asked hoarsely.

"I sent her home so she could change clothes and get some rest."

"Is she coming back?"

"I'd say that's up to you. Mellie knows you like your privacy."

Case winced. "Yeah, I guess she does." He'd certainly hammered home that lesson when he hired her. "I don't know why she stayed with me. I haven't been exactly cordial." In fact, he'd been a bit of a jerk the last time he saw her.

Parker shrugged. "I can hang around until midday. That gives you some time to think it over."

By the time noon came and went, Case had managed a shower with only a little help, had consumed a modest breakfast and lunch, and had realized with no small dose of humility that he had a lot for which to be thankful. Maybe he could salve his conscience concerning Parker by writing another large check to the hospital. Parker got absolutely giddy when he talked about upgrading technology in the NICU.

But what about Mellie?

Parker was on the way out the door when his phone dinged. Case saw his buddy glance down and then look at him.

"What?" Case asked. "Who is it?"

"Mellie wants to know if she needs to come back. What should I tell her?" There was no judgment in Parker's steady gaze.

"I barely know her," Case muttered. "She's not under any obligation to take care of me."

"She's a nice woman. You could do worse."

"Nathan says Amanda will hunt me down and neuter me if I trifle with her friend."

"Trifle?"

"You know. Play around with her."

Parker shook his head in disgust. "I *know* what the word means. Are you tempted to *trifle*?"

"I don't know. Maybe. She's seen me at my worst."

"Is that a good thing or a bad thing?"

"I'm pretty sure Mellie Winslow isn't interested in my money."

"We were talking about you and the flu. Have you changed the subject?"

Case leaned against the doorframe, his knees the consistency of spaghetti. "I need to get back in bed."

"Yes, you do. Your color is lousy."

"Tell her I'll call her after I take a nap."

"You sure?"

Case nodded. "Yeah. Maybe by then I'll have had an epiphany."

"Sounds painful."

"Very funny." Case held out his hand. "Thank you."

Parker returned the handshake. "Glad I could help. If you get worse, don't hesitate to call. Men make lousy patients. Being a hero in this situation is the worst thing you could do."

"Duly noted."

With Parker gone, the house was quiet again. Case stumbled back to his bedroom and fell facedown on the bed. Parker had made him swear to take medicine on schedule. Case intended to keep that promise, but first he had to sleep.

Mellie paced from one side of her smallish living room to the other. Dr. Reese had said that Case would be in touch. But Reese had contacted her right after lunch, and it was now almost five o'clock.

In the interim, she had put together a dish of homemade lasagna and baked that, along with some oatmeal cookies. The house smelled wonderful, but it looked as if she was going to be eating alone.

She could hardly expect Case to be grateful for her help. Men hated feeling vulnerable. Case probably loathed the realization that Mellie had played nurse. Besides, there was a chance he didn't even remember her being there.

But Mellie remembered. Wow, did she. In the middle of the night when Case had finally stopped shivering and his temperature had moderated, she had relaxed enough to doze with him in her arms. She didn't sleep deeply. But when she roused again and again to check on her patient's condition, it had been a shock to find herself entwined with him in a quasi-intimate position.

Gradually, as the night waned, she'd felt something shift inside her. No matter how much she wanted to maintain boundaries for her own emotional protection, after this weekend she would never be able to look at Case the same way again.

The fact that he hadn't called or even sent her a text this afternoon told her he wanted her to stay away. The loud silence hurt. Even though she thought she understood why he hadn't made contact, her feelings were bruised. In truth, she might have to assign someone else to continue cleaning Case's house. The situation was likely untenable.

Telling herself not to be maudlin and foolish, she wandered into the kitchen and found a paper plate and some plastic utensils. She was too tired to worry about cleaning up after herself, and since she had unloaded the dishwasher only an hour before, she didn't want to make a mess.

She was moments away from scooping out a small serving of pasta when her phone made a quiet noise. Her heart pounding, she wiped her hands and glanced at the screen.

Are you busy?

It was Case.

No. Are you hungry?

She told herself she was only being a Good Samaritan. That she wasn't throwing caution to the wind and launching herself willy-nilly into a situation that was wildly inappropriate. Feeding a neighbor in need was a Texas tradition.

Her phone buzzed again.

I'm starving.

I made lasagna. Would you like me to bring you some?

I don't want to interrupt your evening.

She smiled in spite of herself.

It's no trouble. See you soon.

Working rapidly, she covered the casserole dish and wrapped it in towels to keep it warm. The loaf of fresh bread from the bakery in town could be heated in Case's microwave. Even if Dr. Reese had provided lunch for his friend, that was a long time ago. She didn't want Case to wait any longer than necessary.

On the way out to the ranch, she lectured herself. *Stay calm. Don't let him bait you. Treat him like a brother.*

There were two problems with that last suggestion. Number one—she'd never had a brother. And number two—her reactions to Case Baxter bore no resemblance at all to sibling affection. He disturbed her, provoked her and made her want things.

Unfortunately, the trip was not long enough to gain any real handle on the situation. Before she knew it, she was unloading the car and making her way up the steps of Case's home. With her arms full, she had no choice but to ring the bell.

It was almost a full minute before the door opened. Case stood there staring at her, the planes of his face shadowed in the harsh glare of the porch light. "Please come in," he said.

In the foyer, he insisted on taking most of the load away from her. As she followed him to the kitchen, she couldn't help but notice the way his gray sweatpants rode low on his hips. In the midst of the cheery room she had worked so hard to organize, the lighting was better. Now she could see all of Case. His navy cotton shirt was unbuttoned, revealing a white T-shirt underneath that clung to the contours of his muscled chest.

When she could tear her gaze away from all that male magnificence, she saw—as she'd suspected—that he was definitely not 100 percent. His eyes were sunken and his hair was askew. But he smiled.

"This smells amazing, Mellie."

"I hope you like Italian food. I suppose I should have asked about your preferences before I fixed something."

"I'm not a picky eater."

He set the containers on the table and pulled out her chair. "Let me get you a glass of wine," he said. But she noticed that despite his polite manners, he was weaving on his feet.

"Oh, for heaven's sake." She resisted his attempt to make her take a seat. His skin was clammy and his hands unsteady. "You look like you're about to pass out. Sit down, Case. Now."

Surprisingly, he obeyed, but said, "I don't expect you to wait on me." The statement was a shade on the belligerent side.

She handled him the same way she would a fractious toddler. "You're not well. Sit there and rest while I get things ready."

He didn't argue, but his gaze followed her as she moved around his kitchen. His eyes were dark, his unshaven jaw tight. "I owe you an apology," he said. "For what happened when you were here before."

She shot him a look. "You mean last night?"

His jaw dropped noticeably before he snapped it shut. Dark color slashed his cheekbones. "I don't remember much about last night."

For once, she had the upper hand. He was juggling a healthy dose of discomfiture. It was almost funny to see the suave, self-assured cowboy off his game. "Not much to remember." She set a plate of food in front of him. "Eat it before it gets cold."

He grabbed her wrist, not painfully, but firmly. Enough to stop her in her tracks. "I made inappropriate remarks about your clothing. I kissed you. I'm sorry."

Resting her hand on his shoulder, she let herself lean on him. "Don't be silly. You gave me a compliment. I was flattered. And the truth is, you're *not* my boss. You were right. We're equals. A man and a woman."

"And last night?"

When she slept in his bed, holding him in her arms? "Last night was nothing," she said. "You were sick. I couldn't very well leave you here alone. I'm glad you're on the mend."

When she sat down and took a bite of her lasagna, she almost choked at the look on Case's face. His laser stare made her squirm in her seat. There was no way he could know for sure. He'd been too feverish and addled to understand that she had held him like a lover, doing everything she could to give him comfort.

He finally picked up his fork, but he never took his eyes off her. "Parker told me I lost an entire day…that I had a very high fever. He said I might have ended up in the hospital if you hadn't been here to look after me."

"I think your friend exaggerates. It was no big deal."

Case leaned across the table and put his hand over hers. "It is to me. Thank you, Mellie. For everything."

Eight

Case knew he had shocked her. Hell, he had shocked himself. He wasn't a touchy-feely kind of guy. Beneath his hand, Mellie's fingers were soft and delicate. An impression at direct odds with what he knew to be the truth about the woman. She was strong and independent. She didn't need a man to take care of her. Which made it all the more inexplicable that he had the strongest urge to do that very thing.

He forced himself to release her. "Sorry," he muttered. "I didn't mean to make you uncomfortable." She had the look of a rabbit frozen in the grass, trying to appear invisible.

Mellie shook her head. "I'm not uncomfortable. But I'm trying to figure you out."

When he made himself take a bite, he realized how hungry he was. He chewed and swallowed, weighing her words. "I'm an open book."

She snorted and tried to cover it up as a cough. "Um, no."

"Explain yourself, woman." He waved a fork in the air. When Mellie smiled at him, he felt a tug of desire low in his belly.

"First of all," she said, "you're wealthy and available, but you don't date. At least not in Royal."

"How would you know that?" She had him spot-on, but that was beside the point.

"I have my sources." Now her smile was wry.

"Go on."

"You're a self-professed privacy junkie, but you know everyone in town, and you are so popular and well regarded the powers that be elected you president of the Cattleman's Club."

"Liking privacy is not necessarily the same as being a hermit."

"True."

He circled back to the most promising point. "I'm flattered that you've studied me."

Mellie shook her head. "Don't be. Your ego is too healthy as it is."

"Ouch." He paused, realizing that he was deliberately flirting with Mellie. But his sexual overture wasn't necessarily being reciprocated. "Ego is neither good nor bad. I think it's a matter of degree."

"And where would you fall on that scale? Somewhere near the top, I think."

He stared at her, no longer amused. "You might be surprised." Finishing his meal, he stood and poured himself another glass of wine, cursing the fact that his legs were wobbly. Sadly, it had nothing to do with the modest amount of alcohol he had consumed. How long was this damned flu going to keep him down? He had places to go, people to see.

At his best, he would have enjoyed sparring with Mellie

Winslow. But he was definitely not at his best. He brought the bottle with him to the table and collapsed into his chair, trying not to let on that he was light-headed.

Mellie studied him. "You need to be in bed," she said.

"Will you join me?" The words popped out of his mouth uncensored. His subconscious was an uncivilized beast.

His dinner companion gaped. Her mouth snapped shut as hot color reddened her cheeks. "What is it about men?" she muttered, the question apparently rhetorical.

Now he had her measure. If he wanted to keep Mellie off balance and not the other way around, all he had to do was give her the unvarnished truth about what he wanted from her. "What do you mean?"

She shrugged. "You're barely able to stand, and still you obsess about sex."

"It's in our DNA. We can't help it. Especially when a beautiful woman brings us dinner and plays nurse."

"I wasn't playing last night. You were sick."

"I'm only sorry I wasn't able to enjoy it."

"Case!"

Now it was out in the open. He wanted her. And he was almost certain she wanted him, too. But he needed confirmation before he went any further. He would never pursue a woman who wasn't interested.

"There's a strong spark between us. But tell me you don't feel it, and I'll leave you alone. Am I wrong?"

He saw the muscles in her throat work as she sputtered and looked anywhere but at him. "You're not wrong."

Three words. Three damn words, and he was hard as granite. He studied her, unable to come up with a response. She wasn't wearing her uniform. Instead, soft denim jeans outlined long legs and a narrow waist. In deference to the weather, she wore a pale green pullover sweater. The

V-neck exposed a long porcelain-skinned throat and fragile collarbone.

A man could get lost nibbling his way across that territory.

Under other circumstances, he would have stripped her naked and taken her on this kitchen table. Tonight, however, he had to accept his limitations. "Sadly, I don't have the stamina at the moment to follow up on that interesting admission."

"There's no reason you should." She appeared entirely, frustratingly calm...until one noticed the way her lips trembled the tiniest bit.

"We're dancing around this, aren't we?" The woman who almost certainly didn't have casual sex and the man who wanted more than he was able to give at the moment.

Mellie stood, resting her hands on the back of her chair. "I'll come back tomorrow...with more food."

"Don't be afraid of me, Mellie." He meant it. He couldn't bear the notion she might think he was blasé about this. The level of his fascination with her, the depth of his hunger, made no sense. But he wasn't a man to walk away from something he wanted. Even when having her and protecting her seemed to be two diametrically opposed behaviors.

And that wasn't even considering the fact that his actions might spark the wrath of Amanda Battle...or worse, her sheriff husband.

"I'm not afraid of you," Mellie said, her beautiful eyes grave. "Or even afraid of the possibility of us. But I've never started a physical relationship with a man, knowing up front that it had an expiration date."

Her words made sense. He even understood her caution. The feminine hesitation, though, only made his libido fight all the more to be heard. "It's not necessary to plan every turn in the road in advance...is it?"

Temper sparked in her expressive eyes. "Do me the favor of not pretending, Case. If I have sex with you, we both know it will be a physical thing only. No hearts and flowers. No pledges of undying love."

"That's pretty cynical."

"But accurate."

He wanted to argue, but he didn't have a leg to stand on. Mellie had pegged him pretty well. "So that's a no?" Never in a million years would he admit that her harsh assessment of his motives stung. Most women in this situation would be all over him.

But he was rapidly learning that Mellie Winslow was not *most* women.

She shrugged. "Let's take it a day at a time. This flu isn't going to go away overnight. Maybe you'll have the opportunity to rethink your invitation."

"Don't go," he said gruffly. He wanted her here…under his roof. In a way he hadn't wanted anything in a very long time. "It's not like I can seduce you. I can barely hold my head up."

Mellie shivered, though the kitchen was warm. He was doing it again. Winnowing away her good intentions. Trying to pretend that he wasn't the Big Bad Wolf and Mellie a wretchedly willing Red Riding Hood.

"I can't stay the night." That was a lie. She *could*. But she wouldn't.

"A movie, then. I'm sick of lying in bed."

"Such a touching offer. I'm better than boredom."

"You have a smart mouth."

She took pity on him. Beneath his masculine swagger, he was the color of milk. "I'll stay for a while."

"Good."

When he got to his feet, she moved closer and slipped

an arm around his waist, inhaling the smell of warm male. "I don't want to scrape you off the floor again."

He chuckled, the low sound making her catch her breath. "Is that how I got the knot on my skull?"

"Let's just say that you were not the best patient last night."

He kissed the top of her head casually, as if they were an old married couple wandering down the hall to watch a favorite TV program. "You're more than I deserve."

"Damn straight." Making Case Baxter laugh was fast becoming her life's work. But it was either that or give in to the urge to join the handsome, bad-to-the-bone cowboy in his bed.

They had their next argument in the den. Case collapsed on the expensive leather sofa and crooked an arrogant finger. "Come sit with me, Mellie."

"I'll be fine right here." She snagged a spot on the matching love seat, a safe distance away from the heavy-eyed male. "Have you taken your medicine?"

He scowled at her. "Is that all you can talk about? You're a broken record."

"I'll get it," she said wryly. Clearly, he was feeling like roadkill and didn't want to admit it.

When she returned after gathering what she needed from his bedroom and the bathroom, Case was holding the remote, his expression moody as he channel surfed. She put a hand on his forehead, not surprised to find it ferociously hot.

"Take these." She shook a couple of caplets into her palm and held out a glass of water.

"I feel fine."

His big body radiated tension. They had entered dangerous territory. Case was physically frustrated, not only from sexual arousal but because his brain was writing a check his body couldn't cash. As far as she could tell, he was holding himself upright by sheer stubbornness.

She nudged his knee, keeping her tone light and gentle. "Be reasonable, and I'll sit with you. You can put your head in my lap."

It was the perfect opening for some of his sharp-edged sexual innuendo. The fact that he said nothing worried her. He must feel worse than she realized.

When he finished the glass of water—and in the process downed his meds—he stretched full-length on the sofa. Mellie sat down as promised, stroking the hair from his forehead. "Do you really want to watch a movie?" she asked.

He shook his head without opening his eyes. "No. I feel like hell."

"Okay, then…"

After a few seconds, Case's breathing deepened, and she knew he had fallen asleep. The old house creaked and popped as it settled for the night. On the mantel, a beautiful clock ticked away the minutes.

The moment was surreal. How had she and Case transcended so many social barriers so quickly? She was the hired help. He was the rich cowboy. He had one failed marriage behind him. She'd always been too afraid of loss to give marriage a try.

Yet here they were. As intimate together as if they had already become lovers.

With nothing else to command her attention, she traced the shell of his ear with her fingertip, trying to imagine what he would be like in bed. Healthy. Vigorous. Demanding.

She pressed her legs together, her insides shaking with what could only be described as lust. Delicious, quivery, melting need. Heaven help her when Case was back to his old self.

Right now he was like some brilliant sun dimmed by a dust storm. The essence of the arrogant cowboy was still there but muted. The reduced kilowatts made it possible for her to keep up her guard. Maybe it was his vulnerability that stripped away her defenses and misgivings. Perhaps Case Baxter had seduced her without even trying.

The evening waned along with her need to hold him at bay. Would she end up sharing his bed? Why shouldn't she? Becoming Case's lover might well turn out to be the highlight of her adult life.

She knew most of the available men in Royal. Not one of them had sparked more than a fleeting interest in her over the years. So maybe she was destined to be happily single, a focused businesswoman, a dutiful daughter and a generous friend.

Living alone was not a dreadful thought. She understood Case in that respect. There was something to be said for peace and quiet and the chance to spend time with your thoughts. Case valued his privacy. Mellie valued her independence. It was a match made in heaven.

Temporary. Wildly enjoyable. Mutually satisfying.

Regretfully, the two of them were not going to get intimate tonight.

At nine o'clock she eased out from under her not-unwelcome burden and stood to stretch the kinks out of her muscles. Case never made a sound. He was deeply asleep.

His chin was shadowed with the beginnings of a dark beard. Even though she had seen him numerous times with his customary scruffy facial hair, now he looked far less civilized.

She felt guilty for leaving him like this. Still, he was a grown man and she was under no obligation, ethically or otherwise, to stay. Parker Reese would check on him eventually.

After tidying the kitchen and gathering her things, she slipped out the front door and locked it behind her. Unfortunately, when she arrived at home, she found her father sitting on the doorstep again.

Nine

She greeted him with a grimace. "It's late, Dad. What do you want?"

He didn't even offer to help her carry anything into the house. Which, unfortunately, was typical. Harold Winslow spent most of his time worrying about Harold Winslow.

"I need to borrow fifty bucks, baby girl. Just until Monday. I'm good for it."

She'd long since given up keeping track of her father's IOUs. His requests were always modest amounts. Fifty here, a hundred there. Even when she gently reminded him he owed her money, he was all smiles and apologies. But the repayment never took place.

It was her own fault. All she had to do was cut him off, and he would get the message…eventually. But regardless of his failings, Harold was her father. He'd helped raise her, and he'd been the one she'd clung to when her mother died. He was her own flesh and blood.

"Why do you need the money, Daddy?" She dumped everything on the kitchen counter and confronted him.

Harold gaped, his expression both astonished and cagey. She'd never before pressed him about where the cash went. She hadn't wanted to know.

His bloodshot eyes stared back at her. "I had a lot of bills this month," he muttered.

"Is that why you don't have enough left for drinking tonight and tomorrow?"

"I don't appreciate your tone," he snapped.

She had definitely ruffled his feathers. But at the moment, she was so tired and dispirited she didn't care. "I'm not an ATM. I have expenses of my own and a business to support."

"Where have you been tonight?"

The change of topic caught her off guard. After a split second's hesitation, she saw no reason to dissemble. "I took dinner to Case Baxter. He has the flu."

"Well, ain't that sweet."

Her father's colloquial sarcasm nicked her patience. "I'm tired, Daddy. And it's late. Why don't you go home and have a rum and Coke…without the rum."

Harold's face turned red. "What's gotten into you, girl? If you think hangin' out with that fancy-ass richer-than-God cowboy makes you something special, you're wrong. Big-shot ranchers don't marry women who clean their toilets."

His deliberate crudeness broke her heart a little bit. Was this what they had come to? She refused him one time and he attacked?

Her chest aching with emotion, she reached for her purse, opened it and took out a handful of bills. When she held out her hand, Harold grabbed the money as if he was afraid she might change her mind.

Suddenly, her father was all smiles. "You're good to your old dad. I won't forget it." He folded the money clumsily and stuffed it in his shirt pocket.

She dug her teeth into her bottom lip, trying not to cry. "I'm done, Daddy. This is the last time. I want you to get help."

"I told you…I'm fine. Don't know why you're kicking up such a fuss about a little bit of cash."

"I've been looking at the rental income. You could be living like a king." She helped out with the Winslow Properties business, and though she wasn't in that office very often, she knew enough to realize the incoming cash was substantial. And she also knew that Harold wasn't pouring any of that money back into upkeep and development.

"You worried about your inheritance? Is that it?"

The insult barely registered. She had figured out a long time ago that her father would be lucky not to end up a pauper. "I'm worried about *you*," she said quietly. "And though you may not believe me, I'm done. No more handouts."

He backed toward the door, his posture hunted. "I may sell the Courtyard," he said defiantly. "I've had inquiries from a company called Samson Oil."

The Courtyard was an old renovated ranch several miles west of town. It included a large barn and a collection of buildings that housed a growing and thriving arts community, consisting of both studios and retail shops. The land on which the Courtyard sat increased in value day by day.

"You know selling would be a big mistake." He was threatening her. Manipulating her. Classic addict behavior.

Harold shrugged. "That's your opinion. I gotta go. See you later."

Before she could react, he disappeared. Moments later she heard the front door slam.

She sank into a kitchen chair and buried her face in her

hands. If she had stayed at Case's house, she could have avoided her father tonight.

Scarcely five minutes had passed when her doorbell rang again. *Damn it.* If Harold had come back, she was going to have a little hissy fit. She wiped her eyes with the back of her hand and stood up, grabbing a paper napkin to use as a makeshift tissue.

Rarely did she let her father get to her. But as she blew her nose, she conceded inwardly that his barbs had hit the mark. He was often a mean drunk, and tonight was no exception.

It was a distinct relief to find Amanda Battle on the other side of the door. "Come in," Mellie said.

"I won't stay long. I know it's late." Amanda slipped past her, shivering dramatically. "What happened to the warm days?" The sheriff's wife was tall and slim and full of energy.

"We're headed toward the holidays. It was bound to happen. What's up, Amanda? I doubt you came to see me for a discussion about the weather."

Amanda chuckled. "The guys are playing poker at our house. I had to get out of there for a few minutes. Besides, I need a firsthand report. Nathan called Case a little while ago to see how he's doing, but you know how men are. Case said he was fine."

"You don't believe him?"

"Parker told us Case was in bad shape. He said if you hadn't shown up at the ranch to clean yesterday and found Case, he might have ended up in the hospital."

"Well, I don't know about that. I'm glad I happened to be there. I did take dinner to him this evening. He was grumpy but overall seemed somewhat better." Better enough to flirt, anyway. Not that she was about to tell Amanda that.

"You're definitely a Good Samaritan. But don't worry. Several of his friends and their wives and girlfriends have put together a meal schedule. We won't let him starve. You're off the hook with a clear conscience. And Parker is going to keep tabs on Case's flu symptoms."

"That's great."

Mellie knew Amanda didn't mean to sound dismissive… or as if she were kicking Mellie to the curb. Even so, the unintentional message was clear. Mellie was not part of that tight-knit circle of friends. It was ridiculous to let her feelings be bruised. Maybe because she had recently gone several rounds with her father, she was feeling fragile.

Amanda glanced at her watch and sighed. "I'd better get back. I promised Nathan I'd throw together some nachos."

Mellie raised an eyebrow. "At this hour?"

"When this crew convenes, they like to pretend they're all eighteen again."

"You wouldn't have it any other way. I hear it in your voice."

Amanda shrugged, her expression sheepish. "Yeah. You know me—I love to cook for people. And these guys work so hard it's fun to see them unwind."

"Nathan is lucky to have you."

Amanda's grin was smug. "Yes, he is."

Mellie walked her friend outside, feeling unmistakably envious of Amanda's good fortune. What would it be like to be loved in such a way that you knew the other person would never let you down or disappoint you, at least not in any significant way?

Ila Winslow had been that person for Mellie. But once she was gone, Mellie had been forced to face a few cold, hard truths. Love, true love, whether familial or romantic, was rare and wonderful.

* * *

The next day dawned bright and sunny, which seemed a shame given Mellie's mood. She would have much preferred gray and gloomy so she could blame her low spirits on something other than the fact she was not going to see Case Baxter today.

She attended church and brunch with a friend, then popped by the gym for her regular yoga class. In the locker room afterward as she showered, washed her hair and changed, she felt much better. Case was a blip on her radar. No need to get all hot and bothered about a guy who wasn't even her type.

Yeah, right. Her sarcastic inner woman-child sassed her.

As was her custom, Mellie had left her cell phone in the car. No one ever needed her on Sunday, and she always relaxed more knowing that she was unplugged from the electronic world, even if only for an hour and a half.

It was a shock to return to her vehicle in the parking lot and find that her cell phone had exploded with texts.

My cleaning lady has gone missing.

Twenty minutes after that: I pay double time on Sundays. Are you interested?

Mellie stared at the screen. Interested in what? The shiver that snaked down her spine had less to do with cold air hitting her damp hair than it did the prospect of deliberately placing herself beneath Case's roof during nonbusiness hours.

Then a third text: You've already been exposed. Why not keep me company?

Why not, indeed? She slid into the driver's seat, uncertain how to answer. She decided to go with bland and professional and see what happened. I don't work on Sundays, she texted. Hope you're feeling better. I thought I would stay out of your way for now. Once you're well, I can pick up where I left off.

She made it a habit not to text and drive, so on the way home she ignored the series of dings indicating she had new messages. It wasn't until she pulled into her garage that she let herself read Case's responses…one right after another.

I don't give a damn right now if my house is clean and organized.

I'm bored.

Give a guy a break.

How humiliating was it that her hands shook as she used her phone? Case was telling the truth. He was bored, and he thought Mellie was available. She should ignore him… pretend her cell was turned off…or invent a very important function she simply couldn't miss.

Gnawing her lip, she walked a fine line between cordial and suggestive. You sound grumpy.

Of course I'm grumpy, he shot back. I'm in solitary confinement.

You probably deserve it. Oops. That definitely sounded flirtatious. JK, she added rapidly.

Her phone stayed silent for a full two minutes. She'd offended him. Yikes.

Finally, he wrote back.

Please come see me, Mellie. I'll be on my best behavior. And you don't need to cook for me. I've got enough food here to feed an army regiment.

Well, shoot. She was a strong person, but not strong enough to say no to something she really wanted. She tapped the screen.

Okay…give me an hour. Do you need me to bring anything?

Just you.

As a woman, she was generally low maintenance. An hour should have been enough time to get ready and drive out to the ranch. But she dithered over what to wear. Finally, she chose a charcoal-gray wool skirt with knee-high black leather boots and a scoop-necked black sweater with a gray chevron pattern across the chest. Silver hoop earrings and a silver necklace with a key charm completed her look.

The outfit was probably too dressy. But she could always let him think she had worn this to church. Her mother's voice echoed in her head. *Never pretend to be something you're not, Mellie. Tell the truth, even if it hurts.*

Mellie stared in the mirror, tucking a stray fiery strand behind her ear. For a moment, she contemplated leaving her long hair loose. But that might send the wrong message. Since she wasn't exactly sure what it was that she wanted to communicate to Case Baxter, it was probably smarter not to be quite so…flamboyant.

Her hair was hard to miss. Which was why she often kept it confined to a knot on top of her head or in a ponytail. Neither style seemed appropriate for tonight. She pulled the thick mass of red and gold to the side of her neck, secured it with a hairband and let it fall over one shoulder.

As she examined her reflection in the mirror, she saw

much more than a young woman dressed up for an evening that was definitely not a date. She saw uncertainty. Maybe a slice of anxiety. Most visible, however, was the undercurrent of excitement.

Grimacing, she turned and fled before she could change her mind again about what to wear. She grabbed her coat from the closet by the front door, slid her arms into it, freed her hair and scooped up her car keys.

The early evening had turned foggy. Case's house appeared out of the gathering gloom like a regal old lady, sure of her place in the community. Lonely, perhaps, but unapologetic. A light beside the front door offered a welcoming glow.

Mellie felt her pulse wobble as she climbed the steps to the porch.

Case met her at the top of the stairs, the door half-open behind him. "It's about time," he said. When he grinned, she knew he was teasing.

"You shouldn't be outside," she said. "It's freezing."

He put an arm around her shoulders and steered her into the house. "I had to get some fresh air. It's like a tomb in here."

As he took her coat, she smiled wryly. "Nicest tomb I've ever seen."

He shrugged. "I'm still running a fever. You can't trust anything I say."

And wasn't that the crux of the matter?

She laughed because he wanted her to. Still, the irony was not lost on her. "Do you really have a temperature?"

Case stopped short and bent his head. Taking her hand, he placed it on his forehead. "See."

He wasn't kidding. "How long since you've had medicine?"

"I don't know. Four hours? Five? It's probably time."

"Case…"

"Don't scold me," he said. "It makes me hot, and I'm too weak to ravish you." He urged her along the hallway and into the den. A roaring fire in the fireplace added warmth and color to a room that was sophisticated but comfy. A silver tray laden with an assortment of decadent treats was set up on the coffee table in front of the sofa.

After surveying the chocolate-dipped strawberries, champagne and candied fruits, she shot Case an incredulous glance. "Where on earth did this come from? Your friends have outdone themselves."

He sat down rather suddenly, his face an alarming shade of white. "My friends brought fried chicken and green beans. I ordered this stuff online from a specialty shop in town."

"Ah." The small luxuries seemed an odd choice for a man recovering from the flu. But then again, her personal experience with wealthy men was practically nonexistent. Perhaps for Case, this was the equivalent of buttered popcorn and jujubes at the movie theater.

"Sit down," he said gruffly, his eyes closed. "I'll be okay in a minute."

"Did you actually eat any of the fried chicken?" she asked.

"Not yet. I took a shower."

The unspoken inference was that getting his hand-delivered meal onto a plate was more than he could handle. Poor man. "Rest for a few minutes and I'll bring your meal in here."

"Thanks."

He was trying so hard to act tough, but the flu was no respecter of persons. Even a broad-shouldered, macho, athletic guy like Case Baxter could fight back only so far before admitting defeat.

In the kitchen she saw that Case had piled a few dirty dishes in the sink. On the granite-topped island she found a large disposable aluminum pan filled with an enormous amount of fried chicken. And it wasn't from the chain restaurant in town. This was the real deal.

Her mouth watered. So much for the yoga class. Ignoring her better judgment, she fixed two plates with crisp chicken breasts, home-canned green beans and fluffy yeast rolls with butter. Who knew what her host wanted to drink? But the truth was, he should have plenty of water.

Balancing two bottles she plucked from the fridge, she picked up the plates and carried them back to the den. Her host had fallen asleep again.

She stood there looking at him for long minutes, wishing she could put a name to the yearning that tightened her throat and forced her to blink moisture from her lashes. For years she had kept an eye out, always wondering if there was some special guy out there for her. But Prince Charming never showed up.

Now…here…in the most unlikely of places, she found herself tumbling headlong into an infatuation that was sure to break her heart.

Ten

Case came awake with a start, jerking upright and wondering if he had dreamed Mellie. No…there she was. Sitting across from him. Looking young and sexy and prim, her knees pressed together and her hands folded in her lap.

"Sorry," he grimaced. "I keep doing that."

Mellie lifted a shoulder. "That's the drill. Lots of rest and plenty of fluids."

He ran a hand through his hair, wincing when the restrained motion made his head throb. "How long have I been out?"

"Only forty-five minutes."

Damn it. "And you've probably been sitting here starving."

"If I was that hungry, I wouldn't have waited for you. Give me a minute and I'll put everything in the microwave to warm it up."

"No." Once Mellie left the room, he'd probably crash again. "I'm not that picky. Let's do this."

"If you're sure…"

It occurred to him that sitting up long enough to eat was a daunting proposition, even though he was ravenous. Still, he washed the Tylenol down with the bottle of water and then started in on his chicken.

Mellie ate quietly. She was a restful woman. At least when she wasn't arguing with him. He managed half of the chicken breast, the roll and a few of the green beans before he admitted defeat. Pushing his plate away, he leaned back in the embrace of the sofa and rested his head, telling himself he was on the mend. Mind over matter. That was his mantra.

His companion looked askance at him. "You need the protein," she said.

"I had a mother. I don't need another one."

Mellie blinked, set down her fork and stood. "I'll come back when you're in a better mood."

The careful rebuke hit its mark.

"I'm sorry," he muttered. "Don't go."

She crossed her arms at her waist. "I'm getting mixed signals, Case."

"I know." It was true. He wanted to be alone to wallow in his misery, but at the same time, he was intrigued by Mellie Winslow and charmed by her matter-of-fact caring.

Her hair glowed tonight, the long strands catching light from the fixture overhead. The sweater she wore was fitted but not tight. Even so, he was well aware of her ample breasts.

"Sit down. Please. I have a proposition for you."

The expression on her face told him she was evaluating all meanings of that statement. "Um…"

"Oh, hell, Mellie. I can't even finish dinner. Do you really think I'm going to lure you into my bed?"

"Of course not," she muttered, looking anywhere but

at his face. She sat down hard on the sofa, not so much an act of will as a necessary evil, as if her legs had given out. He knew the feeling.

It was a sure bet she didn't trust him. But he had a plan to win her over. "I'd like to become a silent partner in the Keep N Clean. With my investment, you wouldn't have to wait to expand."

Mellie opened and closed her mouth like a fish gasping for oxygen. She shook her head. "No, thank you."

He stared at her, his pulse far too rapid. "Maybe you didn't understand. I'd like to give you fifty thousand dollars. It's the least I can do to repay you for playing nurse."

Now his dinner guest looked murderous. "The milk of human kindness is not for sale, Mr. Baxter. Some things in life are free."

"Has anyone ever told you that you're incredibly over-sensitive?" Aggravation made his head ache like the devil.

She stared him down, her green eyes chilled to the shade of moss. "You hired me to clean and organize your house. An ordinary business arrangement. I neither want nor need your investment money."

Though it took every ounce of energy he could muster, he levered his body off the sofa and joined her on the love seat. Her spine was so straight it was a wonder it didn't crack under the weight of her disapproval.

He rested his arm behind her shoulders. "Don't make a hasty decision, Mellie. This is what I do. I find it very rewarding to help local businesses grow."

"You don't get it."

They were so close he could see the faint, almost imperceptible veins beneath her fair skin. At her temple... in the dip above her collarbone. "So explain it to me," he urged. "I'm listening." He was trying to listen, though all he really wanted to do was kiss her.

Mellie's head was bent, her profile as simple and sweet as a Madonna's. The feelings she invoked in him, however, were a far cry from religious. More like the temptations of the damned.

She inhaled and exhaled, sliding him a sideways glance that begged for understanding. "The Keep N Clean is *mine*. I've sweated and worried and planned and strategized… every mile of the way. I could have stepped into the family business and worked alongside my father, but I needed something that belonged to me…something he couldn't ruin."

"That's pretty harsh."

"You don't know him." Her smile was bleak. "He's an alcoholic…with not the slightest interest in recovery. People in town make jokes about him. The sheriff has a cell with Harold's name on it. I didn't want to be a part of that, but…"

She ground to a halt, biting her lip, her distress almost palpable.

"But what?" He smoothed a strand of hair away from her cheek, tucking it behind her ear. Her skin was softer than a Texas sunrise, all pink and pretty and sweet.

"I can't bear to see him go completely down the abyss. So I keep giving him money. Which is stupid, because his business pulls in twice what mine does."

Her voice broke as a single tear rolled down her cheek. Mellie seemed oblivious. Case felt something twist inside his chest. He couldn't tell if it was a good feeling or a bad one…maybe just damned scary.

Pulling her head to his shoulder, he stroked her hair, releasing the band that held it and using his fingers to winnow through the fragrant mass. "Sometimes doing the right thing is really hard."

"How would you know?" The question was tart.

He rested his chin on top of her head. "My college

roommate had a drug problem, but he hid it from me for almost a year. I was constantly bailing him out of jail and making excuses for him. Until the night I came home from a date with my current girlfriend and found Toby on the floor of our apartment. Dead. From an overdose."

He recited the tale simply, even though the recounting jabbed at a spot in his heart that had never quite healed.

Mellie pulled back to look at him, her eyes wide and distraught. "Oh, Case. I'm so sorry." She put her hands on his cheeks. "You must have been devastated."

Her simple empathy reached down inside the hard shell he'd worn since his divorce and found purchase in a tiny crack. Emotions roiled in his chest, feelings he hated. It was much simpler when he saw Mellie Winslow as simply a potential bed partner. He didn't want to know her innermost secrets. He didn't want to care.

But he was lost…defeated. Almost before the battle had begun. "I want to kiss you," he said raggedly, "but I can't. I'm sick."

Her smile was both wicked and reassuring. "Then I'll kiss *you*," she whispered.

Never in his life had he let a woman take the initiative. Though he didn't mind an aggressive woman in bed if the mood was right, he liked to lead the dance. Even so, it was damned arousing to submit, even momentarily, to Mellie's slightly awkward affections.

She started with his stubbly jaw, her tongue damp against his hot skin. The feminine purr of pleasure sent every drop of blood to his sex, leaving him hard and breathless.

"Mellie?"

She ignored him. Leaning into his embrace, she nuzzled his ear, kissed his brow, traced his nose with a fingertip. When her mouth hovered over his, he protested. "No." It might have been more convincing if he hadn't been dragging her against his chest. "I don't need your pity."

"But you want to kiss me."

It was a statement, not a question. He shuddered, his arousal viciously demanding, relentlessly insistent. *Take, take, take.* "Of course I want to kiss you," he said, the words sandpaper in his throat. Any living, breathing heterosexual male would want to kiss her.

Carefully, telling himself he was still in control, he slid a hand beneath the edge of her sweater and found the plane of her belly with his fingertips. Mellie's sharp intake of breath spurred him on. When she didn't move, not even a millimeter, he found her breast and palmed it.

Hell. Her curves were all woman. Beneath a layer of silky stuff and lace, he felt her heat, her life force. Wanting turned him inside out.

Moving slowly so as to not alarm her, he eased them into a reclining position, Mellie on her back, Case on his side—against the couch—his upper body sheltering hers.

She stared up at him, wide-eyed. "We can't do this."

He unfastened the button on the side of her skirt... lowered the zipper...exposed her practical cotton undies. "I know."

"Wait." She put a hand on his wrist. "Weren't you supposed to woo me with champagne and strawberries?"

He was shaking. Either his fever was back or he was out of control. "Dessert," he said, the words barely audible. "In a little while."

His hand moved of its own accord, breaching the inconsequential narrow barrier of elastic on her bikini underpants and sliding lower.

Mellie whimpered. There was no other word for it. In that raw, needy sound, he heard every last one of his scruples and reservations spelled out. This was insane. *He* was insane.

He swallowed hard. "Shall I stop?" She would never know what the question cost him.

She held his hand against her body, gripping his wrist until her fingernails dug into his skin. The spark of pain drove his lust a notch higher. "Don't you dare."

When he found the moist cleft of her sex, they both groaned. As he stroked her gently, he felt her lift against his hand.

He was dizzy...hungover...and he hadn't even popped the cork on the bubbly. "Close your eyes, Mellie."

Mellie panted, her chest rising and falling rapidly. Why hadn't he removed her sweater? Hell, he couldn't stop now. It wouldn't be fair.

"I want to see you naked," he said urgently.

"Please, don't stop..." The three words were raspy, but ended on a sharp cry.

Watching and feeling Mellie find satisfaction was humbling. No pretenses. No big show. Just a woman experiencing pleasure—deep, raw gratification.

When she could breathe again, he rested his forehead on hers. "I want you."

She licked her lips, her expression befuddled. "You've been desperately ill. Maybe your heart's not healthy enough for sex." She dared to tease him.

"My heart's fine," he groused, not amused by her joking allusion to a television commercial. "And I don't appreciate the reference. I have the flu, not ED."

She curled her arms around his neck, smiling drowsily. "You're gorgeous even when you're sick. It's not fair. And PS, I've never done it with a cowboy."

"You *still* haven't done it," he pointed out, his disgruntlement tempered only by the fact that he felt like hell.

"They say anticipation is half the pleasure."

"I'd like a chance to find out."

"The first day you're well, I swear. We'll drink that champagne and go for it."

"Cheap advice from a woman who just—"

She clapped her hand over his mouth. "Don't be grouchy. Your time will come. In fact, if you think you're up to it, I'm right here. Carpe diem and all that."

He thought about it. Seriously. For about ten seconds. But a quick assessment of his head-to-toe misery settled the argument. "No," he sighed. "I want to impress you with my carnal prowess."

"Is that really a thing?"

"You'll have to wait and see, now, won't you?"

She frowned, examining his face, no doubt spotting the damp forehead and the sudden lack of color. "You need to be in bed," she said firmly. "Alone."

He wanted to argue. He *really* wanted to argue. But damn it, Mellie was right. "I don't want you to leave," he said. "You keep me occupied."

"That's one word for it." She sat up, forcing him to, as well. When they were hip to hip, she took his hand. "I think it's best if I put cleaning your house on hold…give you a week to recover without anyone underfoot. If you're better by the end of the week, we'll talk about resuming our original schedule."

"I *have* to be better by the weekend," he said.

"Why?"

"The club is throwing a big party Saturday night to honor me as the new president."

"Ah."

"That's all you have to say…*ah*?"

She cocked her head. "What do you want me to say?"

"You could at least act interested."

"I don't follow."

"Oh, for God's sake, Mellie. You know I want you to go with me."

She stood abruptly. "I most certainly do not. We're barely acquaintances."

"Aren't you forgetting what just happened? When I rocked your world?" He smiled to let her know he was kidding about the world-rocking thing.

Mellie actually winced. "Aside from your Texas-sized ego, what you and I have been dancing around is the possibility of a fling, *not* any kind of official status. That's crazy."

"Why won't you go with me? It's a single social occasion, not a relationship."

Her reluctance dinged his pride. It wasn't boasting to say that any one of a large number of women in Royal would be pleased to attend the upcoming party as his guest. Mellie looked as if he had offered to take her to a funeral.

"I like my life just fine, Case. Other than the occasional run-in with my dad, I'm pretty happy with the way things have turned out for me. I own a business I love… I have a lot of interesting friends. I'm not interested in finding a man to take care of me."

His temper started a slow boil. "We're talking about a *party*, Ms. Winslow. It's hardly a basis for what you're thinking about."

"True. But if we end up in bed together, I'd rather no one else know about it. That way when we're done, there won't be any messy explanations to deal with."

When we're done… Maybe if he hadn't felt so rotten, he might have been able to understand why her blithe prediction about their future bothered him so much.

"Fine," he said, his jaw clenched. "I won't ask again. If you want me, you'll have to say so. I'm done here."

Eleven

If you want me, you'll have to say so. Mellie replayed those words in her head a thousand times over the next four days. Her departure from Case's house Sunday evening was not her finest hour. He had stormed out of the room, and she had left without saying goodbye.

She was ashamed of her behavior. Her only excuse was that, even sick, Case Baxter made her jittery and uncertain about things she had always seen as rock solid in her life. For one, her assumption that having an intimate relationship with a man was something she didn't have time for.

Honestly, she worked so hard and kept so busy, she rarely thought about what she was missing. She dated now and then, but with only a couple of exceptions over the years, she'd never felt an inescapable urge to have sex just for the sake of having sex.

She thought about it. Alone at night. In the privacy of her bedroom. But her fantasy lovers were compliant and undemanding...exactly the opposite of Case Baxter.

What did he want with her?

By the time she closed the office for a late lunch on Thursday afternoon, she had brought her books up to date, signed contracts with three new clients and worked herself into a mental frenzy of uncertainty. Instead of heading home, she pointed her car in the direction of the diner.

She had to talk to someone, or she'd explode. Amanda was the logical choice.

Fortunately, the sheriff's wife was in her usual spot, smiling and swapping jokes with her regular customers. Mellie had purposely waited until almost two o'clock, hoping that the noon rush would be over and Amanda would have time for a chat. Because of the subject matter, Mellie snagged the booth in the far back corner, hoping to talk quietly without being overheard.

When the other woman headed her way, Mellie waved a hand at the opposite side of the booth. "Do you have time to take a break? I need some advice."

Amanda said a word to her second in command and slid onto the bench seat with a sigh. "Success is killing me," she said. But the smug pride on her face told a different story.

"You love it," Mellie said.

"True. What's up, girlfriend? It's not like you to drop by in the middle of the day."

Mellie played with the saltshaker, feeling the tops of her ears warm. This was embarrassing. "I may have done something stupid."

Amanda leaned in, her elbows on the table, hands clasped under her chin. "Do tell. Are we talking five-hundred-dollar-shoes stupid or forgot-to-thaw-the-chicken-for-dinner stupid?"

"It's more of a personal matter."

"Oh. My. Gosh. You've had sex."

"*No.* Well, sort of. But not really. You're missing the point."

Amanda raised an eyebrow. "Do I need to give you a lesson about the birds and the bees? Was there nudity involved? Skin-to-skin contact? At your age, I'd think you'd be pretty clear about the definition."

Mellie glanced around wildly, making sure no one was in earshot. "Lower your voice, please," she hissed. "I'd rather this not end up on the evening news."

"Who is it?" Amanda demanded. "The new wrangler over at Hartley Ranch? Or, no, it's the dentist…right? He's asked you out a half dozen times and you finally said yes."

Mellie smiled, despite her turmoil. "It's not the dentist. He kept wanting to whiten my teeth…not at all romantic."

"Then who?"

"Back up," Mellie said. "I didn't have sex. Or at least not all the way. More like teenagers in the back of a car."

Amanda appeared to be struck dumb, her eyes wide with astonishment. "It's like I don't even know you," she said.

Mellie wondered suddenly if she should have kept things to herself. But she couldn't move forward without at least an amateur second opinion. She decided to come at the situation from another angle. "I've been invited to the party at the Cattleman's Club Saturday night."

"Okayyyy… So what's the stupid thing you did?"

"I said no."

"Ah. And now you want to change your mind."

"Maybe. But what if he's already asked someone else?"

"Is that likely?"

"I'm not sure. He was mad when I turned him down. Said he wasn't going to ask again. That I would have to tell him if I wanted to go." She fudged a bit. That wasn't exactly how Case had phrased it. He'd said Mellie would have to say she wanted *him*.

"I still haven't heard a name." Amanda's brow creased.

"The *who* isn't important. Because even if I decide to contact him, I don't have a dress to wear."

"That part's easy." Amanda sat back and took a sip of the iced tea she'd brought with her to the table. "Last year when Nathan and I were invited to the governor's mansion for a law enforcement ball, I bought a dress I never wore. I decided the color didn't work for me and the skirt was way too long and too hard to hem. But the dress was on clearance, so I couldn't return it. You and I are about the same size. Plus, you're taller, so I think it will work. Why don't I bring it by your house this evening?"

"That would be great." Except that Mellie had been counting on a lack of wardrobe choices as her reason not to go to the party.

Amanda glanced at her watch. "I've gotta get back to work. I'll text you when I'm on my way…okay?"

"Sure."

Amanda stood and tapped the table with her finger. "You can't keep his name a secret forever. If the dress works, the price for my fashion donation is full disclosure."

"I don't know why you're making such a big deal about this. If I end up going, you'll find out who it is. You and Nathan will be at the party…right?"

"Of course…but I hate surprises. So you might as well tell me tonight."

By 6:00 p.m. Mellie chickened out and sent a text to Amanda.

Changed my mind about the party. Thanks anyway.

Amanda was not so easily dissuaded. She showed up at Mellie's house half an hour later, garment bag in hand.

When Mellie answered the door, Amanda frowned at her. "I never figured you for a coward."

Mellie stepped back, shrugging helplessly. "I'm not a coward. But it's complicated."

"Isn't it always?" Amanda placed the long black bag on Mellie's coffee table and sat down on the sofa.

Mellie took the chair opposite. "I've waited too long to say yes. It's a moot point now. Sorry you came for nothing."

Amanda stared at her. "Tell me who it is."

"Case." Even saying his name out loud made Mellie shiver with a combination of anticipation and dread.

"Case who? Your boss?"

Apparently, Mellie was right. The idea that Case Baxter might invite his housekeeper to the most important event of the year was inconceivable. "Yes."

At last Amanda grasped the enormity of the situation. Her jaw dropped. "Case Baxter invited you to be his date for the party honoring him as the new president of the Texas Cattleman's Club and you turned him down?" That last part ended on a screech.

Mellie winced. "Yes."

Silence reigned for long minutes. Amanda looked at Mellie as if she were some kind of alien being. "I didn't think you even knew Case until you started cleaning his house."

"I didn't. But when he got sick and I helped him out a bit, we...um..."

"Fell madly in lust with each other?"

Mellie couldn't decide if Amanda was scandalized or delighted. "I didn't even like him at first," Mellie said. "He's arrogant and bossy and opinionated..."

"In other words, a Texas male. It's in their DNA, Mellie."

"Maybe."

"But you got past that first impression, obviously."

"I still think he's all of those things, but when he was so sick, I saw another side of him. A human side. A vulnerable side."

"Oh, dear."

"What?"

"You're falling for the guy."

"Don't be silly. He's handsome, and when you get to know him, not so bad, but this isn't about anything long-term."

"So why did you turn him down?"

A very good question. "He's the guest of honor Saturday night. He'll be in the spotlight. I'm not a center-of-attention kind of girl."

"So?"

"I shouldn't even have mentioned this to you. I'm not going, so it doesn't matter."

"Try on the dress. And don't argue." Amanda could be like a dog with a bone when she wanted something.

"Fine. But only because you won't leave me alone until I do." Mellie snatched up the dress in its protective covering and hurried down the hall to her bedroom, trying to ignore Amanda's mischievous smile.

When she unzipped the garment bag, she sucked in a breath. The gown was amazing. It was halter necked and backless. The chiffon-and-silk fabric almost glowed. The color started out as sea-foam green at the bodice, edged into a slightly darker hue at the hips and continued the length of the dress, sliding from one shade into the next as the mermaid-style skirt fell in a dozen layers of tiny ruffles.

No woman could resist trying it on. With a few contortions, Mellie managed the zipper on her own and slid her feet into strappy high heels. One look in the mirror told her the gown was made for her.

Amanda called out from the living room. "I want to see it. Come model for me."

"Give me a minute." Mellie stared in the mirror, trying to imagine the expression in Case's eyes if he saw her in this dress. She didn't suffer from false modesty. Her body was nice…average. But in this confection of multishaded green, she felt like a princess.

Amanda actually stood up and clapped when Mellie walked into the living room. "You look amazing. And I was right. The length is perfect."

"I can't wear a bra." Her shoulders and back were bare.

"You don't need one. I'm so excited you're going to the party."

Mellie held up a hand. "I haven't even tried to contact Case, and if I do, he's probably asked someone else already."

Amanda chuckled. "Why don't we find out?"

"Now?"

"Of course now. The event is less than forty-eight hours away."

"I'll text him later tonight. Let me change out of this and we can grab some dinner. Didn't you say Nathan was working tonight?"

"Yes. But I think my stomach can wait five minutes for a meal. Quit stalling."

"Be honest, Amanda. Don't you see that this could be a disaster? Gossip spreads faster than wildfire around here."

Amanda hugged her, careful not to muss the dress. "It's a very simple question. If he enjoys your company and you like being with him, all that matters is whether or not you can keep from getting hurt."

"It won't last long. He's not interested in anything serious."

"That's all the more reason to enjoy it now. You work hard, Mellie. And you deserve an exciting evening with one of Royal's premier eligible ranchers."

"Sounds like a B-grade reality show."

"I'm serious. Do the Cinderella thing for one night. And come Monday, everything can go back to normal."

"You make it sound so easy."

Amanda picked up Mellie's cell phone. "Here." She held it out. "Do it before you get cold feet."

"I already have cold feet," Mellie complained. But she took the phone and pulled up Case's contact info. Hastily, without overthinking it, she clicked out a message.

If the invitation is still open, I would like 2 go with you to the party Saturday nt.

Suddenly, she felt like throwing up. It was going to be so embarrassing when he told her it was too late…that he had invited someone else. Every passing second made her want to climb into a hole and hide.

Even Amanda seemed abashed, her romantic soul shriveling in the loud silence.

Suddenly, Mellie's phone dinged.

I'll pick you up at 6:30. Glad you changed your mind.

Heart pounding, Mellie replied.

Only about the party. Just so we're clear.

Chicken?

No. Practical. How R U feeling?

100%. Good enough to rock your world. ☺

"What's going on over there?" Amanda asked when Mellie giggled.

Who knew a man like Case Baxter would use an emoticon?

Mellie sat down on the sofa, her legs suddenly too weak to hold her up. "Um, nothing special. He says he's glad I changed my mind."

"Well, there you go. You were worried for nothing."

Maybe. Or maybe her worries were only beginning.

Twelve

Friday flew by in a blur. Mellie subbed for one of her ladies, worked on her scheduling for three weeks out and at the end of the day went for a mani-pedi at her favorite salon.

That night she fell into bed, too exhausted to worry about her upcoming date with Case. But Saturday morning, the day of reckoning arrived. She and Amanda met after lunch to get their hair done.

They had booked simultaneous appointments. Amanda requested that her hair be arranged in a soft knot on top of her head with tendrils framing her face. She would look adorable.

The salon owner and Amanda ganged up on Mellie when Mellie asked for a similar style. "Yours needs to be down and wavy," Amanda insisted. "That gorgeous color will pop against the green of the gown."

"And who says I want to *pop*?"

The other women ignored her, their plan already in progress.

An hour later it was done.

Mellie had asked for a trim, but her hair still swung softly against her shoulders. She paid for her session and waited as Amanda did the same. The truth was, she *did* feel a little bit glamorous.

They saw several other women in the shop, as well— ranchers' wives mostly, with a few girlfriends thrown in. Tonight these would be the people observing Case and his date.

On the sidewalk, Mellie parted company with Amanda. "Promise you'll rescue me at the party if things get weird."

Amanda laughed, her cheeks pink from the heat inside. "Nothing is going to get weird, but yes… Nathan and I will look out for you."

After that somewhat reassuring promise, Mellie went home and second-guessed her decision a thousand times. When she was stressed, she liked to clean, so that's what she did. After a couple of hours, her house was spotless. But she was still jittery.

When Case arrived to pick her up, Mellie felt as awkward as a preteen on her first date. She opened the door and managed not to swoon. He stood there filling the entryway…tall, incredibly handsome, king of his domain in the conservative tux that fit his long, lean body to perfection. Clearly, he was on the mend.

His lazy grin lit a spark deep inside her. She wanted to gobble him up but at the same time had the urge to run away.

He must have nicked himself shaving. She could see the tiny red spot where he had managed to staunch the trickle of blood.

As she stepped back so that he could come in, his warm

gaze raked her from head to toe. "Hello, Mellie." His tone was low and intimate. "You look stunning." The words held a level of intensity she hadn't anticipated.

"Thank you," she muttered. "I'm ready. All I need to do is grab my wrap."

Case was fully recovered from the flu, but he still felt a little unsteady on his feet. Mostly from lying around all week. Inactivity wasn't his usual style.

The fact that Mellie had changed her mind about being his date tonight gave him great hope for the culmination of the evening. Now that he was well, he wasn't about to let her get away a second time. All he'd been able to think about as the days dragged by this week was how amazing it had been to hold Mellie and kiss her and how desperately he wanted to do so much more.

If it had been up to him, the club wouldn't be throwing a party in his honor this evening. But he understood that his new title came with certain social obligations. Having Mellie at his side would go a long way toward making the evening's festivities palatable. Despite her reservations about being seen in public with him, he was going to be proud to have her on his arm tonight.

Thank God he was finally well. Everything was going according to plan.

As she disappeared down the hallway, he watched her go, taking note of the way her dress dipped low in the back. His breath came faster and his forehead was damp, but his symptoms had nothing at all to do with the flu. Mellie Winslow was a smart, gorgeous, funny woman.

And for tonight she was his.

By the time he had tucked her into his vintage sports car, he realized two things. One, he should have brought the larger Mercedes. He and Mellie were so close in this small space he could have leaned over and kissed her with no trouble at all. Given the fact that he was already hard just from looking at her and inhaling her light scent, he was in trouble.

Secondly, Mellie was as nervous as a long-tailed cat in a room full of rocking chairs. She seemed pale, but maybe that was a trick of the light. "Relax," he said. "We're going to a party. I want you to have fun."

Mellie half turned in her seat. "I don't know why I let you talk me into this." Her eyes were huge. The pulse at the base of her throat beat rapidly.

He smiled, ruefully aware that he was in far deeper than he wanted to admit. What he was about to do would make them late, but it would be worth it. Leaning across the gearshift, he held her chin in one hand and slid his other hand beneath her masses of golden-red hair to cup her nape. "I can't wait all night to taste you."

He kissed her slowly, even though he wanted to do the opposite. Her lip gloss would have to be repaired, but that was a minor inconvenience. She responded instantly, moving toward him and sighing as his tongue mated with hers. Her skin was soft and warm, her kiss feminine and eager.

Damn. His memories hadn't been exaggerated by his illness at all. Here he was, stone-cold sober, fever-free and wildly out of control already. He inhaled sharply and released her, pausing only to run his thumb along her trembling lower lip. "Say something," he demanded.

Her faux-fur wrap had fallen away. Mellie retrieved it and huddled into the warmth. "Like what?"

Now that her bare shoulders were covered, maybe he could manage a coherent conversation. "I want to strip that dress from your body and drag you into the backseat."

So much for conversation.

Mellie managed a smile. "I'd invite you inside, but I

think it's probably a terrible faux pas for the newly elected president of the Texas Cattleman's Club to miss his own party."

He gripped the steering wheel, needing to refute her statement but knowing she was right. "Afterward. Tonight. I want to stay over."

The silence lasted several beats too long for his peace of mind. Mellie wrinkled her nose. "I'd rather you not. My neighbors are nosy."

Hell. "Be honest with me, Mellie. Are you objecting to the venue or to the idea of you and me?"

This time her answer was even slower in coming. "The venue only, I suppose. I'd like to think I could say no to you, but I won't lie to myself. I want you, Case. But we seem to be at an impasse, because I know you don't have women spend the night out at the ranch."

A knot inside his chest relaxed. "For you, I'll make an exception." He meant his response to be light and teasing, but the six words came out sounding like a vow.

Mellie nodded slowly. "Okay, then. We can swing by here later, and I'll pack a bag. If you're sure."

He wasn't sure at all…about anything…except that before midnight, Mellie Winslow was going to be in his bed.

Mellie felt as if she had fallen down the rabbit hole. Suddenly, her career seemed far less important than her love life. Since when did she calmly make plans to spend the night with a man? She hadn't had sex in over two years. Maybe she should warn Case that she was rusty. Or maybe he knew enough for the both of them.

As they pulled up in front of the imposing Texas Cattleman's Club, a uniformed parking valet hurried forward, ready to take the keys and whisk the car away. Case helped

Mellie out of the low-slung vehicle, both of them taking care not catch her dress on anything.

When she stood at his side, her stomach full of butterflies, he slipped an arm around her waist. "You ready?"

She nodded, but her heart plummeted. Out at the ranch, Case had simply been a sick male who needed her help. Now…here…it was going to be impossible to ignore who he really was.

That truth was hammered home with a vengeance as they stepped through the doors of the club. Camera flashes went off in chorus. Reporters shouted questions. Case gave the press crew an easy smile and a good sound bite, even as he kept his arm curled protectively around Mellie and steered them toward the ballroom, stopping only to drop off Mellie's wrap and clutch purse at the coat-check counter.

Another doorway, another entrance.

This time there were no cameras, but instead a surge of well-wishers who wanted to congratulate Case. It was inevitable that he and Mellie would end up separated. She smiled and wiggled her fingers at him to let him know she was okay. It was actually kind of sweet to see how many people gathered around him to say hello.

As she waited for the crush to subside, Mellie looked around the room with curiosity. This was only the third time in her life she'd ever been inside the club, and the other two occasions had been long ago.

The building was a century old and had been cared for well over the years. Tradition mingled with luxury seamlessly. It was fun to see so many people dressed to the nines and ready to party.

Mellie smoothed her skirt and kept a smile on her face. Just as she was planning to go in search of an out-of-the-way corner, strong fingers gripped her elbow. "You're not getting rid of me that easily."

"Case." She was startled to find him at her side. A moment ago he'd been surrounded by a small crowd of people.

"I want you to meet Mac McCallum," he said. "And his sister Violet. Mac is an energy technology whiz. Violet keeps their family ranch running smoothly."

Mellie shook hands with each of the attractive McCallum siblings. "Lovely to meet you both."

Violet grinned. "I think this is going to be a short-lived conversation. They're motioning for the two of you to lead out the first dance of the evening."

Mellie's mouth went dry. She looked up at Case as they made their way to the center of the room. "Do you even know how to dance?" she whispered. "'Cause I'm not exactly a professional."

"My mother and grandmother were old school. Young men had an obligation to learn the ways of gentlemen. Dancing was at the top of the list."

"I'm impressed."

The orchestra stuck up a dreamy tune as Case swept Mellie into his arms. At some level she was aware that she and Case were alone in the middle of the floor. Overhead, a priceless chandelier sparkled, showering them with small rainbow flashes of light. The crowd was four- and five-people deep, pressed back around the edges of the room.

But in Case's arms she forgot to be either nervous or self-conscious. He held her confidently, steering her easily in a waltz. His hand was warm on her back. "Thank you for coming with me tonight," he said, his smile a flash of white in his tanned face. "You've made this a lot more fun for me."

"You didn't really need a date," she pointed out. "There

are all sorts of women in this room who would love to dance with you."

He dipped her skillfully and laughed when she couldn't stifle a small gasp. "I didn't want any of them," he said. "I only want you."

After that, the song ended and everyone took the floor as the next song began.

Case bent to whisper in her ear. "Let's get something to eat."

She nodded, even as he extricated them from the mass of bodies nearby. Fortunately, the air was cooler and the people fewer as they approached the buffet tables. Mellie filled her plate with boiled shrimp, beautiful canapés and various hors d'oeuvres. "This looks amazing."

Case served himself three times as much, but then again, he was a big man who needed a lot of fuel. He found a table for two. "Eat fast," he joked. "More of my friends want to meet you."

Mellie knew the moment alone wouldn't last long. It seemed as if every eye in the room was on them. Her earlier reservations about being seen in public with Case Baxter came flooding back. "It's easy to see why you were elected," she said. "You're very popular."

He lifted an eyebrow as he wolfed down a spicy meat-ball. "It would be the same for anyone who holds this posi-tion. People like knowing they have access to influence."

"That's a pretty cynical statement."

"But true. I learned a long time ago not to believe my own press. When a man has money and power, people flock around like bees to honey. Underneath it all, I'm just a Texas cowboy."

"If you say so." Maybe he was being modest and maybe he really believed what he said. Either way, he wasn't see-ing clearly. There was something special about Case…

something that made her want to be with him for more than a single night. Something elemental. Something real.

She didn't particularly enjoy the barrage of eyes trained on their table at the moment. The avid interest made her worry about finding food in her teeth or spilling wine on her beautiful dress. Still, it was a relief to know that she didn't feel as out of place as she had expected.

When they finished eating, Case began to introduce her to an endless stream of his friends, including Jeff Hartley, a local rancher who appeared to be without a date for the party, and Drew and Beth Farrell, to name a few. Some of them—such as Dr. Reese—Mellie knew already, at least in passing.

Royal wasn't all that big. Families tended to own the same land for generations. Drew and Beth shared the story of how they had been not-so-friendly neighbors until the wicked F4 tornado stranded them together in a storm cellar.

All of Case's circle of friends were interesting people. Beneath the social chitchat, though, Mellie knew what Case was thinking. Because she was thinking about it, too. Sex. Naked, wild, exploratory sex. Two people attracted to each other without much else in common.

When Case was pulled into a conversation that seemed to be more business than pleasure, Mellie hung back on the far edges of the room, listening to the band and chatting with Amanda and Nathan. Unfortunately, her support team was heading out early.

Amanda hugged Mellie. "It's been a fun evening, but Nathan was up at five this morning. We're going home."

Mellie returned the hug. "Thank you again for the dress. I think Case likes it."

Nathan snorted. "Every man in the room likes it. You're a knockout, Mellie Winslow."

"Hey." Amanda pinched her husband's arm. "I'm standing right here."

He scooped her up and gave her a thorough kiss, one that left Amanda pink cheeked and starry-eyed. "Mellie knows I only have eyes for you, sweetheart. Don't you, Mellie?"

"I do. And she feels the same way about you. Now go home before you get arrested for public indecency."

Their laughter was equal parts smug and rueful.

Watching the Battles walk across the dance floor to the exit gave Mellie a funny twinge in her chest. Amanda and Nathan had known each other forever. Their relationship was rock solid, and they were more in love today than they had ever been.

What would it be like to have that kind of security and trust in a relationship?

She was still rattling that question around in her head when a young cowboy came up to her and asked for a dance. He couldn't have been more than twenty-one or twenty-two. Mellie felt ancient in comparison, but his earnest invitation was sweet.

They moved around the dance floor in silence. The young cowhand seemed nervous, because he glanced in Case's direction now and then. "Mr. Baxter is giving me the evil eye," he said.

"Don't mind him. You and I are having a nice dance. Nothing wrong with that."

"Your dad is Harold Winslow, right?"

Mellie stumbled slightly. "Um, yes. Why do you ask?" Now the invitation made more sense.

The kid cleared his throat. "My cousin owns one of the shops out at the Courtyard. Word got around this week that your dad is thinking of selling the place. It's made folks nervous about their businesses. When I saw you here tonight, I thought I'd get an answer straight from the horse's mouth."

"You might want to rethink that comparison," Mellie said drily.

The cowhand blushed. "You know what I mean. Is it true?"

Mellie mulled over her answer. "It may be true that my father has been talking big and throwing his weight around. But I'm part owner of the company, too, and as far as I know, there are no plans to sell. Who is your cousin, anyway?"

"Raina Patterson. She owns the antiques store Priceless."

"Oh, yes… I know her. Please tell Raina I'll be out to see her in the next couple of weeks to set things straight. And tell her she has a sweet cousin."

Now the wrangler's neck and ears were as red as the stripe in his Western shirt. "Thank you, ma'am. Nice dancing with you."

Mellie had no sooner grabbed a glass of punch than Case appeared at her side again. For a big man, he surely was quiet and fast when he wanted to be. "Should I bow or salute?" she asked. "Now that you're officially the president and all?"

He snagged her glass and took a sip, his lips landing exactly where hers had been. "I saw the young pup encroaching on my territory. Don't you know you're supposed to throw the small ones back in the water?"

"Very funny. He's a sweetheart."

"I'll bet. He was one of the brave ones. Every unattached guy in this room is thinking about doing what he did."

"You do know how to flatter a girl." She smiled, her confidence buoyed by Case's wry observations.

Case lifted an eyebrow when a tall man with shaggy brown hair and green eyes approached them. The man gave Mellie an appreciative glance. "I don't know how you ended up dancing with Case," the man said, "but I'd be love to take a turn on the dance floor with you, pretty lady."

"Well, I—"

"This one's taken," Case said, glowering. He glanced at Mellie. "Meet my buddy Logan Wade. He likes fast horses and fast women, not necessarily in that order."

Mellie laughed. "Nice to meet you, Logan."

Logan shook her hand, his grip warm and firm. "Don't listen to him. I'm harmless. Case is the ladies' man in our group. At least I'm not opposed to marriage on principle."

From the look on Case's face, he wasn't amused by his friend's ribbing.

Case glanced at his watch. "I've done my time," he muttered. "Mellie and I are going to get out of here. This crowd will party for several more hours."

Logan kissed Mellie's hand theatrically. "When you get tired of this guy, give me a call."

Thirteen

Case's mood soured. Was Mellie tempted by Logan Wade's offer? Surely not. But the other man was definitely popular with women. They loved his easy-going personality.

Case shoved aside the unwelcome realization that Mellie might be looking for something more than Case wanted to offer. He had enjoyed the evening more than he'd thought he would. But right now he was focused on the after-party.

He hoped Mellie was on the same page, because he was wired and hungry. For a brief moment he thought about heading straight to the ranch. It was possible once they got to Mellie's house, she would change her mind.

At a stop sign, in the glare of a streetlight, he studied her profile. "Penny for your thoughts," he said lightly. Surely she wasn't actually thinking about Logan's smooth flirtation. The other rancher was only trying to needle Case.

When she gave Case her full attention, her luminous,

deep eyes drew him in. For a moment, he thought she wasn't going to answer. Then she drew a visible breath. "Will you tell me about your wife?"

The question was way down on the list of things he'd expected her to say. "Is that a prerequisite for tonight?"

"I didn't mean to make you angry."

"I'm not angry," he said, gripping the steering wheel. "But it's old news."

"I'd still like to know. Please…"

He shrugged, wishing he had loosened his bow tie. "I was young and stupid. Leslie worked for my dad. She saw me as a meal ticket, I guess. Dad tried to warn me… suggested a prenup. But I refused. We'd been married for six months when Leslie cleaned out two of my bank accounts and skipped the country."

"I am so sorry. You must have been devastated."

"She didn't break my heart, if that's what you're thinking. But she sure as hell damaged my pride and my self-respect."

"Because you couldn't see through her?"

"Yeah. I guess I wanted to believe I was irresistible."

"You are, as far as I'm concerned. I'm not in the habit of having *sleepovers* with men I've known all of about ten minutes."

In her voice he heard an echo of the same reservations that plagued him. He pulled up in front of her house and put the car in Park. "This isn't the norm for me, either, Mellie. And I might point out that I offered you fifty grand as an investment, but you turned it down. So I'm hoping it's my charm and wit that won you over."

As an attempt at humor, it fell flat.

Mellie's small white teeth worried her lower lip. "Maybe that was a ploy on my part to get you to trust me."

"Go get your toothbrush," he urged, his voice hoarse. "I can't wait much longer."

She stared at him, her hands plucking restlessly at the tiny ruffles on her skirt. Despite their current locale, she reminded him of a mermaid, luring a man into the deep.

"Is this a one-night stand, Case?"

"It's not anything yet." He sighed. "I can't imagine letting you go after only one night."

"But you agree that the two of us are temporary."

His temper boiled over, exacerbated by lust and uncertainty. "Damn it, Mellie. Do you want this or not?"

She swallowed, and he saw her chest rise and fall. "Wait here," she said. "I'll be back."

Twelve minutes and thirty-seven seconds. That was how long it took. When he saw the door to her house open, he jumped out of the car and met her, taking the small overnight bag and tossing it in the trunk.

She was still wearing her mermaid gown, which was a good thing, because he had fantasies of all the ways he wanted to peel the silky fabric away from her creamy-skinned body. He helped her into the car, waited until she tucked her skirt inside and closed the door.

The drive out to the ranch was silent. The miles ticked by rapidly. His brain was a jumble of wants and needs and more angst than was warranted in advance of a simple sexual encounter.

When he pulled up in front of his house, he realized he'd forgotten to leave a single light on. Through the windshield, he saw the night sky punctuated with a million stars. One of the many things he loved about living in Texas was the immensity of the universe overhead.

Every male instinct he possessed urged him to drag Mellie up the stairs and into his bed ASAP. But he wanted to woo her, to win her trust, to make her comfortable with him.

"Can you walk in those shoes?" he asked.

She nodded. "As long as we're not talking a marathon."

"I want to show you something."

Once they were out of the car, he took her hand in his and led her toward the small corral to the left of the house. Though it was often empty, tonight a single horse stood sentinel.

"This is Misty," he said. "I bought her recently. I thought you and I might ride together sometime."

The small mare whinnied and cantered toward them, her tale swishing in the cool night air.

Mellie leaned on the fence rail, her expression animated. "She's beautiful. But I don't know how to ride."

Case raised an eyebrow. "A Texas woman who can't handle a horse? Shame on you." He lifted her by the waist and set her on the railing. Her skirt fluttered around his arms like a swarm of butterflies. "I'd love to teach you… if you're willing."

His guest's smile was demure. "I'm sure you could teach me all sorts of things."

And just like that, he reached his limit. Moving between her legs, he dragged her head down for a kiss. Hot and hard and deep. The mare lost interest and wandered away. Case lost his head and wandered into dangerous territory.

Mellie in the shimmer of the moonlight was just about the prettiest thing he'd ever seen. Her hair was more pale gold than red in this moment. And her skin glowed like pearls.

"Inside," he groaned. "Where there's a bed."

Her husky laugh inflamed him. "I thought you'd never ask."

As he lifted her down from her perch, he couldn't bear to let her go. Instead, he scooped her into his arms and carried her toward the stairs that led to the porch.

Mellie curled one arm around his neck. He smelled her, felt her, tasted her on his tongue. Everything about the night turned mystical and enchanting. And he'd never once seen himself as a whimsical man.

He caught his toe on the second step and nearly sent them both to disaster. But he managed to find his balance. "Sorry," he muttered.

She put a hand on his cheek, her fingertips cool against his hot skin. "I'm not complaining. This is my very first experience with being swept off my feet. I think you're doing just fine."

Managing the final few stairs with only a little hitch in his breathing, he set her down long enough to fish the house key out of his pocket. "*Fine* is a sucky adjective."

He pulled her into the house and flipped the lock, backing his lovely guest up against the barrier that separated them from the outside world. Taking one of her delicate wrists in each of his big hands, he raised her arms over her head and pinned her to the door. "I don't know where to start," he said, utterly serious. "I've dreamed about you every night for a week."

"I hope the reality isn't a disappointment. I haven't done this in a very long time."

His lips quirked. "I'm told it's like riding a bike."

"Or a big, strong cowboy?" The deliberately naughty challenge nearly broke him.

"It's a long night," he said. "I don't want us to peak too early."

"*Peak*? Interesting choice of words."

"Shut up and let me kiss you," he groaned. He wasn't holding her all that tightly. One wiggle or protest from

Mellie and she would be free. But to his everlasting relief, she didn't seem to mind being his captive.

He pressed the weight of his lower body against hers. Still holding her arms over her head, he kissed the side of her neck, nuzzled the spot just below her ear. "You put something in my food last week," he complained. "Some drug that makes me want you incessantly."

She nipped his chin with sharp teeth. "I'm no femme fatale. Maybe you've been on a celibate streak. Maybe I'm available. Maybe you're grateful that I didn't leave you alone to suffer that first night."

He had to let her go so he could touch her. Reverently, he covered her breasts with his hands. Clearly she wasn't wearing a bra. And just as clearly, her firm, young flesh was made for his caress. Her nipple budded beneath the silky fabric as he brushed his thumb back and forth.

"I don't know what it is," he admitted. "And I don't care. But I need you tonight, Mellie. More than you know."

Again he picked her up, and again her head came to rest over his heart. He traversed the halls of his quiet dark house by memory, avoiding furniture and other pitfalls. In his bedroom, he paused. Mellie hadn't said a word. Was she shy? Having second thoughts?

"Talk to me," he said. "Tell me what you want."

The drapes at the windows were open wide. In the ambient light he saw enough of her smile to be reassured that she wanted the same things he did, though she didn't obey his demand for her to speak.

Gently, he set her on her feet and spun her around until he could reach the single fastening at the nape of her neck. He slipped the beaded button free of the buttonhole and eased the entire bodice of the dress to her waist.

The room was hushed, every molecule of air quivering with anticipation. Opposite them, the mirror over his dresser reflected a ghostly tableau. When he embraced her from behind and dragged her back against his pelvis, they both groaned.

It was torture to shape her bare breasts with his hands. He wanted to see her fully, but there was something wickedly sensual about their dim, shadowy figures in the glass.

At last he turned her to face him. A few inches of zipper at the base of her spine gave way beneath his questing fingers, and then he held her hand as she stepped out of the dress.

She tapped his throat with a fingertip. "Your turn."

He had to wait, chest heaving as she fumbled with his bow tie and unfastened the studs down his front. When that was done, he shrugged out of his jacket and shirt and tossed them aside far more recklessly than he had her soft gown.

With Mellie standing in front of him clad in nothing but stilettos and undies, he was a wreck. "Time out," he croaked.

At this particular moment he didn't have either the patience or the fortitude to make it through a slow undressing. He kicked off his shoes, ripped off his socks, and shucked his pants and boxers in short order.

Totally nude, he snagged her wrist and drew her back into his embrace. "Leave the shoes on," he begged.

"Whatever you want, cowboy." Her voice was warm as honey on a summer day. He heard arousal and humor in equal measures.

His erection bobbed eagerly against her belly, but she didn't seem to mind. He ran his hands over her satin-covered butt, imagining all the ways he was going to take her. "This first round might be fast and furious, but we've got all night." It was a promise and a reminder to himself. He could afford to be patient...maybe.

One last time, he indulged in the pleasure of carrying her, this time to the king-size bed. He flipped back the covers and deposited her on the mattress. After striking a match to the small candle on the bedside table, he lowered himself at her side and splayed a hand against her flat belly. "I have condoms," he said flatly. "I would never take chances with you."

He wanted her to know she could trust him.

Mellie wasn't shy. At least not anymore. One hand closed around his shaft and stroked lazily.

He sucked in a sharp breath, mortifyingly close to embarrassing himself. "Let's save that part for later, darlin', when I'm not so trigger-happy."

She released him. "If you say so."

The only reason he'd been at all able to hold himself in check was that he'd let her keep her last item of clothing. But now it was time for the panties to go. When he slid them down her legs, the nylon snagged on the sharp heel of one shoe. "I'll buy you more," he swore. "A dozen pairs in every color of the rainbow."

Without warning, she rolled to her stomach, arms cradling her head. "You could massage my back," she said, her voice muffled. "All that standing and dancing in heels isn't easy." She bent her knees and crossed her ankles in the air, taunting him with the sexy pose.

At least he thought that was what she was doing. Maybe she didn't understand how damned sexy she looked. Telling himself he was no rookie kid in the bedroom, he straddled her waist and settled his thumbs on either side of her spine. With firm pressure, he moved from her bottom to her shoulders in steady increments.

Mellie's hands fisted in the sheets. "Damn, you're good," she mumbled. "This is better than sex."

He caressed every inch of her back. Up and down. Back and forth. "Not even close."

When her body was lax and warm, he reached for the handful of small foil packets he'd put in easy reach. He sheathed himself rapidly, then flipped her to her back and positioned himself between her legs.

Mellie watched him, eyelids drooping, cheekbones flushed with color, arms over her head. "You're a very beautiful man," she said quietly, her gaze raking him from chest to groin.

Gripping her hips, he shoved deep in one forceful thrust. He didn't realize he had closed his eyes until he saw tiny yellow spots of light that pulsed in time with his heartbeat. The fit was perfect.

In retrospect, perhaps he should have started with something more original than missionary position sex. But honestly, his brain circuits were shot to hell and back. Already he needed to come. Needed it more than air and water and food. But he battled the urge.

He wanted Mellie as hungry as he was…and as desperate for the pleasure that hovered just out of reach. His hands were dark against her white skin. He liked touching her…liked the notion that she had come to his home… to his bed.

Later, perhaps, he would remember his rules. And wonder why he'd broken them for someone he'd met only a few weeks ago. But now it didn't matter.

Now she was everything he wanted and needed.

He moved in her slowly, controlling the joining of their bodies with a firm grip, loving the way her eyelids fluttered shut as her breathing quickened. "This is only the beginning," he muttered.

Mellie arched her back, her rose-tipped breasts quivering as he picked up the pace. "Promises, promises."

How could she make him smile in the midst of blind lust? He changed the angle slightly and felt the moment she caught her breath. Knowing she was with him, teetering on the brink, he let go, shuddered and collapsed into the storm.

Fourteen

Mellie couldn't breathe. The problem originated in one of two sources. Either her condition was the aftermath of a wildly lush and powerful orgasm, or it was due to the fact that a large, heavy man lay on top of her, apparently comatose.

She allowed herself a smug smile. For a woman who was out of practice in the bedroom, she hadn't done half-badly. Of course, in all honesty, most of the credit had to go to Case. Alpha males might be stubborn and aggravating and impossibly bossy, but in certain situations, it was nice to have a man with confidence. A man who could play a woman's body as if only he knew the tune.

In the quiet of the bedroom, she cataloged the situation. She needed to go pee, but she didn't want to move. She took in Case's bed…Case's bedroom…Case's big warm frame sprawled in her arms. If she were a cat, she'd be purring right now.

A river of feelings moved through her veins. Relaxation. Joy. Quiet amazement. For once, she had ignored her cautious instincts and let nature take its course. Most of the time, she ran a tight ship. Work. Home. Work and more work. Losing her mother as a teenager had left her with a need for security. And Harold was never going to be any help there.

But holding things together all the time was difficult. She'd become a grown-up before she had a chance to make teenage mistakes. Maybe she was regressing. Maybe Case Baxter was her adolescent blunder. Sleeping with a client wasn't exactly the most professional move she'd ever made...

Suddenly, her lover groaned and rolled onto his back. She held her breath until he settled back to sleep. When his breathing was even and deep again, she slipped from the bed and tiptoed naked into his bathroom, then eased the door shut behind her.

After taking care of business, she found a thick navy robe on the back of the door and slid her arms into it. She had to roll up the sleeves and belt the waist tightly, but it at least gave her some protection from the vulnerability of prancing around stark naked.

Her reflection in the mirror made her wince. Wild hair, mascara smudges, whisker burns on her neck. Her thighs tightened at the memory of Case nibbling his way from her ear to shoulder.

In hindsight, it might have been prudent to actually bring her overnight case *inside*. Fat lot of good it was doing her out in Case's car. But then again, she and Case had been too busy cavorting in the romantic moonlight to worry about pedestrian realities like toothbrushes and nighties.

When she turned out the bathroom light and prepared to

slip back into bed, her stomach growled loudly. She'd been too nervous to eat much at the party, and lunch today had been slim, as well. Fortunately, she knew her way around Case's kitchen. And she knew how much food his friends had brought over while he was sick.

As she reached into the fridge for a container of cold chicken, two big hands grabbed her butt. She yelped and spun around. "Case!"

He gave her a mock scowl. "I woke up and you were gone." Then his eyes narrowed. "Is that my robe you're wearing?"

She flushed. Case had on nothing but a pair of cotton pajama pants. His big bare feet were sexy, which meant she was in real trouble. Because she'd never been turned on by feet before. "My overnight bag is still in the car."

Case grabbed the ends of the terrycloth belt and drew her against him. "My robe never looked so good." He lowered his head and kissed her, long and sweet, making her toes curl against the cold ceramic-tile kitchen floor.

She twined her arms around his neck. Without shoes, the difference in their height was magnified. He made her feel fragile and cherished. She'd always been proud of her self-sufficiency. But it turned out there was something to be said for the notion of allowing a big, strong man to take charge once in a while.

She buried her nose in his bare shoulder. He smelled of soap and warm male skin and sex. "I was raiding your leftovers," she said.

He chuckled, the sound reverberating through her when he kissed the top of her head. "You don't really want cold chicken, do you…"

It was more a statement than a question. She raked her fingernail across his flat copper-colored nipple. "Is there a better offer on the table?"

"Maybe." He inhaled sharply. "If I feed you popcorn, will you come back to bed afterward?"

"I could be persuaded."

He picked her up by the waist and set her on top of the butcher-block island. Moments later he had the microwave humming. The scent of hot popcorn filled the air.

When it was done, Case opened a bottle of wine, poured two glasses and hopped up to sit beside her, handing her the bowl of popcorn. "It doesn't take much to make you happy, does it?"

Mellie shrugged. "We all have our weaknesses. But I like to think I'm a realist. The most important things in life are free."

He was quiet for a long time. What was he thinking?

This huge, wonderful house was a lonely cave for a man to rattle around in. He should have a wife and several children to keep him company. Then again, some guys liked being bachelors.

"May I ask you a personal question?" she asked.

Case drained his wineglass and set it aside. "Sure. Fire away."

"With your parents gone, how do you celebrate Thanksgiving?" The holiday was less than a week away.

"I don't really." Case shrugged. "I have an aunt and uncle in Austin. They always invite me, and sometimes I accept. Other years I go skiing with friends in Colorado."

"Have you celebrated any holiday in this house since your parents died?"

"No."

When he didn't elaborate, she knew she had hit a nerve. "Would you let me cook for you next week? Nothing fancy…just turkey and dressing and maybe a pie or two."

"You don't have to feel sorry for me, Mellie. I've been thinking about Thanksgiving, too. But I thought we could head down to Key West for the long weekend. Rent a boat. Sail around the islands. Eat fresh seafood and dance under the stars."

"Sounds like a movie. Way too good to be true." Did he feel the need to impress her? Or was the idea of having a woman cook for him too domestic...too *familiar*? "Never mind," she said lightly. "It was just a thought."

When he put a hand on her bare knee, she jumped. The sides of her robe had gaped, allowing him a glimpse of her legs covered in gooseflesh.

"We need to get you back in bed," he said. "Before you catch pneumonia."

The change of subject was awkward, but she let it slide. "Bed sounds nice." And maybe round number two. Her snack had revived her. Leaving the door open for other hungers to be sated.

They walked hand in hand to the bedroom. A yawn caught her unawares.

Case laughed. "I'll let you sleep first."

"First?"

"Before round two."

Scrambling onto the mattress, she shed his robe and held out her arms. "I can sleep when I'm dead."

This time she took the initiative. She pulled Case by the wrist. "Lie down on your back," she said. "It's my turn to play tour guide."

"Whatever the lady wants."

The words were playful, but the fierce light in his eyes was anything but. His hard body quivered, poised for action. When Mellie reclined beside him and delicately licked the head of his shaft, he cursed and groaned. It was heady stuff to make the mighty Case Baxter weak and needy.

She stroked him with two hands. He was a big man everywhere.

Moments later he grabbed her wrist in an iron hold. "Enough." The glazed expression in his eyes told her what he wanted.

With only a second or two to decide if she was feeling sexually adventurous tonight, she moved over him and sat on his upper thighs. "I like having you at my mercy," she whispered. The sense of being in control was false. She knew that. Case Baxter might be a Texas gentleman, but in certain situations, the veneer of civilization wore thin.

His chest rose and fell rapidly. His cheekbones carried a flush of color, and his eyes were so dark the pupils were barely discernible. "I'll let you call the shots on this one, Mellie. Be my guest."

The words were lazy and compliant, but his hands fisted at his hips and cords of muscles flexed in his arms. The lion wasn't sleeping…merely biding his time.

After she reached for a condom, she opened it and rolled it over Case's erection. Then rising onto her knees, she lowered herself and took him deep. He'd given her one outstanding orgasm already, but she was greedy. She wanted more.

Case cursed and grabbed her ass in a bruising grip. "Don't move," he begged.

Was he really so susceptible to her charms? It seemed unlikely. Mellie possessed a healthy self-esteem, but she knew Case had access to more women than was good for him. Money, good looks, Texas cowboy charm…the trifecta wasn't really fair to the female sex.

She had to question his ex-wife's intelligence.

Mellie rested her hands, palms flat, on her lover's chest, feeling the heat of him, the light dusting of hair, the tough, muscled breadth of him. She'd told herself a hundred times that she could play this game and not get hurt. But suddenly, a knot lodged in her throat.

When had she let him become so human? When had he ceased to be the wealthy, powerful president of the Texas Cattleman's Club? When had she forgotten he could buy and sell the Keep N Clean a hundred times over and never miss the cash?

Her enjoyment of the intimate moment wavered.

Case—damn him—noticed instantly. "What's wrong?" he demanded.

"Nothing."

He grimaced. "The universal female response. And you don't sell it any better than the next woman. Talk to me, Mellie."

Unexpectedly, a wave of bittersweet regret rolled over her. Hot tears stung the backs of her eyes, but she'd have died before letting him see. "I'm fine," she whispered. "Great, in fact. Just tired."

"I'll let you sleep soon," he swore. "But first, my turn…"

Case knew this time was different. Earlier, he and Mellie had come together in the heat of a mutual passion. Reckless. Unabashed. Grabbing for what they wanted… wringing every drop of physical sensation from the experience. The sex was some of the best of his life.

And yet now he felt a shift in the force. A ragged tear in the veil of pleasure.

He moved on top, taking Mellie with him by the simple expedient of clamping his arms around her waist as he rolled over and maintaining the connection that made their bodies one. Maybe she *was* tired. But he had the sinking feeling that she had slipped away from him mentally.

He'd never asked about other men in her past. She'd told him it had been a long time since she'd been intimate with anyone, and he had believed her. Now he wished he had pressed for more details. After all, Mellie had wanted to know about Leslie.

Despite his mental turmoil, his body seized control. Desperately he entered her, again and again, trying to force her into coming with him, but even as he found his release, he knew he was alone in that moment.

Mellie was unnaturally still. He moved to the side and slung an arm over his eyes, feeling ashamed for no good reason he could understand. Why did women have to be so damned complicated?

Was she asleep? Was she hurt?

"Mellie?" He wasn't even touching her hip to hip.

The candle had long since burned out. Her voice in the darkness was small and shaky. "Will you take me home, please?"

Stunned and angry, he reached for the lamp and turned it on. Mellie winced and turned away, but not before he saw her damp eyes. "God, honey, what is it? What's wrong?"

She had the sheet clenched in her fingers, the soft cotton covering her bare breasts. Though she managed to look at him, it was only a fleeting glance. He saw her throat move as she swallowed. "I thought I could be one of those women who has sex as a lark. You know, just for fun. But I don't think I can. I like you, Case. And I respect you. But I really, really don't want to fall in love with you."

The last sentence was flat. He felt much as he had the time a horse kicked him in the chest. No air in his lungs at all. Coupled with a jolt of pain that would have brought him to his knees had he been standing.

What the hell did she want him to say? The days were long gone when he said the *L* word with no thought of the consequences. Hell, he didn't want to fall in love either. Did he?

He was angry and confused and dangerously close to taking her again just to prove how good they were together.

Perhaps he should have talked to her quietly, explained all the reasons she was panicking for nothing. But his limbs still trembled. He'd come hard, out of control, needing everything she had to give.

And now this.

"Fine," he said, the word like glass in his throat. "Put on your dress and I'll drive you home."

He grabbed up his things and carried them across the hall, leaving Mellie the privacy of his room. Alternating between fury and despair, he dressed rapidly and went to stand in the front foyer. He was afraid if he lingered in the hallway, he would bust through the door and drag her into bed again.

Part of him wanted to make promises…anything to get her to stay. But he'd made a fool of himself once over a woman. Any man who let himself be manipulated by female emotions deserved to fall on his ass. That was a young man's lesson.

Case Baxter was older and wiser now.

He had his keys in his hand when Mellie appeared. Her face was pale, her expression composed. But her posture was somehow broken, as if she were leaving the field of battle. Her beautiful dress was rumpled. She carried nothing, not even a purse. He'd been in such a hurry to make love to her they'd left everything in the car when they came in earlier.

"I'm ready," she said.

He opened the door and stepped aside for her to precede him down the steps. Only then did he realize that Mellie's fur wrap lay in a heap on the porch. Neither of them had noticed it fall. They had been too focused on each other to care about inconsequential things.

Mellie bent and picked up the stole, pausing only long enough to drape it around her shoulders and hold it tight. The temperature had plummeted after dark. With her bare toes and all that bare skin, she must be freezing.

"The car heats up quickly," he muttered.

His companion didn't answer. She moved rapidly down the steps, slipped into the passenger seat and closed her own door before he could help. Earlier, the interior of the small sports car had created intimacy. Now it only magnified the gulf between the two adults who had started the evening with such enthusiasm.

In front of Mellie's house he reconsidered. "Do you want to tell me what's really going on?"

Her hands twisted in her lap. "I'm not playing games. Merely having second thoughts. I think tonight scared me a little bit. We've moved so fast I'm feeling wobbly on my feet."

"Are you saying I pressured you?" That thought left a nasty taste in his mouth.

Mellie turned toward him. "Oh, no…no…no… This is about me, not you. It was sweet of you to ask me to the party, and I enjoyed every moment of tonight."

"But you're done."

"Can we call it a strategic time-out?"

"If this is a ploy to secure my interest by playing hard to get, I should tell you it won't work."

Fifteen

Silence fell like a hammer in the wake of his stupid, belligerent remark. Mellie unlocked her door, picked up her tiny purse from the console between the front seats and got out. "I'd like my bag, please." He'd felt winters in the Rockies that were warmer than her icy request.

"Damn it, Mellie. You know I didn't mean that. You're making me crazy."

"My suitcase, please." She stood there like a queen waiting for a peon to do her bidding.

Gritting his teeth, he reached into the backseat and extricated the bag. He pulled up the handle and passed it to her. "It's three a.m. Nothing makes any sense at this hour. Let's talk tomorrow. Dinner. I'll fly us to Dallas in the chopper. You'll love seeing the city from that viewpoint."

She raked a hand through her hair, looking like a weary angel doing battle with a recalcitrant sinner. "I appreciate the invitation, but I can't. And I think it would be best if I assign another one of my ladies to clean your house. You run with the big dogs, Case. I'm just an ordinary woman who never really believed in the Cinderella story."

"What in the hell does that even mean?"

"I was supposed to clean and organize your house. You got sick. I felt sorry for you. We bonded over chicken soup, and both of us were a little curious. So now we know. Tonight was fun."

"And?" He couldn't believe she was giving him the brush-off. Particularly after the incredible sex they had shared. Didn't she know how rare it was to have that kind of physical connection right off the bat? He'd felt comfortable with her and at the same time eager for more.

"And I think it's best if we stop before things get too intense. You don't even know me, Case. Not really. And I don't know you."

He was too proud to argue. And too self-aware to deny she was telling the truth. When Leslie trashed his life, he had stopped letting so much of himself be vulnerable.

"I'll walk you to the door," he said quietly.

Mellie's brief nod ended the conversation.

Her little house was neatly kept. The front door was recessed at the back of a narrow concrete stoop. In the dark, neither of them saw the obstacle. Mellie stumbled and would have fallen if Case hadn't grabbed her arm.

"What the hell?" His protective instincts kicked into high gear.

Mellie groaned. "Oh, no. It's my father."

The pile of dark clothing on the tiny porch rumbled and moved. Harold Winslow sat up, reeking of whiskey and some other less definable odor. "'Bout time you got home, my girl. Leaving your old pop out in the cold isn't nice."

"Why are you here, Daddy?"

Case noted the total lack of inflection in Mellie's voice.

Harold made it to his feet with Case's assistance. "Came to see you. You weren't here. Didn't have any cash for cab fare to make it home."

"Let's get him inside," Case said in a low voice. "You said your neighbors gossip. Maybe we should keep this quiet before we wake up the whole street."

Once they'd all made it into Mellie's living room and turned on the lights, Case stifled a groan of pained amusement. They were a sad-looking trio. After walking Harold to the sofa and helping him sit down, Case shrugged out of his tux jacket and tossed it on a chair. His shirt was open down the front because he hadn't taken the time to refasten the studs.

Mellie was definitely bedraggled. Her hair was tangled in a just-out-of-bed style that was actually damned appealing. When she looked across the room at him, he had no choice but to go to her and put an arm around her waist. When he touched her, he could feel the trembling she couldn't control.

She lowered her voice. "May I speak with you in private, Case?"

"Of course."

Harold seemed oblivious to any byplay, so Case and Mellie left him to his own devices. In the glare of the fluorescent overhead light in the kitchen, Mellie appeared distraught. "I am so embarrassed," she whispered.

Case shrugged. "Alcoholism is a terrible disease. Have you ever gotten him to an AA meeting?"

"Again and again. But when he's sober, he's the most sensible man in the world. And can argue a person blind. I can't tell you how many times he's convinced me he's absolutely stopped drinking. I'm his daughter. I know him better than anyone. But that's how good he is."

"He's probably able to be convincing because he believes it himself. He believes he can stop anytime he wants to."

"I suppose."

"Would you like me to take him home for you?"

She shook her head slowly. "No. He's my parent. My problem. But thank you for offering. I'm sorry our evening ended this way."

Case leaned against the counter, yawning. "Turns out you had already kind of jacked it up anyway, so no harm done."

Mellie gaped at him and then burst out laughing, which was exactly the response he'd been hoping for. Anything to get that look of sick defeat off her face.

"I can't believe you said that to me, Case Baxter."

"I've been told I have a dark sense of humor." Her smile affected him to an uncomfortable degree. He grimaced. "Will you be okay with him?"

"Yes. He'll sleep it off on the sofa. Maybe tomorrow morning I'll find out why he's here."

"Will you loan him more money?"

Her expression was hunted. "I said I wouldn't."

"It's hard. I know it is." Case brushed her cheek with his thumb. "I don't want to leave you. Hell, I didn't want you to leave my house. You make it feel like a home."

"That's just the furniture polish I use. It probably reminds you of your grandmother."

For a moment he thought she was serious. Then he saw the tiny spark of mischief in her eyes. "Trust me, Mellie. *Nothing* about you reminds me of my grandmother."

He kissed her cheek and hugged her briefly. Nothing more. He didn't want to pressure her, particularly not after the encounter with her father.

By unspoken consent they returned to the living room. Harold was hunched over the remote, squinting at the numbers, trying to find a channel he wanted. He looked up when they appeared. "You staying the night?" He addressed his question to Case.

Mellie winced, but Case took the old man's query in stride. "No, sir. I'll say goodbye now."

He took Mellie's hand and dragged her with him to the front door and outside onto the dark stoop. "I'd like to kiss you good-night, Mellie."

"You kissed me in the kitchen."

"Not like that. Like this." Sliding a hand on either side of her neck, he used his thumbs to lift her chin. He brushed her mouth with his…pressed his lips to hers…breathed the air she breathed.

Mellie sighed and went lax in his embrace. Case kept an iron rein on his libido. Now was the time for tenderness. For understanding.

"I do care about you, Case," she whispered, sending his stomach into a free fall. "But we aren't right for each other."

It was not the occasion to argue the point. She met him kiss for kiss, the embrace lasting far longer than he had planned. So long, in fact, that he now had a painful erection with no hope of appeasing his need for her.

It took everything he had to pull away. "Good night, Mellie."

"Good night, Case." She waved as he strode out to his car.

Mellie would rather have done just about anything than walk back inside her house. Harold was a millstone around her neck. As she gave inner voice to that thought for the hundredth time, she felt like a lousy person. Other people's parents had cancer or even worse challenges to face.

At least Harold was healthy. Of course, there was no telling how long his liver would hold out.

Her intention was to walk past her father with a brief good-night. She wanted a hot shower and her own bed. In that order. Harold had pulled this stunt too many times. Even so, she fetched pillows and blankets so he wouldn't have to sleep on the bare sofa.

As she leaned down to pick up her small evening purse, she saw something that made her stomach curl with dread. A billfold. A familiar billfold, half-hidden beneath her father's leg.

"Oh, Daddy. What have you done?"

Her father tried to stare at her haughtily, but the effect was ruined by the fact that his eyes were glazed over. "I don't know what you mean."

Perhaps she might not have recognized the wallet in other circumstances. Many men's wallets were similar. But she had seen this particular one earlier tonight when Case took it out of his pocket to retrieve the coat-check ticket for Mellie's wrap and purse at the club.

"Give me that," she cried. Hands shaking, she flipped open the expensive leather. "How much did you take?"

Harold stood and nearly fell over. "Are you calling your own flesh and blood a thief?" He was wearing a leather jacket that Mellie's mother had given him twenty years ago. The coat no longer buttoned around his expanding waist, but he refused to give it up.

Gritting her teeth, Mellie reached into the nearest pocket of her father's jacket and wanted to bawl like a baby when her hand came back out with a couple of hundred-dollar bills. "Oh, God, Daddy. How could you?"

At that very moment, a knock sounded at her front door. Given the hour, it was a safe bet she knew who it was. She shoved the bills back in Case's wallet and glared at Harold. "Is there any more?"

She wasn't even sure he heard her. He had dropped back onto the sofa and was sprawled facedown, snoring like a grizzly bear.

Mellie took a deep breath and told herself no harm had been done. She opened the door and managed a smile. "I bet you're looking for this."

Case nodded, his expression relieved. "It must have fallen out of my jacket pocket."

She didn't say a word, and Case didn't seem to notice. He looked past her to the noisy houseguest on her couch. "You sure you don't want me to take him home?"

"We're good," she said, her throat tight.

"Okay. I don't suppose this qualifies for another kiss?"

She shook her head, wanting him to leave so she could fall apart in private. "You've had your quota. Good night, Case."

He sketched a salute and walked away from her a second time, taking part of her heart with him. She closed the door and leaned against it, tears already dripping from her chin.

Tonight was the worst thing she had ever seen her father do. Stealing? Was it a thoughtless crime of opportunity, or was Harold more lost than she realized?

Bracing herself, she searched every pocket on his person. He never even woke up. Thankfully, there was no more money to be found. Maybe this could be chalked up to a near disaster.

In her bedroom, she locked her door for no other reason than that she needed to feel the world was at bay for a few hours. She took a shower and tried not to imagine Case's big gentle hands caressing her body. How could one twenty-four-hour period hold so much joy and heartache in equal measures?

When she tumbled onto her bed and climbed beneath the covers, she clutched the extra pillow to her chest and told herself she didn't have a broken heart.

Not even the pitiful lie could keep her awake anymore.

Sixteen

Case was in a bitch of a mood. Mellie was avoiding him. By phone and in person. It was as if she had up and vanished off the streets of Royal. Four days had passed since the night of the party. On Monday another Keep N Clean employee had shown up bright and early to do the second story of his house. The lady was a pleasant middle-aged woman with a no-nonsense attitude.

He showed her around and gave her carte blanche to carry out the careful list of chores her boss had spelled out. Then he saddled his favorite horse and spent the rest of the day riding his property and brooding about how one ornery redhead had made his life miserable.

Fortunately, he did have a number of things to do at the club. Because of his illness, he was behind in learning his new duties. Gil Addison had blocked off some time on Tuesday to show Case files and paperwork and to introduce him to the young assistant who held court inside the imposing club offices.

Tami knew who got in to see the president and who didn't. She also was extremely efficient and very good at her job. "I'll look forward to working with you," Case said. She smiled politely, already turning back to her desk to resume her work.

Gil nodded. "She'll be the continuity you need, especially if I'm not around to answer questions. But you'll get the rhythm of things pretty quickly."

"I hope I can do the job as well as you have." Gil was a straight-arrow kind of guy, and Case respected the hell out of him.

Gil's careful smile took years off his age. "I'm looking forward to spending some extra time with my family. You'll do a great job as president, Case. Everyone is delighted to have you at the helm."

By midmorning on the Wednesday before Thanksgiving, the club was virtually empty. A lot of people traveled for the holiday, and the ones still in Royal were busy baking and entertaining out-of-town company. Case decided to put in a few hours on the computer and then head home.

He'd have football to watch and movies to enjoy. Lots of men would envy him.

Around eleven o'clock Tami's voice came over the old-fashioned intercom. "Mr. Baxter? There's a Harold Winslow here to see you. He doesn't have an appointment."

Case rubbed the center of his forehead. Surely he owed Mellie this much. "Will you show him in, Tami? I'll give Winslow fifteen minutes. As soon as we're done, you and I can both lock up everything and leave." The club would be shut down from noon today until Friday morning to give employees time to spend with their families.

A couple of minutes later, Tami escorted Harold into Case's small office and excused herself. Case stood and held out his hand, not at all sure Harold would remember Saturday night's fiasco.

Harold grimaced as he shook Case's hand. "Thank you for seeing me on such short notice, Mr. Baxter."

"Please call me Case. And have a seat."

Harold was dressed impeccably today in a sport coat, crisp slacks, and a shirt and tie. The metamorphosis was astonishing. The older man leaned forward, elbows on his knees. "I hope you'll accept an apology for my behavior the last time you saw me. Not my finest hour. But I'm working on it."

Case shrugged. "We all have our issues. What can I do for you today?"

Harold sat back in his chair and crossed his legs. "I've had inquiries from an investor about purchasing this property. So I think it's in your and my best interests to discuss the current lease payments."

"Wait a minute." Case did some quick mental backflips and remembered Nathan telling him that the club sat on land belonging to Winslow Properties. But Case hadn't thought anything about it at the time. He'd assumed there would be legal papers on file somewhere outlining the agreement. Since he didn't know that for sure, he decided to tread carefully. "You're talking about Samson Oil, right?"

Harold's genial smile never faltered. "You've heard of them, I see. Their offer is very generous. But on the other hand, I'd hate to see the club have to move."

Case flinched inwardly. The other man clearly thought he had the upper hand. "I've only just taken over as president," Case said. "I'm still in the process of learning the ins and outs of the club's operations. I wasn't aware that it was time for contract negotiations."

"My great-grandfather offered this property to the club years ago for a nominal fee. But we've never had more than a gentleman's agreement. This might help." Harold extracted a folded spreadsheet from his inside breast pocket. "Here's the info from my files. The rent over the years has been very reasonable, as you can see. But we're deep into a new century now, and I can't let sentiment overrun my need to turn a profit."

Case studied the figures, his expression impassive. In his chest, his heart pounded a warning rhythm. If there was no written agreement, Harold Winslow had the legal right to increase the lease payments anytime he saw fit.

"According to this schedule," Case said slowly, giving himself time to think, "the rent has seen modest increases every two years. What did you have in mind?"

Harold named a figure that was twenty times the current lease payment. "I realize that's a big jump, and I don't want to make trouble. Still, think about what could happen. If I sell to Samson Oil, they might tear down this building entirely. All that history…gone in a flash."

The threat was not even veiled. Harold Winslow had resorted to blackmail. And Case, who had been the new club president for all of ten minutes, was completely caught off guard.

"I'd have to convene my board," Case said. "To talk this over."

Harold smiled. But the calculating gleam in his eyes told Case this was not a friendly conversation.

"Not much to talk over," Harold said. "Either you accept my terms, or you start looking for a new location to build the club."

"Why would an oil company want land that was checked for oil over a century ago and found dry?"

Harold shrugged. "Don't know. Don't care. I'm a businessman. Money talks."

"And it doesn't bother you that the community might see you as greedy and unsympathetic and run you out of town?"

"Afraid not."

"Royal would never let a new owner move the club from its present location. Have you talked to your daughter about all of this?"

Harold looked him straight in the eye. "Of course I have. Mellie wants money to expand her business. This was her idea."

Direct hit. *Goddamn it.* "How do I know you're telling the truth about that?"

"Women lie all the time. They manipulate you and make you believe what they want you to believe. Ask her how you happened to leave without your wallet the other night. See what she says. I think you'll be surprised."

Case drove back out to the ranch in a daze. Though Nathan had been the one to tell him that Mellie's family owned the land on which the Texas Cattleman's Club sat, Mellie herself had never actually mentioned it. The omission seemed painfully suspicious in light of today's revelations.

And he got even more suspicious when he pulled up in front of his house and found Mellie sitting on the top step.

He got out of the car slowly, his mind racing. Memories of Leslie's lies and machinations filled his throat with bile.

Mellie didn't move. Instead, she waited for him to walk up the staircase. When she patted the seat beside her, he shook his head. "I'll stand. Why are you here, Mellie?"

Her smile faltered. "I was feeling bad about the way we argued the other night. Tomorrow is Thanksgiving. I'm renewing my offer to cook for you."

"No, thanks." He didn't dress up his refusal.

"Am I missing something?" she asked.

"Why didn't you tell me your family owned the land where the TCC sits?"

She had the gall to look puzzled instead of guilty. "It's not a secret. I guess it never came up. Or I thought you already knew."

"And one more question. It wasn't an accident that I lost my billfold at your house Saturday night, was it?"

This time the guilt on her face was clear. His heart shriveled in his chest, even as pain choked him. How could she look so open and sweet and plan to blackmail him?

"My father took it," she said, "while you and I were in the kitchen. When I realized what he had done…after you left, I made him put the money back. That's when you showed up at the door."

"So, to be clear, you chose to protect your father rather than tell me the truth." The incident wasn't such a big thing by itself. But combined with Harold's demand for an exorbitant rental increase, Case had to wonder what other things Mellie had been hiding from him.

Mellie went white, her expression agitated. "It all happened so fast. No harm was done. He does such stupid stuff when he's drinking. I'm really sorry, Case."

"My hat's off to you, Mellie," he said. The pain was gone now, replaced by a raging need to hurt her as much as she had hurt him. "You even told me what you were doing. Winning my trust little by little so you could blackmail me and line your pockets. It makes perfect sense that you turned down my fifty-thousand-dollar offer. You had bigger plans…much bigger."

She stood shakily. Since Case was a few steps below her, they faced each other eye to eye. "You've got this all wrong, Case. I don't want your money."

"Not mine, it seems. But your father just stood in my office and demanded a new Cattleman's Club lease at twenty times the price. Threatened to sell the property out from under us if I don't agree to his terms. You *do* want money. But far more than I was offering. And you don't mind dragging my reputation through the mud to get what you want."

"I'll talk to him," she swore. Ashen and trembling, she was very convincing.

"No more theater," he said. "I know it was your idea. He told me so. The thing is, Mellie, if you hadn't overplayed your hand, you could have ended up with a ring on your finger. I was falling for you. Hard. But I had a narrow escape. You and your dad have a nice little scam going. Maybe you even arranged for him to be on your front porch when I brought you home. I actually felt sorry for you."

She reached for him. "I've been falling for you, too, Case. Please don't let my father ruin what we have."

Her touch burned his arm. Jerking away, he tried not to think about how it felt to rest in her arms. "What we have is *nothing*, Mellie. Nothing at all. You gambled and you lost. Now it's over."

Mellie drove back to town and later didn't remember doing so. She was in shock. In denial. Case had looked at her with such cold fury and contempt she felt dirty.

Her first instinct was to hole up in her little house and hide. Thanksgiving came and went. Her father neither called nor came by. He was avoiding her, no doubt. Only on Friday did she find the strength to do what had to be done.

She went to her father's office and found it empty. But everything she needed was on the computer and written on notepads in her father's messy scrawl. Rapidly, she made a list of all the property to which the Winslows still held title. At one time, Harold had been one of the largest landowners in downtown Royal.

But in the past two years, he had sold off more and more, leaving him with only a dozen small tracts and two significant parcels of land—the one on which the TCC sat and the slightly larger one outside of town where the Courtyard was located.

After locking up the office, she went to her father's house, where she found him passed out on the sofa. His condition was a reminder that she was doing the right thing. Though she had been prepared to have a knock-down, drag-out confrontation, she left without disturbing him.

Nathan Battle and one very cranky judge were next on her list. Judge Plimpton didn't like being disturbed on the golf course.

Fortunately, Mellie had legal rights. Mellie's mother had left her portion of Winslow Properties to Mellie and not Harold. So although Harold ran the company, Mellie was an equal partner.

By bedtime that night, all her plans had been set in motion.

Case was already regretting his election as club president. What was supposed to be a largely ceremonial title had landed him in a hell of a mess. It was the Tuesday after Thanksgiving, and here he sat in a room with two lawyers and the nine-member board.

One of the lawyers was speaking, shaking his head. "Sadly, Mr. Winslow is on firm ground in this instance as far as I can tell. As he told you, Mr. Baxter, the original lease arrangement from years ago was a gentleman's agreement with Winslow's ancestor. Unfortunately, subsequent generations saw no reason to add more official parameters. Gil Addison remembers a conversation with Harold Winslow at the beginning of his tenure, but at that time there was only a two percent increase in rent."

One of the board members chimed in. "What if we were to offer to buy the land from Winslow?"

"With what?" Case had already combed through the ledgers. "The club has spent quite a bit of capital in the last few years, first on renovations and more recently to repair tornado damage. The financial bottom line is healthy but certainly not adequate to purchase a piece of property this size."

The second lawyer checked his notes. "So what do we know about this Samson Oil company? Are we sure they would evict you immediately?"

Case ran a hand inside the back of his collar, feeling the walls closing in. "We don't know much, unfortunately. Only that they have been quietly buying up property in and around Royal…and giving fair prices as far as I can tell. The thing is, though, a new landowner could choose to present us with even worse terms than those Winslow is offering."

Everyone in the room fell silent. Though no one would blame Case for the current situation, in his gut, he felt guilty. If he hadn't gotten involved with Melinda Winslow, she and Harold might never have concocted this scheme that might possibly cost the club its identity.

The first lawyer reinforced Case's worst fears. "Mr. Baxter is right. Even if the entire town were to rise up in protest, there would be nothing to stop a legal landowner from doing anything and everything with this property. Without a written lease covenant, we're in murky waters."

Case pressed his temples, a pounding headache building. To move the club intact was impossible. The history within these walls was the history of Royal itself. It made him sick to think of how much they stood to lose.

"Let's break for lunch," he said. "We'll reconvene at one." In the meantime, he had no choice but to confront Mellie again and persuade her to reconsider.

He was too angry and upset to eat anything at all. So he locked himself in his office and dialed Mellie's cell number. Time after time, his call went to voice mail. Hearing her speak was a knife to the heart.

But she never answered.

When he finally gave up, he rested his head in his hands and tried to think clearly. Mellie knew her father was an alcoholic. Why would she collude with him in such a distasteful maneuver?

Unless he was completely mistaken, and maybe he was, this scheme didn't sound like Mellie at all.

When the lawyers and board members returned, Case was no closer than ever to a solution. He could live with embarrassment. He could even live with the fact that once again a woman had used him for financial gain. What he couldn't bear was knowing that his community had placed their faith in him, and the club might lose everything on Case's watch.

Discussion raged helplessly for three more hours, circling back again and again to the fact that Harold Winslow held all the cards. One by one, each man and woman in the room came to the same conclusion. The Texas Cattleman's Club was facing a crisis as stark and painful in its own way as last year's killer storm.

Suddenly, a knock on the door drew Case to his feet. Tami's smile was apologetic. "I'm so sorry, Mr. Baxter. But this registered letter was just delivered, and it's marked Urgent."

"Thanks, Tami."

Case turned to find the group progressing without him. He had no problem with that. It gave him a chance to tamp down dread before he opened the very official-looking envelope.

He read the brief message once, twice…a third time. All of his instincts went on high alert, looking for a further threat. The document made no sense.

Without explanation, he handed it over to one of the lawyers. Conversation ceased as everyone around the table sensed something of import going on.

The lawyer scanned the contents and showed it to his colleague. Both of them studied the letter before finally looking up wearing smiles. Lawyer number one shook his head. "It seems your problems are over, ladies and gentlemen. According to this, Winslow Properties has agreed— in writing— to keep the current lease price in place for the next five years. And they have no intention of selling the land to Samson Oil or anyone else."

"But why?" One of the board members voiced the bafflement they were all feeling.

The second lawyer folded the letter and handed it back to Case. "Who knows? Maybe there was never really an offer at all. But the point is, the crisis has been averted."

Case frowned. "Why would Harold threaten me and then back down? It doesn't make sense."

Gil Addison shrugged. "Maybe he had second thoughts. Maybe he was drunk when he came up with his plan to gouge the club. Who knows? But that's his signature. So why look a gift horse in the mouth?"

And maybe Mellie had been telling the truth. Maybe she'd had nothing to do with Harold's ploy. Case nodded, but inside, his stomach churned.

The room cleared out quickly after that. Case spoke

briefly with the two legal professionals, making sure there wasn't anything more Case needed to do at the moment. Soon Case was the only one left.

He stood by the window, looking out at the crisp autumn day. Across the street, city workers stood on ladders beginning to hang this year's Christmas decorations on the lampposts.

The momentum of the holiday season was in full swing. Even with all the activity going on up and down the busy thoroughfare, Case saw none of it. The only image burned in his brain was the memory of Mellie's face when he tossed accusations at her.

Good God. What had he done?

He snatched up his keys and strode outside to his car, determined to see Harold Winslow face-to-face and demand the truth. The Winslow Properties offices were open, but inside, no Harold. Only a pleasant thirtysomething receptionist.

"Hello," Case said, giving the woman his most nonthreatening smile. "I'm here to see Harold Winslow."

"He's not here," the woman said. "May I take a message?"

"Do you know when he'll be back?"

"Not for some time, sir. Miss Melinda will be running the business in her father's absence."

"I see."

"Are you by any chance a friend of the family?"

"You could say that."

"Shall I give you her phone number?"

Case swallowed. "I have it. Thanks."

He wandered outside and leaned against the brick facade of the building, his heart in his boots. The enormity of his arrogant blunder stood before him…irredeemable… unforgivable. It was entirely possible he had ruined the best thing to ever happen to him. And all because he'd been hung up on the fact that his first wife had never really loved him…that when people looked at him, they saw dollar signs and not the man he was.

If the topic of his downfall had been any less personal and painful, he might have been tempted to ask one of his married buddies for advice. But this situation was deeply intimate, and he knew in his heart that Mellie wouldn't want her name and the nature of her relationship with Case bandied about. She was a very private person.

In a few days, it would be December. The nights would grow longer and the days shorter. Christmas cheer would fill the streets of Royal, Texas. But for Case, this holiday season loomed bleak and empty. He'd been given the most precious gift of all…a woman's trust.

And he had thrown it away.

Seventeen

Mellie was exhausted. Running two businesses at the same time required her utmost attention. During the day she bounced back and forth between both offices. At night she fell into bed too wiped out to do more than say her prayers. At the top of the list was an urgent plea that her father was not going to hate her for what she had done.

It had required a concerted effort by a number of people, but Mellie had managed to more or less kidnap her father and check him into a wickedly expensive but highly successful rehab facility about a hundred and fifty miles from Royal.

Her father had been sober and shaky when she left him there. She'd given him an ultimatum. Either dry out and learn how to make a change, or resign himself to the fact that Mellie was going to run the family business and there would be no more handouts for Harold.

The rules at the facility were very strict. For the first

thirty days, Mellie would have no contact at all with her father. It wasn't until later that she realized those rules meant she would be spending Christmas alone.

She had many friends, of course, but she would not intrude during family time. She was a grown woman, and she could get along on her own.

Today was Friday. The letter from her lawyer had been delivered to the Texas Cattleman's Club on Tuesday. Case had to have seen it by now. And yet nothing. Seventy-two hours, with not a peep out of him.

The total lack of communication indicated more clearly than anything else that Case Baxter had no intention of either forgiving Mellie or continuing their relationship. She should have told him right away that her father had taken the wallet. Her lie of omission had caused Case to question her motives...to doubt her sincerity. And he already had trust issues when it came to women.

Mellie's first instinct had been to protect her father, even though he didn't deserve it. But her misstep had cost her dearly.

Gradually, though, as the hours and days passed, her regret changed to anger. Case *should* have trusted her. It had been far too easy for her father to drag her into his little blackmail scheme. If Case had really cared about her, he wouldn't have been so quick to believe Harold's lie. She had given Case her body and her heart and yet it hadn't been enough.

Because he didn't love her.

At the moment, despite her own personal heartache, she was driving out to the Courtyard because Raina Patterson had sent an agitated email asking for a meeting. Apparently, Mellie's indirect reassurances via Raina's cousin had not been enough.

When Mellie pulled up and parked, she was struck again by how charming and appealing this little cluster of studios and shops had turned out to be. Mellie found Raina inside the big red barn, frowning over a cash register receipt.

Raina looked up when the bell over the door tinkled. "Miss Winslow," she said. "Thank you so much for coming to see me."

"It's a beautiful day," Mellie said lightly. "No hardship at all. What can I do for you? In your email you sounded upset."

Raina grimaced. "I don't know quite how to say this because I thought the matter was settled. But I received a letter from your father saying that our rents were going to quadruple. I think it must have come last week, because I found it in a stack of mail on my desk that I had overlooked. He said he had a good offer for this property, but he'd be willing not to sell if we all agreed to the new terms."

Mellie held on to her smile grimly, disguising her utter disgust with her father's methods. "I think I can relieve you on that score. That letter would have been mailed before I checked him into rehab. I'm running the business now, and we have no plans to increase the rent. In fact, you and all the other tenants will receive a registered letter to that effect on Monday from *me*, stating the new terms. I'm sorry my father caused you sleepless nights."

Raina's relief was almost palpable. "Thank you, Miss Winslow. I'm very sorry about your father, but you don't know how much this means." She handed Mellie a small clay pot glazed in shades of ochre and midnight blue. "Please accept this as a thank-you. I think I speak for all the artists here when I say it's hard to make a living via a creative endeavor. With a stable rent, we'll be able to keep our books in the black."

"The Courtyard shops and the farmers' market are helping make Royal a center for tourism and the arts. What you do is very important. I hope your business will continue to grow."

Though Mellie chatted with Raina for several more minutes, her heart wasn't in the conversation. Eventually, she said her goodbyes and returned to her car.

Though she had reassured the shop owner, it was little consolation for her own situation. She felt as if her whole world had caved in. Even though she had convinced herself that she and Case weren't suited, his lack of faith hurt more than she could have imagined.

Until now she had never understood that heartache could be an actual physical ailment. Remembering the hours she had spent in Case's bed was nothing less than torture. He'd been so gentle with her and at the same time hungry and demanding, drawing a response that stunned her. Until Case she hadn't understood the human body's capacity for pleasure. Sex with Case had opened her eyes to how narrow she had made her life.

It would be a long time before she got over this. A very long time. But perhaps one day she would be given another chance at happiness with a man who was worthy of her heart and her trust.

Grabbing up her purse and briefcase, she got out of the car and stopped dead when she saw Case sitting on her doorstep.

He held up a hand, his expression impassive. "Don't worry. I parked the car two streets over at the grocery store. I know how much you dislike gossip."

She realized he wasn't kidding. Good grief.

It seemed prudent to halt a good six feet away. Her decision-making skills always took a hit when she got too near Case Baxter.

His jaw was shadowed, his eyes sunken with exhaustion. Stress lines she hadn't noticed before bracketed his mouth. "I need to talk to you, Mellie."

She folded her arms across her waist. "So talk."

"Privately. Please."

It seemed dangerous and stupidly hopeful to let him into her house, but she couldn't help it. "Very well."

In her living room it was impossible to forget what had happened in this spot just two weeks before. Humiliation washed over her, reddening her throat and face.

Case must have been affected strongly, as well, because he frowned. "I'd rather not do this here. I have some snacks and a picnic blanket in the car. Will you go for a drive with me?"

"It's chilly outside." She teetered on the edge of uncertainty. Even if Case forgave her and she forgave him, they still weren't suited as a couple. Wouldn't she simply be inviting more heartache if she dragged this out?

Case had his hands shoved in his pockets. His jeans were soft and worn and conformed to his hips and legs like a second skin. His yellow cotton shirt was a button-down with the sleeves rolled up above his broad wrists. "Please, Mellie," he said. "It's important."

"If it's so important, why didn't you talk to me on Tuesday? You did get the letter…right?"

He nodded slowly. "I did. And I went to find your father and demand an explanation."

"But he was gone. My assistant told me you came around asking questions. You didn't try to find *me*, though."

"That's true. I wanted to think about things before I saw you again."

"I checked my father into rehab. And gave him an ultimatum. He blows through money when he drinks, and apparently, he'll stoop to anything to scrape up cash. Including blackmailing good tenants who have never done him any wrong."

"You didn't know what he was doing…"

"No." She grimaced. "And unfortunately, it wasn't only you he targeted."

"So will you come with me so we can talk?"

"If it's that important. But I'd like to change first."

She switched outfits rapidly, going by Case's appearance as a guide and changing into jeans of her own. She grabbed up a scoop-necked sweater in a shade of teal that flattered her pale skin and then slipped her feet into black flats.

A quick check of her face in the mirror, and she was done, though her pulse raced with uncertainty and fear.

When she returned to the living room, Case was standing where she had left him. He didn't smile, even now. In fact, his sober demeanor rattled her quite a bit.

Without speaking, they exited the house and walked for fifteen minutes until they came in sight of an old dusty Land Rover parked at the curb. "This is Betsy," Case said. "She can go anywhere, anytime."

Mellie was glad he hadn't brought the sports car. She'd managed to maintain her composure up until now, but she needed to keep some physical distance between her and Case.

She didn't ask where they were going. That would involve conversation, and apparently, Case was fresh out of that. They drove out toward his ranch, leaving her to won-

der if that wasn't their destination. But Case flew right past
the B Hive gate and kept on going.

At last he turned onto a narrow rutted lane. Now it was
clear why he'd brought the Rover. Though the tire tracks
were deep and well defined, wild grasses growing in the
middle dragged at the bottom of the vehicle.

Finally, the car came to a stop. Nearby, a small stream
rippled and gurgled. Across the creek, a gentle rise, likely
one of the highest places in Royal, drew attention to a single large oak, its branches flung wide in what would be
wonderful shade in the summertime.

While Case grabbed up a few items from the back of
the vehicle, Mellie shaded her eyes and scanned the area.
She couldn't see another soul for miles around. The sense
of peace and isolation was stunning.

Case looked her way. "Come on," he said. "I want to
show you something."

She followed him toward the creek and across a small
bridge. Even then Case didn't take her hand. It was as if
he was afraid to touch her.

When they approached the rise, she could see two
small tombstones at the top beneath the tree. She and Case
climbed the hill, and he spread out the blanket. He indicated the small stone markers. "My mom and dad are buried here. I used to come out and talk to them a lot. Haven't
done that much lately. But I wanted you to see this place."

"It's beautiful," she said. "Absolutely perfect." She bit
her lip, shivering slightly, though not so much from the
cold as from her jangled emotions.

"Mellie…" He stopped, his jaw working.

'What?"

"I am so damn sorry. I never should have believed him.
You even told me how convincing he could be. But when

he said that raising the lease price was your idea, I was furious and hurt and—"

"And you thought I had betrayed you."

"Yes." His face reflected grief and sorrow.

"You jumped to that conclusion pretty quickly...almost as if you were expecting me to hurt you."

"It doesn't reflect well on me, but I've had a hard time with women since Leslie. No, that's not exactly it. I've had a hard time with *me*. I have a tendency to be arrogant and in charge, so back then when I let myself be blinded by Leslie's come-ons, it made me doubt myself."

"Your marriage was over a long time ago."

"Yes. But I've never really wanted to be close to another woman until I met you. Suddenly, there you were in my house and in my bed and I couldn't help falling in love with you."

She blinked. "What did you just say?"

"I'm in love with you, Mellie." His smile was lopsided.

"Love doesn't happen so quickly."

Finally, he took her hands in his. "Maybe not for you. But I'm willing to wait."

She wiggled free of his hold, mostly because she wanted so badly to nestle against his chest and feel his heart beating beneath her cheek. She wrapped her arms around her waist, feeling as if she might fly into a million pieces like dandelion seeds dancing on the wind.

"You and I both live in Royal," she said. "Always have... probably always will. And now you're the president of the Cattleman's Club in addition to being one of the wealthiest ranchers in the state. My father will always be my father. He's in rehab, that's true, but you and I both know that the statistics for full recovery aren't stellar."

"What are you saying, Mellie, my love?"

Hearing him say the words brought tears to her eyes and a painful lump to her throat. "I *can't* be in love with you," she said, the words hoarse. "You may not ever be able to trust me completely. And my father may come between us down the road."

Case took Mellie by the wrist and reeled her in. "I'll never doubt you again," he said, utter certainty in his voice. "When we made love to each other, *that* was the real us... no masks, no barriers. We were the only people in that bed. And that's the way it's going to be. You and I against the world. Forever. If you say yes, of course."

His expression let her know that he was not completely sure of her response. Her knees wobbled. "Sex doesn't solve all the problems," she muttered, even as her stomach pitched and rolled.

Case held her close, tipping up her chin so he could settle his lips over hers. "I need you, Mellie," he whispered, his breath warm on her cheek. "Like I need air and food and a place to lay my head at night. I need your wonderful entrepreneurial spirit and your gifts of organization. I need your independence and your work ethic and the way you go above and beyond the call of duty. I need your compassion and your kindness. But most of all, I need your love."

"Oh, Case." He wasn't being fair.

"Oh, Mellie." He mocked her gently as he pulled her down onto the sun-warmed quilt. "Forgive me for doubting you. Make love to me. Let me show you how the world stops when we're together, flesh to flesh, heart to heart."

He waited an eternity for her answer.

"I don't want to rush into anything," she said. "I need us to be sure."

"But do you love me?"

The vulnerability on the face of this big, strong man

broke her heart a little bit. He'd opened himself up to her, had been the first one to speak words of love. It was a pretty good apology…a very nice way of making amends.

"You're everything I've ever looked for in a man, Case," she said. "You're the other half of me."

Eighteen

They undressed each other slowly, shoes first and then the important stuff. The afternoon was chilly, but the heat between them was sufficient. Case shivered when he felt her hands on his bare chest. He'd come so close to killing something wonderful, so close to losing the one person who could make him want more than a bachelor's existence in a big empty house.

With steady hands, he lifted her sweater over her head and then unfastened her bra. Soft, firm breasts filled his hands. "You're beautiful, Mellie."

Big green eyes looked up at him, searching his face as if she expected to find something she didn't like. "Please be sure about this, Case. I can't change who I am… I can't change my father."

He eased her onto her back and undid the snap on her jeans. "You're perfect just the way you are. And Harold will be the only grandparent our children have, so you and

I will just have to keep him on the straight and narrow and make sure he has plenty of little ones to spoil. I want you, Mellie. Now and always."

Her jaw dropped. "Children?"

"Children. Marriage. The whole package. That's what I want. What I need."

He slid his hands inside her pants, dragging them and her underwear down her legs. When she lifted her hips, he eased the tangled clothing away.

Mellie's skin was covered in gooseflesh. He stood and stripped, vowing to warm her up or die trying. He'd be lying if he said he didn't enjoy the way Mellie's eyes widened as she took in the evidence of how much he wanted her.

Seconds later he moved between her thighs and then cursed when he realized he'd forgotten the condom. Mellie laughed softly while he scrambled for his discarded pants and found the item he needed.

And then the waiting was over. He moved in her with his heart burning and his brain marveling that a man could be so clueless about what was important in life.

Mellie wrapped her legs around his waist, taking him deeper, kissing him wildly until neither of them could breathe. Her skin was soft and warm. He felt as if nothing he said or did was enough. He was helpless to make her see what a miracle she had wrought inside him.

He fought for control, even as his body drove mindlessly to a pinnacle that promised physical bliss.

But beneath it all, some tiny rational still-functioning part of his brain noted an important omission. Mellie hadn't said she loved him.

Shoving the thought aside, he concentrated on the feel of her sex as it squeezed him. When he felt the tiny ripples that told him she had reached the end, Case let himself go, giving a muffled shout and burying his face in her shoulder.

* * *

Mellie felt out of control. The contrast to her usual state of mind was sobering. She could barely cobble together a coherent thought, much less a mature, informed opinion about whether or not Case was in his right mind.

She wanted to believe him. She really did. She wanted to plunge headlong into the fairy tale where the girl who sweeps up the cinders meets her prince.

Idly, she stroked Case's hair. It was thick and silky and warm from the sun. His weight was a welcome burden. His body was the only thing tethering her to the ground at the moment.

Case loves me. She said it again inside her head, rolling the three words around and around until she made herself dizzy.

Finally, he moved, rolling over onto one elbow. "I told myself I was going to withhold sex until I got the answer I wanted."

Mellie laughed out loud at the disgruntlement on his handsome face. "Show me a man who can withhold sex, and I'll call Guinness World Records. Besides, what answer are you talking about? I didn't hear any question."

His smile made her stomach curl. "I don't need you to say anything you don't mean, but strictly as a matter of information, do you think you might fall in love with me eventually? Despite the fact that I acted like a giant horse's ass?"

"No." Mellie didn't have to think about it.

Case flinched. "I see."

"You don't see anything, but that's okay, because I like this abjectly groveling version of Case Baxter."

The man growled. He actually growled. "Explain yourself, woman."

His narrow-eyed glare made her shiver. In the best possible way. She put a hand on his cheek, trying not to fixate on the fact that Case was spectacularly nude. "I won't be *falling* in love with you, because I'm already there. How could I resist a sweet-talking cowboy like you?"

"Say it the right way," he demanded. "Now."

"I. Love. You."

His chest rose and fell. "Well, all right, then." He twisted a lock of her hair around his finger. "We could build out here. A woman should have her own place."

"I love the ranch house, Case. But you keep skipping parts of the script. Either that or I'm getting sunstroke."

"Nobody gets sunstroke in November." He teased her nipple with his fingernail.

Oh, wow. She wet her lips with her tongue. "Was there something else you wanted to ask me?"

"Hmm?" He seemed easily distracted.

"Case? I don't think the president of the Texas Cattleman's Club should live in sin. It sets a bad example."

"Whatever you say, my love."

"Case!"

He flopped over onto his back and spread his arms wide, his big masculine body a thing of beauty under the hot Texas sun. Shielding his eyes with one hand, he gave her the smile that had been her undoing. "Melinda Abigail Winslow…will you marry me?"

"You know my middle name?"

He grabbed her wrist and pulled her down on top of him. "I do…"

She felt him against her, chest to chest, thigh to thigh. "Do you also know that I'm partial to engagement rings?"

"Patience, my love. I have a plan."

She nibbled his ear. "Do tell."

"Tomorrow is December 1," he groaned. The pained

sound evidently had something to do with the way she was rubbing against him.

"Go on."

"I want to spend the entire month making you happy. And I thought we'd start by flying to Paris and picking out an obscenely large solitaire for your left hand."

Mellie reared up in shock? "Paris, France? But you have work to do…and a brand-new position. And I have two businesses to run."

He rubbed her bottom in lazy circles. "Don't say *position*. It gives me ideas."

She scooted away from him and started dragging her clothes on, despite Case's muttered protests. "I think you've had a relapse. We need to get you home. You and I are responsible members of the community. We can't fly off to Paris on a moment's notice."

"You're such a spoilsport."

"One of us has to be practical." When she was decent again, she stood up and stretched, shaking her head to make sure she wasn't dreaming.

Case put his arms around her from behind, a small red leather box in his right hand. "Well, in that case, I guess you'll have to settle for this."

She spun to face him, frowning. "What is that?"

"A ring."

She took the box but refused to open it. "How did you know I'd nix the Paris idea?"

Case shrugged, his smug patronizing smile making her want to smack him or kiss him or both. "I *know* you, Mellie Winslow. And I love every inch of your sensible, hard-working, down-to-earth self."

"You make me sound boring as hell."

"Au contraire, my sexy, beautiful housekeeper. Open the box and you'll see what I think of you."

Mellie was scared. But she opened the box anyway. "Oh, Case…"

"I love how you say that." He kissed her softly and pulled the ring out of its velvet nest. "Give me your hand."

Mellie trembled visibly as Case slid an enormous square-cut emerald onto the appropriate finger. The ring was amazing and exotic. "But this is…" She swallowed hard.

He cradled her in his arms, resting his chin on top of her head. "It's how I see you, Mellie. Stunning. Unique. Incredibly feminine. As precious and rare as the earth itself."

She wiped her nose on his sleeve. "You're a poet," she whispered. "And I never knew. I thought you were bossy and arrogant and—"

He put his hand over her mouth. "We'll work on how to give compliments later."

Without warning, he stepped back and went down on one knee. "I'm going to do this again, just to make sure. Mellie, will you be my wife and make babies with me and create new holiday memories to replace our sad ones? Will you work by my side and warm my bed at night and grow old with me?"

Her face was wet and her heart was bursting. "Yes, Case. All that and more. I love you. Now get up and take me home."

* * * * *

LONE STAR
HOLIDAY PROPOSAL

YVONNE LINDSAY

As always, I'm strengthened by the support of my fellow authors when working on a project like this, whether they are directly involved in the continuity or not. In particular I would like to dedicate this book to Soraya Lane to thank her for her constant cheerleading and encouragement, and for challenging me to bigger, better word counts than I ever dreamed I could achieve in a single day. Deadlines become so much easier when you're haranguing me from the sideline! Thank you.

One

Nolan rolled to a stop in the parking area at the Court-yard and looked around. The four-mile drive out of Royal had been pleasant, quite a difference from the Southern California freeway traffic that was a part of his daily grind back home.

Home. He grunted. Royal, Texas, was really his home, not the sparsely furnished luxury apartment he slept and occasionally ate in back in LA. But he hadn't lived here in Royal, or even been back, in coming up on seven years. Even now he'd chosen to check into a hotel rather than stay with his parents. The reminders of his old life and old hopes were still too fresh, too raw. He gave his head a slight shake, as if to jog his mind back on track, and pushed open the door to the brand-new SUV he'd hired for his visit. He alighted from the vehicle, grabbed his suit jacket from the backseat and pulled it on before taking a moment to adjust pristine white shirt cuffs.

The wind cut right through the finely woven wool of his

suit. It seemed even Armani couldn't protect you from a frigid Texan winter breeze. Nor were highly polished hand-made shoes immune to the dust of the unsealed parking lot, he noted with a slight grimace of distaste. But when had he gotten so prissy? There'd been a time when even baby spit hadn't bothered him.

A shaft of pain lanced through him. It still hurt as if it was yesterday. Nolan buttoned his jacket and straightened his shoulders. He'd known coming back would be hard, that it might rip the scabs off wounds he'd thought already healed. But what he hadn't expected were these blindsiding moments when those old hurts threatened to drive him back down on his knees.

Pull it together, he willed silently, clenching his jaw tight. He'd lived through far worse than these random memories that were all that was left of his old life. He could live through this. It was time to harden back up and get to work.

As private attorney for Rafiq Bin Saleed, Nolan was here to do a job for one of Rafiq's companies, Samson Oil. He loved his work—particularly loved the cut and parry of entering into property negotiations on behalf of his boss and friend. The fact that doing so now brought him back to the scene of his deepest sorrow was tempered only by the fact that he also got to spend some time with his parents on their home turf. They weren't getting any younger and his dad was already making noises about retiring. From personal experience working there, Nolan knew that his dad's family law practice was demanding, but he couldn't quite reconcile himself to the fact that his dad was getting ready to scale down, or even walk away, from the practice he'd started only a few years out of law school.

Again Nolan reminded himself to get back on track. Obviously he'd have to work harder. Being back home after a long absence had a way of derailing a man when he least expected it—but that wouldn't earn him any bonuses when it came to crunch time with his boss. He looked around the area that had been christened the Courtyard. The name fit, he decided as he took in the assembly of renovated ranch buildings that housed a variety of stores and craftsmen. His research had already told him that the tenants specialized in arts and crafts with artisanal breads and cheeses also on sale, while the central area was converted into a farmer's market most Saturday mornings.

To Nolan's way of thinking, it was an innovative way to use an old run-down and unprofitable piece of land. So what the hell did Rafiq want with it? He knew for a fact that there was no oil to be found in the surrounding area. Hell, everyone who grew up in and around Royal knew that—which kind of raised questions as to what Samson Oil wanted the land for. So far, Rafiq's quest to buy up property in Royal failed to make economic sense to Nolan.

Sure, he was giving owners who were still battered and struggling to pull their lives together after the tornado a chance to get away and start a new life, but what did Rafe plan to do with all the land he'd acquired?

Nolan reminded himself it wasn't his place to ask questions but merely to carry out the brief, no matter how much of a waste of money it looked like to him. Rafiq had his reasons but he wasn't sharing them, and it had been made clear to Nolan that it was his place to see to the acquisition of specific parcels of land—whether they were for sale or not. And that's exactly what he was going to do.

Regrettably, however, it appeared that Winslow Properties, despite their shaky financial footing, were not open to selling this particular parcel of land. It was up to him to persuade them otherwise. He'd hoped some of the tenants would be more forthcoming about their landlord but so far, on his visits to the stores, he'd found them to be a closemouthed bunch. Maybe they were all just scared, he thought. Royal had been through a lot. No one wanted to rock the boat now.

There was one tenant he'd yet to have the opportunity to talk to. He recalled her name from his memory—Raina Patterson. From what he understood she might be closer to Mellie Winslow than some of the other tenants. Maybe Ms. Patterson could give him the angle he needed to pry this property from the Winslow family's grip.

He began to walk toward a large red barn at the bottom of the U-shape created by the buildings. The iron roof had been proudly painted with the Texas flag. The sight of that flag never failed to tug at him; as much as he'd assimilated to his California lifestyle, he'd always be Texan.

Looking around, Nolan understood why the Winslow family had, after initial interest in Samson Oil's offer, grown cagey at the idea of selling this little community and the land it was on. For a town that was still rebuilding, this was an area of optimism and growth. Selling out from underneath everyone was bound to create unrest and instability all over again. Not everyone here could just pick up and create a new life in a new town or state like he had.

Damn, and there he was again. Thinking of the past and of what he'd lost. His wife, his son. He should probably have sent someone else on the legal team to do this job but Rafiq had been adamant he handle it himself. He mentally shrugged. It was the price he paid for the obscenely high salary he earned—he could live with that as long as he didn't ever have to live here again, with his memories.

Raina made a final tweak of the pine boughs and tartan ribbons she'd used to decorate the antique mantelpiece and looked around her store with a sense of pride and wonder. *Her* store. Priceless by name and by nature. She'd been here in the renovated red barn a month now. She still couldn't quite believe that a year after the tornado that had leveled her original business and much of the town of Royal, she'd managed to rebuild her inventory and relocate her business rather than just fold up altogether.

It certainly hadn't been easy, she thought as she moved through the store and let her hand drift over the highly polished oak sewing table she'd picked up at an estate sale last week—but it had been worth it.

Now all she had to do was hold on to it. A ripple of disquiet trickled down her spine. Her landlord, Mellie Winslow, had been subdued yesterday when she'd visited Raina but had said she was doing everything she could to ensure that her father's company, Winslow Properties, didn't sell the Courtyard.

Raina needed to know this wasn't all going to be ripped away from her a second time. She didn't know if she had it in her to start over again. Losing her store on Main Street, and most of her underinsured inventory of antiques, had just about sent her packing from the town she'd adopted as her own four years ago. She had to make this work, for herself and for her little boy.

No matter which way she looked at it, though, she still couldn't understand why anyone would be interested in buying the dried-up and overused land, let alone an oil company. If only Samson Oil—who'd been buying land left, right and center around Royal—would go away and let her have the peace and security she'd been searching for her whole life. Heck, it wasn't even as if they seemed to be doing anything with the properties they'd bought up. At the rate Samson Oil was going, Royal would become a ghost town.

"Mommy! Look!"

Raina turned and smiled at her son, Justin, or JJ as he was known, as he proudly showed off the ice cream cone her dad—his namesake—had just bought him. JJ was three going on thirteen most of the time, but today he was home from day care because he'd been miserable with a persistent cold. He was back to being the little boy who wanted his mommy and his "G'anddad" most of all. The theory had been that he'd rest on the small cot she had in her office out back, but theory had been thrown to the wind when JJ had heard his beloved granddad arrive to help Raina move some of the heavier items in the store.

Looking at JJ now, she began to wonder if she'd been conned by the little rascal all along. The little boy had protested his granddad's departure most miserably, but he was all smiles now with an ice cream cone and the promise of a sleepover on the weekend.

"Lucky you," she answered squatting down to JJ's eye level. "Can I have some?"

JJ pulled the cone closer to him, distrust in his eyes. "No, Mommy. G'anddad said it mine."

Raina pouted. "Not even one little lick?"

She saw the indecision on his face for just a moment before he proffered the dripping cone in her direction. "One," he said very solemnly.

Raina licked off the drips before they hit the floor and theatrically sighed in pleasure. "That's so yummy. Can I have more?" she teased, reaching for JJ's wrist.

"No more, Mommy! Mine!" JJ squealed and turned and ran, laughing hysterically as Raina growled and lumbered playfully behind him.

Through her son's shrieks of delight, Raina heard the bell tinkle over the main door, signaling a potential customer.

"Justin Junior, you stop right there! No running through the store," she called out, but it was futile. JJ was barreling away from her at top speed.

She rounded the corner just in time to hear a muffled "oof!" as JJ ran straight into the man who'd just entered the store. The man was wearing a very expensive looking suit, which, she groaned inwardly, now wore a fair portion of JJ's ice cream cone, right at the level of the man's groin. JJ rapidly backed away. The stranger looked up, a startled expression on his face as his eyes met hers. A frisson of something she couldn't quite put her finger on ran between them like a live current. It unnerved her and made her voice sharp.

"JJ! Apologize to the gentleman, right now."

She couldn't help it—even though it was her fault for chasing him, she couldn't prevent the note of censure that filled her voice. And she still felt unsettled by that look she'd just exchanged with a total stranger. A look that left her feeling things she had no right to feel. Raina dragged her attention back to the disaster at hand and searched around for something to offer the man to help him clean up.

The only pieces of fabric she had close by were a set of handmade lace doilies from the early twentieth century. She certainly couldn't afford to lose inventory, but then again, nor could she afford to lose a potential customer either.

JJ turned his little face up to hers. His blue eyes, so like her own, filled with tears that began to spill down his still-chubby cheeks. His lower lip began to quiver. He dropped what was left of his cone on the floor and ran to her, burying his face in her maxi skirt as if he could make himself invisible.

"Hey, no harm done," the man said, his voice slightly gruff and at odds with his words.

Raina definitely noticed a hint of Texas drawl as she glanced from her son to the customer, who, despite that initial look of shock, now appeared unfazed by the incident. He reached into his suit pocket and pulled out an honest-to-God white handkerchief. Was that a monogram in the corner? Raina didn't think they had such things anymore.

"I'm so sorry, sir. Here, let me," she started, reaching for the cotton square.

"Might be best if I handle this myself," the man replied.

Oh, heavens, she was such an idiot. Of course he'd have to handle it himself. It was *his* groin, after all. She had no business touching any man's trousers, let alone there. She gently set JJ to one side and got busy picking up the cone that he'd dropped on the floor, gathering the sticky mess in her left hand.

"JJ, can you go fetch me the tea towel that's hanging up in the kitchen?" she asked her son. "And no running!"

It was too late. JJ raced away as if he couldn't wait to put distance between himself and the mess he'd created.

"Kids, huh?"

The stranger finally smiled and Raina looked up at him—really looked this time—and felt a punch of attraction all the way to the tips of her toes. Before she could answer, JJ was back and, ridiculously glad of the distraction, Raina used the cloth to wipe up the residue from the floor and then wrapped up the cone in the towel to deal with later. Her customer had likewise dealt with the mess on his trousers.

"See, all cleaned up," he said, rolling up the handkerchief and shoving it in his pocket again.

Raina cringed at the cost of getting all that fine tailoring back into pristine condition again. "But the stain. Please, let me get your suit dry cleaned for you."

"No, seriously, it's no bother. Is this your boy? JJ is it?"

She nodded and watched as the man squatted down so he was at eye level with JJ, who had cautiously turned his head around when he'd heard his name. She couldn't help but notice how the fabric of the stranger's trousers caught snugly across his thighs and, despite hastily averting her gaze, she also couldn't stop the disconcerting rush of acute feminine awareness that welled inside her.

"Hey, JJ, no harm done, except to your ice cream. I'm sorry about that, champ." When Raina started to protest that he had nothing to be sorry for, he merely put up one hand and kept his attention on her little boy. "Are you okay?"

JJ nodded.

"But you lost your ice cream. Maybe I can talk to your mommy about buying you another one. Would you like that?"

Again Raina went to protest but the man shot her a glance and a smile that made her hush. As embarrassed as she was by what had happened, she found herself prepared to follow his lead.

JJ nodded again and the man put out one hand. "Good," he said with another smile. "Sounds like we have a deal. You want to shake on that?"

Raina felt a tug of pride as her son extended his grubby little hand to be engulfed in the stranger's much larger one. But pride was soon overtaken by something else as she noticed the man's hands. They were tanned and broad, with long fingers and neatly kept nails. Definitely an office worker, she surmised, and not from around here, but—oh boy—there was that swell of attraction again. What on earth was wrong with her? After Jeb, she'd sworn off men. She couldn't trust her own judgment anymore.

The man rose to his full height, which dwarfed Raina's own five foot seven by a good several inches. He held out his hand toward her.

"Nolan Dane, pleased to meet you."

Automatically Raina took his hand but realized her mistake the moment she did so. A sharp tingle of electricity sizzled up her arm the second their palms met.

"I... I'm R-Raina. Raina Patterson."

She groaned inwardly. Great, now she sounded like a complete idiot. Her heart skittered in her chest as she noticed he was still holding her hand. She gently pulled free and fought the urge to rub her palm on the fabric of her skirt. "Welcome to my store, Priceless. Were you looking for something in particular? Perhaps I can help you," she asked, forcing herself to put her business voice on.

His first reaction to her had been instant, visceral and totally unexpected. Now Nolan could barely tear his eyes from her. She looked so much like his dead wife, Carole, it was uncanny. Her shoulder-length hair was the same shade of glossy brown that hovered between dark chocolate and rich espresso. She had the same shape of chin and brows. But it was only once he looked more closely at her that he saw the differences that set them apart.

The woman before him now wore only a bare minimum of makeup, letting her natural beauty shine, whereas Carole had been so caught up in projecting the right appearance that even he had rarely seen her without makeup on. Even at breakfast. Carole's argument had been that while he'd comfortably slipped into a law practice with his father, she'd had a harder road to travel, proving herself against the good ol' boys in one of Maverick County's corporate law firms. She'd needed all the armor she could get.

But there was something in the way that Ms. Patterson carried herself, too, and the sweetly serene smile she wore, that continued to remind him of his late wife. Raina presented a strong and untroubled facade to the world. A facade that he already knew hid a vulnerability that had been evident in her hesitant introduction and which had appealed to the protector in him with surprising force.

Hell no, he reminded himself forcibly. No matter how much she fascinated him, he absolutely couldn't go there. Women like Raina Patterson were completely out of bounds. Even if she wasn't married—which she probably was—she had a kid, and he had strict rules about not complicating his life any further. He'd already had his heart torn out and shredded to pieces once and he would bear those scars for the rest of his life. Dating was strictly for brief respites—and this woman did not look like the type for a quick roll in the sheets followed by an even quicker farewell.

"Thank you," he said, finally pulling himself together. "I just came to look around, to be honest. The Courtyard hasn't been operating long, has it?"

"No, not terribly long. It stopped being a working ranch a few years ago. The ongoing drought forced the original owners to sell and the new owners, the Winslows, came up with the idea to convert it to shops and studios. It's helped a lot of us get back on our feet after the tornado."

Nolan nodded as he processed the information and matched it up with what he knew already. "And you're selling antiques here?"

"Yes, and running craft classes out back. My first one is tonight. Would you be interested in signing on for a lesson in candle making? They're going to be a hot gift item for Christmas this year in Royal."

She laughed softly and, unexpectedly, he delighted in the sound. It was refreshing. Genuine amusement wasn't often heard in the circles in which he moved, at least not without some malice in it somewhere.

"I'll take a rain check," he said with a wink, and he was delighted to see a faint blush color her ivory cheeks.

"A shame," she said averting her head slightly. "I'm sure all the ladies would have been thrilled to have you."

And then he felt the heat of a blush on his cheeks, as well. Ridiculous, he thought. He hadn't blushed since the day he'd asked Carole out in high school and yet here he was with cheeks aflame. The memory was just the cold dose of reality he needed. It was time to get out of here before he made a complete fool of himself and broke his own rules about dating and asked the enticing Ms. Patterson out. He made a show of looking at his watch and made a sound of surprise.

"I need to get on my way, but first I should remedy the demise of JJ's ice cream."

"Oh, please don't worry. He'll be fine and, besides, the homemade ice cream store will be closed now."

"And I'm holding you up from closing, too, I see," he said, gesturing to the face of his watch. "I'll head off."

"Please, don't rush away. Look around—you never know—something might grab your attention. We'll be a little while closing up anyway."

Despite his determination to put some distance between them, Nolan found himself agreeing to prolong his visit.

"Okay, thanks. Let me know when you want me out of your way."

She nodded and gave him another of those serene smiles that delivered a solid whack to his solar plexus.

As he moved among the pieces she had on display, he reexamined his options. He was here to do a job. Part of that job was gathering information. He hadn't missed the spark of interest in her eyes. Perhaps he could use that interest to his advantage. Ms. Patterson, whether she knew it or not, had just become his best opportunity to get an angle on Winslow Properties and hopefully the leverage he'd need to pull off this purchase. Somehow, he needed to get past his emotional barriers and see her purely as a means to an end. If he didn't, all bets were likely off, and he'd have to deliver Rafiq his first failure in this acquisitions venture. Nolan's need to succeed pushed through. He could do this. And he would.

Nolan could hear Raina moving around toward the back of the store. He flicked a look her way and saw her laying out egg cartons and wicks and precut blocks of what he assumed was wax. JJ was doing his best to help. Raina moved quietly behind him and straightened up the things he laid out for her, and every now and then she paused to wipe his little nose.

She did everything with grace and an effortless elegance that mesmerized Nolan, and he had to force himself to look away and remind himself he was here to gather intel about the Courtyard, not spend his time mooning over one of the proprietors. He was on the verge of leaving the store when he overheard Raina talking to JJ.

"Well, how about that?" she said, putting her hands on her hips and looking around the workroom. "We're all done, JJ. I couldn't have done it all so fast without your help."

Nolan fought back a smile. He had no doubt she'd have had it done in half the time, but it tugged at his heart to see how she took the time to make JJ feel special and his efforts valued. Then came a fresh debilitating wave of sorrow as he remembered all he'd lost. Even so, he still couldn't tear himself away from the tableau in front of him.

"I'm a good boy, aren't I, Mommy?" JJ said, his little chest puffed out with pride.

"Yes you are. The very best. And you're all mine!" She reached out to tickle him and he giggled and squirmed out of reach. "How about, as a reward, I take you to the diner for dinner before your sitter comes tonight."

The little boy nodded vigorously. An idea occurred to Nolan. This was an opening he could use. He still owed JJ an ice cream. What better opportunity to fulfill his promise to the kid and to *accidentally* bump into his mother again and draw her back into conversation.

She'd mentioned a sitter. Did that mean there was no Mr. Patterson around? He gave himself another mental shake. Whether there was or not, it made no difference.

This would merely be another opportunity to ask her more questions about the Courtyard and Winslow Properties.

At least that's what he told himself.

Two

Raina heard her cell phone ring in her handbag as she was securing JJ in his car seat. Whoever it was would just have to leave a message, she thought as she did up his harness and checked to make sure he was snug. Finally satisfied, she got in the driver's seat and turned on the ignition.

"Seat belt, Mommy!"

She smiled at JJ in the rearview mirror. "Yes, sir!"

He giggled in response, the way he always did, and it made her heart glad. She thanked God every day for the gift of her son. Jeb Pickering might have been a useless no good son-of-a-bitch but he'd left her with a gift beyond price. While it would have been her ideal wish to have provided JJ with both a mommy and a daddy who loved him, she was happy to parent alone. In fact, given Jeb's reliability, or lack of it, and his predilection for gambling and drink, JJ was better off not knowing the man even existed. Of course, being a single mom running a business brought its own issues, including relying on sitters when her dad wasn't free to help out. Which reminded her—the phone call. Maybe it had been her sitter calling.

"I'm just going to check my phone, JJ, then we'll head to the diner, okay?"

"C'n I have nuggets 'n' fries?"

"You sure can."

"Yum!"

Satisfied that he could have his favorite meal, JJ hummed quietly to himself, kicking a beat on the back of the front passenger seat while he waited. Raina stifled the admonition that sprang to her lips when he started to kick. She didn't want to enter into an argument with him now. Instead, she reached into her bag and dragged out her phone. One missed call, unknown number. A sick feeling of dread crept into her gut. Quelling the sensation, she listened to the message.

"Hey Rai, it's Jeb. I hear you got your little shop up and running again. That's good, 'cause I'm in a bit of a bind. I really need some money, honey." He sniggered and Raina cringed. He sounded drunk, again. "Anyway, I owe some guys… I, uh, well, I'll tell you when I see you. Soon, babe. By the way, how's that kid of ours? Later!"

Raina deleted the message instantly, her skin crawling. She felt as if she needed a long hot shower. Hadn't it been enough that he'd emptied out her bank account and skipped town when she'd been at the hospital in labor with JJ? And what about the extra five grand she'd given him early last year for what she'd told him was absolutely and totally the last time ever?

"Mommy, I'm hungry!" JJ demanded from the back, his kicks picking up in tempo.

Raina reached across to still his little legs. "JJ, what's the rule about kicking in the car?"

His little mouth firmed in a stubborn line. *Pick your battles*, Raina reminded herself, morphing into distraction mode instead. "Are you having ketchup with your chicken nuggets?"

"Yay! Ketchup!"

"Let's go then," she said with a smile as she put the car into gear.

It was a short drive into Royal but traffic was heavy. Raina was lucky to get a parking spot on the road about a block away from the diner. JJ skipped and jumped, holding her hand, as they walked along the pavement. Judging by his energy levels, she hoped he'd be okay to go back to day care tomorrow.

When they entered the Royal Diner, JJ hopscotched along the black-and-white checkerboard linoleum floor. They took a booth near the back and settled in on the red faux-leather seats.

"Be with you soon, hon," a waitress said with a smile as she poured glasses of water and left them with the sheet menus that everyone knew by heart but still pretended to study anyway.

Raina's appetite was gone, but she decided on a green salad with ranch dressing because she knew if she didn't eat, she'd be running on empty by the time her craft class started in a couple of hours. Shoving all thoughts of her ex to the back of her mind, she focused instead on her son and the evening ahead.

All going well, JJ would eat his dinner and she'd take him home to shower before the sitter arrived. Once the sitter was there, she'd be able to head back to Priceless to open up for her first class. Bookings had initially been slow but they'd picked up in the past day or so, and she hoped the simple candle-making class would be well received and that word of mouth would bring more students. With more students would come more overhead but she'd done her homework. After the initial outlay was met, the classes would bring in more sorely needed income, as well.

A movement across the booth made her look up from the menu she was staring at but had stopped actually seeing several minutes earlier. JJ was waving at someone. Thinking it might be their waitress returning for their order, Raina looked up with a smile, only to feel it freeze on her face and the hairs at her nape prickle to attention as she recognized the man walking toward them. Nolan Dane. What was he doing here? Surely he was more likely to be dining out at the Texas Cattleman's Club, or at the hotel in town?

It took only a few seconds to notice that he'd changed. His jeans were new and fit him perfectly, and the black Henley he wore under a worn leather jacket seemed to stretch across his chest as if it caressed him. Her cheeks flamed at the thought.

"Mommy! Man!" JJ said from his booster seat, and he waved again.

"Hey there," Nolan said as he drew next to the table.

"I'm having nuggets 'n' fries," JJ informed him importantly. "You wanna eat with me?"

"Oh, no, JJ. I'm sure Mr. Dane has other plans," Raina said quickly, feeling her blush deepen on her cheeks.

"Please, call me Nolan and, actually, no, I don't. But I don't want to intrude. I can eat at another table."

Raina felt terrible. She'd all but told him he wasn't welcome to sit with them. JJ's face fell. How bad could it be? she asked herself.

"Oh, please sit down. Seriously, it's okay. We haven't ordered yet, anyway. Join us."

"Well, if you're sure."

She nodded and gestured to the empty space next to JJ's booster seat. Nolan slid into the booth and stretched his long legs out under the table. She shifted slightly as his leg brushed hers.

"Do you guys eat here often?" Nolan asked.

"No, this is a treat for JJ. Aside from the mess with your suit, he's been a really good boy for me today, haven't you, JJ?"

JJ nodded emphatically and reached for his water glass. Nolan helped him steady the large glass as he drank and then put it back on the table for him.

"You're good at that," Raina commented. "Do you have kids of your own?"

A bleak emptiness appeared in his eyes, its presence so brief she wondered if she'd imagined it, but it was enough to make her realize she'd been prying where she had no right to.

"Oh, I'm sorry. I shouldn't be so rude. I didn't mean to pry."

"No, it's okay," Nolan brushed off her concern. "Maybe we should just put it down to self-preservation. I've seen how lethal he is with an ice cream cone."

Nolan watched Raina from across the table and silently congratulated himself on managing to keep his past locked firmly where it belonged. The waitress came by and took their orders, distracting Raina from asking any further questions. She was less relaxed than she'd been when he'd left the store. Was it his presence at the table that did that to her, he wondered, or was it something else? The waitress returned promptly with JJ's order, and while the little boy dug in, Nolan thought it time to ease conversation back to the Courtyard.

"So tell me a little more about the Courtyard," he started.

"The idea for it really only took off a few months after the tornado. A lot of us lost our stores and several of Royal's local artisans lost workshops and homes. The Courtyard gave us all a fresh start—gave us a new community to be proud of." Her eyes grew worried and a frown marred the smoothness of her forehead. "There's talk that some oil company is looking to buy the land. It worries me."

"Why's that? What difference would a new landlord make?" Nolan probed.

Raina looked away, her face thoughtful, before directing her blue gaze straight back at him. "The Courtyard actually became a symbol of hope for a lot of us. A chance to get our feet back firmly on the ground and get us back to normal in a world that got turned upside down in one awful day. You can't put a price on that. We need stability now. We need to be able to know from one day to the next that after all our hard work, we aren't simply going to be turned out.

"An oil company isn't going to want to keep us as tenants, you can be sure of that. They'll want the land for testing, although why they think there's oil there, I don't know. I haven't lived in Royal all that long and even I know the land is barely suitable for grazing, although with the drought that's questionable, too."

She fiddled with the salt and pepper shakers in front of her. "No, the Winslows did the right thing turning the ranch buildings into the Courtyard. Mellie assures me they're not selling. I only hope nothing happens to change her mind. None of us there can afford to have our businesses fold or see our rents increase. What with the cost of increased insurance premiums and setting up all over again, it wouldn't take much to destroy us."

A pang of guilt pulled at him. If he was successful in changing the Winslows' minds, and Rafe got hold of the Courtyard, Nolan knew there were no guarantees that his boss would keep the tenants. And it was true. Raina had a point—while the greater Maverick County area had yielded some successful oil fields, none had been in this general area. Nolan shifted uncomfortably. For the first time he was seeing the personal face of his assignment:

someone who'd be directly and negatively impacted by his boss's plan. And he didn't like it. Not one bit.

He took a sip of his water and decided a change of subject might be in order.

"So, the tornado. That must have been terrifying. People are pretty resilient here, though," he commented.

Raina smiled and once again he was struck by how natural and effortless her beauty was.

"Sometimes I think Royal is the epitome of the 'get down and get on with it' ethic. Some people have moved on, which is completely understandable, but most have just licked their wounds and carried on. And of course there are also the lucky ones who are benefiting from the damage. Tradesmen have been at a premium in the district and we've seen an influx of out-of-towners coming in to fill demand. Bit by bit Royal has found its way back to a new normal. Is that what brings you here? The rebuild?"

Nolan was saved from immediately answering as their waitress dropped their meals in front of them with a smile. "Good to see you back, Nolan," she said before racing off to her next customer.

Raina looked taken aback. "You're local?"

"No, not anymore. I'm here to see family."

"You grew up here, then?"

He nodded. "Yeah, but I've been living in California for several years. I'm only here for a visit."

"Then I'm sure you would have heard all about the tornado from them." Raina's voice held a note of reserve that had been missing before.

"From their point of view, yeah. Dad's in family law, and he said he's seen an unfortunate upswing in business in the wake of the tornado. Families breaking up under the strain of trying to put their lives back together—more domestic abuse."

Raina nodded. "Yeah, it's sad. So often these events

pull people closer together, but if they don't they seem to have the complete opposite effect. I guess I'm lucky I didn't have to factor that in. It's just me and JJ, and my dad. Dad's retired and usually travels around the country, but he came to stay in the trailer park just out of town so he could be on hand to help me reestablish Priceless and get me and JJ back on our feet again."

Nolan couldn't help it: a swell of relief that there was no partner in Raina's life bloomed from deep inside. He pushed the sensation away. She was still out of bounds. She was the kind of woman who had long-term written all over her, while he was only planning to be here long enough to complete the land purchases to Rafiq's satisfaction.

And then there was the kid. He certainly didn't want to take on a package deal of mother and child, no matter how much his libido sizzled like a drop of water on a hot skillet whenever he was anywhere near Raina. He needed to keep his eye on the main goal. He was here to do business, not dally with the locals or become emotionally involved in the town he grew up in. He'd made his choice to walk away from Royal and all the pain it represented seven years ago. He had no plans to stick around. Even so, he perversely wanted to know more about the woman sitting opposite him.

"So, what brought *you* to Royal?" he asked.

She laughed, the sound self-deprecating. "I followed a man. He left and I stayed. It's as simple as that."

Somehow Nolan doubted that it was quite as straightforward as she said.

"Mommy, my hands dirty." JJ spoke up from beside him.

"Use your napkin, JJ."

"But it dirty," he grumbled.

"Here, use mine," Nolan offered.

JJ held his hands up for Nolan to wipe them. "P'ease?" he implored.

Nolan automatically enveloped JJ's hands with the large paper napkin and made a game out of cleaning the little boy's fingers. When he was done, he wiped a bit of sauce from JJ's chin, as well.

"Hey, you're good at that," Raina said with a smile. "Are you sure you don't have kids?"

Nolan swallowed. This would be the perfect opportunity to segue into the past, to admit he'd had a wife and child, but he couldn't bring himself to say the words. It just opened up the floor for too many questions—questions that had no answers and only evoked pity, which he hated.

"Maybe I'm just a clean freak," he joked, scrunching up the used napkin and tossing it on the table.

"Can we go now, Mommy?" JJ asked.

"No, son. Mr. Dane and I haven't finished our meals."

For a second it looked as though JJ would object, but then Nolan remembered his earlier promise.

"What about some ice cream? You never got to finish the one you had before, right?"

"Oh, but I said you didn't need—" Raina began to protest.

"Need doesn't enter into it when ice cream is concerned," Nolan interrupted her smoothly. "What do you say, JJ? Do you want a junior sundae?"

"Wif sprinkles?"

"Sure, my treat." He looked across at Raina. "How about you? Do you want a sundae with sprinkles, too?"

JJ laughed next to him. "Mommy doesn't have treats, she's a mommy!"

Nolan read the subtext in JJ's words. It didn't take a rocket scientist to figure out that Raina went without so that her son could have little treats every now and then. How much had she foregone to ensure her son could still enjoy special things while she rebuilt her business and kept a roof over their heads? Again that urge to protect swirled at the back of his mind.

"Even mommies like treats sometimes, don't they?" he asked, looking straight across the table at Raina.

"Not tonight, thank you. I need to get back to Priceless. My first class starts this evening and I can't be late, not even for a treat."

"Another time then," Nolan promised, and as he called the waitress to order JJ's sundae, he found himself wondering just how soon that might be.

Three

Another time? Did he mean to ask her out on a date? Raina wasn't quite sure how she felt about that. She hadn't dated since Jeb—hadn't even been interested in dating as she came to grips with his betrayal, single parenthood and running a business. It had been a painful irony that she'd been duped by the person she'd thought would stand by her, exactly as her father had been.

She had never known her mother and pictures of her had been few and of poor quality. Raina's enduring memory of the woman who'd borne her was the story of how she'd come home from the hospital with Raina, put her in her bassinet and gone out to buy some milk and never returned. Growing up, Raina had always had more questions about the whole situation than answers and, in retrospect, she could understand why she'd been drawn to the losers.

Despite all the security and love her father had poured into her, Raina's sense of self-worth had been low. She'd found herself desperate to be accepted by others, only to be walked all over again and again. Jeb had been the last in a string of disastrous relationships, and when he'd cleaned out her bank account while she was in labor with his son, she'd finally learned her lesson—and with it, who she was and where she belonged in her world. Now, she was at peace with her decision to focus her energies on JJ and provide a home for them. She finally, at the sage old age of thirty, felt grown up.

Her friends still teased her about her dating moratorium but she'd avoided all potential setups they'd thrown her way. And in the aftermath of the tornado, it had made far better sense not to get involved with anyone. Life had become incredibly precious and despite her need to nurture and to try to "fix" broken souls, aka the losers she'd dated previously, she'd had to draw a line somewhere.

But a date with Nolan Dane? He was nothing like the guys she'd been out with before. He owned a suit, for a start, and showed the kind of manners her father had always told her to expect from a man.

She looked across the table and noticed that JJ had made short work of his sundae and was now rubbing his eyes and fidgeting in his booster seat. She glanced at her watch—a 1920s timepiece she hadn't been able to bring herself to sell after she'd discovered it in a boxed lot she'd bought at an estate sale a couple of years ago. If she didn't get on her way soon, she'd be running late for the sitter and for her class.

"This has been lovely," she said, gathering her bag and searching for her wallet. "But JJ and I really must get going. Thank you for joining us."

"No, thank *you* for *your* company. Please, let me get this. It's the least I can do for crashing your dinner together."

"Oh, but—"

"Please, I appreciated having someone to talk to over my meal."

Before she could say anything, Nolan left several bills on the tabletop, including a generous tip, and helped JJ from the booth.

"Are you parked far away?" he asked as they walked toward the exit.

"No, not far. A block."

"Let me walk you," Nolan said, falling into step beside her on the sidewalk outside the diner.

"Mommy, up," JJ interrupted, and he lifted his little arms in the air.

"Sure, sweetie," she said, bending to lift him into her arms.

She wouldn't be able to keep this up for too much longer. JJ was getting so big and most of the time she had trouble keeping up with her energetic wee man. The fact that he wanted her to carry him spoke volumes about how tired he was. She reminded herself to cherish these moments while they lasted.

They were halfway down the block when she had to readjust JJ's weight in her arms.

"He looks heavy," Nolan commented. "Can I carry him for you?"

"No, it's fine, I can manage," Raina insisted, even though her back was starting to ache a little.

"Man carry me, Mommy."

JJ squirmed in her arms, almost sending her off balance.

"Are you sure you don't mind?" she asked Nolan.

In response, Nolan effortlessly hefted her son from her and propped JJ on one hip. "Of course not."

At the car, Nolan waited on the sidewalk while she strapped JJ into his seat.

"Thank you for dinner, and for your help with JJ. You didn't have to," Raina said as she straightened from the car and held her hand out to Nolan.

He took it and again she was surprised by the sizzling jolt of sensation that struck her as his hand clasped hers.

"Honestly, the pleasure was all mine," he replied, his eyes locked on hers.

She found herself strangely reluctant to let his hand go and Nolan seemed to feel the same way, but then a group of people coming along the sidewalk forced them apart. Thankful she could disengage before things got awkward, Raina gave him a small wave and settled herself in the car.

Her hand still tingled as she reached forward to put the key in the ignition. It had been a long time since she'd felt anything like this at a man's touch. As she drove away, Raina made herself keep her eyes on the road in front of her. She wouldn't look back. Looking back only invited trouble, she told herself, and she'd had bushels of that already in her life. No, she'd promised herself to keep moving forward the right way, and that didn't involve complicating her life with a relationship or fling with someone who was passing through.

Nolan watched from the sidewalk until he couldn't see Raina's taillights any longer. Why had he done this to himself? he wondered as he hunched deeper into his jacket and began to walk back to his hotel. Carrying JJ had brought back a wealth of hurt and repressed memories of his own son, Bennett.

Holding another small body in his arms…it had been a more bitter than sweet experience. He reminded himself very firmly that using her for information about the Winslows was one thing, but he was in no way embarking on any kind of friendship with Raina. It would be too easy, he knew that. He was already attracted to her, already felt that surge of physical awareness every time she smiled or her gaze met his. From the moment he'd laid eyes on her he'd been drawn to her and he'd been unable to get her out of his thoughts.

Being there in the Royal Diner with Raina and JJ had felt too much like his old life. The life he'd vowed he would never turn back to. No, his home was Los Angeles now. Royal held no allure for him anymore even though everything here still felt so achingly familiar.

He acknowledged the doorman at the hotel with a smile and went straight to his room. It was early. Any other time he'd have stopped in the bar and had a drink. Maybe enjoyed a bit of casual female interest before heading to his room—or hers. The mobile nature of his role as Rafiq's personal attorney gave him leeway in his life that he'd never allowed himself before and while casual hookups had never been his style, a man had needs—and clearly the women he'd met had needs, as well. But while those encounters may have left him physically sated, there always remained an emptiness deep inside him.

His thoughts flickered back to Raina Patterson. She was definitely not the type for a casual hookup. She exuded stability and comfort. A man could fool himself that he belonged in the softness of her arms, but only until he broke her heart by leaving again. Nolan promised himself he would not be that man.

He threw himself on the bed and reached for the TV remote. Maybe he'd be able to numb his mind and his awakened libido by watching some mindless sitcoms or movies until he was ready to sleep. But distraction was a long time coming that night, and he couldn't stop his mind wandering back toward the woman who'd so captured him.

Raina was glad she'd taken the time to prepare the workroom before she'd left Priceless earlier that day. JJ had been surprisingly clingy when she'd left him at home with the sitter, making her wonder if their company over dinner had unsettled him. It had certainly unsettled her.

Her students began to arrive, right on time, and once everyone was there and introductions were complete, Raina started the lesson. She'd decided to keep it simple for the first session, changing the style of the candles each week as they carried on. She smiled as she made eye contact with one of JJ's previous babysitters. Hadley Stratton was only a couple of years younger than Raina and had a delightful way with children.

"Okay, ladies, thank you all for coming along tonight. I see you all received my email with the instructions for preparing for this evening's lesson. Does anyone have any questions so far?"

Hadley spoke up. "You said we could dye the egg shells, but what if we could only get brown eggs?"

"No problem," Raina assured her. "You can choose to keep your candles in the shell and decorate the shells, or you can break the shell away after the candles have set and simply burn them in a container—like an eggcup or something like that. It's entirely up to you."

"I'm so brain dead after nannying all day and studying all night that I think I can only go as far as filling a shell. Is that okay?" Hadley laughed. "Maybe I can leave decorating to another lesson."

Several other women joined in with Hadley's laughter, obviously empathizing with her. Raina nodded in acknowledgment.

"How many of you would prefer to decorate or color?"

About half the women in the room put their hands up.

"Okay," Raina said. "How about we split into two groups for tonight? Decorators this side of the workroom, and plain beeswax candles on the other."

The women good-naturedly shifted around and, after showing the group doing plain candles how to start the process of melting their beeswax, Raina discussed with the group of decorators how to dye their egg shells or hand paint them with freestyle or stenciled designs. As everyone set to work, Raina began to feel a sense of excitement. The lesson was really going well and the atmosphere was both lighthearted and creative at the same time.

She stopped by Hadley's table for a minute, while making the rounds of the class to check that everyone was on track.

"It's good to see you, Hadley. We miss you."

"I miss you guys, too. But you know what it's like balancing everything."

"You always make everything look so effortless when you're with kids. You should really have some of your own one day," Raina teased with a friendly smile.

Hadley laughed out loud, drawing attention and several smiles from the people around her. "I've got so much on my plate right now I'm quite happy to put that off for a while longer. Besides, there's the important prerequisite of finding the right man for the job, y'know?"

Raina felt her smile slip a little, but she knew Hadley hadn't meant anything by her comment, that she hadn't been referring to Raina's poor choice of partner in Jeb.

"You make sure he's the right one, then," Raina said, with a light touch on Hadley's arm.

"Don't you worry, I will. When the time is right. In the meantime, at least I have your classes to look forward to on Tuesday evenings. This is about as far as my social life extends. Getting to spend time with other adults and relax and unwind is like gold to me right now, plus I get to make some cute Christmas gifts at the same time. What more could a woman want?"

With a murmur of agreement, Raina moved on to her next student. Hadley was right. What more could a woman want than to be surrounded by people she enjoyed being with and doing something creative? Even so, Raina felt an unexpected yearning that pulled from deep inside. She wanted that "right one" in her life one day. The man who would be her partner in everything and help her to guide JJ on his path in life. Right now, while JJ was small and so dependent on her, it was easy to imagine that she'd be able to cope forever. But sometimes she wished for more. For herself, as well.

Nolan Dane popped immediately to mind and Raina quashed a startling swell of desire as adequately as she was able. This was ridiculous. She'd only met the man today and she was already spinning a tale of happy ever after in her mind? Clearly she wasn't busy enough with her life already. Pushing all thoughts of men to the back of her mind, she went to assist one of her students with the placement of her candle wicks.

By the time the class finished, everyone was proud of their results—Raina most of all. Not only had she successfully pulled off tutoring her first official craft lesson, but everyone had commented how much they were looking forward to returning the following week when they'd be making mason jar candles filled with oil. Some were even talking about classes in the New Year and how they'd like to bring other friends along.

When everyone had cleaned up and gone, and Raina had locked up, she drove herself home. After paying the sitter and checking on JJ, she decided to run herself a luxurious deep bath. She'd earned the hot soak, she decided as she stripped and pulled on a robe while waiting for the bath to fill. In fact, she'd earned a celebratory glass of wine to go along with it. After a quick trip to the kitchen she was soon back with a glass of merlot. She disrobed and lowered herself into the soothing water.

Everything was going to be okay, she told herself. While the antiques business was a little slow in getting off the ground again, she knew it wouldn't take too long before her old customers would discover her new location. A bit of careful advertising across the county would help, and now, with the popularity of the craft classes, as well, she could afford to place those advertisements. She took a sip of her wine and allowed the mellow flavors to roll across her tongue before she swallowed.

Yes, everything would be fine from now on. She and JJ wouldn't want for anything. Or anyone.

Later, as she readied for bed, she checked her phone for messages. She'd turned it off during her class and hadn't gotten around to turning it back on yet. A bit of the shine of happiness from the evening's success dulled when she saw she had another missed call from Jeb and that he'd left another message. Her finger hovered over the button to simply delete the message, but she couldn't bring herself to do it. Instead, she listened and felt her happiness dull a little more.

"Rai, c'mon, babe. Call me back. I really need some money fast. I know you're good for it. Look, this is pretty urgent. Call me."

Raina closed her eyes in frustration. When would she ever be rid of the man? She'd taken all the legal steps she could to have sole custody of JJ, so she knew the little guy was safe from his father. But what would it take for Jeb to leave her alone?

Stop giving him money. The words echoed in her head as clearly as the last time her father had uttered them to her. Not for the first time she wondered why she continued to help her ex. It wasn't because she still bore any love for him. That had died long ago. Was it because she felt beholden to him because of JJ? No. She'd made the decision to go ahead with raising him, knowing it was unlikely that Jeb would provide any support. Maybe it was just because, despite herself, she couldn't help but reach out when she

knew a man was down. Her father had often teased her
about her need to make everyone happy and feel safe. The
thing was, if she kept helping Jeb, when would he ever
learn to stand on his own feet and accept some responsibility for everything that happened in his life?

She came to a decision. This ended here and now. She'd
no longer be Jeb's cash cow or his go-to person. She deleted the message and shoved her phone in her purse and
climbed into bed. Let that be an end to it, she thought as
she closed her eyes and drifted off to sleep.

Four

Nolan strolled around the Courtyard the next afternoon, telling himself he wasn't there to see Raina Patterson at all, he was merely doing his job and finding out a bit more about the other tenants. If he could present the acquisition of this parcel of land to Rafiq as an ongoing business concern rather than merely as a land purchase, maybe he could preserve the jobs and incomes of these hardworking people.

He was taken by the work in the silversmith's shop. The delicacy of the silversmith's designs was exquisite and Nolan knew his mother would love the pendant designed to look like a peacock tail with tiny cabochon amethysts and peridots inset at the ends of the feathers. He eyed the price tag and decided that the cost didn't matter. His mother's pleasure on opening the gift would bring its own reward. She'd had little enough joy from him in the past few years as he'd avoided returning to Royal. Maybe this would help show her that despite his withdrawal from home, she was still very much in his thoughts.

The shop assistant was effusive about his choice, almost talking him into purchasing a matching set of earrings, but he knew that less was very definitely more when it came to his mother's tastes and that she preferred a few well-chosen pieces to a cacophony of color and design.

"Is this a Christmas gift?" the woman asked.

"No, just something my mom will enjoy," he answered.

"Ah, that's lovely. Would you still like me to gift wrap it for you?"

"Please."

"Are you new to the area?" the assistant asked as she deftly wrapped the pendant in tissue and wrapping paper.

"I grew up here but I've been away for a while. Just here to see my family."

"Oh, that's lovely," the woman said with a friendly smile. She tied off a length of organza ribbon around the little packet and popped it in a gift bag. "Well, thank you for supporting the Courtyard with your purchase. I hope we see you back before you head home."

Murmuring a note of assent, Nolan took the gift and left the store. It was only midweek but the parking lot was almost full of vehicles and people were bustling around, their arms filled with bags emblazoned with the local artisans' logos. This place really was a gold mine. Yesterday he hadn't spent enough time wandering about, getting a real feel for the place—it was something he was determined to remedy today.

A flash of color caught his eye and he turned his head to see Raina Patterson outside her store, assisting a customer putting a small side table in the back of their car. He felt a now-familiar wallop of awareness as he took in the way her bright red sweater dress clung to her feminine curves and skimmed her hips like a lover's caress.

His body heated and sprang to life, arousal beating a low thrumming pulse that reminded him all too much of the dreams he'd endured last night.

Dreams where he'd begun to make love to his late wife, but when she'd turned toward him it had been Raina's face before him instead.

Nolan swiftly veered into the nearest store, determined to bring his body back under control and rid himself of the desire to walk those few yards toward the big red barn and spend time again with its proprietor. He wasn't here to embark on an affair, he reminded himself. He was here to work.

Raina looked up, surprised to see Nolan Dane on the other side of the Courtyard. She raised a hand to wave, but it appeared that he hadn't seen her as he abruptly turned and headed into the cheese maker's store. She told herself it didn't matter, that she hadn't hoped to see him again anyway. Even so, she felt a tiny twinge of disappointment that she forced herself to rapidly shove aside. She had enough on her plate for today as it was. The class she had lined up for tonight was mosaic work, and she had yet to check the inventory of stock she'd ordered for her students to buy and use for their lessons. The simple mirror frame kits would hopefully be a quick and easy project for her students to tackle, all of them first-timers to mosaic work, and she was looking forward to the class.

A prickle of uneasiness ran down her spine—the sense of disquiet making her look around before heading back into the store. She must be imagining things, she thought, pushing the feeling away and delving into the boxes of stock she'd left on the workroom tables. Last night's message from Jeb was making her paranoid and goodness knew she had little enough time for that.

* * *

The week went quickly and her classes were going from strength to strength. As a side bonus, several of her students were also avid collectors of a variety of antique items including some of the delicate English china she had on display. She was excited to have sold several pieces already and had requests to look out for more. Things were going better than she'd anticipated.

By the time Friday night rolled around, she was really beginning to feel the strain of carrying the responsibility of the store and the classes on her own, and she wanted nothing more than to sit at home with JJ, tucked up in front of the fire and reading a few of his favorite storybooks. But she'd already promised him that they'd go downtown to the Christmas tree lighting ceremony organized by the Texas Cattleman's Club. It was her goal to one day be sponsored to join the club. Of course, she'd need to make a better than average income before she could afford to do that.

While the club had been a solely male domain when it was founded, in recent years women had become members and the club had become more family-oriented in general. And they did such good work in the community, too. Something she hoped to be able to participate in when the time was right. It was important to give back.

The evening air was cold and Raina made sure JJ was bundled up snug and warm in a jacket and hand-knitted wool beanie that one of her customers had made for him. He looked as cute as a button with a few dark tufts of hair poking out from beneath the beanie.

She helped him from the car when they got to downtown Royal, and for a second she felt a pang of regret that Jeb couldn't be a part of JJ's life. But JJ deserved a father he could rely on. Not one who drank and gambled and drifted from one town to the next, looking for work to support his habits.

She'd been blind to Jeb's faults for a long time and forgiven him time and again, believing his well-spun lies, right up until the day he wasn't there when she needed him most. JJ's birth had been a roller coaster of emotions: intense joy to finally hold her child in her arms and meet him face-to-face that was tempered by the realization that the only people Raina could honestly rely upon were herself and her dad. She'd grown up a heck of a lot that day. She'd thought herself so mature at twenty-seven, so ready to be a mother.

"Will there be gifts under the tree, Mommy?" JJ asked as he skipped along beside her on the sidewalk, holding her hand.

"Not real ones, my boy."

"Not even one for me?"

Raina laughed and tugged his beanie more securely over his little ears. "Not even for me either! But don't worry. I'm sure that Santa will remember exactly where we live and will bring you your gifts in time for Christmas."

Satisfied with her answer, JJ turned his attention to the growing crowd. In the distance, Raina caught sight of Clare Connelly. The chief pediatric nurse at Royal Memorial Hospital had been a wonderful support when JJ had been severely jaundiced after his birth and Raina had worried herself sick over him. Newly abandoned by her partner and with her father still on his way to Royal, Raina had had a severe dose of the baby blues as she began to doubt her ability to look after her newborn son. It had been Clare's confident and capable manner with the babies in her care, not to mention the gentle support she'd offered to the new mothers, that had made Raina begin to believe she could do this parenting thing all on her own.

Raina caught Clare's eye and waved a hello. Clare was involved in what appeared to be a very intense conversation with one of the pediatricians who'd also attended JJ at the hospital, Dr. Parker Reese. Raina raised her eyebrows in surprise. Was there something going on between the petite blonde nurse and the sometimes prickly pediatrician? The thought brought a smile to her lips. It had been a joke among the mothers in the hospital that Dr. Reese would make a great husband for someone one day—if he could ever let go of his work and develop a social life. The man was dedicated to his career but everyone needed some balance in their life.

The reminder of balance prodded at Raina's thoughts. Lately everything had been JJ and work for her. There'd been no time for herself, but she was okay with that. One day, maybe, when JJ was a bit older and when her business was on a stronger footing, then yeah, she might think about dating. Until then, she had to stay focused on keeping her financial footing and being the best mother she could be for her little boy.

"Mommy, I can't see," JJ complained, tugging at her arm. "Up?"

"Sure, baby."

Raina bent and lifted JJ into her arms, settling him on one hip. It probably didn't make a world of difference to his line of sight but it was all she could manage.

"Still can't see," he fretted, twisting in her arms and making her clutch his jacket to stop him from falling.

"JJ, settle down. Trust me, when the lights go on, you'll see everything."

"Here" came a familiar male voice. "Maybe I can help?"

"Man!"

JJ flung his arms toward the newcomer with an exuberance that dismayed Raina and almost sent her off balance. Nolan Dane loomed up beside her. She should refuse his offer of help, but JJ was already transferring himself into Nolan's arms and was soon deposited high on Nolan's shoulders.

"Better now?" Nolan asked, looking up at JJ who was holding on tight to Nolan's head.

JJ nodded.

"What do you say, JJ?" Raina prompted.

"T'ank you."

"You're welcome." Nolan turned his smile to Raina. "I hope you don't mind. You look tired and I could see he was getting heavy."

Raina's lips twisted into a smile. "It's okay, thank you."

So, he thought she looked tired, huh? Wow, way to build a girl up, she thought, then immediately chastised herself for being so churlish. She did look tired. The three late nights this week with the classes, on top of everything else, had taken a toll. She made a mental note to try to get to bed earlier on the nights she wasn't working.

The crowd around them thickened as the local singers and dance groups performed on the makeshift stage that had been set up for the evening. Raina's gratitude to Nolan for taking JJ increased. There was no way JJ would have seen the show, or enjoyed it, from her arms; nor would she have been able to hold him for this long.

The night sky was fully dark and the atmosphere quickly became one of excitement as, over the loudspeakers, the master of ceremonies and the newest Texas Cattleman's Club president, Case Baxter, led the countdown to the lighting of the tree. Everyone in the crowd counted with him.

"… Three, two, one!" Raina shouted along with the rest of the crowd, then she joined them in the oohs and ahhs of delight as the switch was thrown to bring a multitude of colored lights to life in the massive tree that now dominated downtown Royal. Tearing her eyes from the tree, Raina looked up at her son, whose face was a picture of enchantment. A deep sense of contentment filled her.

She might not own the world, but it sure felt like it when she could still put a look like that on her little boy's face.

A choir began to sing "Joy to the World," and bit by bit the crowd joined them. Nolan had a surprisingly pleasant tenor, Raina discovered as he unselfconsciously added his voice to the singing. As the song wound to its end, the mayor of Royal took the microphone and thanked Case Baxter and the Texas Cattleman's Club committee for sponsoring the tree lighting ceremony, and he concluded by wishing everyone the very best for the season and inviting them to support the retailers who'd set up stalls around the square.

Raina turned to Nolan. "Thank you. I really mean it. I'm sure he'll remember tonight for a long time to come and that's because you helped us out."

"Only too happy to oblige y'all," Nolan answered. "Say, do you have to race home right away? How about a churro and some hot chocolate from one of the stalls over there?"

"Yummy, churro!" JJ crowed from on top of Nolan's shoulders.

"Manners, JJ!" Raina admonished. "What have I told you?"

"T'ank you, man," JJ dutifully responded.

Nolan laughed and Raina felt her heart skip a happy beat at the sound.

"His name is Mr. Dane, not man, JJ," Raina gently admonished.

"I think you should let him call me Nolan. Mr. Dane sounds so stuffy."

Raina nodded her head. "I'll try but I can't guarantee it. He can be pretty stubborn when he decides on a word."

Through the crowd, she spied Liam Wade. The rancher was clearly in demand with the ladies and looking none too thrilled about the prospect. A group of very determined looking mommas with single daughters in tow had circled him like a wagon train, ensuring he had no easy way out. A chuckle escaped her lips, prompting a question from Nolan.

"What's so funny?"

"Oh, just poor Liam. He's one of Royal's most eligible bachelors," she said, pointing him out in the crowd, "and one of Royal's most reluctant at the same time. I think he'd be happy if he never had to leave his ranch."

Nolan chuckled in sympathy. "Yeah, I guess when you have an operation like the Wade Ranch you're pretty self-contained. I can see why he wouldn't want to leave, especially if he gets mobbed whenever he sets foot outside his property line."

"Sure, but everybody needs somebody, don't they?" Raina countered without thinking.

Raina caught Nolan looking at her—a strange expression on his face as if he was weighing her words. Did he need somebody? His eyes lingered on her mouth and she fought not to lick her lips in nervous reaction. But it made her wonder: What would his lips feel like on her own? She immediately shoved the thought away. Here he was with her son on his shoulders and she was thinking about him kissing her? What was wrong with her?

Nolan shifted his gaze. "And what about you? Don't you need somebody, as well?" he asked.

She felt color flood her cheeks. "I have JJ," she said, her voice staunch. "He's all I need."

Nolan made an indeterminate sound and guided Raina toward one of the stalls off to the side. He swung JJ down to the ground and rolled his shoulders a few times before marching up to the counter and placing an order. Had she upset him by saying that JJ was all she needed? It was hard to tell. And besides, she reminded herself, it shouldn't bother her if it had upset him. She wasn't in the market for a relationship. Even so, it didn't stop her watching him as he picked up the tray with their hot chocolate and churros and led them over to a seating area that had been set up to one side.

"Don't let it all get cold," he warned gently as he set the tray down on the table in front of them.

"Thank you so much for this," Raina said, transferring some of JJ's hot chocolate to a sippy cup she'd pulled from her bag. "Sorry, I just like to be on the safe side with drinks when we're out. I know he's probably old enough to do without—"

"Hey, no need to apologize," Nolan interrupted. "You're his mom, you know what's best for him. I'm hardly in a position to judge."

By the time they'd finished their treats, JJ was getting cranky and tired. There was no way he'd make the trek back to where Raina had parked so when Nolan offered to carry him for her again, she didn't object. Weariness pulled at her, too, but the thought of curling up in her bed was tempered by the need to get up early the next morning. Saturdays she opened late, because they were her yard- and estate-sale mornings when she rose before dawn to try to pick up the occasional treasure to resell at Priceless. Her dad always came over super early to take care of JJ for the day so she could go straight to the store after doing her rounds of the sales.

At the car, Nolan stood to one side while she settled JJ into his car seat. Poor kid, he was almost asleep already, she noticed. Straightening from the car, she closed JJ's door gently and turned to Nolan.

"Thank you so much for your help tonight. I really do appreciate it."

"I enjoyed it. It's always fun seeing the lights through a child's eyes. Kids make everything so simple, so basic and enjoyable, don't they?"

Raina smiled at him, then struggled to stifle a yawn. "Oh, my. I'm sorry. Please excuse me. It's been a heck of a week. I'd better head off and get JJ into bed."

Nolan nodded and then stepped a little closer. "Raina, I'd really like to see you again. To take you out to dinner or the movies?"

Raina's breath caught in her throat. He was asking her for a date? For the briefest of moments she cherished the idea but then her practical nature set in. She shook her head gently.

"Nolan, I'm flattered. Truly I am. But I don't date. My life is too busy as it is. It's really not a good time for me to be thinking about stretching myself any thinner. I'm sorry."

"No, it's okay," Nolan said, his brown eyes gleaming under the streetlamp. He reached into his back pocket and pulled out a card holder. "I'm disappointed but I understand. If you ever change your mind, make sure you let me know, okay? My private number is on the back."

He slid one pristine white business card from the holder and pressed it into her hand. The instant he touched her, that familiar tingle came back, except this time it quivered through her veins along with something else. Something that felt curiously like desire.

She held on to the feeling for the briefest moment, wondering when had been the last time anyone had made her feel like a desirable woman, before ruthlessly quelling it again. She couldn't—no, shouldn't—entertain the idea. It was best that she didn't see Nolan again. Every relationship she'd ever had had extracted a price whereby she'd lost a little bit of herself in the process. She daren't do that to herself, or to JJ, again. Not now. Not ever. And yet she still found herself wishing she could say yes.

"How long are you prepared to wait?" Raina joked with a nervous laugh, unable to stop herself from asking the question even though she had no intention of taking Nolan up on it.

"As long as it takes," Nolan said with a slow smile that sent curls of delight all the way to her extremities.

Oh, yes. She was well-advised to steer completely clear of Nolan Dane. She'd only met him four days ago and he was already heating her blood.

Unable to think of a suitable response, Raina muttered a swift good-night and got into the car. She gave Nolan a small wave as she pulled away from the curb and drove away. A red light at the intersection halted her retreat and she glanced in the rearview mirror. Nolan still stood there on the sidewalk, his hands shoved in his jacket pockets, watching them go.

She couldn't stop thinking of him during the journey home to their little rented house and, even after she'd put JJ to bed and found refuge between her own sheets, Nolan Dane remained front and center in her thoughts. The way he looked at her made her feel like a woman. Not just a mom, not just a retailer or a tutor, but a warm, desirable and wanted woman. She'd pushed the idea away so hard and so vehemently after Jeb that it had become a concept she'd almost forgotten. Seeing that attraction reflected in Nolan's face empowered her. It was a sensation she liked.

She twisted in her sheets, her body aching with unexpected longing. Nolan Dane affected her in ways she hadn't wanted to acknowledge but now that she'd opened the door on those feelings, they'd all come rushing out. She liked everything about him so far—his manners, his careful way of speaking, even the tone of his voice. And his eye-catching looks didn't hurt either. He carried his height with confidence, with his broad shoulders set straight, and he met a person's gaze square on with no subterfuge—no lies. Having been on the receiving end of those looks Raina had come to realize that a woman could get happily lost in those deep brown eyes of his.

And then there was his manner with JJ. Even at the store, on the first day she'd met him, he'd been so good with her little boy—so understanding after the disaster with the ice cream. Nolan was an out-and-out gentleman, there was no denying it. And he treated her like a lady. Going out on a date with him would be something special. Suddenly Raina was swamped with regret that she'd said no to his invitation. She shifted in the bed again and thumped her pillow into shape. If only she could as easily reshape her life, she thought as she settled back down.

Nolan was the last thing on her mind as she drifted off to sleep. Nolan, and the knowledge that the next time he asked her out, *if* he asked her out again, she might even say yes. After all, what harm could it do?

Five

Nolan walked back to his hotel rather than grab a cab. He was filled with an energy that demanded release—although walking wasn't the first activity that sprang to his mind. No, his mind was filled with the image of a certain dark-haired, blue-eyed storekeeper who had somehow inveigled her way into his thoughts and lodged there like a burr under a saddle.

He could still see the flare of awareness that had dilated her pupils when they'd touched only a short while ago. Hell, he could still feel it within himself. The only other person he'd ever felt that way about had been Carole. The reminder was a daunting one, and it should serve as a reminder that Raina Patterson was not the kind of woman he needed in his life. He'd been there and done that. He'd lived and loved within a perfect marriage with his perfect woman and they'd had the perfect little family—until it all fell apart.

Nolan went to step off the curb and was jolted into awareness by the blast of a car horn. Damn, he needed to keep his wits about him and Raina had managed to scatter said wits to the four corners of the earth. She was definitely not what he was looking for. He didn't even know why he'd asked her out, except that, for all his mental flagellation, deep down he still wanted her.

He nodded to the doorman as he entered the hotel and headed for the elevators. The sounds of music, conversation and laughter echoed across the marble-floored lobby from inside the hotel bar, catching his interest. He looked at his watch. It certainly wasn't too early to return to his suite but he was sick of his own company right now. Perhaps a distraction could be found elsewhere—one that would hopefully erase or at least dull the throb of desire Raina had left him with.

At the bar he ordered a brandy. It wasn't long before he had company. A blonde woman took the stool next to his and cast him a smile. He reacted in kind automatically and waited for the flicker of heat that usually signified an initial burst of interest. As they embarked on conversation there was no mistaking her interest in him, and yet he couldn't seem to kindle an answering response in himself.

Instead, before he'd even finished his brandy, Nolan excused himself and went up to his suite. And as he lay staring at the dark sky through his open bedroom windows over an hour later, he wondered if sleep was as distant for Raina as it was for him. He forced his eyes closed, but even then all he could see were still shots of her beautiful face—sometimes smiling, sometimes pensive.

Nolan reached into his memory for the sense of loss he'd carried with him since losing Bennett and Carole, but it was further away than it had been before. Instead, he found his thoughts drawn to another woman, one whose gentle personality and sensual warmth somehow had begun to fill a hole inside him he didn't even want to acknowledge that he had.

It was late when Nolan finally rose the next morning. As he shaved, he considered his next step. He'd always prided himself on being a man of action. It was what had gotten him through the bleak empty horror of the death of his son soon followed by that of his beloved wife. And if something was worth doing, it was worth doing well. He also had never been one to take no for an answer.

As soon as he'd finished getting ready and had enjoyed a late breakfast in the coffee shop next door to the hotel, he was in his rental and heading out to the Courtyard. He didn't even bother trying to mentally dress this visit up as being in the course of his work.

Fact-finding mission be damned. He'd had a niggling feeling that Raina was merely going through the motions when she'd turned down his invitation to a date yesterday. The words had fallen all too easily from those sexy lips of hers. As if she'd trotted the phrases out often enough for them to become automatic. That left him with two options. The first was to find out if she really meant what she said and the second, to discover what it was that she'd left unsaid.

As he drove out to the Courtyard, he considered his strategy for getting the truth out of Raina. Sure, he could go in and ask her straight out but he had a feeling that the shield she'd built around her was pretty darn strong and could withstand anything he could metaphorically throw at her. No, he'd go gently, softly. Try to understand where she was coming from and why she was so adamant about not dating.

He shook his head. Why was he even bothering? It wasn't as if he planned on hanging around after he'd finished his job for Rafiq. There'd be more dragons to slay back in Los Angeles, or maybe even somewhere else.

A smoldering ember of desire sparked deep inside him. That's why he was bothering. He wanted Raina. It was as impure and as complicated as that. He smiled a little at his twist on the old saying of things being pure and simple. Given that what his boss planned for Royal could mean eviction for Raina's store, Nolan should stay well back. But he couldn't.

He had to at least try with her, didn't he? Maybe it was a just physical thing, something he needed to get out of his system. But maybe it was something more.

As soon as he gave the thought a moment in his mind, its tendrils secured themselves as tightly as a stubbornly clinging vine. The analytical side of him demanded that he define what that "something more" could be, especially when he'd spent the past seven years telling himself he wasn't interested in long-term ever again. He'd lived the life he'd always dreamed of right up until the day it had turned into a nightmare his family had never recovered from. He owed it to them, to their memory, to keep what they'd had sacred. To keep it in the forefront of his thoughts so that he never let down another person or another family like that again.

He totally understood the pain that had driven Carole to take her own life. After all, didn't he choose to live with it every day and face it like the demon it was?

All of which brought him back to why he was so persistent about seeing the delightfully warm and sensual Ms. Patterson. Even he knew this attraction was more than a simple itch to be scratched. One look at Raina and he'd seen complicated all the way.

Before he realized it, Nolan was parked in front of Priceless. Through the windows he could see Raina moving about inside. His gut clenched on a swell of need that took him completely unawares.

He wasn't a man who'd ever taken rejection well, and that was probably what made him so good at his job. If one method failed, then there was always another, and another. Strategy, for him, was all about finding the weak points, then mercilessly exploiting them. His lips pulled into a wry grin. Wow, like that sounded sexy and irresistible. What woman could refuse an approach like that?

He was still smiling as he pushed open the door to the store and heard the chime of the bell above announcing his arrival. Raina lifted her head with a smile on her face to welcome him. Her smile froze for a moment, her blue eyes wide and vulnerable, before she composed herself and straightened from her task to greet him.

"Good morning. What brings you here today?" she asked, setting down the cloth she'd been using to polish the top of a box she was cradling in her other arm.

In pristine condition, the box housed a fountain pen with nibs and a crystal inkwell with an engraved silver lid. It was a beautiful set and, by the look of it, had barely been used. She left the lid open to better display its contents and set the case down on a nearby table.

"Christmas shopping," he improvised, moving closer to take another look at the writing set. "For my mother. I was hoping you'd be able to help me. Say, that looks interesting."

Was it his imagination or did her pupils dilate a little as he stepped closer? Raina had her hair pulled back into a ponytail today. The style exposed the delicate curve of her neck and the soft line of her jaw. What he wouldn't do to be able to take his time and lay a line of sweet kisses along those very contours, and more.

She took a half step back. "It's a writing set, from the

1920s, I think, judging from the art deco design on the pen."

"It's beautiful," he said, tracing the engraved pattern on the silver with a fingertip. He wondered what sort of price tag she had on the set.

"I recognize that look in your eye," Raina said on a short laugh.

"Look?"

"Of longing. I feel that way with pretty much everything in my store. Regrettably, I can't keep it all. Are you looking for something like this for your mom? It's a bit masculine. Or does your mother collect anything in particular?"

"Egg cups," he said abruptly after racking his brain and coming up with the first thing he could remember. "She loves English china egg cups."

Raina's smile returned. "Oh, then you're in luck. I have a few you can choose from."

She gestured for him to follow her across the broad plank flooring of the store toward a glass-fronted display cabinet. Selecting a key from the chain she kept hooked at the waistband of her jeans, she opened the cabinet and pointed out the exquisite pieces.

"These two are English. One Staffordshire, which as you can see comes with a salt pot and pepper shaker in the stand, and the other is Royal Winton, hazel pattern, with the toast rack, as well. This one here, though, is French."

She pointed to a delicately patterned gold-edged porcelain tray with six matching egg cups arrayed around a carry handle in the shape of a porcelain chick.

"Good grief," Nolan exclaimed. "And people use these?"

"Well, given their age it's safe to say people more likely used these in the past, while they collect and display them now. Would you like me to lift them out so you can take a closer look?"

Nolan nodded and bent to peer at them when Raina put

them on top of a nearby sideboard. As he studied them, Raina gave him a little commentary.

"The Staffordshire piece certainly looks the more sturdy, doesn't it?" she asked. "This one is from the nineteenth century."

"So old?"

She laughed. "Well, this is an antiques store."

He found himself smiling back at her and this time there was no mistaking the dilation of her pupils or the slight blush of pink on her cheeks as they made eye contact. She was attracted to him, he knew it as well as he knew the face that greeted him in the mirror every time he shaved.

"Good point," he conceded as she briskly looked away. "Which one is your favorite?"

She hesitated a moment before speaking. "While the Staffordshire is an exceptional example, with no chips or cracks, and the Royal Winton is also, I prefer the whimsy of the French pieces. Yes, they're a little more worn, but that comes with use and for me, use brings character to a piece. I like to imagine the family who might have enjoyed these egg cups, the children who might have touched the chick coming out of its china eggshell as they enjoyed their breakfast."

She gave an embarrassed laugh. "But then, that's me. And you said your mom collects English china, didn't you?

He nodded. "Maybe it's time she diversified across the channel to France, as well."

He studied the pieces again and then gave a decisive nod. "The French one it is."

"Nolan, you didn't even ask me how much it is!"

He shrugged. "Does it matter? It's for my mom. She'll love it, and probably for the exact same reasons you do."

Raina nodded in acceptance and then carefully put the other two breakfast sets back in the cabinet.

"Would you like me to gift wrap it for you?" she asked, carrying the tray to the counter.

"Please. And double the bubble wrap for me, would you? I'm terrified that I'll break it before I give it to her."

Raina eyed him teasingly. "You don't strike me as a careless man."

"Accidents happen," he said without thinking, his voice sharper than he intended. He knew that for a truth...all too well.

"Bubble wrap it is then. Plus I think I have a box out back that would be perfect. Would that suit you?" she said, picking up on his change in mood and making her tone more businesslike than before.

"Thank you," he replied, determined to inject more warmth into his voice. "I really appreciate it. Mom will be thrilled, I'm sure."

"I'm glad. It's always nice to know things will continue to be appreciated when they leave here. I kind of feel like a custodian for them, you know. Like I have a responsibility to the original craftsmen and -women to see that their hard work continues to be loved as it changes hands."

Her words summed her up perfectly, he thought. She cared about things and about people. So why then did she keep herself so aloof? It was time to find out.

"I imagine that you don't get a lot of time to yourself," he said leaning against the scarred countertop that looked as if it had seen many years of service somewhere in its life. "What with the store and JJ and all."

She kept her head bent and her attention on her task but he saw the slight change in her posture. As if she was shoring up her defenses.

"I get enough. In fact I get most Saturday evenings to myself when my dad is in Royal and takes JJ for a sleepover. That is plenty for me. I wouldn't change anything in my life for something as ephemeral as time alone and definitely not at the expense of my son."

"You sound like a woman who knows her own mind."

"I like to think so. Now, at least. I wasn't always this certain, but I guess when you've learned the hard way, you tend to take things a little more seriously."

"The hard way?"

Raina finished wrapping his mother's gift and swiftly tied a cheerful Christmas bow around the wrapping paper. "There you are. All done. Now, will that be cash or credit?"

She was avoiding answering him. That much was clear. He slid his platinum card from his card holder and passed it to her before placing both hands on the countertop and leaning toward her.

"Raina, I meant what I said last night. I really would like to see you, to get to know you better."

She looked up at him, a little flustered and a lot startled. He realized how much he was encroaching on her space and straightened up from the counter again.

"I… I told you last night, Nolan. I don't date. I just don't have time."

"What are you afraid of, hmm?" he coaxed.

Her eyes shone with what he suspected—hell, *hoped*—was yearning. He pressed forward with what he saw as his advantage.

"At least tell me why. You can't let me go away with a complex. Just think of what that could do to a man like me."

His deliberate foolishness earned its own reward when she laughed, openly and honestly and from the heart.

"Oh, I think your ego is completely safe from me," she said, passing back his card. "But if you really must know, I haven't exactly had the best taste in men. Take JJ's father for example. I met him near where we lived, over in the next county. He swept me off my feet and dazzled me with his grand plans. We moved to Royal when he got work here as a ranch hand, but he never quite seemed to be able to hold down a job for more than a few months at a time. Then he left me broke after cleaning out my bank account. I promised myself, there and then, that no man would ever leave me that vulnerable again."

Nolan sensed there was a great deal more behind her words than she was letting on.

"You never pressed charges?"

"He's JJ's father. Of course I didn't. I just hoped that he'd taken enough money that he'd never need to come back. But—" she cut herself off abruptly and seemed to gather her thoughts back together "—but that's all in the past," she said with false brightness.

Nolan could read between the lines and he knew there was much more to her story than the potted history she'd just given him. But it could wait. Instead, he latched on to something she'd said a few minutes ago. "You mentioned your dad has JJ on Saturdays?"

She nodded slowly.

"Today?"

She nodded again. Nolan felt a glow of excitement light up in his chest.

"So, if I asked you if you could break your no-dating rule and have dinner with me tonight, could I persuade you to consider it?"

Raina pursed her lips and crossed her arms but even though her body language was all about the "no," the yearning he'd seen in her eyes before was still very much in evidence. He held his breath while she took her time making her decision.

"Okay," she said on what sounded like a long held sigh. "Yes, I'd like that. But just dinner."

He smiled and fought the urge to fist pump the air in delight.

"Just dinner," he agreed. "Where and when can I pick you up?"

Raina gave him her address and they agreed on the time he would pick her up. He knew the area. Not the worst in town, but not the best either. Still, after what she, and the rest of Royal, had been through just over a year ago, at least she and JJ had a secure roof over their heads.

He could do so much better for her. The thought hit him from nowhere and left him reeling. He pushed it back. Looking after Raina Patterson wasn't his business; she'd made that abundantly clear. She was a strong and independent woman.

Which only made her all the more appealing.

Six

Nolan pulled up outside the address Raina had given him. The area was worse than Nolan remembered and he hit the automatic lock on his car key as he got out and walked up the path toward the house. Raina answered the door before he'd so much as lifted his finger to the doorbell. As excited to see him as he was to see her, perhaps? He certainly hoped so.

He let his gaze roam her body. She looked beautiful. Her silky dark brown hair shone loose and long as it fell about her shoulders, and she'd done some incredible magic with eye makeup that made her blue eyes even brighter and more intense than he'd ever seen them. There was a faint hint of blush on her cheeks and her lips had a delicious watermelon-colored sheen. He ached to lean forward and see if those lips tasted as good as they looked.

She wore a long sheer burgundy blouse, with a matching camisole beneath it, over slim-fitting black pants and high heels. A fine gold chain graced her neck and small pear shaped gold drops hung from her ears.

"I'm so sorry," she started, and for a second he thought she was going to pull out of their date. But then she said, "Dad dropped JJ back home earlier. He has a leak in the trailer right where JJ's bed is and since he had JJ with him all day he didn't get a chance to repair it. When I told him I'd planned to go out he said he'd be back to sit for me, but he's not here yet."

Nolan felt himself relax. Waiting for her father to return was no problem.

"That's okay. We have plenty of time," he assured her.

"Man!" JJ slid to a halt on the polished wooden floor in front of him.

"JJ!" Raina admonished. "His name is Nolan, not man."

"No'an." JJ tried the name out for size, then reached for Nolan's hand. "Come see Spider-Man."

Nolan looked to Raina for approval. She shrugged. "If you don't mind?" she said helplessly. "He's certainly fixated on you. Dad said all he talked about today was 'man' and the Christmas tree."

"I don't mind," Nolan assured her before looking down at JJ's eager face. "C'mon then, JJ. Show me Spider-Man."

The sensation of the little boy's fingers so trustingly wrapped within his own somewhat soothed the ache Nolan felt in his heart. Bennett had been only eighteen months old when he'd died. Less than half JJ's age. Would he, too, have been a fan of comic-book heroes? Nolan would never know.

JJ's excited chatter yanked him back into the present and Nolan fell into an easy banter with the garrulous child. Sure, JJ still struggled with some syllables but his overall command of language made him easy to understand as he bounced around his room in excitement—dragging one thing and then another from his shelves and drawers to show Nolan.

Down the hallway, Nolan heard sounds of another person arriving. A man with a deep voice. When he got to JJ's room, Nolan took him for Raina's dad immediately. He had the same piercing blue eyes and that determined set of the jaw. Raina stood behind him, looking a little uncomfortable.

Nolan rapidly got to his feet and extended a hand to the newcomer.

"Nolan Dane, pleased to meet you."

"Justin Patterson. Can I have a word with you before you leave with my daughter?"

The man's eyebrows pulled into a straight line and the no-nonsense look in his eyes set Nolan back a bit. He hadn't seen a look like that in a father's eyes since he dated back in high school—and he hadn't missed the proprietary use of the word *my* when referring to Raina either.

"Sure," he answered smoothly. "Just let me help JJ put his things back."

"I can do that," Raina said, stepping into the room. "You go talk with Dad, then we can leave for the restaurant."

"I'll only need a minute," her father said dourly from the doorway.

Justin Patterson didn't take long to get to the point. The moment they were out of earshot of JJ's bedroom, he bluntly told Nolan exactly what he expected.

"Treat my daughter with respect."

"You have no worries on that score, sir. Raina is a wonderful woman."

"I don't know what your intentions are toward her, but I will tell you this. If you break her heart, or if you hurt her in any way, I will come after you."

Raina's dad was Nolan's equal in height and had at least twenty pounds on him. He had the look of a man used to hard work and Nolan had no doubt that he meant every word.

"Thank you for being honest with me. Now let me be honest with you. I know Raina doesn't normally date, and we haven't even known each other very long, but I have no plans to hurt her. We're going out for dinner tonight, and that's all."

"Humph." The older man crossed his arms over his chest. "Make sure that *is* all you do."

Nolan understood where Justin Patterson was coming from, especially based on what Raina had said to him earlier. "I'm not in town for long and I respect your daughter too much to try to take advantage of her—although you misjudge her if you think she'd let me. So far, I think it's safe to say that we like each other and I enjoy her company. JJ's, too. Raina is safe with me."

Justin narrowed his eyes at Nolan. "Dane, you said. Your father is Howard Dane?"

Nolan nodded. His father was well known in Royal and his family law practice was well respected.

"He's a good man. Let's hope the acorn didn't fall far from the tree."

With that, Justin turned and went into the kitchen where Nolan could hear him bustling around and putting the tea-kettle on. Raina came into the room with JJ trailing behind.

"Go see what Grandpa is up to, JJ," she urged. "Maybe he's making hot chocolate for bedtime."

As the little boy scampered toward the kitchen, she looked at Nolan with an apologetic expression on her face.

"I'm sorry about that. He's kind of protective."

Nolan put up a hand. "No problem. He's your dad. He's entitled to be protective of you. So, are we okay? Shall we go?"

She nodded and called out, "We're on our way, Dad. Call me if you need me!"

Judging by Justin's grunt they were free to go.

Nolan helped Raina into her coat and held the front door for her as they went outside. Streetlamps shone like golden orbs in the air, casting light onto the road beneath them. He guided her to his SUV and closed the passenger door for her once she was settled.

As he climbed into his seat, Nolan saw a furtive movement near a bush a few yards away. His eyes strained to see what it was but it appeared there was nothing there. He shrugged it off as something he'd either imagined or perhaps an animal that was now long gone. But as he began to drive down the street, he caught a glimpse of a man briskly walking down the sidewalk.

There was something about the way the man carried himself and how he kept to the shadows that made Nolan's instincts go on alert. As they cruised by in the SUV, the man furtively kept his face averted and hunched his shoulders. Sure, it was cold tonight—certainly too cold to be out casually walking anyway—which could explain the man's posture, but even if he was out for a constitutional stroll, why was he doing his best not to be recognized? In his work Nolan had seen a lot of characters and to him it was clear that this guy didn't want to be noticed.

Nolan didn't want to alert Raina to his concerns. She was busy looking out the window at the other side of the road and therefore oblivious to what he had seen, but he remained uneasy. Had the guy been watching Raina?

The idea plagued him during the drive to the restaurant, even while Raina kept up a patter of general conversation, asking him about growing up in Royal. By the time they were seated and perusing their menus, Nolan had decided to put thoughts of the walker, whoever he was, from his mind. He was here to enjoy Raina's company and he didn't want anything to detract from that.

Later, when they were about to make their selections

for dessert, his cell phone began buzzing persistently in his pocket.

"I'm sorry," he said, sliding the device out to see who the caller was. Rafiq. Damn. His boss was hardly the kind of person he could hold a conversation with in front of Raina. "Will you excuse me a moment? I really need to take this call."

"No problem." She waved him on with a smile. "I need some time to decide on dessert anyway."

He excused himself and, lifting the phone to his ear, he answered the call.

"Rafe, what can I do for you?"

"You can tell me how things are going with the Courtyard acquisition for a start," his boss said without preamble.

"The Winslow woman is very resistant to selling."

"The Winslow woman? What happened to Homer Winslow?"

"He has been removed by his board for mismanagement," Nolan said, summarizing how Melanie Winslow had wrested control. He strongly suspected the proposed buyout of the Courtyard had been the catalyst for that. "Ms. Winslow now heads Winslow Properties."

"But she's a maid, isn't she?"

Nolan fought back a smile. Rafiq was very modern and forward thinking in many ways, but in others he was still a throwback to his family's roots in ancient Al Qunfudhah, on the coast of the Red Sea.

"Ms. Winslow has a very successful business providing house-cleaning and house-sitting services. She is quite a bit more than a maid, and she is proving to be adamantly opposed to the sale of the Courtyard."

"Offer her more."

"Are you sure you want to do that? When word gets around, and it will in a place like Royal, any other owners of property you're interested in will simply increase their asking prices accordingly."

Rafe made a sound of annoyance and Nolan could just imagine the expression on his boss's face.

"They still owe money on that land, don't they? Can we get any leverage through their lenders?"

"It's an avenue I'm looking into now. Rest assured. If we can buy the Courtyard, it will most certainly be yours."

"There is no 'if,' Nolan. I want that land."

Not for the first time, Nolan started to bite his tongue against the question of why Rafiq was so adamant about his acquisitions around Royal. To hell with it, he decided. He wanted to know and, as Rafe's agent in all of this, he damn well deserved to know.

"Why, Rafe? What's so important about that or any other piece of land you're buying?"

"My reasons are my own. Do not overstep the bounds of our friendship, Nolan. I'll be in Holloway next weekend. We will meet Saturday at 10:00 a.m. at the Holloway Inn."

It was just like Rafiq to make a demand rather than a suggestion. But Nolan was well used to his boss's manner.

"I'll be there."

"Good. I expect to hear more progress has been made on the situation then."

With that closing statement, his boss ended the call. Rafiq hadn't said as much but the implication was clear in his tone. Friendship or no, if Nolan wasn't happy to continue to act for him, there were plenty of other lawyers who would. He slid his phone back into his pocket and returned to the table.

Raina looked up as Nolan approached.

"Everything okay?" she asked, as he settled back down into his chair. "Was that work?"

"What makes you ask?" he said, evading her question.

"Probably that frown you've got right now."

He forced himself to relax and smile. "Better?"

"Much. Seriously though, is everything okay?"

"Sure, nothing that can't wait until tomorrow anyway."

He picked up his dessert menu and briefly scanned the contents without even really seeing them. Rafe's unwavering determination to purchase the Courtyard and the barren acreage it sat on didn't sit comfortably with him at all. In fact the whole business was beginning to leave a bad taste in his mouth. Sure, Royal had changed a lot since the tornado. It certainly wasn't the town he'd grown up in anymore, nor was it the one he'd left seven years ago. But deep down, the values and the lifestyles remained the same. What kind of impact would Rafe's plan have on all of that?

And what of the traders, like Raina, who'd picked their lives back up after total devastation and who needed the stability and continuity the Courtyard provided? Did Rafe plan to continue to run it as it currently operated, or did he plan to scuttle everything? There were just so many questions buzzing around like angry bees in Nolan's brain right now. It made it hard to recapture the pleasure he'd felt in Raina's company only a few minutes ago.

It was clear her trust in him was growing and he appreciated that far more than he'd believed possible. But by acting for Rafe, he was betraying that trust and he didn't like it.

"What have you decided on?" Raina prompted from the other side of the table.

"What are you having?" he countered.

"It was a tough decision to make," she said with a short laugh. "But I think I'll go for the white chocolate cheesecake."

He closed his menu card and laid it back on the table. "Same for me."

By unspoken mutual consent, they lingered over their coffees and dessert. Nolan didn't want to break the fragile spell that had rewoven itself around their evening by drawing things to a close, but when he caught Raina stifling another yawn, he knew it was time to take her home. Despite Rafiq's interruption, Nolan had thoroughly enjoyed the evening. And he knew without a doubt that he wanted to get to know Raina better.

Their drive back to her house was done in a companionable silence and, once they got there, Nolan walked Raina up the path to her front door. Haloed by the porch light, she looked like a beautiful angel but his thoughts and intentions toward her were anything but angelic.

"Thank you for this evening," Raina said. "I'd forgotten how much I enjoy adult conversation and company that's not related to kids or work."

There was a smile on her face that was wistful and it sent a pang to Nolan's chest. He could imagine she had little enough time to herself, let alone to share with another person.

"It was absolutely my pleasure."

Afterward he couldn't be certain who had made the first move. But it didn't matter one bit. His senses filled with her—her scent, her taste, the feel of her in his arms and, above all else, the beauty of her kiss. A sense of rightness filled him as their lips met, as his hand lifted to thread through her hair and to cup the back of her head. Inside him a knot began to unravel and he knew, in that moment, that he wanted Raina in his life. That he could finally begin to let go of the pain of the past that had kept him in emotional isolation.

He traced the softness of her lips with his tongue as they parted beneath him. Desire unfurled through his body, doubling on itself until it consumed his thoughts. When Raina's hands pushed through his hair and held him to her, he knew she felt the same. She pressed her body against his and heat flared between them.

Nolan deepened their kiss. His tongue probed her mouth and she responded in kind. A shudder of need pummeled him and he felt an echoing tremor from her.

Overhead the light flicked off and then on again.

He felt Raina pull away. Her lips were swollen and curved into a grin.

"I can't believe this. My father is obviously letting me know it's time for me to come inside." She gave a half-embarrassed giggle before leaning forward to kiss Nolan sweetly, and all too swiftly, on his lips. "I'm sorry. I'd better go in before he comes out with a shotgun."

"You're kidding about the shotgun, right?"

"Of course I am, but he's very protective. Thank you again, Nolan. For everything."

"We'll see each other again," he stated firmly.

"Yes, I'd like that."

"Soon."

She nodded and laughed, her breath leaving a misty cloud in the air between them. "Yes, soon. How about Monday night? Dinner here, with JJ and me."

"I'd really like that," Nolan said. Even though every minute he'd spent with JJ so far reminded him all too much of all the things he'd missed out on with his own son, he enjoyed the little guy's company and his simple enthusiasm for life. It was a poignant reminder that he needed to inject some of that enthusiasm back into his own. And maybe, just maybe, he needed to consider telling Raina about the wife and son he'd lost, too. "Monday, then."

"Is six o'clock okay with you?"

"Perfect. I'll be there. Can I bring anything?"

"Just yourself is fine. See you then."

She turned, put her key in the lock and opened the front door. Then, with a small wave, she was gone from sight. Nolan shoved his hands in his pockets and jogged down the path to his car. He drove back to the hotel, his mind only half on what he was doing while the other half raced ahead and churned over a million different thoughts.

Sleep would be a long time coming tonight. He hadn't expected anything like this when he'd returned to Royal. Hadn't wanted it. He'd been meticulous about his relationships in the past and particularly about avoiding any emotional entanglements. But somehow this attraction had found him and lodged itself within the gaping hole of loneliness he had come to accept as being as much a part of him as every breath he took.

And it felt good. In fact, it felt better than good—it had brought back to life something he hadn't experienced in far too long—hope, which left him between a rock and a hard place when it came to the job he was really here to do. Did he compromise his professional integrity for this fledgling relationship or should he focus on the role he was here to complete and then walk away at the end of his time here in Royal, knowing he could be walking away from the best thing that had happened to him in a very long time?

Seven

Raina woke the next morning still locked firmly inside the bubble of joy that had enveloped her last night. Her father had taken one look at her face as she'd come into the sitting room and had shaken his head.

"I don't suppose there's any point in telling you to be careful," he'd growled from behind his beard.

She'd merely smiled and thanked her father for taking care of JJ. To his credit, he hadn't given her a lecture. Something he was inclined to do even though she was thirty years old and a mom herself. Instead he'd merely hugged her, pressed a kiss on the top of her head and, after telling her he loved her, made his way home to the trailer park.

Now Raina felt her heart skip with happiness as she made pancakes and bacon for breakfast. They needed to get some groceries this morning, her one day off, and she didn't want to waste any more time on the humdrum chore than was absolutely necessary. Today was a precious day with her boy and she wanted to make the most of it. Coaxing JJ out of his Spider-Man pajamas and into clothing suitable for the outdoors took a bit of doing but a promise to buy a new movie to add to his growing collection seemed to give him the impetus he needed.

She was in the process of buckling him into his car seat when she caught a dark movement from the corner of her eye. Raina quickly straightened up from what she was doing to see who it was who'd come up beside her. The second she did, her happy bubble burst.

Jeb.

"What are you doing here?" she demanded. "You promised you'd stay away."

"Where's my money, Raina?"

Raina quickly shoved the car door closed in an attempt to prevent JJ from hearing anything more from the man who'd done no more for him than provide a few strands of DNA.

"I don't owe you anything, Jeb Pickering. Now, please, get off my property and leave me alone."

"The boy's looking good. Growing fast. Does he ever ask about his daddy?"

"No, he doesn't," she responded flatly. God help her when JJ started asking those kinds of questions. How did you explain to your child that his father was no more than a lying no-good drifter plagued by gambling debts?

"I think it's time we met then."

"Are you threatening me?" Raina asked, her hands now clenched in tight fists of impotent rage.

Jeb had signed all the papers relinquishing his rights to any form of visitation with JJ two years ago but she should have known he'd renege on their agreement. His eyes narrowed speculatively as he looked at her car and then toward the house.

"You're doing pretty well these days, girl. I've been out

to that store of yours, too. Seems to me you could afford to help out the father of your only child, don't it?"

"You helped yourself plenty in the past. I'm done giving you money, Jeb."

Jeb's arm snaked out and his hand closed tight around Raina's wrist. She tugged against his grip, trying to free herself, but his fingers closed in a painful vice.

"Stop it. Let me go. You're hurting me," she said, pitching her voice low so there was no chance JJ could hear her. She didn't want to alarm him and from over Jeb's shoulder she could see his eyes were fixed on his mommy and the strange man talking to her.

"I need that money, honey." He gave her a crooked grin. "I'm in a bit of trouble. I need to get away. Maybe for good."

Did he mean it? She didn't dare believe him. If she showed one sign of weakness, just one, he'd exploit it. He turned back to the car and waved with his free hand toward JJ, who weakly waved back. Through the car window she could see JJ was getting upset and his muffled "Mommy?" tore at her heart.

"For good?" she pressed.

"Maybe."

"Maybe's not good enough for me, Jeb," Raina insisted, yanking her arm free. Her wrist throbbed with pain but she wouldn't look to see what damage he'd wrought. He'd done enough to her already without adding a few bruises to the list. "I don't want to ever see you again."

"Then give me my money."

His money? She stifled the urge to shove her hands hard at his chest and push him away. Give him a taste of his own medicine for a change. When had he ever had any money by honest means? She certainly couldn't remember.

"I'm mortgaged to my eyeballs with the house and I have rent to meet on my business. Pretty much everything else I have is tied up in inventory now. I don't have a lot to spare, Jeb."

"Whatever you can give me, then. And it had better be soon."

There was an urgency to his voice. An underlying thread of something he wasn't telling her, not to mention a significant threat in his tone.

"Jeb, what have you gotten yourself into now?" she sighed.

"Look, I owe a guy some cash is all. I want to clear my debts and make a fresh start."

How many times had she heard him say that? So many that she'd stopped believing him a long time ago. And look at him now. He was jittery and unkempt. Even at his worst he'd never looked this bad before. Was it really just owing money or had he gotten involved in something worse? Whatever it was, she needed to get him away from JJ as quickly as she could.

"I'll see what I can do," Raina said in defeat.

She knew it was just pandering to his dependence on her, but right now she didn't see any other way of getting rid of him. She knew she didn't have the kind of money he expected but he'd just have to make do with the couple of thousand dollars she'd put aside for emergencies when she had a chance to withdraw it from the bank. Just the thought of leaving her account empty again made her stomach burn with anxiety. All she'd ever wanted was to be able to provide her son with the same security her father had provided her—love, combined with a roof over his head, food in his belly and a warm bed at night. Was that too much to ask?

"Thanks, Rai."

"How will I be able to reach you?" The number on the mobile phone he'd been using was blocked.

"I'll be in touch."

And with that, he flipped up the collar of his jacket and began to walk away. Was it her imagination, or was he darting furtive glances left and right as he walked up the street—almost as if he expected someone to jump out of the bushes at him at any moment. She shook her head. What on earth had he got himself into, now?

She hurried to the car and, after giving JJ a shaky smile through the window, got into the driver's seat.

"Bad man, Mommy," JJ pronounced from the backseat with all the solemnity of a frightened three-year-old.

She didn't know what to say. Jeb wasn't all bad, just misguided and selfish. She settled for an indistinct murmur as she fastened her seat belt and put her key in the ignition.

"I don' like bad man. I like No'an," JJ continued.

Raina smiled at her little boy in the rearview mirror. "I like Nolan, too, honey bun. C'mon, let's go get our groceries and then the rest of the day is just for you and me."

"Yay," he crowed in happiness, his fear already forgotten.

The next morning Raina was putting out her signs at Priceless and trying to quell her excitement about the night ahead. She'd woken earlier than usual, and with an energy she could only put down to looking forward to seeing Nolan again. Even the shadow of Jeb's visit yesterday and his demands, coupled with the bruises he'd left on her wrist as a reminder, couldn't overshadow her joy in planning their dinner tonight. She'd serve lasagna with garlic bread and salad. Simple fare, and filling and, best of all, easy to prepare ahead of time so she didn't have to get herself all flustered before Nolan arrived.

As she straightened and surveyed the parking lot, she spied Mellie Winslow walking toward her. She gave the other woman a wave.

"Good morning!" she called as Mellie drew closer. "It's a lovely clear day, isn't it?"

"It is," Mellie agreed.

Her landlady looked cute today in a forest-green coat that emphasized her clear green eyes and gorgeous soft red hair. Raina envied Melanie her curls.

"Would you like to stop in for a cup of coffee?" Raina asked. "I've just put a pot on."

"I'd love that, thank you."

Mellie pulled off her gloves and shrugged out of her coat as they entered Raina's tiny lunch room. She shoved the gloves inside her coat pocket and hung the garment on one of the ornately curved brass hooks on the rack by the door.

"I love this," she said, gesturing to the rack. "And I especially love that it has an umbrella stand, as well. Is it yours or is it for sale?"

"Everything here is for sale, except me," Raina laughed in response.

"What kind of wood is it?"

"Oak. You see a lot of replicas these days, but this is the real deal."

"Hmm, maybe I should get it for Case for Christmas."

"Things are that serious?" Raina asked.

In response, Mellie thrust out her left hand, exposing a beautiful ring on her engagement finger. The large square-cut emerald gleamed under the light and Raina gasped in surprise.

"Oh, I'd say that looks very serious. Congratulations!"

"Thanks, it was all rather complicated, what with everything that went on last month, but I'm so happy."

And she looked happy, too. There was a glow about her that Raina hadn't seen before. She tried to ignore the tug of envy that plucked at her along with a wish that her own life could have followed a more traditional path. But she quickly shoved it away. Traditional or not, her life was what it was and without the choices she'd made—both good and bad—she wouldn't have JJ or be where she was now, doing something she loved.

Mellie sat down at the small table in the center of the room. "I'm glad I have a chance to talk to you today. I just wanted to let you know that I'm definitely not letting the Courtyard go. It's not for sale. Not now, not ever."

Raina felt a swell of relief flood through her. "You're serious? Everything's going to be okay?"

She'd heard, along with everyone else in town, about Homer Winslow's financial issues and how he'd put Winslow Properties into financial jeopardy. It had only served to increase her anxiety about her position here.

Mellie nodded. "Definitely. Even if Winslow Properties' resources won't stretch far enough, and I believe that with some restructuring they should, Case has assured me that he will back us financially if need be."

Raina didn't quite know what to say. She filled two coffee mugs, put them on the table with shaking hands and sank into her chair. This was incredible news.

"I'm sure you know how much this means to me, Mellie. Thank you for telling me now. It's the best Christmas present I could have imagined."

"I thought it best to give you peace of mind as soon as I knew, and I wanted to do it myself. I know how much it means to you to be here and how hard you've worked."

"But what about Samson Oil? Are they going to back off now? Seems they've been busy buying up everything that's for sale around Royal and some of what's not."

Mellie nodded her head. "Yeah, I know. It certainly looks that way, doesn't it?"

"And why? Everyone here knows the land isn't worth squat for oil, and with the drought even ranching isn't so viable. What are they thinking? Do you know who is behind it all?"

"No, all I know is that their attorney, Nolan Dane, is one stubborn guy. Every time we say no to selling, he bounces straight back with another offer. Honestly, if I hadn't taken over from Dad, Winslow Properties' portfolio would be looking very slim indeed."

Raina gasped out loud and reeled at the name that had come from Mellie's mouth. *Nolan Dane?* A giant fist clutched at her chest and squeezed tight, making it nearly impossible to draw breath.

"Raina? Are you okay?"

"I'm fine," she replied, feeling anything but. She forced herself to take a breath, drawing it all the way in before letting it out again. "A-are you sure Nolan Dane is their attorney?"

"He's certainly the person we've been dealing with. And I've heard from a few of the stall holders and retailers here that he's been sniffing around, asking all sorts of questions about the operation and about Winslow Properties. He won't have any excuse to come out here now though. Our lawyers sent him a message today categorically stating that the Courtyard is not, and never will be, for sale. At least not as long as I'm running things," Mellie confirmed before taking a long sip of her coffee. "Ah, this is good—just what I needed. I have a meeting with our board in—" she glanced at her watch "—oh, heck, twenty minutes. I'd better fly! Thanks for the coffee. I'll see myself out."

Raina remained glued to her chair in shock as Mellie put her mug in the sink, grabbed her coat and headed out of the store. Nolan was acting for Samson Oil? Did that mean that everything he'd done had been in the pursuit of getting an edge on Winslow Properties and buying the Courtyard?

She felt sick as she remembered how open she'd been about her situation. About how much all this meant to her here, to be able to start up her business again after the hellish year she'd had. And all the time he'd been planning to rip it all out from under her. Pressure built up inside her chest, growing bigger and more painful until a sob broke free. She clapped a hand over her mouth in a futile attempt to hold back the grief she felt at Nolan's betrayal.

She'd really thought he liked her—and JJ. And all along he'd simply been using them both. This hurt far worse than anything Jeb had done. He'd made empty promises, sure, but never anything like this.

Raina tipped her head back and stared at the ceiling of the old barn, willing the burning in her eyes to stop before the tears that already blinded her began to fall. Man, she could pick 'em, couldn't she? Did she have some sign over her head, visible only to losers and liars that said, "Soft touch and fool"?

After Jeb she'd sworn never again. She wouldn't make the same mistakes—not when she had JJ to consider. She'd guarded herself and her privacy, spurning male attention on the occasions it had been offered, making it clear that her son and her business were her sole priorities. Until Nolan.

He'd managed to charm his way past her barriers, slowly and gently peeling them away and exposing her vulnerability. It had been more than just the physical attraction she'd felt toward him; there'd been an emotional connection there, too. It had been so tangible that she would have sworn he felt the same way. Man, had he ever taken her for a ride.

Just went to show what an appalling judge of character she was after all. Raina dashed away an errant tear from her cheek. No. There'd be no more tears over men whose sole purpose in life was to break her heart—or worse, her hope for the future. She was better than that and she deserved better than that, too.

Raina pushed herself up onto her feet and put her mug

in the sink alongside Mellie's. She was grateful the woman had come to see her today to tell her the news. What if it had been tomorrow, or even next week? Heck, she had invited Nolan to her house for dinner with her and JJ, and who knows where that might have led given the heat of their kiss on Saturday night?

She pressed trembling fingers to her lips. It took very little stretch of her imagination to relive the pressure of his lips on hers. To remember the taste of him, the strength of his arms around her and how safe and protected he had made her feel. And that hadn't been all. He'd wanted her, she'd felt it in the hard lines of his body, and to her shame she'd wanted him back with all the heat and hunger she'd ignored for too long.

Damn him for doing this to her. For sliding under her skin and for making her want things she had no right wanting.

With a sound of disgust, Raina reached for her bag and snatched her cell phone. She pulled up Nolan's number and viciously tapped the call button on the screen. He wasn't welcome at her house anymore, let alone anywhere near her son. She had to tell him tonight was off. Tonight and every other night in the future.

Eight

Nolan pulled up outside Raina's house and sighed. Today had been tough. They'd closed on several private deals today. While on the one hand he'd known that, under the guise of Samson Oil, Rafiq was offering many people a way out of a situation that had become untenable since the tornado—people who'd been underinsured and overmortgaged and living hand-to-mouth since the disaster—he also knew he was taking them from a way of life that had been in their families for generations.

It had taken a toll—seeing relief tempered with failure, hope for a new start tempered with sorrow at leaving behind the past. These were families and people whose kids had gone to school alongside him here in Royal. And now they were scattering to the winds, some leaving Royal altogether and others settling for a life they'd never believed they'd live in one of the new suburbs. Sure, there were those who'd ecstatically accepted Rafiq's money and were eager to move forward with new lives. But the majority were people whose pride had been beaten down by so much loss that they had no fight left in them. It had been there in every hollow-eyed stare, every line of strain on their faces.

The shining light in his day today had been the knowledge that he'd see Raina again. His body had been buzzing with suppressed energy ever since Saturday night, and he'd realized that for the first time since Carole's and Bennett's deaths, he'd begun to be able to think about them without the sharp stab of pain that always accompanied the memories. Instead, he saw two new faces. Faces that he knew were fast becoming equally special to him.

Nolan got out of the SUV, hit the autolock and reached into his jacket pocket for his mobile phone before remembering he'd forgotten to charge it last night and that he'd heard the warning beeps before it shut down earlier today. It had been a blessing in disguise, he'd thought at the time, that he hadn't had to deal with the text messages and emails while he'd dotted all the *i*'s and crossed all the *t*'s on each individual contract that signaled the end of life as many people had known it. He strode up the front path—eager now to rid himself of the clinging mental residue of the day.

He'd no sooner knocked when the door was flung open. He was assailed by two things. JJ's effusive greeting, as the little boy almost knocked him off his feet with a powerful hug around his legs, and the sound of Raina's stern admonition to let her get the door. Nolan reached down and tousled JJ's mop of dark hair. An unexpected surge of tenderness swelled inside him as JJ lifted his happy little face.

"Hi, No'an."

This was what a man's life should be filled with. Moments like this that were precious and memorable for their simplicity and purity. This was what he'd been missing for far too long.

"Hey, JJ. How're you doing?"

"Good!" The little boy disengaged from Nolan's legs and began hopping from one foot to the other. "We're having lasagna for dinner. Yum!"

"JJ, let me talk to Mr. Dane," Raina interrupted, coming up behind JJ and putting a hand on his shoulder to restrain him.

Nolan's senses went on full alert. He was back to being Mr. Dane? Something was very wrong. The chill that surrounded Raina cut through JJ's excitement and the boy stilled as he looked from his mommy to Nolan in confusion.

"Do you want money from my mommy, too?" JJ asked.

Raina's eyes flared wide at her son's words, and Nolan saw the shock that streaked across her face.

"Hush, JJ. Mr. Dane doesn't want anything from me."

Oh, she was very wrong there, he thought, but he didn't miss the silent message in her words or her tone. Nolan squatted down to JJ's level and gave the little guy a reassuring smile.

"No, I don't want money from your mommy."

"You sure?"

Nolan nodded. "Of course I'm sure."

"Bad man hurt mommy."

Nolan heard Raina's gasp of shock. "JJ, don't be telling stories."

"But it true," the little boy protested.

Nolan thought it a good time to interrupt before the atmosphere got any more difficult than it was already. "Hey, JJ, look at me. I would never hurt your mommy. I promise. Okay, champ?"

JJ nodded slowly and Nolan rose to his full height again. As he did, he caught a glimpse of Raina's arm. She'd pushed the sleeves of her long-sleeved T-shirt halfway up her forearm and there was no mistaking the livid bruising around her wrist. The second she was aware he'd noticed, she pulled the sleeves down but it was too late now. He couldn't unsee what was there and he wasn't a fool. He knew fingermarks when he saw them. He'd seen marks like that, and worse, often enough when he was working alongside his father at his family law practice.

"You okay?"

Nolan chose his words carefully, even though he wished he had the right to demand who the hell had dared to lay a hand on her—and then hunt them down for some payback. Before she could answer him, though, JJ jumped up and down and started to speak.

"No'an! No'an! I'm gonna be Spider-Man at the C'istmas show!"

"Settle down, JJ," Raina admonished her son. "What he means is he's been chosen to play one of the shepherds at his day care's Christmas pageant this year."

"Yeah!" JJ interrupted again, unable to contain his excitement. "Can you come, No'an?"

"I'm sure Mr. Dane will be far too busy to attend the pageant, JJ."

Raina gave Nolan a fierce look, warning him not to contradict her. In response he squatted back down to JJ's level and put one hand on the little boy's shoulder.

"I'm sorry, JJ. Your mom is right. I'm working that night."

"I hate work!" JJ shouted, before turning tail and running down the hall toward his room.

"You mind telling me what that was about?" Nolan asked as he rose again to his full height and met Raina's chilling blue gaze full-on.

From the second he'd arrived, he'd felt a cold vibe coming from Raina that was at complete odds with the way they'd parted last time they'd been together. What the hell had gone wrong between then and now? He could have sworn that they were both heading in the same direction and now it seemed that she was slamming on the brakes. Did it have something to do with those marks on her wrist?

Again Nolan felt the slow burn of anger flicker inside at the fact that anyone had dared to lay a hand on Raina. But it was nothing compared to the irritation he felt at being manipulated into letting JJ down just now.

Raina lifted her chin and crossed her arms in front of her. Her body language was clear. She was shutting him out in more ways than one.

"Sure," she said abruptly. "I don't mind telling you. I *know* why you're here."

For a split second he was confused and then it dawned on him. She'd found out about his connection to Samson Oil. "I'm guessing it's not because of your invitation to dinner, right?"

"Don't you dare try to make a joke of it. You used me."

Nolan couldn't refute her accusation. "I'm sorry about that. Believe me, I—"

"Believe you?" she interrupted with an incredulous expression on her face. "No way. Not ever. You may have missed this in Lawyer 101, Mr. Dane, but where I come from belief comes along with trust, and I don't trust you anymore. Not now. Not after what you've been doing."

"Raina! Please? Listen to me."

"No way. Do you even understand what you were doing to me? You were working to take away my sole security. If I can't run my business at the Courtyard, JJ and I will lose everything I've worked to provide for us—we're barely making ends meet now as it is. My son deserves a bright future, one that only I can give him because God knows there's no one else there for him. By doing what you were doing, attempting to buy out that land, you threatened everything I hold dear. So, no, I won't listen to you. Not now and not ever again. Get out of my house. I don't want to ever see you here again."

Her voice broke and there were tears in her eyes as she finished her impassioned speech.

"Look, Raina, you have to let me explain—"

"The time for explanations was when you met me. Before you started pumping me for information about the Courtyard and about Royal. Not now."

The fact that she was totally right made her scorn no less galling or painful.

"Can I at least say bye to JJ?"

"No, you may not."

Raina stepped toward the front door and hauled it open. The chill air outside rushed in, enveloping them both in its icy swirl. He stared at Raina's face for a moment, but her expression remained implacable. He knew he had to pick his battles. This was definitely not the time to press her.

Silent, he passed her and went out the door. Before his feet had even struck the paved path to the road, he heard the door slam resoundingly behind him. He didn't look back, not even when he climbed into the SUV and pulled away from the curb.

On the drive back to his hotel and during a lonely dinner, he couldn't stop thinking about those bruises Raina had so swiftly hidden and who might have been responsible for them. The very idea that someone had felt they had the right to harm her like that made his blood boil and roused every protective instinct in him. Who was the bad man JJ had referred to and what was he to Raina? Was it the ex she'd said so little about? Nolan was suddenly reminded of the shadowy figure he'd seen the other night. Was it him? The thought left a sour taste in his mouth and made him determined to get to the root of what had happened to her, one way or another.

Nine

Raina was still bristling mad about Nolan's lies two days later. It had been tough breaking it to JJ that Nolan wouldn't be staying for dinner. He'd gone to bed that night grumpy and woken yesterday morning in the same state. It seemed her little guy could hold a grudge, and he laid the blame for his new idol not being around very firmly at her feet. She could only hope that the rehearsals for the pageant would distract him from his disappointment.

She thanked her lucky stars that she hadn't had time to let things go any further with Nolan than they already had. One kiss, that's all it had been—*but what a kiss*, her subconscious reminded her uncomfortably. She shoved the thought to the back of her mind and tried to focus on her preparations for the mosaic class she had scheduled tonight. Her group had enjoyed getting started on their mirror frames last week and she had no doubt that a few of them would finish gluing their pieces tonight and be ready to grout them.

She felt another flush of anger at Nolan as she remembered how his actions, if successful, would have taken all of this away from her. She hadn't been kidding when she'd told him on that first night that the Courtyard had become a symbol of hope for so many people. But then hope was obviously a cheap commodity for a man like him, along with belief and trust.

No matter how angry she was, though, she couldn't help but feel a numbing sense of loss. Her attraction to him had come out of the blue, startling her with its intensity. "Hormones, just hormones," she growled under her breath as she did her final checks around the room. Obviously she'd never learned her lesson about the kind of guy she should be attracted to. In the future, if there was any spark at all, she'd take it as a warning and then run a mile in the opposite direction. Fast.

"Hi, Raina!"

She looked up and greeted her students as they came in through the workroom's exterior door. In no time the workbenches were full. She'd had to restrict numbers on this class, as well as her Thursday night stained-glass classes purely because people needed to be able to spread their tools and supplies out while working. It was something she needed to consider when she came up with costing out her next cycle of classes in the New Year. While this first cycle had been a short one, geared mainly toward making gifts in time for Christmas, for her to maximize earnings and rebuild that little nest egg she'd had to withdraw for Jeb, she might need to have two evenings with large classes focused on smaller crafts and only one evening devoted to the larger projects.

"Okay, ladies," she said once everyone was there. "You all know where your projects are stored. I've already set out all your tools and the pots of glue and scrapers, so let's get to it!"

The noise in the workroom steadily built and conversation began to flow between the women. As Raina did her rounds, checking to make sure that everyone had what she needed and offering advice where necessary, she was startled to overhear Nolan's name being mentioned. She hated eavesdroppers but in this case she couldn't help it; she hovered near the women talking about him.

"I have to say it was a surprise to see him back in town," one of the older women said. "Apparently even his own mother didn't know he was coming back."

"Do you know why he's here? I know he's not staying with his parents. They're neighbors of mine and I've barely even seen Nolan there," replied another.

Raina interrupted them both. "He's with Samson Oil. He's the legal counsel for their land grabbing."

Her words were laced with bitterness and more than one pair of eyes swiveled to watch her as she spoke.

"Really? Oh, that's a pity. He was such a nice boy and he grew up into a fine young man."

Raina was hard pressed not to snort at the woman's remark. Fine? Sure, physically maybe. Certainly not as far as his integrity went.

The woman continued. "It was such a shame about his wife and son. A thing like that is bound to change a man. Makes him harder."

A general murmur of assent rose around her and, as if by silent mutual agreement, the women turned their conversation in a different direction. Numbing shock overwhelmed Raina, holding her paralyzed in its grip. Buzzing filled her ears. She felt herself sway a little, as if she was losing her balance, and she put out a hand to a chair to steady herself. Breathe, she told herself. Breathe. After a few seconds, she felt as if she was regaining control. Had anyone noticed how she'd completely zoned out?

She looked around the workroom. Apparently not. Her

students seemed intent on their tasks and were happily chatting among themselves while they worked. Raina drew in another breath and walked slowly to the back of the workroom where she leaned against the wall. The buzzing in her ears began to subside, but as it did, questions began circling in her mind.

A wife and son?

Nolan had never so much as mentioned his parents, let alone anyone else. Sure, he'd made vague reference to visiting family in town, but that had been it. So who was she, this wife of his? Could she have been a customer of hers, or maybe Raina had passed her in the street somewhere? And his son—how old was he?

Suddenly it all became very clear to her why Nolan was so good with her little boy. Why he hadn't been grossed out by JJ's snotty nose on the day they'd met. Why he'd so competently cleaned JJ's hands at the dinner table that night. Why he'd so easily fallen into conversation with JJ about his Spider-Man obsession.

So, were he and his wife amicably separated or bitterly estranged? Which one was it? The latter would certainly explain him staying away from Royal for so long and probably would also explain him not bringing them up in conversation. Raina clenched her hands into tight fists of frustration, digging, her fingernails into her palms. She welcomed the pain. It was a distraction from the pain of the betrayal she'd felt on learning he was working for Samson Oil—and realizing she'd let herself begin to fall for him. Hard. Physical pain she could deal with. It healed. It was the emotional pain and the toll it took that were harder to recover from.

A new thought bloomed in Raina's mind. Maybe his wife had cheated on him. Would that have been the catalyst that sent Nolan to another state? Had he sought to escape the pain of a relationship breakdown by moving away? Was that why he'd never said anything to her about a wife and child?

Whatever his circumstances, no matter whether they were justified or not, nothing excused the way he'd sought her out under false pretenses. He'd deceived her about the Courtyard. Why wouldn't he do the same about a wife and child, too? It wasn't her problem. Not anymore. She'd sent him on his way and it was highly unlikely their paths would cross again.

Nolan was glad of the excuse to quit Royal, even if it was for only one day to meet with his boss in Holloway. He'd known coming back to Royal would be tough, would force him to face a lot of his personal demons, but he hadn't expected, or wanted, to find someone to whom he was so strongly attracted.

He struck the steering wheel with the heel of his palm and cursed aloud in the cabin of the SUV. How could he have handled things differently with Raina? No matter how many times he examined everything they'd said and done since he'd met her, he still couldn't see anywhere he could have prevented what happened. Short of telling her exactly why he was in Royal on the day he'd introduced himself at the Courtyard, of course. And he'd just bet how well that would have gone down.

Besides, the confidentiality clause in his contract with Rafiq prevented him from disclosing Samson Oil's business with anyone other than the party with whom he was negotiating. His hands had been tied.

Even though he'd rationalized everything, he still couldn't erase the look on Raina's face when she'd told him to get out of her house. He'd dealt with a lot of angry people in his time, but never before had there been such a palpable level of anguish beneath the anger. It had tortured him to know he'd put that look on her face.

He knew he should have stepped away the moment he'd recognized the fierce attraction he'd felt toward her. How often had he told himself that she was everything he *wasn't* looking for?

A speed limit sign shot by his window and Nolan realized that he'd been so lost in his thoughts that he'd lost track of what he was doing. He eased off the accelerator and focused on his surroundings. He was almost there. As much as he wasn't looking forward to imparting the news to Rafe that the Courtyard was completely off the table, it would at least be some respite from constantly thinking about Raina.

The entrance to the Holloway Inn wasn't what Nolan had expected. From the moment he pulled up outside, he wondered if somewhere along the line he hadn't somehow traveled thousands of miles to England. The white stucco walls, with dark wooden battens, reminded him very much of a Tudor inn he and Carole had stayed in outside London during their honeymoon, although, he noted as he entered the lobby, that's where the similarities ended. There'd be no ducking to clear doorways here. He walked up to the reception desk and smiled at the receptionist.

"Good morning. Nolan Dane to see Mr. Ben Samson," he said, using the name Rafe had assumed while the property negotiations were ongoing.

"Welcome to the Holloway Inn, Mr. Dane. Mr. Samson is waiting for you in his suite."

The young woman smiled and gave him concise directions to the suite, and Nolan located the rooms without any trouble. His knock was quickly answered by Rafe himself. The fact his boss was alone was unusual but not entirely unexpected given how secretive he'd been about his involvement with Samson Oil from the outset.

"Good morning," Rafe said, shaking Nolan's hand and gesturing for him to enter. "Knowing how punctual you always are, I took the liberty of ordering coffee already. Help yourself."

"Thank you."

Nolan stepped inside, his feet sinking into the plush carpeting. He looked around the suite. It was no more and no less than he'd come to expect. The main living room was spacious and well lit. A fifty-inch flat-screen television took pride of place on one wall and a number of oversize leather sofas and chairs were grouped around it. Across the room, a dining table, large enough to comfortably seat twelve, was covered in what looked like a map of Royal and several stacks of papers.

He gave Rafe a look. His boss was as immaculately turned out as ever but there were shadows under his eyes.

"Hard night?" he asked, as he poured himself a coffee and helped himself to a Danish pastry from the white-linen-draped room-service cart.

"I met someone."

Rafe's terse response was characteristic of the man himself, but the second he reached for the cuff of his sleeve and gave it a tug, Nolan knew there was a great deal of meaning behind those three words. Rafe was a controlled man and generally very reserved. In fact, the first time Nolan had met him he'd been a little unnerved by the guy's intensity until he learned to appreciate the keen intelligence and mind for business that lay behind it. But he had his familiar mannerisms, as well, and Nolan knew this one— something had made Rafiq uncomfortable. Something... or someone.

"A woman?" Nolan pressed before taking a sip of his coffee.

"Of course a woman," Rafe laughed. "An intriguing and beautiful one at that."

"Have I met her before?"

"I only met her myself last night."

For a second Rafe's eyes got a faraway look, as if he was remembering something intensely personal.

In all the time Nolan had worked for his boss, he'd never known the man to indulge in anything as impulsive as a one-night stand. He wouldn't mind meeting the woman who'd managed to put that look in his boss's eye.

"She must have been something else, huh?" he probed.

"Yes, she certainly was." Rafe appeared to shake off whatever memory had gripped him and gathered himself together. "But that's in the past. We're not here to discuss my after-hours activities. Come, sit at the table. Bring me up to date. What's happening with Winslow Properties?"

Shaking his head, Nolan settled into a chair while Rafiq took one opposite. "No movement there at all. We don't stand a chance under the new management. It's like arguing with a wooden Indian."

Rafe raised one dark brow and Nolan waved a hand in response.

"Local terminology," he explained. "Basically, pressing forward with Winslow Properties is a waste of time. They're not selling."

Rafe didn't look pleased. "You're certain?"

"Absolutely."

To his credit Rafe accepted the news with better grace than Nolan had anticipated. Perhaps he realized that sometimes it was better to step away. Rafe pushed a folder toward Nolan.

"Let's move on these, then."

Nolan lifted the folder from the table and opened it. He ran his eye down the list on the first sheet. Not entirely surprising, he thought, and from what he'd seen and heard in Royal already, he had no doubt they'd manage to acquire these properties without too much hassle. His eye stopped on the name of one ranch, though, and a frisson of disquiet tickled at the back of his mind.

"All of these?" Nolan asked, looking up from the documents.

Not a man to waste words, Rafe merely nodded.

"This one—the Wild Aces ranch—what do you want with that?"

Again Rafe raised one brow. "I don't pay you to ask questions."

Nolan's sense of unease increased. He'd done plenty of research both before he returned to Royal and since he'd been there. He knew who was vulnerable and he knew who'd had enough hardship to be coaxed off their land and sent to newer pastures. And he knew, without a doubt, that with the right amount of coercion, the owners of the Wild Aces would in all likelihood accept a reasonable offer for their land.

"That's true," Nolan conceded. "But if I'm to perform my role properly, I need to know the background."

Rafe met Nolan's gaze full-on, not giving an inch and continuing to say nothing. Eventually Rafe made a sound of annoyance and leaned forward, placing his elbows on the table between them and steepling his fingers.

"Why is it so important to you all of a sudden to know why? It hasn't been an issue for you up until now."

"I'm your boots-on-the-ground man. As such, I'm a lot closer to the people of Royal."

"Which is exactly why I appointed you to this role. You grew up there. You know how best to attain my goals."

"But I don't know why you're doing this. People are already asking questions. Questions I can't answer."

"And you don't have to."

"No, that's true. But my parents still live there. My father still practices there. I would hate there to be any fallout for them."

"There will be no fallout. Are we not helping people by relieving them of useless assets? Offering them good money and a fresh start before they're forced to move on when their banks foreclose?"

"We are. But if the assets are so useless, why do you want them so badly?"

Rafe said nothing.

"If I'm to continue to act on your behalf I need to know."

Rafe leaned back in his chair again. "A threat, Nolan?"

"No, a statement of fact. Take Wild Aces for example. Most of that land is leased out to another operation, the McCallums', because their stored water supply was compromised after the tornado and with the drought they haven't been able to replenish their water stock. To keep their herds at optimum levels, they're leasing this land here." He stabbed a finger at the map on the table. "If your offer to purchase the land is accepted by the owners, do you intend to continue with the lease already in place?"

"My plans are mine alone. I don't disclose my reasons." Rafe paused before adding, "To anyone."

Nolan carefully closed the folder in his hands and, equally carefully, placed it on the table. "Then I cannot continue to work for you."

"You're serious?"

"Never more so. I will not represent Samson Oil unless I have a better understanding of what your aims are in relation to the land acquisitions. Like I said, people are beginning to ask questions and I have a few of my own."

"It is no one's business but mine."

There were times when Rafe's privileged background shone through—times like this when he held himself above others and believed his will was law. That might be the case back in Al Qunfudhah, his homeland, but the last time Nolan checked it certainly wasn't that way in Texas.

"Then I'm sorry, but I'm forced to resign. Effective immediately."

"We have a contract, Nolan," Rafe reminded him. "You are bound to honor that, are you not?"

"A contract I drew up," Nolan said on a sigh. "And under the terms of the exit clause, I believe you'll discover that I'm within my rights to do this. I'm sorry, Rafe. I've always liked you and admired your business acumen, but I can no longer continue to work for you. Not under these circumstances. I hope we can still be friends."

He rose and extended his hand. Rafe hesitated a moment before also getting to his feet and clasping Nolan's hand in return.

"I, too, am sorry it has come to this. Can I ask you one thing?"

"What's that?"

"Why? You were happy to continue working under my instructions before. What changed?"

Nolan gave Rafe a bitter smile. "I met someone."

Ten

Nolan drove away from Holloway with a sense of lightness he hadn't felt in a very long time. It was as if walking away from his contract with Rafiq had freed him from an invisible cell. It wasn't that he hadn't enjoyed his work, because he had. He'd always loved the cut and thrust of law, and property law had brought its own challenges to keep him sharp. But he'd never truly stopped to consider the peripheral effect of what he was doing. Not until he'd met Raina.

Would she allow him back into her life? He wanted to tell her he was no longer acting for Samson Oil, but after the way they'd parted, he seriously doubted that he could just pull up to her front door and expect her to see him.

He activated the hands-free calling in his car and spoke her name. Through the speaker he heard the phone at the other end begin to ring.

Pick up, he silently willed her. *Pick up*. But after a few short rings, the call was diverted to voice mail. He was disappointed but not surprised. In fact, he wouldn't have put it past her to have blocked his number altogether.

Nolan left a message anyway, asking her to please call him when she had a chance. As he ended the call he wondered whether she would call him back. Maybe she'd simply delete his message without listening to it. Well, he'd call her back again. Not too soon, of course. Even he respected that he'd done a serious amount of damage when it came to her trust in him. He had a lot of work to do before he won it back.

At a bit of a loose end, Nolan decided to drop in on his parents. Maybe his dad needed some wood chopped. He sure hoped so, because he suddenly had a burning urge to work off some energy and wood chopping felt like just the chore for it.

When he got to his parents' house, he sat in the car a moment and stared at the home where he'd grown up. He had so many memories from when he was a kid and more from when he'd reached his teens. He still remembered, clear as day, the first time he'd brought Carole over to meet his mom and dad. He and Carole had been in their last year of high school, each with the same goal for their future. Even then they'd hoped to build that future together.

Would he have changed anything if he could? He'd known Carole for what felt like forever, but he still remembered the day when he'd seen her and everything had changed. It was as if a switch had been thrown in his mind and from that moment forward he'd known she was the one for him. It turned out that he'd been a little slow on the uptake. She'd decided long before that she wanted him, too, and she'd waited patiently, biding her time until he woke up to the fact that they'd been made for one another.

Strange how he could think about her now without it hurting. Yes, he still missed her and he probably always would, but he could also remember the good times—the fun times before life got so frenetic and busy and pressured and everything fell apart. Before their son had died and she'd taken her own life in a cruel combination of guilt and grief and hopelessness.

A movement on the front porch of his parents' house dragged Nolan from his reveries. His dad—standing there in the cold, quite happy to wait until his son was ready to get out of the car in which he'd been sitting for, he now realized, upward of twenty minutes while his thoughts wandered.

Nolan finally got out of the SUV and walked up the front path. His dad greeted him with a hug. Although Nolan was a grown man, he still took succor from his father's grasp, from the warmth and unconditional love.

"Everything okay, son?" Howard Dane asked him.

Nolan met his father's brown eyes, so like his own, and smiled. "Yeah, Dad. Everything's okay."

His father gave him a nod. "Your mother was worried when she saw you parked out front. You know what she's like."

"I was thinking. About Carole and Bennett."

His father's eyes dulled with unspoken pain. "Thought as much. It's why we left you to it."

"So," Nolan said, clapping his father on the back as they turned and walked toward the front door. "Got any wood that needs chopping?"

His father laughed. "In that suit? I don't think so."

"Maybe you can loan me something to wear."

Howard Dane eyed him up and down. "Maybe I can. You look like a stuffed shirt, son."

"Not anymore, Dad. Not anymore."

Nolan's back and shoulders ached like he couldn't remember and the blisters on the palms of his hands reminded him he'd grown soft during his time in California.

It had been good to do some manual labor. It gave him plenty of time for thinking. His mom had brought out some lunch for him and his dad, who was busy stacking the firewood as Nolan split the logs. Once they were done and came inside, Nolan looked across the sitting room and saw the new gas fireplace installed where the old open fire had once been. He turned and looked at his father.

"You didn't tell me you'd gotten rid of the old fireplace."

His father shrugged. "Sometimes a man just has to chop wood."

Nolan gave his father a look. "Why'd you have it removed?"

"Debris from the tornado damaged the old chimney. We decided to remove the whole thing, fireplace and all."

"You might have told me." Nolan laughed.

His dad shrugged again. "It's no bother. Besides, the wood should come in handy come summer. Your mother made me buy one of those fancy brazier things for the back patio. We'll use it for that."

Nolan laughed again. This was what he'd missed living so far away. His father's quiet acceptance and solid support. It didn't mean he was a pushover. No sirree. In fact, Howard Dane was known through several counties as a tough lawyer who could be relied on to stand up for his clients.

Nolan's mother came through from the kitchen.

"Are you staying for dinner?" she asked, wiping her hands dry on a tea towel.

"I'd like that if you have room for me," he said with a wink that he knew would earn an eye roll in response. He wasn't disappointed.

"Go get cleaned up and I'll see if we can squeeze you in at the table," his mother teased, flicking the tea towel in his direction.

Over dinner, Nolan told his parents about his decision to quit Samson Oil.

"So what are you going to do now?" his mom asked with a worried frown on her still-pretty face.

"I haven't given it a lot of thought yet, Mom. I just made the decision today."

"But it's not like you not to have a plan beforehand. What on earth prompted you to do such a thing?"

Nolan eyed both his parents before answering. "I didn't feel comfortable with it anymore. Yes, I know we were doing a lot of good, giving people a way out they didn't have before. But somewhere along the line, others would get hurt and I figure Royal's seen enough hurt already. I just couldn't do it anymore."

His father narrowed his eyes at him and Nolan shifted in his seat. Howard was a man of few words but when he chose them, you generally listened.

"What changed?"

Not, why did *you* change, Nolan observed of his father's question. It made him think carefully about his response.

"I guess it mattered to me more."

His father continued to look at him in much the same way he had back when Nolan was a kid and had done something wrong. Howard knew that silence was a very effective weapon.

"I met someone. Someone who reminded me of what it's like to feel." Nolan heard his mother's gasp of surprise, but he kept going. "Someone who potentially was going to be put at a major disadvantage both financially and emotionally if things had continued the way they were. Regrettably, I withheld information from her. I abused her trust. I don't like the man who did that and I don't want to be that person anymore."

"Good to hear, son. So who do you want to be now?" Howard said quietly.

"The man who makes things right again."

Nolan watched his father take a sip of his wine and set the glass carefully back down on his mother's crisp white linen tablecloth.

His father sighed and looked up at him again. "And if you can't?"

Nolan shook his head. Failure wasn't an option. He wouldn't be his father's son if it was. "I will succeed. It won't be easy, but I'll get there."

"Does she know about your old life here?"

"No, and I need to address that. She deserves to hear it from me. It's just...not easy talking about them."

"You'll find the right time, son, and the right words," his father said encouragingly.

"Does this mean you're moving back to Royal for good?" his mom asked while she gathered up the plates from the table.

"I hope so," Nolan answered. "No, I know so. LA isn't the right place for me. Not anymore. It was a good place to run to. It let me grieve at my own pace and in private. But I'm back now."

Howard shifted in his seat. "You planning to set up a property law practice here?"

Nolan shook his head. "No. In fact, I think I'm ready to go back to my roots, to family law." He gave his father a half smile. "Do you know anyone looking for a lawyer?"

His father's smile was slow to come but when it did, it shone with a world of approval and joy. "I think I might know of a space. You'd have to brush up a bit, jump through a few hoops, untie some red tape."

"Oh, Howard, stop teasing the boy," Nolan's mom protested. "You know you need him back at the practice. It hasn't been the same since he left."

Nolan met his dad's gaze and stood as Howard rose to his feet. The older man extended his hand across the table and Nolan grasped it firmly, exactly the way his father had taught him more years ago than he could even remember.

"Then, welcome back aboard, son. We've missed you."

"It's good to be back, Dad. Thank you."

And Nolan knew the words were more than just that. Inside he felt as if everything had clicked back into place. Almost everything, he corrected himself. There was still some rebuilding to do, if that was even possible. But, like he'd reminded himself before, failure wasn't an option.

Number withheld. Raina stared at her cell phone screen and debated taking the call. It was quiet in the store; she had no reason not to take it, and yet there was a knot in her stomach that made her hesitate. She knew it wasn't Nolan. He'd been leaving messages every day since Saturday asking her to call him. She wished she had the courage to call him back and tell him to stop calling her, or even had the courage to block his number, but something always held her back. That same perverse something that gave her a quiet thrill of attraction every time she heard his voice.

Her phone went silent in her hand and a few seconds later the icon popped up telling her she had a voice message. With a sigh of frustration, Raina checked it. And there it was, she thought as she listened. Yet another call from Jeb. She'd already told him how much money she could give him but he insisted on more. Telling her his life depended on it. When she'd pressed him for details, he'd explained about the gambling debts he'd incurred in New Mexico. The loans he'd taken out with some guy who was now impatient to be repaid. The sum had staggered her. Surely Jeb couldn't have gambled it all away?

She had the impression that for all the things he'd told her, he was still holding something back. She decided it was time to get to the root of it and dialed the number he'd given her in his message.

"Rai, about time," he growled in her ear.

"What aren't you telling me?" Raina demanded, not wasting any time on pleasantries.

"Babe, I've told you everything you need to know."

Need to know? She looked to the ceiling of the old barn and prayed for strength. "Look, I might be able to borrow some money from my dad. But you have to tell me the truth, Jeb. Why so much?"

He laughed, a grating sound that was devoid of even an ounce of mirth. "I've gotta get out, Rai. Disappear and never come back. That costs."

Disappear? Never come back? Heck, if she believed— even for one minute—that he'd never be back it would be worth paying him what he was asking. To think that she wouldn't have to be wondering and waiting when the next call or visit would come. The next demand for more money. But what on earth had he done that was so bad?

"Forever?" she asked, the word slipping from her mouth before she even realized she'd said it.

"Aw, Rai, don't tell me you're gonna miss me. Or is it maybe that you really don't want to see me ever again?"

Raina shuddered. He was back to playing his word games, twisting everything around, including her, until she didn't know which way was up anymore.

"How much? Tell me, Jeb. Exactly how much do you need?"

He named a sum that had her rocking back on her heels. "I can't do that."

"That's what it's gonna take, Rai baby. And I need it by tomorrow."

"Tomorrow?" She couldn't get that kind of cash together by tomorrow and she doubted that even if her dad was prepared to lend her the money he could either. Besides, tomorrow was JJ's pageant. She didn't want Jeb anywhere near her or her son on what was a very important day for her little boy. "That's far too soon! Give me a few days."

"I don't have a few days." Jeb's tone became more urgent and a shiver of fear trickled down Raina's spine. "I'll see you tomorrow. Look out for me."

With that he hung up, leaving Raina staring at her phone and shaking. How on earth had she ever let things get to this? She should have drawn the line on being his cash cow years ago, but somehow it had always been easier just to pay him and send him on his way.

Raina stared at her phone and knew she had to do this. She dialed her father's number. He answered on the second ring.

"Dad, I need your help."

Eleven

Raina had been on tenterhooks all day. Her father, bless him, had come to see her at the store earlier in the day with a wad of bills. That he'd done such a thing, even knowing that the money was for Jeb, filled her heart with gratitude. No matter what happened in her life, she had him as her rock. When her mother had abandoned her, he'd been there. When Jeb had abandoned her, he'd been there. Every minute of every day that she needed him. But he wasn't getting any younger and it was time she was that rock for him, not the other way around. She needed to be able to stand on her own two feet.

And then there was the anxiety of carrying several thousand dollars in cash on her person for the rest of the day. Every time someone had come into the store and set the bell above the door ringing, she'd virtually jumped out of her skin. By the time she'd closed up shop and headed home, her nerves had been stretched so taut she felt as if the slightest thing would see her fracture into a million pieces.

"Mommy! Mommy! Look, I'm Spider-Man!" JJ zoomed around the house in his costume, looking like no shepherd any children's pageant had ever seen.

"JJ, we've talked about this. You can't be Spider-Man in the pageant," she said wearily and with an edge to her voice that JJ didn't miss.

"I am, Mommy. I am!"

His face took on a petulant look that reminded her all too much of his father, and Raina was hard pressed to remind herself not to visit her frustrations over Jeb's sins upon JJ. She had to pick her battles.

"How about you be Spider-Man in the car and then a shepherd when we get to the hall?"

"Spider-Man!" JJ shouted and hopped on one foot.

"C'mon," Raina said, fighting to hold on to her temper. "Let's get your coat on. If we don't go soon we'll be late."

By the time she had them both bundled up and in the car her hands were shaking. She took in several steadying breaths before putting the car in Reverse and backing out of the drive, all the time keeping an eye out for Jeb. But he was nowhere to be seen. She didn't know whether to be relieved or sorry.

Luck was finally with her when they got to the hall where the pageant was being staged and she parked her car in the last vacant space in the lot. Uttering a silent prayer of thanks, Raina helped JJ from the car and grabbed his shepherd's costume before heading toward the foyer. Inside was a cluster of angels on one side, shepherds on the other and all other variety of pageant costumes in between. And Spider-Man, Raina told herself. Don't forget him.

A tingle of awareness spread through her body as she sensed a movement to her right-hand side. Jeb?

"No'an!" JJ cried.

Raina felt her body sag. Was it in relief or in shock that he'd come? Right now he was definitely the lesser of two evils.

"Raina, I hope you don't mind me being here, but I didn't want to let JJ down."

"The pageant is open to everyone," she replied. "Just a small donation is requested for the local food bank."

"I know, I've already donated," Nolan said.

Just then, someone jostled her from behind, making her lose her balance, and Nolan immediately steadied her, his large warm hands at her shoulders. He let go of her just as soon as she was steady on her feet and for some stupid reason, tears sprang to her eyes. Raina blinked furiously to rid herself of them. She'd weathered tough days before and this one wasn't any different, she reminded herself.

A call went out for the shepherds to assemble and to go with one of the day care teachers.

"C'mon, JJ," Raina said, shaking out his costume. "Let's get you changed."

"No. I'm Spider-Man, Mommy."

JJ's voice was raised and Raina saw several faces turn toward them. Her cheeks flushed with embarrassment.

"Maybe we should just go home," she muttered to herself but JJ overhead her and pitched his voice so that everyone in the foyer could hear him.

"No! Not going home!"

JJ was normally an even-tempered child but when he threw a tantrum it had force equal to the tornado that had leveled so much of Royal more than a year ago. On top of everything she'd dealt with in the situation with Jeb, this was one thing too many for Raina. She reached for JJ's hand, determined to take him back out to the car, drag him if she had to, but Nolan put a hand on her arm.

"Maybe I can help," he offered, taking the shepherd

costume from her and squatting down in front of JJ. "Hey, champ, you've blown your cover."

JJ eyed Nolan with a wary but intrigued expression.

Nolan gave JJ a serious look. "No one knows who Spider-Man really is, right? He hides his suit until his special powers are needed, doesn't he?"

JJ nodded slowly, his eyes growing wide.

"Quick," Nolan suggested. "Before anyone notices. Let's cover you up."

To Raina's stunned surprise, JJ let Nolan dress him in the rough cotton overshirt, complete with rope belt, and secured the tea towel she'd brought for his head with another length of twine.

"Great work," Nolan whispered to the little boy. "I think your secret is safe."

"Raina, is JJ ready?" one of the day care teachers asked, clipboard in hand and a harried expression on her face. "Oh, great, I see he is. That's everyone accounted for. I'll bring him out back so you can go and take your seat."

Before she knew it, JJ was amiably holding hands with his teacher and walking away. But all of a sudden he broke free and ran back to Nolan and beckoned for him to lean down. Her little boy whispered something in Nolan's ear and gave him a massive hug around his neck.

This time Raina couldn't hold back the tear that spilled over and traced a line down her cheek. She brushed it away but not before Nolan noticed it.

"Thank you," she said to him, her voice shaking just a little.

Nolan didn't say anything right away, just pushed his hands in his trouser pockets and looked at her. Raina self-consciously looked away. She wasn't at her best tonight. A sleepless night followed by the tension of today, capped off by JJ's behavior, had left her feeling more raw and vulnerable than she had in a long time.

"Raina, we need to talk."

"No." She shook her head. "No we don't. Thank you for settling JJ for me, but we've said all we need to say to one another. And, to be honest, the time for you to *talk* to me was when we met. Not now."

She turned to go but Nolan caught the sleeve of her coat.

"Please, Raina. Just give me five minutes. You won't answer or return my calls—what else was I supposed to do but turn up to see you?"

"So you didn't come here for JJ then?" She challenged him with an angry glare.

"Of course I came for JJ. But I'd have been stupid not to want to see you, too."

Raina crossed her arms over her chest. "Fine. Say what you've come to say."

Nolan looked around the busy foyer full of parents and family members of the performers all milling about. "Can we step outside for a bit of privacy?"

He held his breath, waiting for Raina's reply, and felt a surge of relief when she gave him a brief nod and headed toward the main doors. They found a spot outside under the portico where they wouldn't be in the way of people coming into the hall. She still had her arms crossed and her eyes kept flicking this way and that, as if she was on the lookout for someone.

"Thank you," he said. "I appreciate it."

"Just get to the point, Nolan. What is it that you're so determined to tell me?"

While she still sounded as if she was madder at him than a wet hen, he could see she was barely holding herself together. Lines of strain pulled around her mouth and eyes and she looked exhausted.

"I've quit Samson Oil," he started, thinking he may as well get to the point from the beginning. She definitely wasn't in a mood to mess around. "I thought a lot about what you said and you were right. It made me look at myself with fresh eyes and I didn't like what I saw anymore."

Raina didn't respond, so he continued.

"I've decided to move back to Royal, to rejoin my father's practice. I know I can do good there and while I feel that I did a lot of good with Samson Oil, I also hurt a lot of people, too. Especially you. I'm sorry for that, Raina. It was never my intention to cause you any harm either directly or indirectly. Nor could I just stand aside and let my boss potentially harm people like you anymore."

Raina shifted from one foot to the other and rubbed her upper arms with her hands. It was clear she'd heard about all she was prepared to listen to.

"Why is this any of my business, Nolan? What makes you think I care where you live or what you do?"

The hurt was there, loud and clear in every word she spoke even though she'd kept her tone even.

"I'd like to think it's your business because before I messed everything up, you started to have feelings for me." At her sound of protest he continued. "The way I have feelings for you. Hear me out, please. Raina, I think I'm falling in love with you. Yes, I know it's sudden and that we barely know one another but from the first moment I laid eyes on you I knew you were someone special. Someone who had been missing in my life. Please, give me another chance. Give *us* another chance."

He waited for her response for what felt like forever, even though he logically knew it could only have been a minute or so. Her face had changed, become unreadable even to someone like him who was used to studying every nuance of expression for answers. Finally, she took in a breath and spoke.

"I can't make a decision about something like that here and now."

He took solace in the fact that it wasn't a direct no.

"I accept that. Look, right now it's enough that you're prepared to think about it."

"I need to get inside. They'll be starting soon."

She pushed past him and he let her go. It would probably be too much to expect her to sit with him. Nolan watched her go in the front doors and started, more slowly, to follow. He didn't care if he stood at the back of the hall for the duration of the pageant, but he would be there for JJ. As he made his way to the door, he saw a shadow detach itself from the bushes near the road. Nolan watched as the man walked toward the parking area. There was something about the shape and size of the man, and the way he moved, that was vaguely familiar. In a rush, Nolan remembered the person he'd seen on the road near Raina's house.

Every sense in his body went on full alert. He followed the man to the lot where he saw the guy draw to a halt by Raina's car.

"Can I help you?" he called out and was surprised when the guy wheeled around to face him rather than run away.

The man's face might once have been handsome, Nolan thought, but the dissipation wrought by hard living, no doubt compounded by too much alcohol judging by the smell coming from him right now, had left its mark.

"I know you," the man said. "Seen you sniffing around Raina's place. She's a fine piece of ass, isn't she?"

Nolan's hands curled into fists at the familiar way the man spoke about Raina.

"What's it to you?" he demanded.

The guy laughed. "She hasn't told you about me, has she? Her dirty little secret."

Suddenly it all started to slip into place. This guy was Raina's ex—and JJ's father. Nolan instinctively wanted to shield them from this guy—to make sure he didn't touch or tarnish their lives again. But, last he checked, murder was still illegal in the state of Texas.

"I know about you," Nolan said, taking scant satisfaction in pricking Jeb Pickering's bubble of confidence. This was the man who'd left Raina's wrist looking black and blue. Nolan itched to deliver a dose of the same thing to the bastard but he knew there were ways and means of dealing with lowlifes like him—and he was going to make sure he never hurt Raina again. "You're not wanted here. Get on your way."

"I got every right to be here. More right 'n you, anyways. JJ's my boy. Not yours."

Jeb's stance altered and he drew himself up to his full height in an effort to intimidate Nolan. While the guy had an inch or two on him, Nolan knew that if it came to it, he'd still best Pickering in a fight. That, however, would be a last resort.

"Now you want to claim him?" Nolan sneered. "A bit late, isn't it?"

"It's never too late," Jeb challenged in return.

"It is when you're a no-good waste of time. You think you're a man but you're nothing. A real man doesn't treat a woman the way you've treated Raina."

Jeb's expression grew ugly under the lamp light, his mouth twisting into a harsh line. "You don't know nothing 'bout what happened."

"I know enough."

The look on Jeb's face changed again, going from belligerent to sly in one breath.

"A man can change his mind, can't he? Although—" he paused and rubbed at the stubble on his chin "—I guess that would mess up your plans, wouldn't it?"

"My plans?"

Nolan inwardly cursed himself for falling into Jeb's verbal trap.

"Yeah, your plans with my girl and my son."

"Look, you might be his biological father but be honest, that's where your attachment to JJ begins and ends. As for Raina, she's not your girl. Not anymore."

"Ah, but she's not yours either, is she? Not yet."

Jeb looked smug and Nolan's hands itched to wipe that expression off his face.

"Besides," Jeb continued. "She owes me."

Nolan shook his head. "I don't see how she owes you anything."

"Money, doofus. She owes me money. We have, what you would say, an agreement."

"Haven't you already taken enough from her? What kind of man are you anyway, constantly leeching off a woman that way?"

The insult fell on deaf ears. "I'm here to get what's mine. Mind you, since you're the one who has the hots for Rai, maybe *you* should be the one paying me."

He could imagine the gears grinding in the back of Jeb's mind as the man took in Nolan's appearance, the quality of his coat, the expensive haircut and his handmade boots. Since money was the man's major motivator, Nolan hoped that maybe he could save Raina the additional pressure of ever having to see Jeb again. Maybe.

"How much?" Nolan demanded.

"Look, man, this is between Raina and me," Jeb started, rocking back on his feet slightly. "But if you wanted to pay what she owes me—hell, I'm an equal opportunity kind of guy. Your money is as good as hers."

"If I give you anything, you have to give me your word, such as it is, that you won't bother Raina again."

"Hey, man, no need to insult me," Jeb protested, suddenly the picture of a man affronted when his integrity has been called into question. But then he laughed. It was an ugly sound that revealed his true avaricious character. "Whatever. When can you pay me?"

"First you have to tell me how much."

Jeb named a figure and Nolan didn't so much as bat an eyelid. "I can do that. Give me your bank account details."

"I don't have no bank account, man. I need cash and I need it now."

"I can get it to you tomorrow night. But on one condition."

"What's that?"

"That you get away from here now and stay away from Raina and JJ."

"It's not like I want to see them," Jeb scowled. "She owes me, is all. But, yeah, I'll do as you say. She won't see me—tonight anyway."

"Good. But if I hear that she's caught so much as a glimpse of you after our talk tonight, the deal's off." Nolan glared at him to make his point clear. "And I'll make sure she doesn't give you anything either."

Jeb looked at him, as if trying to figure out whether Nolan could influence Raina that much. Obviously he decided that Nolan could. He lifted his chin in acceptance of the terms.

"Where d'you want to meet?"

Nolan named a parking lot in back of some buildings downtown. Jeb nodded. "I know it. I'll be there. Six o'clock tomorrow night. Don't be late or the deal's off and I'm back to my original plan."

"Oh, I'll be on time, don't you worry about that," Nolan affirmed, staying outside to watch Jeb as he headed off down the street and faded from sight.

Nolan went back to the hall. The lights gleaming on the front porch were a welcome contrast to the darkness of the man he'd just seen leave. He wondered what the hell Raina had ever seen in Jeb Pickering, but then again, knowing her even as little as he did, he could see why the lost boy inside Jeb would appeal to her nature to nurture and mend what was broken. She certainly had mended what was broken within him, Nolan thought, and made him dream of a new future.

He quietly let himself into the hall and scanned the rows of seats, trying to spot Raina. There she was. Again that familiar wave of protectiveness swept through him. Dealing with Jeb would be an unpleasant business, but he'd do whatever it took to keep Raina safe from that creep and anything or anyone else that threatened her. Raina and JJ both.

As if she'd sensed his presence, she turned and their eyes met. She gave him a tentative smile and waved him to come toward her. Nolan realized she'd saved him a seat. The knowledge eased loose the knot he'd been carrying in his chest since she'd confronted him and told him to get lost, and for the first time in a long time, Nolan admitted he felt hope.

Twelve

From the moment Nolan sat down next to her, Raina felt every nerve and cell in her body become attuned to his nearness. The seats were close together so his broad shoulder brushed against hers. In the end, it was easier to give in to the occasional contact and stop trying to hold herself apart from him.

Who was she kidding anyway? Yes, she was still mad at him and, yes, she still felt betrayed, but he'd extended an olive branch tonight. While her first instinct had been to reject it, and him, in an attempt to save herself from any further hurt or heartbreak, didn't she owe it to herself to give him another chance? If what he said was true, and he'd quit Samson Oil, maybe that was the genuine measure of the man himself.

She glanced toward him and caught him looking back at her. His brown eyes were alight with joy and she felt her body relax even more.

"Our Spider-Man is doing great, don't you think?" he whispered to her, leaning in closer.

Her nostrils flared as his scent wafted toward her, making her insides twist with suppressed need. It was all she could do to smile and nod an acknowledgment and return her eyes to the stage where JJ stood as tall and proud as he could, his little face turned to the crowd and his gaze searching for her among the many faces. She saw the moment he picked her out in the crowd and he beamed at her, and then his eyes drifted to where Nolan sat beside her and she thought JJ's face might split with happiness.

She felt a telltale prickle of tears in her eyes. She'd tried so darn hard to be everything that JJ had needed in his young life. But his obvious joy at having Nolan present made her realize that she couldn't be all things to her son, no matter what she did. Not being able to ensure he had the best of everything life had to offer frustrated her. She wanted him to have it all.

If Nolan's words were true, if he was really falling in love with her, then she had to know how he felt about JJ, too. They were a package deal.

But what of the wife and child she'd heard mention of earlier this week? How could she casually bring that up in conversation without it sounding as if she'd been snooping into his life? Of course, she rationalized, she had a right to snoop—she had more than herself to consider—but snooping had never been her thing. She'd always been a "live and let live" type of person, someone who tried to always see the good in people.

But hadn't that very facet of her personality caused her to make some of the worst decisions in her life, as well? Decisions like Jeb and the loser boyfriends she'd had before him? No—no matter which way she looked at it, she couldn't regret her time with Jeb no matter how much it had cost her and how much heartache he'd wrought. Without him, she wouldn't have had JJ. Becoming a parent had made her realize just what her father had sacrificed for her all these years and deepened her love for him a thousandfold. Her dad had worked hard to make up for her mother's abandonment, and while he'd had lady friends come and go through the years, Raina had never felt as if she'd lacked for not having her mother with her growing up.

Which brought her to even more questions. Was it in JJ's best interests for her to keep allowing Nolan access to them both if he was going to abandon them like he might have done already with his own family? Raina had learned the hard way, time and time again, what abandonment felt like, how much it hurt. Could she even consider risking that for JJ? He was still so young. Still so reliant on her to protect him.

And what of Nolan's wife? Was she someone Raina had met before? Someone she came across in her day-to-day life? She hated the thought that for some poor soul she might become the other woman.

Her mind was whirling with so many worries that she barely noticed the pageant was up to the final number. The children were singing "Silent Night" and the audience had joined in. Beside her, the sound of Nolan's tenor forced her attention back to the present. Sometimes, she reminded herself, you simply had to let go and let God. Maybe it really was as simple as that.

She felt herself begin to relax a little as she joined in for the final lines of the carol. But then a jarring thought sideswiped her. For all her ponderings she hadn't stopped to consider the situation with Jeb or the very large sum of money she had in her purse right now.

With the pageant over, people began to rise from their seats and jostle one another on the way to the main doors. Raina felt Nolan's hand at her elbow, steadying her in the crush as they filed out of their row of seats. Raina turned to him.

"I have to go out the back and collect JJ. Please don't rush off. I know he's going to want to see you."

"And you? Do you want to see me?" Nolan asked, pulling Raina to one side so the crowd could eddy past them without bumping them again.

"I'll be honest—I really don't know. Part of me says, yes, but—"

"I understand. If you'd rather, you can make my apologies to JJ."

She could see the hurt in his eyes, watched the light in them dim a little. It made up her mind.

"Come back to our house for a hot chocolate with JJ. He's going to take some time to unwind before getting off to bed tonight anyway."

Nolan looked at her and she saw the slight curl at the edges of his lips. "Are you sure? I understand if you—"

"No." It was her turn to interrupt him. "I'm sure. Look, he's waiting. I'll see you back at the house, okay?"

"I'll wait for you in the parking lot," Nolan said in a voice that brooked no argument. "And I'll follow you home."

Knowing he'd be there, waiting in the darkness outside, made Raina feel warm inside. And when Jeb showed up for his money, either outside the hall or later, back at her house, she'd deal with it then. Actually, thinking about it, having Nolan handy might make the whole process go more smoothly. She doubted Jeb would try anything stupid with another person there.

"Okay, that's good of you. Thank you."

Later, with JJ in tow and wrapped up again in his winter coat and beanie, they walked quickly to the car. As good as his word, Nolan had pulled up his SUV alongside hers and was waiting in the frigid air.

"Did you see me, No'an?" JJ asked excitedly as they approached the car.

"I did, champ. You were great."

Her little boy's smile made Raina glad she'd asked Nolan back to the house. JJ had had enough of her short-tempered company this week. Goodness only knew, if Nolan hadn't been there tonight, she wouldn't have thought twice about taking JJ home—no doubt kicking and screaming—over the costume issue.

She looked around the parking lot for Jeb. But among all the families loading their preschoolers into their cars and saying bye to their friends, there was no sign of him. Maybe he'd turn up at the house, she decided as she drove along the road toward home. She flicked her eyes to the rearview mirror, reassured by the sight of Nolan's vehicle following her at a safe distance. She was all over the place as far as he was concerned. If only she could trust her heart and they could discover exactly where this complicated relationship of theirs could go. But she'd trusted her heart before and look where that had landed her. She didn't want to ever go through that again.

At the house, Nolan offered to supervise JJ as he changed into his pajamas while she made the hot chocolate. Raina gratefully accepted. As she heated milk on her stove she could hear JJ's excited tones tempered by Nolan's calmer deeper voice down the hall and closed her eyes for just a moment, wondering what it might be like if this were to become a regular, even daily event. How did that make her feel?

A commotion at the kitchen door made her turn as she started to fill the mugs. Nolan had given JJ a piggyback ride from his bedroom and the two of them were laughing. Raina couldn't help but join in.

"Who wants marshmallows?" she asked as she finished pouring the hot drinks.

"Me!" JJ crowed from his perch. "And No'an, too."

Raina looked to Nolan for confirmation. "Are you a marshmallow man?"

"Through and through," he said.

His word were simple at face value but she found herself left wondering if he'd meant more by that. She had to stop overthinking everything. It was time to just let some things find their natural course. She dropped marshmallows in each of the mugs and put them on a tray to carry through to the sitting room.

"Let me take that for you," Nolan offered, swinging JJ down to the floor.

"Thanks."

Raina followed Nolan and JJ and relished just how good it felt to share something as simple as carrying a tray, rather than being responsible for everything herself. But even so, she couldn't allow herself to simply give in to the comfort of this moment. Nolan still had secrets and until he was prepared to share them with her, she had to guard her heart.

Even as she thought it, she knew it was too late. Her heart was already a lost cause when it came to this man. Had been from the moment he'd kissed her. It was why discovering his subterfuge had been so painful.

She watched from the door as Nolan encouraged JJ to kneel on the floor by the coffee table to sip his drink. Obviously sensing her scrutiny, he looked up.

"You okay?" he asked.

She smiled and nodded. "I think so," she answered, and stepped forward to accept the mug he held out for her.

It wasn't long before JJ was drooping with exhaustion. To Raina's surprise he made no argument when she said it was bedtime. He asked to be carried to bed and she lifted him comfortably into her arms and held him close as she went down the hallway to his room. It was a constant marvel to her that this growing child had come from her body. A marvel and a precious gift.

So much responsibility came with parenthood. She had to be certain she was making the right decisions for herself, sure, but for JJ most of all. He deserved only the very best in life. Did that include a second chance with Nolan? she wondered as she supervised JJ brushing his teeth and then carried him to his bed.

JJ was out like a light before she'd even made it to his bedroom. She left the door ajar for him so the nightlight in the hallway could provide enough light should he stir, and she walked slowly back toward the living room. Nolan was sitting on the couch, his mug on the table in front of him.

"Your hot chocolate is cold," he commented. "Can I reheat it for you?"

She shook her head. "It's okay, I'm used to that."

A distant look passed through his eyes as he nodded and gave a short laugh. "Yeah, I bet. Seems that when you have kids nothing is ever eaten or drunk hot or chilled, right? Room temperature is your best friend."

Was he talking about his own child, his own life? He seemed to understand what it was like. Raina couldn't speak for fear that she'd just come straight out and ask him about the little she'd overheard about his wife and kid, but a sense of self-preservation made her hold her tongue. She wasn't even sure that she wanted to know. She knew that made her sound selfish, at least in her own mind.

She drank her lukewarm chocolate and let Nolan steer the conversation to a review of the evening's performance. And while she laughed and talked and agreed with him, she found herself thinking how very much she wished this kind of evening could become a regular event for them. She looked at the clock, startled to see that another full hour had passed since she'd put JJ to bed.

Nolan followed her gaze and made an exclamation. "I'm sorry, I'm keeping you up."

Raina felt a flush of heat and awareness suffuse her body, along with a longing that when she went to bed, they could go together. She shoved the thought to the back of her mind. It was ridiculous. She needed to get her crazy hormones under control. Desire was clouding rationality, and it was that very rationality that got her through every day without falling apart. If she lost that, where would she be?

"Thanks for coming tonight," she said, standing up and putting the mugs on the tray to return them to the kitchen.

Nolan stood also and reached once more for the tray. His fingers brushed hers and her already jangling nerves surged to awareness, making her jerk the tray away.

"It's okay, I can manage," she insisted before turning away from him before he could see the rush of color that stained her cheeks.

Raina set the tray down on the kitchen counter and looked at her reflection in the dark window above. This was ridiculous. She'd barely seen him in the past week and a half and now she was a jittering mass of contradictions in his company. She'd told herself she was better off without him, that she didn't need a man like him in her life, but no matter what her head said, her body told a different story. Even now her breathing was slightly ragged and she felt aware of every brush of her clothing over her sensitized skin. If this was how she reacted when he did nothing more than touch her with a fingertip, she'd be a complete and utter mess if they went any further.

"Raina? You okay? I'm heading off now. Thanks for the drink."

She took a steadying breath and went back to the sitting room.

"You're welcome and thanks again for defusing that

situation with JJ before the pageant. I couldn't have done that without you."

"Only too happy to help out."

He walked toward the door and Raina followed. In the entranceway he paused a moment and then turned to face her.

"Raina, I meant what I said to you earlier tonight. Can I hope that you'll give me another chance to prove to you that I'm not all bad?"

Raina gave him a twisted smile. "I don't have a particularly good track record with bad men."

He smiled back in return but she could see the hurt in his eyes. The knowledge that she was categorizing him with the other deadbeats she'd fallen for in the past.

"Then let's set the record straight, together," he murmured and leaned forward.

She hadn't known he was going to kiss her, at least not consciously. But while her mind may have been slow on the uptake, her body certainly wasn't. She leaned into him, meeting him more than halfway and closing the gap between them. His arms wrapped around her, one hand lifting to spread through her hair.

The second his lips touched hers, she knew she was lost. What was life for if you couldn't take second chances? His lips upon hers were electric, sending a pulse of longing through her body that made her tremble in response. He tasted of hot chocolate and more. Of something darker, spicier, deeper and more forbidden. Logic told her she should pull back, end this. End all of it. But logic took a backseat to the sensation and the promise that poured through her body at this gentlest of caresses.

Raina raised her hands to Nolan's chest. Was it a subconscious attempt to keep some barrier between them, or was it so she could feel the hard strength of his lean muscles beneath the finely woven cotton of his shirt? Her hands tingled as she touched him, as her fingers spread out and her palms soaked up his heat. She ached to feel his skin, to touch him all over, but she daren't ask him to stay. It was too soon. Too much. And she still had far too many questions.

When Nolan pulled back and let his hands drop away from her, Raina felt physically bereft.

"I'll call you tomorrow, okay?" he said, stepping away and opening the front door.

Words failing her, Raina could only nod. After he'd closed the door behind him she stood there for several minutes, the fingertips of one hand pressed to her lips as if she could hold on to the moment—the sweetness, the promise—they'd just shared. But, like everything good in her life, the sensation was a fleeting one, gone before she heard his car start up outside and pull away from the curb.

She wanted him. She knew that. Acknowledged it with an honesty that brought tears to her eyes. But could she have him? Dare she?

Only time would tell.

Thirteen

If the staff at the sheriff's office thought that Nolan looked like someone who'd pulled an all-nighter then that's probably because he had. When he caught sight of his reflection in the outer doors, the red eyes and scruffy jaw, he grimaced. Certainly not his usual *GQ*-style appearance but then it wouldn't be the first time Nolan had looked a bit frayed around the edges.

He'd never felt quite as invested in the result of his work as he had with what he'd done last night. The work itself, and his reasons for doing it, had made one thing abundantly clear to him. He wasn't falling in love with Raina Patterson. He was already there. He loved her. There was no question about it. Yes, it was fast; yes, it had surprised him; and, yes, he'd fought it. But it's what had kept him going at about two this morning when he was questioning his sanity in finding out all there was to know about Jeb Pickering.

Raina was his reason for being here—both at the sheriff's office and in Royal altogether. While his work had sent him here, she was what would keep him. He only needed to convince her of that fact. A cakewalk, right? He snorted under his breath and earned a stern glance from a passing deputy.

"Can I help you, sir?" a woman behind the front counter asked.

"Yes, I know I don't have an appointment but I need to see the sheriff, if he's in. It's urgent."

"Just about every man coming in to see the sheriff says the same thing," she answered with a roll of her eyes. "Your name?"

Nolan gave it and thought he saw a glimpse of recognition in the woman's eyes.

"Howard Dane's boy?"

He nodded. He might be a grown man but he'd always be his father's son in this town—and proud of it, he realized. "Yes, he's my dad."

The receptionist nodded. "Take a seat over there. I'll see if Sheriff Battle's available."

Nolan sat down on a hard vinyl-covered seat against the wall and drummed his fingers on his leg. He was lucky he didn't have to wait long.

"Nolan Dane?" The sheriff had come out to the reception area himself. "Welcome home."

"Thanks," Nolan answered, rising to his feet and offering his hand.

"What brings you to my office?"

"Can we talk in private?"

"Sure, c'mon back."

Once they were seated in a private room, Nolan didn't waste any time.

"I have information on a man named Jeb Pickering. He's got a long list of convictions for petty crime but right now he's wanted in New Mexico on third-degree felony charges."

"Tell me more," Sheriff Battle said, leaning forward with his elbows on the desk between them.

"He's the ex-partner of Raina Patterson, who runs Priceless out at the Courtyard."

The sheriff nodded. "Yeah, I know her. Lost her store in town in the tornado. Brave woman. Has a little boy. He'd be about three now, I guess."

Nolan was impressed that the man could recall one of the people of Royal so easily, but then again that's probably why Nate Battle was reelected each term. He cared. Nolan was counting on that to help him rid Raina of Jeb's shadow forever.

"That's the one. Pickering skipped out on her but keeps coming back for handouts. Seems he has a bit of trouble with gambling and drinking."

"Not the best of combinations but not necessarily a crime, unfortunately."

"No," Nolan agreed. "However, we can now add manslaughter while driving under the influence of alcohol and skipping bail to his list of charms."

The sheriff let out a low whistle. "I see. And you know this how?"

Nolan quickly explained, showing the sheriff the information he'd gathered. After reading it carefully, the sheriff looked up.

"D'you know where he is now?"

"Not exactly, but I know where he'll be tonight."

The anger he was feeling at Jeb Pickering's callous disregard of life added cold hard inflection to his words as Nolan outlined his confrontation with Pickering last night.

"So he thinks you'll be there to give him money so he can head on his way out of state again." The sheriff nodded. "I think we can work with you."

"I was hoping you'd say that." Nolan smiled and leaned back in his chair.

"Give me the details and I'll get a couple of my men together, and I'll alert the New Mexico authorities that their chicken will be coming home to roost."

Nolan stamped his feet against the cold as he waited in the parking area for Jeb to show. So far Nolan hadn't seen a sign of anyone, although he had every confidence that Nate Battle and his men were nearby.

The skitter of a stone on the pavement made Nolan turn around.

"Pickering," he acknowledged as the man slipped out from the shadows.

"You got my money?"

Nolan ignored his request. "I've been doing a bit of research on you, man. It seems you're a wanted criminal."

Jeb's face turned nasty. "What the hell do you know? I've been doing a bit of research of my own. You're just some fancy-pants lawyer who couldn't even keep his wife and son alive. Now give me my money," he demanded as he yanked one hand from his pocket and shoved it in Nolan's direction.

Nolan fought to ignore the man's gibe but even so, it cut deep. The truth always did. He forced himself to focus—to do what was right for Raina. Yes, he might not have been able to save Bennett and Carole, but he'd be damned if he ever saw another person he loved hurt when he could do something about it.

He took a step closer to Jeb. "Turn yourself in, man. You know the authorities are going to catch up with you sooner or later."

"Not if I get to Mexico they won't. With that money I reckon I can disappear for a while."

"Oh, you'll disappear for a while, all right," Nolan

agreed as he spied Nate Battle and a couple of his deputies move silently up behind Jeb.

Jeb grinned, but then he realized that Nolan's words had held a double entendre. "Whaddya mean?"

"I mean there is no money. Not from me and not from Raina either."

Jeb started to swear and launched himself forward at Nolan, both fists now swinging in fury. Nate and his deputies closed the distance between them and wrestled him to the ground, but not before a punch caught the edge of Nolan's jaw making his head snap back. But one shot was all the other man got and it was with a great deal of satisfaction that Nolan watched the deputies cuff Jeb and haul him to his feet to read him his rights then lead him to their car—as he loudly and energetically protested the whole way.

"I think we can add resisting arrest to his list of charges, don't you?" Nate Battle commented as he straightened his jacket.

"Yeah," Nolan said, rubbing his fingers along his jaw where Jeb's fist had connected.

"You want to press charges for that?"

"No." Nolan shook his head. "I'm pretty sure he has enough charges against him now to ensure that he won't bother Raina again."

The sheriff gave him a piercing look. "Like that is it? You're soft on Raina Patterson?"

Nolan nodded.

Nate reached out a hand to Nolan. "As I said this morning, good to have you back in Royal."

Nolan shook the sheriff's hand. "Thanks. It really is good to be back."

"I guess we'll be seeing more of you."

"If you mean, am I staying in town, the answer is yes. And I'm rejoining dad's practice, too."

"That's good. We need men like you and your dad fighting for the vulnerable people in this town."

With that, Nate tipped his hat and turned and walked toward his car.

Nolan stood there in the darkness, oblivious now to the cold that whipped around him. Home. He really was home again and he had the approval of the sheriff. It probably didn't get much better than that in terms of acceptance. There was just one more obstacle to overcome. Raina. He'd taken care of her past, now he needed to share his own. And for the life of him, he didn't know how he was supposed to do this right.

Raina checked the floor safe in the shop for the umpteenth time to reassure herself the money she was holding for Jeb was still there. Well, where else would it be? She closed the door and spun the dial before pulling the trap door down over it again. It had been a couple of days since she'd promised him she'd have the money ready. It wasn't like him not to show and the waiting was making her jumpy.

Even his phone calls and texts had stopped. So what on earth had happened to him? She didn't dare hope that he'd left and forgotten all about it. That wasn't his style at all.

Raina got to her feet and went over to the cheval mirror she had propped in the corner of her small office and checked her appearance. Nolan was picking her up soon and taking her out for dinner. Her dad had JJ at his place for one of their much anticipated Saturday nights together and for some stupid reason Raina felt more nervous about tonight than she had on her very first date with a boy.

This is Nolan, she kept telling herself. *You know him. You trust him...mostly.* She shook her head. She trusted him, she just didn't know everything she needed to know about him yet. There was a difference. Of course he had secrets, so did she, didn't she? She sighed. Maybe that was her trouble. She trusted too darn easily.

She studied her reflection in the mirror. The long floral skirt she'd teamed with a pair of high black boots made her feel feminine and pretty, although after a day on her feet, her toes were beginning to complain. It'd be worth it, she'd told herself as she examined her reflection and smoothed the soft sweater she'd chosen over her hips. She didn't often wear black but the contrast between the sweater and her creamy skin brought out the light in her eyes. Noticing her makeup could definitely do with a touch-up, she grabbed her makeup bag from her purse and made a few running repairs, eager to look her best for the man who continued to send her pulse flying.

The bell chimed out front and she quickly shoved her makeup bag back into her purse and went out into the shop, a smile already stretching her lips.

"Nolan, you're early!" she exclaimed.

"Would it sound ridiculous if I said I couldn't wait to see you?"

He bent and kissed her cheek and even though the touch was about as innocent as you could get, Raina immediately felt her body flare to aching life. She wanted him so much and it was quite clear to her that he felt the same way.

But why didn't he tell her about his wife and son?

Oh, sure, she could come right out and ask him, but she strongly felt that this was Nolan's story to tell on his own terms—even if waiting didn't sit comfortably with her. She'd learned the hard way not to push a man for the truth. In the past, and with Jeb in particular, men had only told her what they thought she wanted to hear. She didn't want to travel down that road with Nolan. He'd tell her about his family when he was ready, she reminded herself for the umpteenth time.

She pushed the niggling thoughts to the back of her mind, determined to enjoy his company tonight.

"I've been looking forward to tonight, too."

"Is there anything I can do to help you lock up?" Nolan asked.

"No, I'm just about finished. It's been quiet today. I guess not everyone wants to buy antiques for Christmas."

"I'd say that was a shame but if it means we get to spend more time together, who am I to complain?"

Nolan smiled at her but Raina's attention was caught by a dark bruise on the edge of his jaw. She raised a hand and gently touched the mark with her fingertips.

"What on earth have you been up to to get this?" she asked.

Nolan grabbed her hand and kissed her fingertips before letting it go again. "It's nothing. Something just flew up and hit me when I wasn't expecting it."

She searched his face, but he just smiled at her in return.

"Are you ready to go? We can get a drink before the movies if we leave now."

"Sure," she shrugged. "I doubt I'll get any last-minute customers at this stage of the day."

Raina grabbed her jacket and set the alarm system before they left through the front door. She shivered as the cold air outside cut through her.

"It almost feels as if it could snow," she commented as Nolan held open his car door for her and helped her up into the SUV.

"Yeah, it might. But even if it does, I doubt it'll stick. You know what it's like around here this time of year."

They made small talk in the car, mostly discussing JJ and how excited he was about Christmas being only six days away. Nolan was good company, the best male company she'd ever had, she decided. If only he'd open up about his past.

The movie was a comedy, and Raina was glad because she loved to hear Nolan laugh—which he did, loudly and often. Afterward, they walked to a nearby Italian place she'd never been to before. The proprietors greeted Nolan like a long lost son and she didn't miss the glance that passed between the Italian couple when Nolan introduced her.

They were shown to a secluded table with low lighting and the ubiquitous red checkered tablecloth and a candle inserted in a used Chianti bottle.

"This is lovely," Raina commented as they studied their menus. "Do you come here often?"

"Not in a long time," he admitted. "It used to be a favorite."

A favorite with his wife perhaps? Maybe that explained the owners' slightly uncomfortable expressions when he'd introduced her.

"So, can you recommend anything?"

"Let's see," Nolan drawled, running his eyes across the menu card. "The veal scalloppini is always good, especially if you're not crazy about pasta. Hell, I didn't think. You do like Italian food, don't you? I just assumed—"

"I love Italian food, and the scalloppini sounds perfect," she hastened to reassure him.

"Okay. What about an appetizer?" he prompted.

"You choose. I'm pretty much okay with everything."

He nodded and beckoned the waiter over, ordering them a platter of antipasto to start, followed by the veal and a bottle of Chianti to go with it.

Raina was feeling decidedly mellow by the end of the evening. The movie, the food and the company had all been incredible, and when Nolan drove back to her house she knew what her next step was.

"Will you come inside?" she asked as they sat in the car in the pitch-dark night.

"I'd like that," Nolan agreed, and together they walked up the front path to her house.

Inside, she hung their coats up and led him to the sitting room. Her heart was beating double time. She knew what she wanted, but was it what he wanted, too?

"Did you want a nightcap, or a coffee?"

Nolan only shook his head and reached for her, pulling her into his arms. "No, I only want you."

"Then we're in agreement," she said softly, feeling a run of excitement deep inside. "Because I want you, too."

She cupped his face and pulled it down to hers and kissed him with all the pent-up longing she'd harbored since their kiss on Thursday night. Instantly her body leaped to life, her nipples tightening into hard nubs and her breasts growing full and heavy. She pressed against his chest, as if that could somehow ease the aching demand, but instead it only heightened it.

Nolan's hands splayed across her back, holding her to him as if they could be molded together forever. One hand drifted to her lower back and pulled her body more firmly against his. The hard ridge of his arousal pressed against her, sending a thrill of anticipation throughout her entire body and ending in a pulse of longing that centered at her core.

"I want to touch you," she whispered against his mouth. "All of you."

She tugged at his shirt, pulling it from the waistband of his trousers and pushing her hands underneath. His skin was smooth and hot, and he shuddered at her touch. Raina forced herself to draw away slightly so she could work his buttons loose. Eventually she succeeded and she pushed the fabric wide open, exposing his tanned skin. A light dusting of hair peppered his chest before narrowing in a tempting path down his abdomen and lower. She traced that line with her fingers and felt his stomach muscles contract beneath her touch.

"Raina, I—"

Whatever he'd been about to say was lost as she leaned forward and pressed her lips to one nipple, her tongue swirling around the smooth disc and teasing its tip into a taut bud. She raked her nails lightly across the other, eliciting a groan of need from deep inside him. The sound gave her a sense of power and she took her time exploring his upper body with her hands, her mouth, her tongue. When Nolan pulled her up to kiss him again, she was one hot mess of need, and when his hands drifted to the waistband of her top she didn't hesitate to let him remove it for her.

Nolan backed her toward the couch and gently guided her down before joining her there. He held himself up on one elbow as he traced the lacy cup of her bra. His eyes looked darker than usual, his pupils almost consuming the brown of his irises, and a light flush of color stained his cheekbones.

"You are so beautiful," he murmured before leaning down and tracing a line in the valley of her breasts with his tongue.

It was what she wanted and yet it still wasn't enough. Raina squirmed against him, desperate to ease the insistent demand of her body. Nolan reached behind her, unsnapped the clasp of her bra and gently tugged the garment away from her before dropping it to the carpet.

For a moment Raina felt self-conscious. She had stretch marks all over her body, silvered now, but a continuing reminder of the son she'd borne. But her insecurity soon vanished as Nolan paid homage to her breasts, teasing first one tip, then the other, with his mouth and tongue. As he drew one into his mouth and suckled hard, she felt a spear of pleasure drive through her body, almost sending her over the edge. She'd never felt so responsive.

She murmured his name as he worked his way down, tracing the lines of her rib cage with his strong fingers and following each touch with a kiss, a lick, a suck of his mouth. Her nerves were screaming for more and she squirmed under his sensual assault. She'd never felt this much before. Never wanted another human being like she wanted him.

Her body felt empty, demanding to be filled, to be led to the precipice of the pleasure she knew she'd find under his touch. Nolan pulled away and she made a sound of protest, which he silenced with a swift kiss.

"Just making you more comfortable," he said, and then he reached for her boots.

He undid first one, then the other, easing them off her feet and peeling away her stockings and tossing them to the floor to join her top and her bra. When Nolan reached for the fastening on the side of her skirt and eased the zipper down, she lifted her hips, allowing him to slide the garment off.

Dressed only in her panties, she was assailed by a sense of awkwardness and moved her hands in an attempt to cover herself. Nolan merely caught her wrists in gentle fingers and pulled her hands away.

"Don't," he admonished. "I meant what I said before. You're beautiful. Every. Inch. Of you." He punctuated his words with a kiss on her belly. Her hips. The edge of her panties.

Raina let her head drop back against the arm of the couch and closed her eyes, giving herself over to the delicious sensations that poured through her. One moment Nolan's hands and mouth were at the edge of her panties and the next her panties were gone and she could feel the heat of his breath against the soft skin of her inner thighs.

He pressed a wet kiss against her skin, and then blew out cool air. She shivered as anticipation threatened to destroy her mind even as her body coiled in hope and eagerness, awaiting his next touch. She wasn't disappointed. His fingers traced a delicious line from her hip to her groin and back again before moving ever so slowly lower.

She knew she was wet and ready for him and yet when his fingers parted her outer lips and traced the entrance of her body she almost jolted right up off the couch.

"Too much?" he asked softly.

"No, not too much. Never too much," she gasped.

She forced herself to relax and let her thighs fall open, giving him easier access to the secrets of her body. When he eased one finger inside her she murmured her approval and clenched against him involuntarily, sending delight spiraling outward from where he touched.

"You feel so good," Nolan said, his voice growing huskier by the minute.

"You make me feel so much," Raina countered breathlessly.

She could feel her climax hovering just on the periphery and knew, without a doubt, that it wouldn't take much more to send her on a trajectory of pleasure that would shatter her into a million pieces. Nolan eased his finger from her body and then reentered her with two. She loved the sense of fullness it gave her, and as he brushed against that magical part of her, she felt the first pull of orgasm.

Her last rational thought was of his mouth closing over her, of his tongue rolling around the tight bead of nerve endings at her center and of the draw of his mouth as he pushed her gently over the edge and tumbling headlong into bliss.

Nolan gathered her into his arms as the final waves of satisfaction petered away into lassitude, and he lifted her off the couch. She made no protest as he carried her down the hallway and deposited her in her bed, but it wasn't until he pulled the comforter up over her naked body that she realized he didn't intend to join her there, or stay.

"Nolan?" she asked, reaching out for him. "We haven't finished."

He bent and pressed his lips to hers. "We have—for tonight."

"But you… I…" She was lost for words to describe the imbalance of what had happened.

"It's okay. Now sleep. Tomorrow's another day. I'll let myself out."

This wasn't how she'd imagined things ending tonight at all, Raina thought as she lay in the darkness and heard the front door close, shortly followed by the sound of Nolan's car driving away. And, while her body was sated, she still felt as though an essential ingredient was missing. She reached across the vacant expanse of her bed and realized that she already missed him. And still she didn't have the truth.

Fourteen

Raina spent the next few days in a blur of confusion about her feelings for Nolan. Their evening together had been wonderful, truly so. And he'd made her feel cherished and special and all those things that she'd decided, after Jeb, were nonnegotiable. But high on her list was honesty, too. Was withholding things about himself the same as being dishonest? She began to worry that the longer it took, the less likely it was she was going to hear about his past from him. And Raina knew she didn't want to hear it from anyone else.

Even so, it didn't stop her from looking forward to seeing him as she had at lunch on Monday, and then for a quick coffee yesterday afternoon. Her father had cautioned her about rushing into things too fast, with a reminder about where that had left her the last time, and she'd acknowledged his concerns. After all, hadn't he been the one to stand by her through all the fallout from each previous disastrous relationship?

The thought brought her back to Jeb. There had still been no contact from him and when she attempted to call his cell phone, it was disconnected.

At least there were still some things in her life she kept a handle on. She smiled to herself as she adjusted the Christmas display in her store window. The antique Santa and the child's sled had garnered a great deal of comment from passersby, bringing them into the store and boosting her small-ticket item sales quite comfortably. And the sled itself had sold, too—with the new owner planning to pick it up before New Year's Eve.

All in all, her December sales had been very strong. Factoring in the success of her craft lessons, things were definitely looking up for the New Year. Which reminded her, she needed to finalize the newsletter she'd be sending out with the new classes and timetables for January.

Outside the store, a car pulled up in the parking area and Raina noticed a young woman alight. She recognized the petite blonde instantly—Clare Connelly. Raina waved as Clare started to walk toward Priceless.

"Good morning," Raina said with a welcoming smile as she opened the door for her. "Have a day off?"

Clare's role as chief pediatric nurse at Royal Memorial Hospital kept her very busy but if anyone could handle busyness with a liberal dose of chaos, it was Clare. Her no-nonsense approach to her work was well-known around Royal and she held the respect of everyone who'd had babies under her care.

"I'm on a late shift tonight but I needed to get some last-minute Christmas shopping done. I need something special for my elderly neighbor. She's such a darling."

"Does she collect anything in particular?" Raina asked as they walked deeper into the store.

Clare wrinkled her brow in concentration. "Not anything specific. Do you mind if I look around for a bit? I'm not 100 percent sure of what I want but I'm hoping I'll recognize what I'm looking for when I see it."

"Sure," Raina said with a smile. "Holler if you need me. I'll just be out back, okay?"

"Thanks," Clare answered as she turned away with a distracted look on her face.

It wasn't like Clare to be indecisive, Raina thought as she pottered around in the back of the store, wielding her dusting cloth and giving some of the larger pieces of furniture a rub with furniture oil. After a few minutes, she looked up at Clare, who'd barely moved from where she left her. The other woman was staring blankly at a Royal Albert tea set as if she was waiting for some genie to waft out of the teapot's spout or something.

Raina worked her way back toward Clare.

"Are you sure I can't help you find something?"

Clare started and gasped in surprise. "Oh, I'm sorry. I was a million miles away. Yes," she said on a sigh. "I would be glad of your help. I know my neighbor has a thimble collection that she's added to ever since she was a little girl. She used to be quite skillful with a needle and thread from what I understand, and most of the thimbles are well used, but her eyesight's deteriorated as she's grown older, and she's developed arthritis and can't work with her hands anymore."

"That's a shame," Raina sympathized. "We have some beautiful handcrafted lace and linen doilies here from the early 1900s. Do you think she'd be interested in them?"

"They sound gorgeous. Show me."

Raina brought Clare over to a large mahogany sideboard and glass-fronted hutch that she used to showcase several of her better pieces of china. She slid open a drawer and removed a tissue-wrapped package. Her hand shook a little as she remembered the last time she'd handled the doilies, and how she'd almost used one to mop ice cream off the front of Nolan's trousers. A smile curved her lips at the memory. How much further had they come since then? Raina unwrapped the tissue and spread the doilies on the gleaming wooden surface of the sideboard.

"They're rather beautiful, don't you think?"

Each one had a round, finely woven linen center and a painstakingly created lace edge. There were four in total, each one slightly different in pattern from the other but with a floral theme that took Raina's breath away every time she looked at them. Such craftsmanship, such patience. She envied the woman who'd created them because she doubted she would ever have been able to have produced such exquisite work.

"They're gorgeous! And they're perfect. Thank you. I should have known you'd find exactly what I needed," Clare said on a note of relief.

"It's my job to make sure you do." Raina smiled back at her. "Clare, I hope you don't mind me saying this, but you don't seem yourself. Is everything okay?"

"Oh, it's nothing in particular. I'm just really stressed with the reorganization of the neonatal unit at the hospital. I'm sure the pressure will drop a little once the new wing is open next month. It's been a tough year."

Raina nodded. "But we're getting through it."

Clare looked at her and smiled. "Yes, we are. We're nothing if not determined, right?"

Raina smiled back. "Would you like me to gift wrap the doilies for you?"

"Would you? That would save me the bother, thank you."

"Come on over to the counter…unless you'd like to keep browsing?"

"Maybe I'll come in some other time and have a good poke around. Perhaps a day when I'm a bit less distracted," Clare laughed.

"Good idea," Raina agreed and walked over to the counter where she rewrapped the doilies in fresh tissue and put them in a gold box that she covered in a vibrant Christmas paper. "There you are," she said as she finished tying a red bow around the box.

"That looks far better than anything I would have done," Clare said admiringly.

"I get a bit more practice. I'm sure you can still diaper and swaddle a baby faster and more effectively than I ever could."

"You could be right," Clare conceded. "How is JJ?"

"He's doing really great, thanks. Of course he can barely sleep for counting the nights until Christmas."

"Good thing there are only two more to go."

"For my sake as well as JJ's," Raina agreed vehemently.

A thought occurred to Raina. She knew Clare was about the same age as Nolan and probably went to the local high school at around the same time as he would have. She'd told herself she wouldn't probe into his past, but with the opportunity presenting itself, maybe it was time she did a little poking around.

"Say, do you remember Nolan Dane?"

"Nolan? Yeah, sure. Why?"

"You know he was working on behalf of Samson Oil, don't you?"

Clare's mouth twisted into moue of distaste. "Yeah, I know. Seems like Royal is evenly divided about whether Samson Oil is a good thing or not."

Raina nodded. "I know. But he resigned from that position. He's going back to family law."

Clare's face brightened. "Is he? That's great. I know everyone around here was so shocked when he left. Of course, it was totally understandable after what he'd been through but no one really expected him to leave. He'd always been so woven into the fabric of Royal, y'know? Excelled at high school—popular and great at sports. It didn't matter what he put his hand to, he did it brilliantly. Our Nolan was quite the golden boy but never arrogant about it. Everyone liked him."

"What he'd been through?" Raina prompted, even though her stomach curled at what she might be told. Being nosy like this was wrong on so many levels—what if she didn't like what she heard? Raina forced herself to clear her mind of anxiety. Yes, this was Nolan's tale to tell, but to be honest, she was done with waiting. She wanted to know. And she'd have to take whatever she heard and deal with it.

"Oh, you don't know, do you? I keep forgetting that you didn't grow up here. That's a compliment by the way," Clare said with a warm smile. "Like I said, Nolan was always a high achiever but so was Carole, his high school sweetheart. They went to college together and then on to law school. Once they got their degrees they came back to Royal and married, and a year later they had a little boy, Bennett. Nolan and Carole were the couple everyone wanted to emulate. They were successful, sure, but they were also so in love. You couldn't look at them without feeling it."

Raina felt each one of Clare's words as if it was a physical blow but she tried hard not to linger on the pain. He'd had a life before she'd met him. So what on earth had gone wrong?

Clare continued, oblivious to the turmoil Raina was going through. "Carole returned to work soon after Bennett was born and I think he was about eighteen months old when it happened."

Raina hesitated to ask but couldn't help herself. "What happened?"

"It was awful. Apparently Nolan used to take Bennett to day care each morning as part of their routine. This particular day he heard that one of his clients had been severely beaten by her husband the night before. She called and asked him to come into the hospital to see her early, so he did. Of course that meant that Carole had to take Bennett to day care. Trouble was, she was in the middle of some really important negotiations her firm was handling at the same time and apparently she got paged while she was driving. She called her office and completely forgot Bennett was in the back of her car. They think he'd probably fallen asleep, too. Carole drove straight to her office and went to work. It was July and her car was parked in direct sunlight. Bennett died of heat exhaustion."

Raina gasped in horror. She'd heard of forgotten baby syndrome and, while she'd never understood it, she could only imagine how unbelievably awful it would be to have it happen to you.

"Did no one at the day care call to see where the baby was?" she asked.

"Apparently they had a new staff member on and they failed to figure it out at first. It wasn't until lunchtime that someone mentioned him. By then it was too late. Of course, the police were sympathetic but they had to bring charges of manslaughter and felony child abuse. It was just an awful time and it divided a lot of the people here.

"Poor Carole, she couldn't live with what she'd done. Before their case even got to court she took her life. Six months after that Nolan was gone, too—to LA, where he's been ever since."

"No wonder he didn't come back," Raina sympathized. "It must have been awful for him to lose them both."

Clare nodded. "It was a sad time for everyone who knew them but, of course, most of all for him."

The old grandfather clock near the front door chimed the hour and Clare glanced at it in consternation.

"Oh, heck, is that the time? I really need to get going. Thanks so much for the help with the Christmas gift,

Raina. I really appreciate it." She cocked her head and looked at Raina with a funny expression on her face. "You know, you actually look a bit like Carole. Same coloring and similar features. You could almost have passed for sisters. She was beautiful, too. Thanks again!"

Clare was gone in a whirlwind of movement, leaving Raina alone with her thoughts. Her heart ached for Nolan's loss. She didn't even want to begin to imagine what it would be like to lose JJ; just thinking about it was enough to bring tears to her eyes. But hearing Nolan's story brought a lot of things into sharper focus. Like his confidence and ability with her son and his patience. Those were all characteristics of someone who was used to being with a child.

She could almost understand him keeping his past to himself, but for one thing—her similarity to his late and obviously much beloved wife. Was that why he thought he was falling in love with *her*? Was it simply that she and JJ represented all that he'd lost? Were they merely substitutes for the wife and son that had been torn so tragically from his life?

It was impossible to know for sure, at least until he really talked to her. But how could she encourage him to do that? And what would she do if her fears were well-founded? Could she turn him away? It would break her heart if she did, and wouldn't she be breaking his all over again, too? He'd already lost his wife and son. But, she asked herself, could she live her life with him, knowing that he didn't love her for herself, but instead loved her for what she represented to him?

She'd promised herself to never again put herself last in a relationship—that things needed to be on an equal footing or no footing at all. She wouldn't settle for being second best. Which left her where, exactly, with Nolan?

Raina groaned out loud and squeezed her eyes shut. What on earth was she going to do?

Nolan walked up the path to Raina's house on Christmas Eve, ready to collect her and JJ to take them to the service at the nearby church. He'd debated with himself, long and hard, before accepting Raina's invitation to go with them. The last time he'd been here in Royal at Christmas, both Carole and Bennett had been alive. Bennett had been a year old and had been a complete handful in church. Not quite walking but active enough to want to be kept busy through the entire service. The memories were still so bittersweet and painful and yet, today at least, thinking about that time didn't bring the searing shaft of pain it used to. He missed them so very much, but he'd learned he needed to move forward with his life a long time ago. The irony that his moving forward had brought him full circle, and back home, wasn't lost on him.

From the other side of the front door, Nolan could hear JJ's excited chatter as he and Raina got ready. After he rapped his knuckles on the door, JJ's excited shout of "No'an!" came through clear as a bell. Nolan felt his lips turn up in a smile that dispelled any of the lingering doubt or sorrow he'd felt about attending the service tonight. He couldn't help but admit it. It was more than nice to be wanted.

And he wanted in return. Raina opened the door wearing a vibrant red wool coat that complemented her fair skin and dark hair perfectly. He took in her appearance and a jolt of lust rocked him. Since he'd left her in her bed last Saturday, he'd been walking around in a state of semiarousal that had tormented and excited him in equal proportions. He'd wanted nothing more than to make love with Raina that night, to stay wrapped in the comfort of her arms and her body through the dark hours and to wake with her in the morning and know that she was his. But he felt their relationship was still so new, so tenuous, that he'd needed to at least try to take things slower. To allow her time to ease into what he hoped would be their future together before taking what he knew would be an almighty step for them both.

Raina had been hurt before, badly. And he'd hurt her, too. He knew it and regretted it with almost every waking thought. So it was up to him to re-earn her respect. To give her space and time to know that she could love him as much as he already knew he loved her. Which, in a nutshell, meant a whole lot of self-denial on his part. Still, he reminded himself, it didn't hurt a man to be prepared. He patted his jacket pocket and felt the small parcel there. He'd carried it around for a couple of days now, debating when would be the right time, keeping it with him always should the opportunity present itself.

"No'an!" JJ launched himself through the front door and off the top step straight into Nolan's arms.

Nolan caught the little boy and swung him in the air, laughing even as Raina chided the boy for not saying hello properly. After whirling a giggling JJ around Nolan tucked him up on one hip and smiled at Raina.

"Good evening. I take it you're both ready?" he said on a laugh.

"As ready as we'll ever be," Raina said and smiled back.

"No'an! Santa's coming tonight!" JJ squealed excitedly.

"So I hear," Nolan replied, giving the little boy his full attention. "Have you been a good boy all year, JJ?"

For a moment JJ's forehead wrinkled in a frown, then his expression smoothed. "Yup!"

"Then I guess tomorrow morning will be a whole lot of fun for you, won't it?"

"Yup." JJ leaned a little closer to Nolan and cupped a small hand in front of Nolan's ear. "Mommy has a present for you," he whispered loudly. "It's a secret."

Nolan looked at Raina, who was rolling her eyes.

"JJ Patterson, what did I tell you about secrets?"

"That you're not suppos'ta tell other people?"

"That's right."

"But No'an's not other people," JJ protested.

Raina's eyes met Nolan's and the look they shared deepened into something else. Something that made Nolan's heart swell on a note of hope.

"No, honey. Nolan's not other people. He's much more than that."

Silence stretched between them. Nolan wished he could do nothing else but kiss Raina right now. Long and hard and deep. He wanted to demand from her what "more than that" meant to her. But he had to satisfy himself with waiting. Down the street, they heard the church bells begin to chime.

"We'd better get going."

He carried JJ toward his SUV but Raina remained on the front path.

"Shouldn't we take my car? I have JJ's seat in there," she said.

Nolan opened the rear door of the SUV and gestured to the new car seat he'd had installed a couple of days ago.

"You bought a car seat?" she asked, her voice incredulous.

"I thought I ought to," he said simply. "Brand-new and ready for a test drive. How about it, champ?" he asked JJ. "You ready to hop in?"

In answer, JJ scrambled into the car seat and waited to be buckled in.

"You want to check he's secure?" Nolan asked Raina,

who was standing on the sidewalk, a bemused expression on her face.

"No, it's okay. I… I trust you."

The words were simple enough in their expression but they meant the world to Nolan. Now he had only to prove to her that she could trust him in all things—not only with her precious son, but with her heart, as well.

The service at the nearby church was well attended and, given that the congregation was primarily young families, it was kept simple and sweet and involved the children for much of it. He didn't miss the pointed glances Raina received from several people when they saw her at his side. The only sign that she'd noticed anything was the faintest of blushes on her cheeks.

But when the service was over, it was the words of one of the older parishioners that really made her blush.

"Raina Patterson, good to see you've seen sense and have found yourself a decent young man," the old woman said as they left the church with JJ holding both their hands between them.

"Mrs. Baker, Merry Christmas to you," Raina replied courteously, but Nolan could see she was embarrassed by the attention. "This is Nolan Dane. You might have heard of his father, Howard Dane?"

The old lady eyed Nolan up and down as if he was a prime cut of meat before smiling and giving him the benefit of the twinkle in her eye. "I remember teaching your father. He was quite the rascal in his day. Are you a rascal, young man?"

Nolan heard Raina's sharp intake of breath and laughed before replying. "Only when absolutely necessary, ma'am."

Mrs. Baker snorted. "Humph. Cheeky. Just like your father." She leaned across and whispered in Raina's ear. "I'd hold on to this one if I was you, young lady. Good men are hard to find."

Raina was clearly speechless and could do no more than nod. Nolan reached down and gave the old lady a kiss on her wrinkled cheek.

"Merry Christmas, Mrs. Baker. I'll pass your regards on to my dad."

"You do that, young man. You do that."

By the time they left the church and headed home, JJ was still wide-awake and more pumped up than ever. As they arrived at Raina's place, she turned to Nolan, her blue eyes troubled.

"I'm sorry about that, back at the church."

"What for? I enjoyed it."

He held her gaze and watched as the concern faded from her face.

"Hot choclik time!" JJ announced from the backseat.

"Are you coming in for a hot drink?" Raina offered.

"Just try and hold me back."

Inside, Raina put on the TV and tuned in to a channel showing Santa's progress from the North Pole. JJ sat and watched the radar blip on the screen as if his life depended on it.

"Straight to bed after your hot chocolate, JJ."

"Can I stay up and see Santa, Mommy. Please? I be good," JJ pleaded.

"Hey, champ, Santa's a bit of a shy guy. He won't come unless you're tucked up in bed and fast asleep," Nolan answered.

"He won't?" JJ's eyes grew huge.

Nolan assumed a solemn expression and shook his head. "Why don't you come up here and sit with me and tell me what you want for Christmas."

Raina threw Nolan a grateful look. "I'll be right back."

Nolan watched her go through to the kitchen, his eyes caught by the gentle sway of her hips as she walked. Her skirt was not so tight as to be indecent, but not so loose as to hide the perfect shape of her either.

"No'an, you listening to me?" JJ's voice broke through his thoughts.

"Sorry, champ. Yep, I'm listening. What did you ask Santa for?"

"I tol' Santa I want one thing more'n anything else."

"And what's that?"

"It's secret," JJ said with a little frown on his forehead. "Can't tell secrets."

"What about if you just whisper it to me. Like you did before."

JJ mulled over Nolan's suggestion and then got up onto his knees and, leaning against Nolan's shoulder, said in his ear. "I aks'd for you to be my daddy."

Nolan's heart skipped a few beats in his chest. As JJ settled back down beside him he put an arm around the little guy's shoulders to give him a hug. His eyes stung with emotion and the enormity of what JJ had just said.

A rattle of mugs on a tray made him realize that Raina had returned to the room and that she'd overheard JJ's wish for Christmas. She was staring at Nolan, her expression a combination of shock and yearning and something else he couldn't quite put his finger on. He wished he could read her better. Wished he could be sure that she wanted the same thing that JJ wanted.

He chose his next words very carefully.

"That's a mighty special wish, JJ. Being a daddy is a very precious gift. You know what precious is?"

JJ shook his head.

"It's something that means everything to you."

"Like Spider-Man?"

"Even more than that," Nolan said with a smile. "I hope you get your wish, champ, but it's a mighty tall order for poor old Santa."

* * *

Raina set the tray down on the table and passed JJ his small mug of hot chocolate and Nolan his larger one.

"There you go, guys."

She averted her gaze from the question in Nolan's eyes. It was too soon, she told herself, even though her heart and soul screamed otherwise. And, yes, while there was nothing physically holding them back, there was an emotional minefield between them that still needed to be successfully negotiated. How could she even think about the future when she wasn't sure that Nolan had dealt with the past?

She hadn't been lying earlier this evening when she said she trusted Nolan. He was exactly what Mrs. Baker had said—a good man. But if she was going to commit to him she needed better than good for her and JJ. She wanted all of him—all his scars, all his truths, all his fears as well as his successes. Not just the parts he was willing to share. It had to be everything, or nothing.

She had to be sure he wanted her for herself, not because she reminded him of his dead wife or because JJ gave him back the chance to be a dad when his own son had been so cruelly taken from him. They both deserved more than that. If Nolan could be honest with her, she knew she'd have no further hesitation in giving herself to him with everything she had. Having him in her and JJ's life was a glowing beacon of what their future could be like. Which made the prospect of turning away from it, from Nolan, terrifying in its enormity.

Fifteen

After Raina caught JJ yawning more than once, she hustled the little guy off to bed but he insisted on both Nolan and her tucking him in. It brought tears to her eyes when JJ's little arms wrapped around Nolan's neck and he hugged him tight before snuggling under the covers.

"Sweet dreams, champ," Nolan said gently as he disentangled JJ's arms.

"Love you, No'an" came JJ's sleepy reply.

Raina saw the look of shock on Nolan's face at JJ's words and watched as he smoothed JJ's hair off his forehead and pressed a kiss there.

As she followed Nolan out of the room and down the hall, her mind was in turmoil. It was already too late to protect JJ from heartache if she shut Nolan out of their lives. And did she even want to do that?

"I've got something for JJ in the car. Do you mind if I put it under the tree for him for tomorrow?" Nolan asked when they got to the living room.

"Oh, that's kind of you," she answered. "No, I don't mind at all. He'll be thrilled. But won't you be able to give it to him tomorrow yourself?"

"I'll be with my parents first thing, and after that I'm flying back to LA. There are some things I need to sort out."

Raina couldn't hold back the sound of dismay that escaped her. "Oh, I'd hoped…"

"I will return, Raina. I promise you that," he hastened to reassure her. "I'm taking the time now to pack up my apartment and settle a few matters before I move back here permanently. I'll be back for New Year's Eve."

She forced herself to smile. "I guess I'll have to be satisfied with that then."

He pressed a quick kiss to her lips. "I'll go get JJ's gift."

As Nolan went out to the car, Raina quickly retrieved JJ's gifts from where she'd hidden them in her room and put them under the tree. Once that was done, she sank down onto the sofa. She'd thought that life might get easier as she got older but it seemed that the complications only came in different forms. She had so much to consider. Did she, like JJ, love Nolan, too? The answer came back to her with resounding clarity. Yes, she did. Either way she turned it, it was clear to her that both she and her son had lost their hearts to the man who'd come into their lives so unexpectedly.

She heard Nolan come back into the house and stood as he entered the living room, an enormous wrapped parcel in his arms.

"Wow, that's huge. I hope you haven't gone to too much trouble," she said as she eyed the massive gift.

"No trouble at all. The first Christmas that I can remember, I was about JJ's age and got one of these. I always wanted to do the same for my—"

Raina frowned as his voice broke off. "For your…?"

she prompted. Maybe this would give him the opening to tell her everything.

"For another three-year-old," Nolan said on a rush of words. "It's a Spider-Man bike, with training wheels. It might still be a bit big for him but the seat and handle bars are adjustable and JJ's tall for his age. Anyway, I hope he likes it."

"He'll love it, but, Nolan, it's too much."

"No." He shook his head. "Where kids are concerned, it's never too much."

There was now a bleak note to his voice that Raina couldn't miss. She realized the holidays must be so hard for him and stepped forward to comfort him without giving it a second thought. Her arms slid around Nolan's waist and she reached up to kiss him gently on the lips.

"Thank you," she said simply. She studied him carefully, her eyes roaming his serious face with his beautiful brown eyes and straight blade of a nose. And those lips. She wanted to taste those lips again. She wanted... oh, she wanted so much more than that. "Will you stay with me tonight?"

Nolan's face grew even more serious than before. "Raina, I—" He shook his head. "I don't think that's a good idea just now."

"Please, Nolan. You could still stay with me a while tonight, couldn't you?"

Did she sound too needy? Too desperate? She hoped not. Raina held her breath, waiting for Nolan's reply.

"Yes, I'd like that."

"Then that makes two of us," she said with a slow smile spreading across her face.

Nolan kissed her. This kiss so different from the last. It was as if Nolan was trying to imprint himself on her, get lost in her, perhaps. Whatever it was, she welcomed him with equal fervor, her lips parting under his possession like the petals of a flower opening for the sun. Desire licked along her veins like wildfire and with it her body came to aching life.

Her breasts felt full and swollen in the cups of her bra, her nipples wildly sensitive against the lace. Nolan continued to kiss her like a man trying to lose himself in sensation, and Raina was only too willing to meet him head-on, matching his passion with her own.

She yanked his sweater up in the back and shoved her hands underneath, her palms flat on the warm smooth skin of his back. She stroked upward along the muscles that ran parallel to his spine then lightly scraped her nails down again. He shuddered in her arms, a groan coming from his mouth as he tore his lips from hers.

"Raina, I want you so much. I never thought I…" His voice trailed away and Raina pressed another kiss to his lips.

"Me either," she whispered softly against his mouth. "Make love with me, Nolan."

His pupils flared, making his eyes look darker, hungrier than she'd ever seen them. A shiver of need ran through her. Nolan was always so in control, so self-assured. She wanted to see him lose that control tonight, and she wanted to be the reason for it.

"Are you sure, Raina? There're things I haven't—"

Not tonight, not now, she decided. She didn't want another woman in bed with them tonight. Instead, she kissed him again. "I'm sure. I don't think I can say it any clearer than that."

A smile tugged at the corners of his beautiful lips. "I guess not," he agreed.

She shook her head and gave a small laugh. Even with her blood pumping through her body, her lips swollen from his kiss and her senses focused on the pleasure she knew she would attain with this man, he could make her laugh. It was a gift, she realized.

"Let's stop talking. Start doing," she urged, curling her fingers and embedding her nails in his back more firmly.

"Whatever the lady wants."

She led him to her bedroom where she gently closed the door behind them and flowed into his arms as if she belonged nowhere else in the world. And, right here, right now, she didn't.

His lips were teasingly gentle when they kissed this time. He made a sweet exploration of her mouth, her jaw, the sensitive cord of muscle down the side of her neck. She moaned as his lips burned a trail to the neckline of her blouse. He brought his hands up between them, his fingers busily plucking her buttons undone until he could ease the fabric aside. He pushed it off her shoulders and let her blouse drop to the bedroom floor.

Raina watched his face as he looked at her. The desire reflected there was tempered with a look of awe that made her feel invincible. As if his world, his attention, began and ended with her and no one else. This was what she'd always craved. A bond between two people that was so perfect that nothing could tear it apart.

Nolan eyes met hers and she quivered a little at the intensity of his gaze.

"I love you, Raina Patterson. I want you to know that before I show you just how much it's true."

She parted her lips to speak, but no words came out. Emotion closed her throat, making it impossible to speak, but he didn't appear to mind that at all as he slid his hands to her waist and skimmed them upward, his fingertips brushing her rib cage and sending goose bumps all over her skin.

He only took a second to size up the bed behind them. The double bed was small, but more than sufficient for their purposes, he thought as he backed Raina toward the mattress and guided her down onto it.

He eased himself over her body and, propping himself up with one elbow, began to trace featherlight designs on her skin with his fingertips, punctuating them with a kiss, a nibble, a swipe of his tongue. She quivered underneath his onslaught and he could see her pebbled nipples against the soft pink lace of her bra. He'd never been a big fan of pink, but right now it was most definitely his favorite color. Nolan bent to cover one tip with his mouth, sucking hard through the delicate lace. Raina's fingers threaded roughly through his hair and she held him to her. She arched her back, thrusting herself upward. Unabashedly offering herself to him.

Nolan released her nipple and traced the outline of her bra with his tongue. With his free hand he reached to cup her other breast before sliding his hand around to the back and unsnapping the fastening. The garment fell away from her body and he slowly guided the straps down her arms, taking his time, worshipping every inch of her as he did so. She shook beneath him as he paid homage to her beauty, to each scar he discovered, each stretch mark, every curve. When he got to her skirt, Raina lifted her hips so he could ease it from her and expose the delicate pink lace panties that matched the bra he'd already discarded somewhere on the floor.

Her body went rigid as he traced the edges of her panty line, his fingers lingering a moment in the hollow at the top of her thigh, eliciting a moan of delight from Raina. He bent closer to her, inhaling the musky sweet scent that was her signature, and nuzzled at her mound. He was rewarded with a gasp, her hands now at his shoulders, her fingers tightening until he could feel the imprint of her nails on his skin.

"I want to taste you, again," he murmured, nuzzling her.

"I'm yours," Raina replied, her voice strained and her body now as taut as a bow beneath him.

He whisked the last remaining barrier from her body and nestled lower between her legs, his fingers at the top of her thighs, pressing gently into her pale flesh and parting her legs that little bit more. When he sank down and teased her glistening flesh with a flick of his tongue, she moaned again—the sound almost enough to make him want to dispense with this foreplay and race straight to the main event. Inside his jeans his erection strained against the restriction of his clothing. He pressed his hips against the mattress in an attempt to relieve his body's demands but it was a short-lived respite.

To distract himself, he focused solely on the woman in his arms, intent on bringing her the kind of pleasure he dreamed of having the right to give her every day of her life. The taste and scent of her body filled him, exciting him to higher levels and driving him to see her every need fulfilled. He sensed that this—making love here in her bed—was the only time she wasn't holding back. Here in the sanctuary of her room, she was his alone and so he paid homage to the privilege she bestowed upon him. Loving her with every cell in his body until she arched beneath him, her body locked in paroxysms of pleasure before softening and sinking back down into the mattress.

Nolan swiftly stripped himself of his clothes and returned to her. His arousal demanded satisfaction but he waited until Raina's eyes cleared, until she was with him 100 percent.

"How do you do that?" she asked, sounding dazed.

"Give you pleasure, you mean?"

"Yes, that."

"I do it from my heart, Raina. I love you. It's that simple."

And with that, he eased his length within her, hissing a little between his teeth as her swollen wet sheath gripped him. It was almost more than he could stand but still he held himself in check. Raina's eyes were a glittering blue, punctuated by wildly dilated pupils. She met his gaze and reached for him, her hands gripping his hips and pulling him to her. He sank deeper into her body, deeper into pleasure, deeper into love, and with every stroke, every withdrawal, he affirmed that love until they both tumbled headlong into satisfaction.

Nolan watched Raina as she slept. They'd been about as close as two people could be. He didn't want to screw this up. It was too precious. Too important to him. He thought about the small package that was nestled at the bottom of his jacket pocket and the note he'd written to go with it.

The logical side of his brain told him that it was too soon to give it to her, but every other cell in his body told him to do it now. The thing was, he was ready—more than ready—to take the next step with her, to make her his forever. But was she? One word began to echo in the back of his mind. *Time.* He had to give her more time. And, he realized, he had to let her come to her decision at her own pace, without undue pressure from him.

Already he wished he didn't have to return to LA. There wouldn't be much to do. He'd barely existed when he'd lived there and he could tie up the loose ends within the week. Would a week be enough for Raina? Would it give her the time he felt she needed to be certain about them both and give them a chance to forge a future together? He certainly hoped so. And when he came back he needed to face his final demons. He needed to tell Raina about Carole and Bennett. He didn't want any secrets between them any longer. It had been one thing to convince himself that it was okay to hide his past, to bury it where it didn't hurt anymore, but Raina deserved to know everything and she deserved to know it from him.

Nolan eased from the bed and felt around in the dark for his clothes before slipping into the bathroom and quickly getting dressed. It was still pitch-dark outside and the sun wouldn't be up for at least another hour. Maybe it was wrong to be leaving her like this—letting her wake alone after all they'd shared together. But he also respected that she would need her space.

And then there was JJ to consider, as well. The little boy's Christmas wish had plucked at Nolan's heart and he'd wished he'd had the right to tell JJ that his wish could come true. He loved the child as if he was his own, there were no two ways about it. He wanted them both in his life but the decision lay firmly in Raina's gentle but capable hands.

Once he was dressed, Nolan walked through the house to the sitting room. The tree lights glittered with their myriad colors, making the small room look exotic and exciting. He knew it wouldn't be long before JJ wakened and raced to see what Santa had brought him. He wished he could be here to see JJ open his gifts, but with any luck he'd be able to share that delight with the little guy next year, and hopefully every year after that.

Nolan's heavy winter jacket lay over the back of an armchair where he'd discarded it last night. He reached into the pocket and pulled out the small gift and the envelope with the note he'd written for Raina before picking her and JJ up last night. He placed them under the tree, in among the gifts for JJ, then quietly let himself out of the house and into the burgeoning dawn.

Sixteen

"Santa's been here, Mommy. Wake up! Santa's been here!"

Raina opened one bleary eye then the other as JJ's joyful cries dragged her from sleep. She reached for Nolan, wondering how on earth they were going to explain his being there in bed with her, but her hand came up empty, the sheets cold beneath her touch. Raina quickly dragged on her nightgown and a robe and went to the living room where JJ was excitedly hopping from one foot to the other and staring at the bounty under the Christmas tree.

"Merry Christmas, JJ," she said, scooping her son up for a cuddle and a kiss. As she expected, he squirmed in her arms wanting to be put down to get to the serious business of opening gifts. "Remember the rules, JJ. Only one gift now. Granddad will be here to have breakfast with us and you can open all the rest then."

"Just one, Mommy?" JJ asked plaintively.

Raina held firm. She'd explained this all to JJ more than once in the days leading up to Christmas.

"How about you phone Granddad and let him know you're awake? He can let you know what time he'll be here."

JJ raced to do as she'd suggested, pressing the speed dial button on the phone Raina had taught him to use. After a brief conversation, he ran back to the Christmas tree. "Ten minnit!" he announced, hopping from one foot to the other.

"Great, now which gift are you going to open first?"

JJ zeroed in on the massive present Nolan had left under the tree for him. "This one," he said, and began tearing the paper off it immediately.

His squeal of delight was ear piercing when he saw the picture on the box. Raina hastened to help him open it and lift the bike out. There was a little assembly required but thankfully it only took a few minutes. Even better, Raina's dad arrived to do it all for her. He raised an eyebrow in her direction when he saw the bike, knowing it wasn't something she'd been able to afford for her son.

"It's from a friend, Dad," Raina said in explanation.

"Fancy wheels from a fancy man," he commented with a brusque nod, his eyes not budging from her face.

Raina felt the heat of a blush rise in her cheeks and she turned away from her father's piercing gaze.

"Now that you're here, I'll go and grab my shower and get dressed. Then I'll make us all breakfast, okay?"

Without waiting for a response, Raina flew down the hall toward the bathroom. She closed the door behind her and leaned against it for a few seconds, willing her blush to subside. Her father knew her too well. She'd seen that look on his face when she'd believed herself in love before. But this time it was different, she told herself. This time it was real.

Thankfully, her father didn't seem inclined to say any more on the subject, and after they'd had breakfast and opened all the presents under the tree, he went back to his place. Raina started to clean up the mess of wrapping paper and boxes that JJ had strewn all over the room in his exuberance. She'd hoped that he'd have happy memories of this day. Goodness knew she'd tried really hard to make it so. Right now, he was in his room, playing with some of his new toys until Raina could take him outside on the sidewalk with the new bike.

Raina almost missed the small parcel and envelope that had been placed at the tree's base. In fact it was already in her hand with the fistful of discarded paper when she felt it. After sorting through the paper and putting it in the trash bag, she sat down and looked at the items in her hand. Her pulse raced as she examined the small wrapped cube and the simple white envelope that accompanied it. Her name was written in bold black script across the front of the envelope and she traced the letters with a fingertip.

It wasn't her father's handwriting, which left only one other person who could have left it there—Nolan. Butterflies swarmed in her stomach, their tiny wings brushing against her nerves and making her hands tremble. What was this? Despite his words last night, could it be a farewell perhaps, or something else? There was only one way to find out but suddenly Raina found the prospect of reading whatever he had written more daunting than anything she'd ever done before.

Eventually she dragged in a deep breath and slid her finger under the flap of the envelope, tearing it open with a jagged edge. There was a single slip of paper inside, which she took out and unfolded.

Dear Raina,
I know we've only known one another a very short time, but believe me when I say that I'm very serious about wanting you in my life. I guess by now you've

realized that I have something very special to ask you. I wanted to ask you last night, but I know you probably need more time to think about this and to be sure, so I'm giving you this next week—unencumbered by my presence—to consider what we mean to one another and particularly what I mean to you.

For my part, I know I don't want to spend the rest of my life without you by my side. I've learned, the hard way, that the special things in life can be torn from you at a moment's notice and that we need to reach out and grasp those gifts when we can—to cherish them and hold them dear to us, the way I want to cherish and hold you.

I only hope that you want the same as I do and that you'll let me be there with you and JJ, loving and supporting you both for as long as you'll let me. Nothing would give me greater pride or pleasure.

I'll be home on New Year's Eve and I'd be honored if you'd accompany me to the Texas Cattleman's Club function that night. You can give me your answer then. In the meantime, I would like you to open my Christmas gift to you and know that it comes from my heart and with my very best intentions.

All my love,

Nolan

Raina's fingers were wrapped tight around the small box in her hand, so tight that her knuckles whitened and her palms began to ache from the imprint of the edges of the box. Did he mean to ask her to marry him? Black spots began to swim in front of Raina's eyes and she realized she was holding her breath. She forced herself to breathe in and out, and again, until the spots receded.

Panic clawed at her throat. She'd thought she was ready for this but she so wasn't. They'd met less than four weeks ago. How could he be so certain she was what he wanted? How could she when she knew he still hadn't told her about the sadness of his past? There was still so much unsaid between them. The details of her past, of his. But did any of that matter when they loved each other?

Droplets of water dripped onto the sheet of paper in her hand and Raina realized she was weeping. The words on the paper blurred and she quickly refolded the sheet and shoved it back in the envelope. All the while, her heart urged her to take a risk on love again and her mind shrieked its horror in the background.

She'd taken risks on love before and she still bore the emotional scars from that. How on earth could she even contemplate marriage, if that was indeed what Nolan was suggesting, based on her track record with men? Hadn't it been a crazy, hormone-driven attraction that had seen her hook-up with Jeb in the first place? She'd been twenty-six, going on twenty-seven. Hardly a child by any means. She should have known better then—and she certainly knew better now.

Sure, deep down, she knew that Nolan was different from Jeb and the others she'd dated before him. But there was still that niggling sense of not knowing exactly where she stood with Nolan.

JJ would be thrilled at the chance to call Nolan Daddy. She knew that. But she had to be careful. She'd fought Jeb and beaten a tornado to give JJ a stable and secure home, a safe and happy childhood. She couldn't risk throwing that all away. Not now.

A voice in the back of her head reminded her that Nolan had acknowledged his initial deceit, that he'd apologized and done his best to make it up to her. That he'd even re-signed from his job over it. Surely those were not the actions of a man who would stomp all over her heart and then walk away. He said he was back in Royal for good now. And she knew he meant it.

A kernel of hope began to bloom inside her until she reminded herself of the money that still sat in the safe back at Priceless and of the fact that Jeb probably still wanted it. While her ex certainly appeared to have dropped off the radar for now, who knew when he'd be back next or what his demands would be? How would Nolan react then? Would he be prepared to accept Raina with all her baggage?

"Mommy? Can we go outside now?"

JJ interrupted her jangled thoughts and Raina latched on to the chance to distract herself.

"Sure, honey," she said, shoving the envelope and the still-wrapped box in a drawer in the sideboard. She'd deal with it later. Maybe. "Let's get our coats on, okay?"

"Yippee!"

It was New Year's Eve and Raina was still in a quandary about Nolan's letter and the box that sat untouched in the drawer of her sideboard. She'd missed him this week. More because she'd known he was so far away. But he was back today and she'd alternately been filled with excitement and with a major case of the jitters.

"G'anddad's here!" JJ announced from where he'd been watching at the front window for his grandfather to pick him up and take him back to the trailer park to see in the New Year.

"Go and get your bag then, JJ," Raina suggested with a smile, turning away from the mirror where she'd been fussing with her hair for about the seventh time already that evening.

She went to the front door and opened it wide.

"You all right, girlie?" her dad asked, stomping his feet on the step before coming inside.

Raina welcomed her father with a huge hug and inhaled the special scents of his forbidden cigars and Old Spice.

"Yeah, Dad, I'm fine. Just glad to see you."

Her father gave her a sharp look and a small nod. "I heard some interesting news today. About your young man."

"My young…? You mean Nolan?"

"He's why I'm sitting for you tonight, isn't he?"

Raina felt the heat of a blush warm her cheeks and nodded. "Yes, he's taking me out tonight. What did you hear?"

Please don't let it be something bad, she wished with all her heart.

"Has to do with that no good piece of sh—"

"Dad! No swearing," Raina interrupted, glancing toward JJ.

"Well, you know who I mean."

"Jeb?"

"Who else?"

"What has Nolan got to do with Jeb?"

Her Dad gave her a sly smile. "Seems your young man arranged a meeting with the lowlife. Got him arrested and put away. Turns out he was wanted for third-degree felony over in New Mexico. Killed someone while driving under the influence and fled the scene, then jumped bail after that."

"But…how…when?" Raina was at a loss for words. How on earth would Nolan have known who Jeb was, let alone arranged for him to be arrested?

"Happened the night after the pageant, apparently. According to my poker buddy at the sheriff's office, Nolan offered him money to stay away from you, permanently. A goodly sum, so I'm told. That scumbag couldn't resist, of course, but it turns out he was dealing with the wrong person. Nolan apparently used his contacts to find out a bit more about who he was dealing with, and took his information to Sheriff Battle, who was only too pleased to oblige and take that waste of space off the streets. Apparently he put up a bit of a fight."

Did that explain the bruise on Nolan's face? Hard on the heels of that question came the realization that Jeb was in jail. Relief warred with confusion in Raina's mind.

"Anyways, doesn't sound like Jeb's going to be a problem for you again. You can thank your young man for that. I certainly plan to the next time I see him." Her dad fixed her with a steely look. "And I will see him a next time, won't I?"

"I... I don't know, Dad. I'm not sure I'm ready."

Her father harrumphed and pulled her into his arms for another hug. "You'll know when you're ready, my girlie. You'll know in your heart."

"But, Dad, we haven't known each other long en—"

"Time isn't what's important here. What you gotta ask yourself is what would your life be like without him in it."

Raina tipped her head to look up at her father. He'd had plenty of lady friends since her mom had left them, but never anyone who stuck around. "Is that what you asked yourself?"

He nodded. "I did, and I never got lucky enough to meet the lady I'd miss forever. Well, not yet anyway," he concluded with a twinkle in his blue eyes. "Now, where's that grandson of mine?"

After JJ and her dad had gone, Raina paced the living room floor, weighing her father's words and the news that Jeb was in jail. The relief she felt was slow to sink in, but bit by bit, the realization that she no longer had to worry about a random knock at her front door or being accosted on the street or receiving yet another late-night phone call or text began to seem real. A feeling of liberation filled her, a sense of freedom she hadn't known in a very long time—and she owed it all to Nolan.

What kind of man did what he'd done? A good man. An honest one. A man who was reliable and forthright and who looked after what was his to the very best of his ability and who wasn't afraid to ask for help when he couldn't do it alone. He'd protected her from harm, even when she hadn't asked for it. And she knew, deep in her heart, that Nolan would move mountains for her if she needed him to.

No matter which way she looked at it, Nolan Dane was a better person than she'd wanted to believe. She'd been so scarred by the actions of her past that she'd let them hold her back when she was being offered a chance to make a new start, a new beginning—filled with the kind of love she'd always dreamed of.

The sound of a car door slamming announced Nolan's arrival. Raina quickly grabbed the wrapped box from the drawer and slipped it into her evening purse.

He'd given her this week and she'd thought long and hard. And she'd reached her decision.

Seventeen

Nolan strode confidently up the path to the house and felt his heart lift when he saw the front door open to reveal Raina standing there, waiting for him. He'd missed her both physically and mentally. He'd lost track of the number of times he'd picked up the phone to call her, only to remind himself that he was giving her space to think.

Now the time had come for what he hoped would be the answer he'd been waiting for. Despite his eagerness, he wouldn't push. He understood her vulnerability, even though she projected such a staunch and strong face to the world. She needed to come to him on her own terms.

Framed in the doorway, she smiled nervously down at him. He bounded up the front steps to greet her the way he'd been waiting to do from the moment he'd left her bed, and she slid easily into his arms and lifted her face for his kiss. He kept it short and sweet, denying the nearly overwhelming urge he had to forget the night ahead and to simply sweep her off her feet, take her into her bedroom and pick up where they'd left off a week ago.

"I've missed you," he said simply, as he forced himself to release her.

She gave him a shy smile. "I've missed you, too."

"You look beautiful."

"Thank you."

Her cheeks flushed a delicate pink beneath the subtle makeup she wore and Nolan felt his heart squeeze in response. There was nothing he didn't love about her. He only hoped she'd let him tell her that every day now for the rest of their lives.

"You left without opening your Christmas gift," Raina said, reaching behind her to the hall table and passing a long slender parcel to him.

Nolan looked at it in surprise. This was the secret JJ had whispered to him about. "Can I open it now?"

"Sure," she teased, "unless you want to wait until next year."

He tore away the wrapping and instantly recognized the case he'd coveted a few weeks ago. He opened the lid and revealed the writing set inside. Nolan was staggered. Not just by the beauty of the gift, but by her thoughtfulness in giving it to him.

"It's old, of course," she said, sounding worried, "but in excellent condition. I remembered you looking at it and I thought—"

"I love it. Thank you, it's perfect."

He leaned forward to kiss her again. She was flushed when he finally let her go.

"Oh, you like it? Well…that's good then."

He smiled; she still sounded as if he'd knocked her off-kilter. She could barely meet his eyes as she reached into the cupboard behind her for her coat. He helped her into it, taking a moment to inhale the fresh herbal scent of her hair as she lifted it over her collar. He imagined his face buried in that sweet softness again and, as his body throbbed in response, was forced to turn his mind to other things.

"Shall we go?" Raina asked.

Surprised, because he'd hoped they'd talk about the gift he'd left for her before they headed out tonight, Nolan inclined his head. "My chariot awaits," he replied, gesturing for her to take his arm.

She locked the door behind her and they headed to the car where he stowed the writing set safely in the back. The journey to the Texas Cattleman's Club was conducted in silence, briefly punctuated by Raina asking how his trip to LA had gone. By the time Nolan handed his car keys to the valet outside the club, his stomach was a ball of nerves. Still not one word about his letter or his gift. He reminded himself that he was the one who'd set the parameters here. It had been his choice to leave her for this week and give her space and time to think about their future, if indeed they had one.

They circulated among the crowd, stopping and chatting here and there. The club was a large, rambling single-story building made of dark stone and wood that had originally been built in the early 1900s. The interior decor still reflected its Old World men's club heritage, with hunting trophies and historical artifacts adorning the paneled walls but, Nolan noticed, the ceiling had been lifted during the repairs after the tornado, giving the club an airier feel about it, and the colors were brighter and lighter than before. Overall the renovations better reflected the now mixed gender culture of what had long been solely a male domain.

In the great room, the mood was vibrant and celebratory, but Nolan knew he couldn't relax and celebrate until he had the answers he sought. During a lull in conversation with a group of his old high school buddies, Nolan tucked Raina closer to his side and drew her away to a quiet alcove he'd spied.

"Tired of the party already?" Raina teased.

Her cheeks were still softly flushed and her blue eyes sparkled, but he sensed that she was nervous. Possibly even as nervous as he was.

He smiled in response—it was now or never. "Actually, I was wondering what you thought of my Christmas gift."

The smile on Raina's face froze for a moment, before disappearing altogether and Nolan felt his hopes for the future slide inexorably out of his grasp. She reached into her small purse and pulled out the gift he'd left for her under the tree. His stomach dipped as he realized she hadn't even unwrapped it.

Raina looked up at him and he braced himself for the rejection he was sure was coming his way.

"I…" She stopped and chewed at her lower lip for a moment before continuing. "I didn't want to unwrap it without you there. You mentioned intentions in your letter. I need to know exactly what those are, Nolan."

It wasn't what he'd been expecting her to say and for a moment he was lost for words. But then the logical side of his brain kicked in and processed what she'd said. She wasn't rejecting him. She simply needed more reassurance. At least he hoped that's what was happening. He'd felt adrift like this once before in his life and he'd hated every second of it. It was why he'd been so reluctant to embrace the idea of sharing his life with anyone again. But he'd realized that he had to let himself be a little vulnerable if he wanted Raina to trust him. Trust him and love him.

"You know I love you, Raina, don't you?" he asked and felt a tentative swell of hope when she nodded. "I got off on the wrong foot with you to begin with and I can't apologize enough for that. The man I was then, the one who thought he could approach someone with an ulterior motive and damn the consequences—he's not the man I'm meant to be, nor the man I ever wanted to be. Do you believe me when I say that, too?"

Again she nodded and again he felt the tightness ease inside him that little bit more. Nolan led Raina over to a pair of chairs set against the wall in the alcove. They were surrounded by the noise and celebration of the crowd, and yet at the same time they were isolated. Locked in their own private space.

"I walked away from my life once," he began anew. "Things became more than I could bear and I had to leave or lose myself completely. I found a new way of living with myself. Unfortunately it didn't make me a very decent man.

"I like to think that everything in life eventually comes full circle and that fate took a hand in bringing me back to Royal. I wasn't ready to come back, I'll be honest with you about that. And I definitely wasn't ready to fall in love. But I did. Coming home has given me a new start— a chance to lead a good decent life again, a life I want to share with you and JJ, if you'll let me.

"I love you," he repeated and took both her hands in his, bringing them up to his lips to kiss her knuckles.

"I know you love me. I believe you, Nolan," Raina answered him quietly. "My father told me what you did with Jeb. Until I heard what he said and what you'd done, I think I was too afraid to trust my heart and let myself admit that I love you, too." She pressed one hand against his chest. "I know you have a good and decent heart, Nolan, and your actions have proved that to me when I wouldn't listen to what I really wanted to hear. You see, I don't have such a great track record with men. I don't tend to choose the stayers, or the reliable guys. In some ways I think I was just waiting for you to fail at the first hurdle because that would let me let you go."

"And I did fail. I failed you terribly."

"That's in the past, Nolan. You've more than made amends for that. You were acting for your client and, to be honest, even I can see now that you had no other option than to do the best for him at the time."

She looked up at him and Nolan saw tears swimming in her exquisite blue eyes. The sight made his heart wrench at the knowledge he'd put those tears there.

"Raina—" he started, but she put her fingertips to his lips.

"Shh, let me finish. You did what was right at the time, the same way you did what was right when you resigned your position with Samson Oil. I know that now." She took in a deep breath and her voice was so soft when she next spoke, Nolan could barely hear her. "I also know about Carole and Bennett."

The names struck him like a physical blow. "I planned to tell you, eventually," he said, his voice raspy with emotion. "It was more difficult than I thought."

"It's okay, Nolan. I understand that it's probably too painful for you to talk about them. For a while I've held that against you as another secret you were keeping from me. But I've let that go. Even so, there's still something that worries me. Something I need to ask you."

"Ask," he demanded.

"Do you love me and JJ because we remind you of your wife and son?"

Nolan felt her gaze lock on him with an intensity that showed him that everything now relied upon his response. He pushed aside the pain and the hurt, and chose his words carefully. His future happiness depended on how he said this.

"Raina, I will always love Carole and Bennett." His voice cracked on their names and he halted for a moment, closed his eyes and drew in a deep breath. "But they're gone. Losing them— I thought I'd never love again. That I never could. It wasn't just the pain of losing them, it was the risk of putting myself back out there again. Of maybe losing what little I had left of them, as well, if I let someone else into my heart.

"Meeting you has taught me that it's possible to love again without diminishing what I had with Carole, and trust me, I never thought I'd even want to feel about anyone the way I feel about you. You're so strong and so resilient. Life has battered you down and still you've shown your strengths by getting back up and moving forward. You haven't just been an example to me, you've opened my eyes to who I should be and shown me that I can loosen my grip on the past. Doing so allows me to think of a future. It's a future I want with you."

She nodded but remained silent. He looked down at the little packet in her hands.

"Will you open it now?" he asked.

His heart hammered in his chest. She could still return it to him. And he'd accept it and let her go if that was what she really wanted, even though the very thought threatened to tear his heart in two. He held his breath until she'd worked loose the tape that bound the wrapping, exposing the ring box. She lifted the lid and gasped. Inside, nestled against a dark velvet bed, lay his promise to her—a cushion-cut blue diamond edged with brilliant white diamonds and set in delicate platinum scrollwork.

Nolan dropped to one knee on the floor in front of her and lifted the ring from the box, offering it to her.

"Raina Patterson, will you do me the honor of becoming my wife? Will you let me be your husband for eternity and be a father to JJ and any other children we might be lucky enough to have?"

She appeared lost for words until he heard her choke on a sob. Tears rolled down her face but none of that mattered when he heard the words she was so desperately working to get out of her throat.

"Yes. Yes. Yes," she said repeatedly through her tears.

Nolan took her hand, slid the ring onto her finger and stood, pulling her to her feet. Raina lifted her face to his.

"I love you, Nolan. So very much. I was scared, I'll admit it. And probably too quick to look for reasons not to love you. I didn't want you to be able to hurt me and I didn't trust my own judgment anymore. But I do now. I love you and I'd be the happiest woman in the world to marry you. I'm so lucky to have you."

"I'm the lucky one, Raina. I never expected to be given another chance at love and life the way I have with you. And I want to spend the rest of my life showing you how much you mean to me."

He kissed her and, in her arms, found the sense of belonging that had been missing from his world for far too long. Her lips were sweet and tender and tasted of the promise of a future he never dreamed he'd want again. And yet, with Raina, he knew the future would be truly wonderful and that it was something he wanted to grasp with both hands and hold on to and cherish forever.

"They'll be doing the fireworks soon," he commented as they came up for air and he saw the crowd thinning in the great room as people started to move outdoors for the display. "Did you want to go outside to watch?"

Raina shook her head. "No, let's go home instead… and make our own."

* * * * *

NANNY MAKES THREE

CAT SCHIELD

For Jeff and Roxanne Schall of Shada Arabians

One

Shortly after the 6:00 a.m. feeding, Liam Wade strode through the barn housing the yearling colts and fillies, enjoying the peaceful crunching of hay and the occasional equine snort. It was January 1, and because of the way horses were classified for racing and showing purposes, regardless of their calendar age, every horse in every stall on the ranch was now officially a year older.

Dawn of New Year's Day had never been a time of reflection for Liam. Usually he was facedown in a beautiful woman's bed, sleeping like the dead after an evening of partying and great sex. Last year that had changed. He'd left the New Year's Eve party alone.

His cell phone buzzed in his back pocket, and he pulled it out. The message from his housekeeper made him frown.

There's a woman at the house who needs to speak to you.

Liam couldn't imagine what sort of trouble had come knocking on his door this morning. He texted back that he was on his way and retraced his steps to his Range Rover.

As he drove up, he saw an unfamiliar gray Ford Fusion in the driveway near the large Victorian house Liam's great-great-grandfather had built during the last days of the nineteenth century. Liam and his twin brother, Kyle, had grown up in this seven-bedroom home, raised by their grandfather after their mother headed to Dallas to create her real estate empire.

Liam parked and turned off the engine. A sense of foreboding raised the hair on his arms, and he wondered at his reluctance to get out of the truck. He'd enjoyed how peaceful the last year had been. A strange woman showing up at the crack of dawn could only mean trouble.

Slipping from behind the wheel, Liam trotted across the drought-dry lawn and up the five steps that led to the wraparound porch. The stained glass windows set into the double doors allowed light to filter into the wide entry hall, but prevented him from seeing inside. Thus, it wasn't until Liam pushed open the door that he saw the infant car seat off to one side of the hall. As that was registering, a baby began to wail from the direction of the living room.

The tableau awaiting him in the high-ceilinged room was definitely the last thing he'd expected. Candace, his housekeeper, held a squalling infant and was obviously trying to block the departure of a stylish woman in her late fifties.

"Liam will be here any second," Candace was saying. With her focus split between the child and the blonde woman in the plum wool coat, his housekeeper hadn't noticed his arrival.

"What's going on?" Liam questioned, raising his voice slightly to be heard above the unhappy baby.

The relief on Candace's face was clear. "This is Diane Garner. She's here about her granddaughter."

"You're Liam Wade?" the woman demanded, her tone an accusation.

"Yes." Liam was completely bewildered by her hostility. He didn't recognize her name or her face.

"My daughter is dead."

"I'm very sorry to hear that."

"She was on her way to see you when she went into

labor and lost control of her car. The doctors were unable to save her."

"That's very tragic." Liam wasn't sure what else to say. The name Garner rang no bells. "Did she and I have an appointment about something?"

Diane stiffened. "An appointment?"

"What was your daughter's name?"

"Margaret Garner. You met her in San Antonio." Diane grew more agitated with each word she uttered. "You can't expect me to believe you don't remember."

"I'm sorry," Liam said, pitching his voice to calm the woman. She reminded him of a high-strung mare. "It's been a while since I've been there."

"It's been eight months," Diane said. "Surely you couldn't have forgotten my daughter in such a short period of time."

Liam opened his mouth to explain that he wasn't anywhere near San Antonio eight months ago when it hit him what the woman was implying. He turned and stared at the baby Candace held.

"You think the baby's mine?"

"Her name is Maggie and I know she's yours."

Liam almost laughed. This was one child he knew without question wasn't his. He'd been celibate since last New Year's Eve. "I assure you that's not true."

Diane pursed her lips. "I came here thinking you'd do the right thing by Maggie. She's your child. There's no question that you had an affair with my daughter."

He wasn't proud of the fact that during his twenties, he'd probably slept with a few women without knowing their last name or much more about them other than that they were sexy and willing. But he'd been careful, and not one of them had shown up on his doorstep pregnant.

"If I had an affair with your daughter, it was a long time ago, and this child is not mine."

"I have pictures that prove otherwise." Diane pulled a

phone out of her purse and swiped at the screen. "These are you and my daughter. The date stamp puts them at eight months ago in San Antonio. Are you going to deny that's you?"

The screen showed a very pretty woman with blond hair and bright blue eyes, laughing as she kissed the cheek of a very familiar-looking face. Kyle's. A baseball cap hid his short hair, but the lack of a scar on his chin left no doubt it was Kyle and not Liam in the picture.

"I realize that looks like me, but I have a twin brother." Liam was still grappling with seeing his brother looking so happy when Diane Garner slipped past him and headed toward the entry. "But even so, that doesn't mean the baby is a Wade."

Diane paused with her hand on the front doorknob. Her eyes blazed. "Margaret dated very infrequently, and she certainly didn't sleep around. I can tell from the pictures that she really fell for you."

Either Diane hadn't heard Liam when he explained that he had a twin or she saw this as an excuse. While he grappled for a way to get through to the woman, she yanked the door open and exited the house.

Stunned, Liam stared after her. He was ready to concede that the child might be a Wade. A DNA test would confirm that quickly enough, but then what? Kyle was on active duty in the military and not in a position to take on the responsibility of an infant.

The baby's cries escalated, interrupting his train of thought. He turned to where Candace rocked the baby in an effort to calm her and realized Diane Garner intended to leave her granddaughter behind. Liam chased after the older woman and caught her car door before she could close it.

"Are you leaving the baby?"

"Margaret was on her way to see you. I think she meant

to either give you Maggie or get your permission to give her up. There were blank forms to that effect in her car."

"Why?"

"She never wanted to have children of her own." Diane's voice shook. "And I know she wouldn't have been able to raise one by herself."

"What happens if I refuse?"

"I'll turn her over to child services."

"But you're the child's grandmother. Couldn't you just take care of her until we can get a DNA test performed and…"

"Because of health issues, I'm not in a position to take care of her. You're Maggie's father," Diane insisted. "She belongs with you."

She belonged with her father. Unfortunately, with Kyle on active duty, could he care for a baby? Did he even want to? Liam had no idea—it had been two years since he'd last spoken with Kyle. But if the child was a Wade—and Liam wasn't going to turn the child out until he knew one way or another—that meant she belonged here.

"How do I get in contact with you?" Liam asked. Surely the woman would want some news of her grandchild?

"I gave my contact info to your housekeeper." The older woman looked both shaken and determined. "Take good care of Maggie. She's all I have left." And with more haste than grace, Diane pulled her car door shut and started the engine.

As the gray car backed down the driveway, Liam considered the decision his own mother had made, leaving him and Kyle with her father to raise while she went off to the life she wanted in Dallas. He'd never really felt a hole in his life at her absence. Their grandfather had been an ideal blend of tough and affectionate. No reason to think that Maggie wouldn't do just as well without her mother.

He returned to the house. Candace was in the kitchen

warming a bottle of formula. The baby continued to show-case an impressive set of lungs. His housekeeper shot him a concerned glance.

"You let her go?" Candace rocked the baby.

"What was I supposed to do?"

"Convince her to take the baby with her?" She didn't sound all that certain. "You and I both know she isn't yours."

"You sound pretty sure about that."

Liam gave her a crooked smile. Candace had started working for him seven years ago when the former house-keeper retired. Diane Garner wasn't the first woman to show up unexpected and uninvited on his doorstep, al-though she was the first one to arrive with a baby.

"You've been different this last year." Candace eyed him. "More settled."

She'd never asked what had prompted his overnight transformation from carefree playboy to responsible busi-nessman. Maybe she figured with his thirtieth birthday he'd decided to leave his freewheeling days behind him. That was part of the truth, but not all.

"I've been living like a monk."

She grinned. "That, too."

"What am I supposed to do with a baby?" He eyed the red-faced infant with her wispy blond hair and unfocused blue eyes. "Why won't she stop crying?"

"She's not wet so I'm assuming she's hungry." Or maybe she just wants her mother. Candace didn't say the words, but the thought was written all over her face. "Can you hold her while I get her bottle ready?"

"I'd rather not."

"She won't break."

The child looked impossibly small in Candace's arms. Liam shook his head. "Tell me what to do to get a bottle ready."

The noise in the kitchen abated while the baby sucked greedily at her bottle. Liam made the most of this respite and contacted a local company that specialized in placing nannies. Since it wasn't quite seven in the morning, he was forced to leave a message and could only hope that he'd impressed the owners with the urgency of his need. That done, he set about creating a list of things that baby Maggie would need.

Hadley Stratton took her foot off the accelerator and let her SUV coast down the last thirty feet of driveway. An enormous Victorian mansion loomed before her, white siding and navy trim giving it the look of a graceful dowager in the rugged West Texas landscape.

The drive from her apartment in Royal had taken her fifteen minutes. Although a much shorter commute than her last job in Pine Valley, Hadley had reservations about taking the nanny position. Liam Wade had a playboy reputation, which made this the exact sort of situation she avoided. If he hadn't offered a salary at the top of her range and promised a sizable bonus if she started immediately, she would have refused when the agency called. But with student loans hanging over her head and the completion of her master's degree six short months away, Hadley knew she'd be a fool to turn down the money.

Besides, she'd learned her lesson when it came to attractive, eligible bosses. There would be no repeat of the mistake she'd made with Noah Heston, the divorced father of three who'd gone back to his ex-wife after enticing Hadley to fall in love with him.

Parking her SUV, Hadley headed for the front door and rang the bell. Inside a baby cried, and Hadley's agitation rose. She knew very little about the situation she was walking into. Only that Liam Wade had a sudden and urgent need for someone to care for an infant.

A shadow darkened the stained glass inset in the double door. When Hadley's pulse quickened, she suspected this was a mistake. For the last hour she'd been telling herself that Liam Wade was just like any other employer. Sure, the man was a world-class horseman and sexy as hell. Yes, she'd had a crush on him ten years ago, but so had most of the other teenage girls who barrel raced.

A decade had gone by. She was no longer a silly fangirl, but a mature, intelligent, *professional* nanny who knew the risks of getting emotionally wrapped up in her charges or their handsome fathers.

"Good morning, Mr. Wade." She spoke crisply as the door began to open. "Royal Nannies sent me. My name is—"

"Hadley..." His bottle-green eyes scanned her face.

"Hadley Stratton." Had he remembered her? No, of course not. "Stratton." She cleared her throat and tried not to sound as if her heart was racing. Of course he knew who she was; obviously the agency had let him know who they were sending. "I'm Hadley Stratton." She clamped her lips together and stopped repeating her name.

"You're a nanny?" He executed a quick but thorough assessment of her and frowned.

"Well, yes." Maybe he expected someone older. "I have my résumé and references if you'd like to look them over." She reached into her tote and pulled out a file.

"No need." He stepped back and gestured her inside. "Maggie's in the living room." He shut the door behind her and grimaced. "Just follow the noise."

Hadley didn't realize that she'd expected the baby's mother to be ridiculously young, beautiful and disinterested in motherhood until she spied the woman holding the child. In her late forties, she was wearing jeans, a flannel shirt and sneakers, her disheveled dark hair in a messy bun.

"Hadley Stratton. Candace Tolliver, my housekeeper."

Liam cast a fond grin at the older woman. "Who is very glad you've come so quickly."

Candace had the worn look of a first-time mother with a fussy baby. Even before the introductions were completed, she extended the baby toward Hadley. "I've fed her and changed her. She won't stop crying."

"What is her normal routine?" Hadley rocked and studied the tiny infant, wondering what had become of the child's mother. Smaller than the average newborn by a few pounds. Was that due to her mother's unhealthy nutritional habits while pregnant or something more serious?

"We don't know." Candace glanced toward Liam. "She only just arrived. Excuse me." She exited the room as if there were something burning in the kitchen.

"These are her medical records." Liam gestured toward a file on the coffee table. "Although she was premature, she checked out fine."

"How premature?" She slipped her pinkie between the infant's lips, hoping the little girl would try sucking and calm down. "Does she have a pacifier?"

Liam spoke up. "No."

Hadley glanced at him. He'd set one hand on his hip. The other was buried in his thick hair. He needed a haircut, she noted absently before sweeping her gaze around the room in search of the normal clutter that came with a child. Other than a car seat and a plastic bag from the local drugstore, the elegant but comfortable room looked like it belonged in a decorating magazine. Pale gray walls, woodwork painted a clean white. The furniture had accents of dusty blue, lime green and cranberry, relieving the monochrome palette.

"Where are her things?"

"Things?" The rugged horseman looked completely lost.

"Diapers, a blanket, clothes? Are they in her room?"

"She doesn't have a room."

"Then where does she sleep?"

"We have yet to figure that out."

Hadley marshaled her patience. Obviously there was a story here. "Perhaps you could tell me what's going on? Starting with where her mother is."

"She died a few days ago in a traffic accident."

"Oh, I'm sorry for your loss." Hadley's heart clenched as she gazed down at the infant who had grown calmer as she sucked on Hadley's finger. "The poor child never to know her mother."

Liam cleared his throat. "Actually, I didn't know her."

"You had to have…" Hadley trailed off. Chances were Liam Wade just didn't remember which one-night stand had produced his daughter. "What's your name, sweetheart?" she crooned, glad to see the infant's eyes closing.

"Maggie. Her mother was Margaret."

"Hello, little Maggie."

Humming a random tune, Hadley rocked Maggie. The combination of soothing noise and swaying motion put the baby to sleep, and Hadley placed her in the car seat.

"You are incredibly good at that."

Hadley looked up from tucking in the baby and found Liam Wade standing too close and peering over her shoulder at Maggie. The man smelled like pure temptation. If pure temptation smelled like soap and mouthwash. He wore jeans and a beige henley beneath his brown-and-cream plaid shirt. His boots were scuffed and well worn. He might be worth a pile of money, but he'd never acted as though it made him better than anyone else. He'd fit in at the horse shows he'd attended, ambling around with the rest of the guys, showing off his reining skills by snagging the flirts who stalked him and talking horses with men who'd been in the business longer than he'd been alive. His cockiness came from what he achieved on the back of a horse.

"This is the first time she's been quiet since she got here." His strained expression melted into a smile of devastating charm. "You've worked a miracle."

"Obviously not. She was just stressed. I suspect your tension communicated itself to her. How long has she been here?"

"Since about seven." Liam gestured her toward the black leather couch, but Hadley positioned herself in a black-and-white armchair not far from the sleeping child. "Her grandmother dropped her off and left."

"And you weren't expecting her?"

Liam shook his head and began to pace. "Perhaps I should start at the beginning."

"That might be best."

Before he could begin, his housekeeper arrived with a pot of coffee and two cups. After pouring for both, she glanced at the now-sleeping child, gave Hadley a thumbs-up and exited the room once more. Liam added sugar to his coffee and resumed his march around the room, mug in hand.

"Here's what I know. A woman arrived this morning with Maggie, said her name was Diane Garner and that her daughter had died after being in a car accident. Apparently she went into labor and lost control of the vehicle."

Hadley glanced at the sleeping baby and again sorrow overtook her. "That's just tragic. So where is her grandmother now?"

"On her way back to Houston, I'm sure."

"She left you with the baby?"

"I got the impression she couldn't handle the child or didn't want the responsibility."

"I imagine she thought the child was better off with her father."

"Maggie isn't mine." Liam's firm tone and resolute

expression encouraged no rebuttal. "She's my brother's child."

At first Hadley didn't know how to respond. Why would he have taken the child in if she wasn't his?

"I see. So I'll be working for your brother?" She knew little of the second Wade brother. Unlike Liam, he hadn't been active in reining or showing quarter horses.

"No, you'll be working for me. Kyle is in the military and lives on the East Coast."

"He's giving you guardianship of the child?"

Liam stared out the large picture window that over-looked the front lawn. "He's unreachable at the moment so I haven't been able to talk to him about what's going on. I'm not even sure Maggie is his."

This whole thing sounded too convoluted for Hadley's comfort. Was Liam Maggie's father and blaming his absent brother because he couldn't face the consequences of his actions? He wouldn't be the first man who struggled against facing up to his responsibilities. Her opinion of Liam Wade the professional horseman had always been high. But he was a charming scoundrel who was capable of seducing a woman without ever catching her name or collecting her phone number.

"I'm not sure I'm the right nanny for you," she began, her protest trailing off as Liam whirled from the window and advanced toward her.

"You are exactly what Maggie needs. Look at how peaceful she is. Candace spent two hours trying to calm her down, and you weren't here more than ten minutes and she fell asleep. Please stay. She lost her mother and obviously has taken to you."

"What you need is someone who can be with Maggie full-time. The clients I work with only need daytime help."

"The agency said you go to school."

"I'm finishing up my master's in child development."

"But you're off until the beginning of February when classes resume."

"Yes." She felt a trap closing in around her.

"That's four weeks away. I imagine we can get our situation sorted out by then, so we'd only need you during the day while I'm at the barn."

"And until then?"

"Would you be willing to move in here? We have more than enough room."

Hadley shook her head. She'd feel safer sleeping in her own bed. The thought popped into her mind unbidden. What made her think that she was in danger from Liam Wade? From what she knew of him, she was hardly his type.

"I won't move in, but I'll come early and stay late to give you as much time as you need during the month of January. In the meantime, you may want to consider hiring someone permanent."

Despite what Liam had said about Maggie being his brother's child, Hadley suspected the baby wasn't going anywhere once the DNA tests came back. With the child's mother dead and her grandmother unwilling to be responsible for her, Liam should just accept that he was going to need a full-time caregiver.

"That's fair."

Liam put out his hand, and Hadley automatically accepted the handshake. Tingles sped up her arm and raised the hair on the back of her neck as his firm grip lingered a few seconds longer than was professionally acceptable.

"Perhaps we could talk about the things that Maggie will need," Hadley said, hoping Liam didn't notice the odd squeak in her voice.

"Candace started a list. She said she'd get what we needed as soon as you arrived." His lips curved in a wry grin. "She didn't want to leave me alone with the baby."

"Why not?"

"It might seem strange to you, but I've never actually held a baby before."

Hadley tore her gaze away from the likable sparkle in Liam's arresting eyes. She absolutely could not find the man attractive. Hadley clasped her hands in her lap.

"Once you've held her for the first time, you'll see how easy it is." Seeing how deeply the baby was sleeping, Hadley decided this might be a great opportunity for him to begin. "And there's no time like the present."

Liam started to protest, but whatever he'd been about to say died beneath her steady gaze. "Very well." His jaw muscles bunched and released. "What do I do?"

Two

Going balls-out on a twelve-hundred-pound horse to chase down a fleeing cow required steady hands and a calm mind in the midst of a massive adrenaline rush. As a world-class trainer and exhibitor of reining and cutting horses, Liam prided himself on being the eye of the storm. But today, he was the rookie at his first rodeo and Hadley the seasoned competitor.

"It's important that you support her head." Hadley picked up the sleeping baby, demonstrating as she narrated. "Some babies don't like to be held on their backs, so if she gets fussy you could try holding her on her stomach or on her side."

Hadley came toward him and held out Maggie. He was assailed by the dual fragrances of the two females, baby powder and lavender. The scents filled his lungs and slowed his heartbeat. Feeling moderately calmer, Liam stood very still while Hadley settled Maggie into his arms.

"There." She peered at the sleeping child for a moment before lifting her eyes to meet Liam's gaze. Flecks of gold floated in her lapis-blue eyes, mesmerizing him with their sparkle. "See, that wasn't hard."

"You smell like lavender." The words passed his lips without conscious thought.

"Lavender and chamomile." She stepped back until her path was blocked by an end table. "It's a calming fragrance."

"It's working."

As he adjusted to the feel of Maggie's tiny body in his arms, he cast surreptitious glances Hadley's way. Did she remember him from her days of barrel racing? He hadn't seen her in ten years and often looked for her at the events he attended, half expecting her name to pop up among the winners. At eighteen she'd been poised to break out as a star in the barrel-racing circuit. And then she'd sold her mare and disappeared. Much to the delight of many of her competitors, chief among them Liam's on-again, off-again girlfriend.

"I almost didn't recognize you this morning," he said, shifting Maggie so he could free his right arm.

Hadley looked up at him warily. "You recognized me?"

How could she think otherwise? She'd been the one who'd gotten away. "Sure. You took my advice and won that sweepstakes class. You and I were supposed to have dinner afterward." He could tell she remembered that, even though she was shaking her head. "Only I never saw you again."

"I vaguely remember you trying to tell me what I was doing wrong."

"You had a nice mare. Lolita Slide. When you put her up for sale I told Shannon Tinger to buy her. She went on to make over a hundred thousand riding barrels with her."

"She was a terrific horse," Hadley said with a polite smile. "I'm glad Shannon did so well with her."

Liam remembered Hadley as a lanky girl in battered jeans and a worn cowboy hat, her blond hair streaming like a victory banner as her chestnut mare raced for the finish line. This tranquil woman before him, while lovely in gray dress pants and a black turtleneck sweater, pale hair pulled back in a neat ponytail, lacked the fire that had snagged his interest ten years earlier.

"We have a three-year-old son of Lolita's out in the barn.

You should come see him. I think he's going to make a first-class reining horse."

"I don't think there will be time. Infants require a lot of attention."

Her refusal surprised him. He'd expected her to jump at the chance to see what her former mount had produced. The Hadley he remembered had been crazy about horses.

"Why'd you quit?"

Hadley stared at the landscape painting over the fireplace while she answered Liam's blunt question. "My parents wanted me to go to college, and there wasn't money to do that and keep my horse. What I got for Lolita paid for my first year's tuition."

Liam considered her words. When was the last time he'd been faced with an either-or situation? Usually he got everything he wanted. Once in a while a deal didn't go his way, but more often than not, that left him open for something better.

Maggie began to stir, and Liam refocused his attention on the baby. Her lips parted in a broad yawn that accompanied a fluttering of her long lashes.

"I think she's waking up." He took a step toward Hadley, baby extended.

"You did very well for your first time."

Unsure if her tiny smile meant she was patronizing him, Liam decided he'd try harder to get comfortable with his niece. Strange as it was to admit it, he wanted Hadley's approval.

"Would you like a tour of the house?" Liam gestured toward the hallway. "I'd like your opinion on where to put the baby's room."

"Sure."

He led the way across the hall to the dining room. A long mahogany table, capable of seating twelve, sat on a black-and-gold Oriental rug. When he'd overhauled the house six years ago, bringing the plumbing and wiring up to code, this was the one room he'd left in its original state.

"It's just me living here these days, and I haven't entertained much in the last year." The reason remained a sore spot, but Liam brushed it aside. "When my grandfather was alive, he loved to host dinner parties. Several members of Congress as well as a couple governors have eaten here."

"When did you lose him?"

"A year and a half ago. He had a heart condition and died peacefully in his sleep." Grandfather had been the only parent he and Kyle had ever known, and his death had shaken Liam. How the loss had hit Kyle, Liam didn't know. Despite inheriting half the ranch when their grandfather died, his brother never came home and Liam dealt with him only once or twice a year on business matters.

"I remember your grandfather at the shows," Hadley said. "He always seemed larger than life."

Liam ushered her into the large modern kitchen. Her words lightened Liam's mood somewhat. "He loved the horse business. His father had been a cattleman. Our herd of Black Angus descends from the 1880s rush to bring Angus from Scotland."

"So you have both cattle and horses?"

"We have a Black Angus breeding program. Last year we sold two hundred two-year-olds."

"Sounds like you're doing very well."

After a quick peek in the den, they finished their tour of the first floor and climbed the stairs.

"Business has been growing steadily." So much so that Liam wasn't able to do what he really loved: train horses.

"You don't sound all that excited about your success."

He'd thought the abrupt cessation of his personal life would provide more time to focus on the ranch, but he'd discovered the more he was around, the more his staff came to him with ideas for expanding.

"I didn't realize how focused my grandfather had been on the horse side of the business until after his heart problems forced him into semiretirement. Apparently he'd been keeping things going out of respect for his father, but his heart wasn't really in it."

"And once he semiretired?"

"I hired someone who knew what he was doing and gave him a little capital. In three years he'd increased our profits by fifty percent." Liam led Hadley on a tour of three different bedrooms. "This one is mine."

"I think it would be best if Maggie is across the hall from you." Hadley had chosen a cheerful room with large windows overlooking the backyard and soft green paint on the walls. "That way when she wakes up at night you'll be close by."

While Liam wasn't worried about being up and down all night with the infant, he preferred not to be left alone in case something went wrong. "Are you sure I can't convince you to live in?"

"You'll do fine. I promise not to leave until I'm sure Maggie is well settled."

That was something, Liam thought. "If you have things under control for the moment, I need to get back to the barn. I have several calls to make and an owner stopping by to look at his crop of yearlings."

"Maggie and I will be fine."

"Candace should be back with supplies soon, and hopefully we'll have some baby furniture delivered later today. I'll have a couple of the grooms empty this room so it can be readied for Maggie."

Hadley nodded her approval. In her arms, the baby began to fuss. "I think it's time for a change and a little something to eat."

"Here's my cell and office numbers." Liam handed her his business card. "Let me know if you need anything."

"Thank you, I will."

The short drive back to the barn gave Liam a couple minutes to get his equilibrium back. Kyle was a father. That was going to shock the hell out of his brother.

And Liam had received a shock of his own today in the form of Hadley Stratton. Was it crazy that she was the one who stuck out in his mind when he contemplated past regrets? Granted, they'd been kids. He'd been twenty. She'd barely graduated high school the first time she'd made an impression on him. And it had been her riding that had caught his attention. On horseback she'd been a dynamo. Out of the saddle, she'd been quiet and gawky in a way he found very appealing.

He'd often regretted never getting the chance to know anything about her beyond her love of horses, and now fate had put her back in his life. Second chances didn't come often, and Liam intended to make the most of this one.

The grandfather clock in the entry hall chimed once as Hadley slipped through the front door into the cold night air. Shivering at the abrupt change in temperature, she trotted toward her SUV and slid behind the wheel. An enormous yawn cracked her jaw as she started the car and navigated the circular drive.

In order for Hadley to leave Liam in charge of Maggie, she'd had to fight her instincts. The baby was fussier than most, probably because she was premature, and only just went to sleep a little while ago. Although Liam had gained confidence as he'd taken his turn soothing the frazzled infant, Hadley had already grown too attached to the motherless baby and felt compelled to hover. But he needed to learn to cope by himself.

Weariness pulled at her as she turned the SUV on to the deserted highway and headed for Royal. Her last few assignments had involved school-age children, and she'd forgotten how exhausting a newborn could be. No doubt Liam would be weary beyond words by the time she returned at seven o'clock tomorrow morning.

This child, his daughter, was going to turn his world upside down. Already the house had a more lived-in feeling, less like a decorator's showplace and more like a family home. She wondered how it had been when Liam and his brother were young. No doubt the old Victorian had quaked with the noisy jubilance of two active boys.

Twenty minutes after leaving the Wade house, Hadley let herself into her one-bedroom apartment. Waldo sat on the front entry rug, appearing as if he'd been patiently awaiting her arrival for hours when in fact, the cat had probably been snoozing on her bed seconds earlier. As she shut the front door, the big gray tabby stretched grandly before trotting ahead of her toward the kitchen and his half-empty food bowl. Once it was filled to his satisfaction, Waldo sat down and began cleaning his face.

The drive had revived her somewhat. Hadley fixed herself a cup of Sleepytime tea and sipped at it as she checked the contents of the bags a good friend of hers had dropped off this afternoon. After seeing what Candace had bought for the baby, Hadley had contacted Kori to purchase additional supplies. She would owe her friend lunch once Maggie was settled in. Kori had shown horses when she was young and would get a kick out of hearing that Liam Wade was Hadley's new employer.

Hadley had a hard time falling asleep and barely felt as if she'd dozed for half an hour when her alarm went off at five. Usually she liked to work out in the morning and eat a healthy breakfast while watching morning news, but today she was anxious about how things had gone with Liam and Maggie.

Grabbing a granola bar and her to-go mug filled with coffee, Maggie retraced the drive she'd made a mere five hours earlier. The Victorian's second-floor windows blazed with light, and Hadley gave a huge sigh before shifting the SUV into Park and shutting off the engine.

The wail of a very unhappy baby greeted Hadley as she let herself in the front door. From the harried expression on Liam's face, the infant had been crying for some time.

"It doesn't sound as if things are going too well," she commented, striding into the room and holding out her arms for the baby. "Did you get any sleep?"

"A couple hours."

Liam was still dressed for bed in a pair of pajama bottoms that clung to his narrow hips and a snug T-shirt that highlighted a torso sculpted by physical labor. Hadley was glad to have the fussy baby to concentrate on. Liam's help-lessness made him approachable, and that was dangerous. Even without his usual swagger, his raw masculinity was no less potent.

"Why don't you go back to bed and see if you can get a little more sleep?"

The instant she made the suggestion, Hadley wished the words back. She never told an employer what to do. Or she hadn't made that mistake since her first nanny job. She'd felt comfortable enough with Noah to step across the line that separated boss and friend. For a couple months that hadn't been a problem, but then she'd been pulled in too deep and had her heart broken.

"It's time I headed to the barn," Liam said, his voice muffled by the large hands he rubbed over his face. "There are a dozen things I didn't get to yesterday."

His cheeks and jaw were softened by a day's growth of beard, enhancing his sexy, just-got-out-of-bed look. Despite the distraction of a squirming, protesting child in her arms, Hadley registered a significant spike in her hormone levels. She wanted to run her palms over his broad shoulders and feel for herself the ripple of ab muscles that flexed as he scrubbed his fingers through his hair before settling his hands on his hips.

Light-headed, she sat down in the newly purchased rocking chair. Liam's effect on her didn't come as a surprise. She'd had plenty of giddy moments around him as a teenager. Once, after she'd had a particularly fantastic run, he'd even looked straight at her and smiled.

Hadley tightened her attention on Maggie and wrestled her foolishness into submission. Even if Liam was still that cocky boy every girl wanted to be with, she was no longer a susceptible innocent prone to bouts of hero worship. More important, he'd hired her to care for this baby, a child who was probably his daughter.

"Do you think she's okay?" Liam squatted down by the rocker. He gripped the arm of the chair to steady himself, his fingers brushing Hadley's elbow and sending ripples of sensation up her arm.

"You mean because she's been crying so much?" Hadley shot a glance at him and felt her resolve melting beneath the concern he showered on the baby. "I think she's just fussy. We haven't figured out exactly what she likes yet. It might take swaddling her tight or a certain sound that calms her. I used to take care of a baby boy who liked to fall asleep listening to the dishwasher."

"I know we talked about this yesterday," Liam began, his gaze capturing hers. "But can you make an exception for a few weeks and move in here?"

"I can't." The thought filled her with a mixture of excitement and panic. "I have a cat—"

"There's always plenty of mice in the barn."

Hadley's lips twitched as she imagined Waldo's horror at being cut off from the comforts of her bed and his favorite sunny spot where he watched the birds. "He's not that sort of cat."

"Oh." Liam gazed down at Maggie, who'd calmed

enough to accept a pacifier. "Then he can move in here with you."

Hadley sensed this was quite a compromise for Liam, but she still wasn't comfortable agreeing to stay in the house. "I think Maggie is going to be fine once she settles in a bit. She's been through a lot in the last few days."

"Look at her. She's been crying for three hours and you calm her down within five minutes. I can't go through another night like this one. You have to help me out. Ten days."

"A week." Hadley couldn't believe it when she heard herself bargaining.

Triumph blazed in Liam's eyes, igniting a broad smile. "Done." He got to his feet, showing more energy now that he'd gotten his way.

After a quick shower and a cup of coffee, Liam felt a little more coherent as he entered his bookkeeper/office manager's office. Ivy had been with Wade Ranch for nine years. She was a first cousin twice removed, and Grandfather had hired her as his assistant, and in a few short years her organizational skills had made her invaluable to the smooth running of the ranch.

"Tough night?" Ivy smirked at him over the rim of her coffee cup. She looked disgustingly chipper for seven in the morning. "Used to be a time when you could charm a female into doing your bidding."

Liam poured himself a cup of her wickedly strong brew and slumped onto her couch. "I'm rusty." Although he'd persuaded Hadley to move in for a week. Maybe it was just babies that were immune.

"Have you considered what you're going to do if the baby isn't Kyle's?"

As Ivy voiced what had filtered through Liam's mind several times during the last twenty-four hours, he knew he'd better contact a lawyer today. Technically, unless he claimed the child as his, he had no legal rights to her.

"I really believe Kyle is her father," Liam said. "I'm heading to a clinic Hadley recommended to have a DNA test run. I figured since Kyle and I are identical twins, the results should come back looking like Maggie is my daughter."

And then what? Margaret was dead. With Kyle estranged from his family, it wasn't likely he or Maggie would spend much time at Wade Ranch. And if Liam was wrong about his brother being Maggie's father, Diane Garner might give her up to strangers.

Liam was surprised how fast he'd grown attached to the precious infant; the idea of not being in her life bothered him. But was he ready to take on the challenge of fatherhood? Sure, he and Kyle had done okay raised by their grandfather, but could a little girl be raised by a man alone? Wouldn't she miss a mother snuggling her, brushing her hair and teaching her all the intricacies of being a woman? And yet it wasn't as if Liam would stay single forever.

An image of Hadley flashed through his thoughts. Beautiful, nurturing and just stubborn enough to be interesting. A year ago he might not have given her a second thought. Hadley was built for steady, long-term relationships, not the sort of fun and games that defined Liam's private life. She'd probably be good for him, but would he be good for her? After a year of celibacy, his libido was like an overwound spring, ready to explode at the least provocation.

"Liam, are you listening to me?" Ivy's sharp tone shattered his thoughts.

"No. Sorry. I was thinking about Maggie and the future."

Her expression shifted to understanding. "Why don't we

talk later this afternoon. You have a fund-raising meeting at the club today, don't you?"

He'd forgotten all about it. Liam had been involved with the Texas Cattleman's Club fund-raising efforts for Royal Memorial's west wing ever since it had been damaged by a tornado more than a year ago. The grand reopening was three weeks away, but there remained several unfinished projects to discuss.

"I'll be back around three."

"See you then."

Fearing if he sat down in his large office, he might doze off, Liam headed into the attached barn where twelve champion American quarter horse stallions stood at stud. Three of them belonged to Wade Ranch; the other nine belonged to clients.

Liam was proud of all they'd accomplished and wished that his grandfather had lived to see their annual auction reach a record million dollars for 145 horses. Each fall they joined with three other ranches to offer aged geldings, sought after for their proven ranch performance, as well as some promising young colts and fillies with top bloodlines.

At the far end of the barn, double doors opened into a medium-sized indoor arena used primarily for showing clients' horses. One wall held twenty feet of glass windows. On the other side was a spacious, comfortable lounge used for entertaining the frequent visitors to the ranch. A large television played videos of his stallions in action as well as highlights from the current show and racing seasons.

Liam went through the arena and entered the show barn. Here is where he spent the majority of his time away from ranch business. He'd grown up riding and training reining horses and had won dozens of national titles as well as over a million dollars in prize money before he'd turned twenty-five.

Not realizing his destination until he stood in front of

the colt's stall, Liam slid open the door and regarded WR Electric Slide, son of Hadley's former mount, Lolita. The three-year-old chestnut shifted in the stall and pushed his nose against Liam's chest. Chuckling, he scratched the colt's cheek, and his mind returned to Hadley.

While he understood that college and grad school hadn't left her the time or the money to own a horse any longer, it didn't make sense the way she'd shot down his suggestion that she visit this son of her former mount. And he didn't believe that she'd lost interest in horses. Something more was going on, and he wasn't going to let it go.

Three

Hadley sat in the nursery's comfortable rocking chair with Maggie on her lap, lightly tapping her back to encourage the release of whatever air she'd swallowed while feeding. It was 3:00 a.m., and Hadley fended off the house's heavy silence by quietly humming. The noise soothed the baby and gave Hadley's happiness a voice.

She'd been living in the Wade house for three days, and each morning dawned a little brighter than the last. The baby fussed less. Liam smiled more. And Hadley got to enjoy Candace's terrific cooking as well as a sense of accomplishment.

Often the agency sent her to handle the most difficult situations, knowing that she had a knack for creating cooperation in the most tumultuous of households. She attributed her success to patience, techniques she'd learned in her child development classes and determination. Preaching boundaries and cooperation, she'd teach new habits to the children and demonstrate to the parents how consistency made their lives easier.

Feeling more than hearing Maggie burp, Hadley resettled the baby on her back and picked up the bottle once more. Her appetite had increased after her pediatrician diagnosed acid reflux, probably due to her immature digestive system, and prescribed medication to neutralize her stomach acids. Now a week old, Maggie had stopped losing weight and was almost back to where she'd started.

In addition to the reflux problem, Maggie had symptoms of jaundice. Dr. Stringer had taken blood samples to run for DNA, and the bilirubinometer that tested jaundice levels had shown a higher-than-average reading. To Liam's dismay, the doctor had suggested they wait a couple weeks to see if the jaundice went away on its own. He'd only relaxed after the pediatrician suggested they'd look at conventional phototherapy when the blood tests came back.

By the time Hadley settled Maggie back into her crib, it was almost four in the morning. With the late-night feedings taking longer than average because of Maggie's reflux problem, Hadley had gotten in the habit of napping during the day when the baby slept. The abbreviated sleep patterns were beginning to wear on her, but in four short days she would be back spending the night in her tiny apartment once more.

Yawning into her pajama sleeve, Hadley shuffled down the hall to her room. Seeing that her door was open brought her back to wakefulness. In her haste to reach Maggie before she awakened Liam, Hadley hadn't pulled her door fully shut, and after a quick check under the bed and behind the chair, she conceded that the cat was missing. Damn. She didn't want to tiptoe around the quiet house in search of a feline who enjoyed playing hide-and-seek. Given the size of the place, she could be at it for hours.

Silently cursing, Hadley picked up a pouch of kitty treats and slipped out of her room. The floorboards squeaked beneath her. Moving with as much stealth as possible, she stole past Liam's room and headed toward the stairs.

Once on the first floor, Hadley began shaking the treat bag and calling Waldo's name in a stage whisper. She began in the living room, peering under furniture and trying not to sound as frustrated as she felt. No cat. Next, she moved on to the den. That, too, was feline free. After a quick and fruitless sweep of the dining room, she headed into the kitchen, praying Waldo had found himself a perch on top of the refrigerator or made a nest in the basket of dirty clothes in the laundry room. She found no sign of the gray tabby anywhere.

Hadley returned to the second floor, resigned to let the cat find his own way back, hoping he did before Liam woke up. But as she retraced her steps down the dim corridor, she noticed something that had eluded her earlier. Liam's door was open just wide enough for a cat to slip inside. She paused in the hall and stared at the gap. Had it been like that when she'd passed by earlier? It would be just like Waldo to gravitate toward the one person in the house who didn't like him.

She gave the pouch of cat treats a little shake. The sound was barely above a whisper, but Waldo had fantastic hearing, and while he might disregard her calls, he never ignored his stomach. Hadley held her breath for a few tense, silent seconds and listened for the patter of cat paws on the wood floor, but heard nothing but Liam's deep, rhythmic breathing. Confident that he was sound asleep, she eased open his door until she could slip inside.

Her first step into Liam's bedroom sent alarm bells shrilling in her head. Had she lost her mind? She was sneaking into her employer's room in the middle of the night while he slept. How would she explain herself if he woke? Would he believe that she was in search of her missing cat or would he assume she was just another opportunistic female? As the absurdity of the situation hit her, Hadley pressed her face into the crook of her arm and smothered a giggle. Several deep breaths later she had herself mostly back under control and advanced another careful step into Liam's room.

Her eyes had long ago grown accustomed to the darkness, and the light of a three-quarter moon spilled through the large window, so it was easy for her to make out the modern-looking king-size bed and the large man sprawled beneath the pale comforter. And there was Waldo, lying on top of Liam's stomach looking for all the world as if he'd found the most comfortable place on earth. He stared at Hadley, the tip of his tail sweeping across Liam's chin in a subtle taunt.

This could not be happening.

Hadley shook the pouch gently and Waldo's gold eyes narrowed, but he showed no intention of moving. Afraid that Liam would wake if she called the cat, Hadley risked approaching the bed. He simply had to move on his own. In order to pick him up, she'd have to slide her hand between Waldo's belly and Liam's stomach. Surely that would wake the sleeping man.

Pulling out a treat, she waved it in front of the cat's nose. Waldo's nose twitched with interest, but he displayed typical catlike disdain for doing anything expected of him. He merely blinked and glanced away. Could she snatch up the cat and make it to the door before Liam knew what had happened? Her mind ran through the possibilities and saw nothing but disaster.

Maybe she could nudge the cat off Liam. She poked the cat's shoulder. Waldo might have been glued where he lay. Working carefully, she slid her finger into his armpit and prodded upward, hoping to annoy him into a sitting position. He resisted by turning his body to stone.

Crossing her fingers that Liam was as sound a sleeper as he appeared, Hadley tried one last gambit. She scratched Waldo's head and was rewarded by a soft purr. Now that he was relaxed, she slid her nails down his spine and was rewarded when he pushed to his feet, the better to enjoy the caress. Leaning farther over the mattress, she slid one hand behind his front legs and cupped his butt in her other palm when she felt the air stir the fabric of her pajama top against her skin.

Hadley almost yelped as a large hand skimmed beneath the hem of her top and traced upward over her rib cage to the lower curve of her breast. Awkwardly looming over Liam's bed, her hands wrapped around an increasingly unhappy feline, she glanced at Liam's face and noticed that while his eyes remained closed, one corner of his lips had lifted into a half smile.

Liam was having an amazing dream. He lay on a couch in front of a roaring fire with a woman draped across him. Her long hair tickled his chin as his hands swept under her shirt, fingers tracing her ribs. Her bare skin was warm and soft beneath his caress and smelled like lavender and vanilla.

It was then he realized whom he held. He whispered her name as his palm discovered the swell of her breast. His fingertips grazed across her tight nipple and her body quivered in reaction, He smiled. A temptress lurked beneath her professional reserve and he was eager to draw her out. Before he could caress further, however, something landed on his chest with a thump.

The dream didn't so much dissolve as shatter. One second he was inches away from heaven, the next he was sputtering after having his breath knocked out. His eyes shot open. Darkness greeted him. His senses adjusted as wakefulness returned.

The silken skin from his dream was oh so real against his fingers. As was the disturbed breathing that disrupted the room's silence.

"Hadley?"

She was looming over his bed, frozen in place, her arms extended several inches above his body. "Waldo got out of my room and came in here. I was trying to lift him off you when you…" Her voice trailed off. She gathered the large gray cat against her chest and buried her face in his fur.

Liam realized his hand was still up her pajama top, palm resting against her side, thumb just below the swell of her breast. The willpower it took to disengage from the compromising position surprised him.

"I was dreaming…" He sat up in bed and rubbed his face to clear the lingering fog of sleep. "Somehow you got tangled up in it."

"You were dreaming of me?" She sounded more dismayed than annoyed.

He reached for the fading dream and confirmed that she had been the object of his passion. "No." She'd already pegged him as a womanizer; no need to add fuel to the fire. "The woman in my dream wasn't anyone I knew."

"Perhaps it was Margaret Garner."

It frustrated him that she continued to believe Maggie was his daughter. "That's possible, since I never met her." His tone must have reflected his frustration because Hadley stepped away from his bed.

"I should get back to my room. Sorry we woke you."

"No problem." Liam waited until the door closed behind her before he toppled backward onto the mattress.

The sheer insanity of the past few moments made him grin. Had she really sneaked into his room to fetch the cat? Picturing what must have happened while he slept made him chuckle. He wished he could have seen her face. He'd bet she'd blushed from her hairline to her toes. Hadley didn't have the brazen sensuality of the women who usually caught his interest. She'd never show up half dressed in his hotel room and pout because he'd rather watch a football game than fool around. Nor would she stir up gossip in an attempt to capture his attention. She was such a straight arrow. Her honesty both captivated and alarmed him.

Rather than stare sleepless at the ceiling, Liam laid his

forearm over his eyes and tried to put Hadley out of his mind. However, vivid emotions had been stirred while he'd been unconscious. Plus, he was having a hard time forgetting the oh-so-memorable feel of her soft skin. With his body in such a heightened state of awareness, there was no way Liam was going to just fall back asleep. Cursing, he rolled out of bed and headed for the shower. Might as well head to the barn and catch up on paperwork.

Three hours later he'd completed the most pressing items and headed out to the barn to watch the trainers work the two-year-olds. At any time, there were between twenty and thirty horses in various stages of training.

They held classes and hosted clinics. For the last few years, Liam had taught a group of kids under ten years old who wanted to learn the ins and outs of competitive reining. They were a steely-eyed bunch of enthusiasts who were more serious about the sport than many adults. At the end of every class, he thanked heaven it would be a decade before he had to compete against them.

"Hey, boss. How're the colts looking?" Jacob Stevens, Liam's head trainer, had joined him near the railing.

"Promising." Liam had been watching for about an hour. "That bay colt by Blue is looking better all the time."

"His full brother earned over a quarter of a million. No reason to think Cielo can't do just as well." Jacob shot his boss a wry grin. "Think you're going to hold on to him?"

Liam laughed. "I don't know. I've been trying to limit myself to keeping only five in my name. At the moment, I own eight."

Until Hadley had shown up, he'd been seriously contemplating selling Electric Slide. The colt was going to be a champion, but Liam had more horses than he had time for. If only he could convince Hadley to get back in the saddle. He knew she'd balk at being given the horse, but maybe she'd be willing to work him as much as time permitted.

"Thing is," Jacob began, "you've got a good eye, and the ranch keeps producing winners."

Liam nodded. "It's definitely a quality problem. I've had a couple of good offers recently. Maybe I need to stop turning people down."

"Or just wait for the right owner."

"Speaking of that. Can you get one of the guys to put Electric Slide through his paces? I want to get some video for a friend of mine."

"Sure."

As he recorded the chestnut colt, Liam wasn't sure if he'd have any luck persuading Hadley to come check out the horse, but he really wanted to get to the bottom of her resistance.

Lunchtime rolled around, and Liam headed back to the house. He hadn't realized how eager he was to spend some time with Maggie and Hadley until he stopped his truck on the empty driveway and realized Hadley's SUV was absent.

Candace was pulling a pie out of the oven as he entered the kitchen. Her broad smile faded as she read the expression on his face. "What's wrong?"

"Where's Hadley?"

"Shopping for clothes and things for Maggie." Candace set a roast beef sandwich on the center island and went to the refrigerator for a soda. "The poor girl hasn't been out of here in days."

"She took Maggie with her?"

"I offered to watch her while she was gone, but the weather is warm, and Hadley thought the outing would do her some good."

"How long have they been gone?"

"About fifteen minutes." Candace set her hands on her hips and regarded him squarely. "Is there some reason for all the questions?"

"No."

Liam wondered at his edginess. He trusted Maggie was in good hands with Hadley, but for some reason, the thought of both of them leaving the ranch had sparked his anxiety. What was wrong with him? It wasn't as if they weren't ever coming back.

The thought caught him by surprise. Is that what was in the back of his mind? The notion that people he cared about left the ranch and didn't come back? Ridiculous. Sure, his mother had left him and Kyle. And then Kyle had gone off to join the navy, but people needed to live their lives. It had nothing to do with him or the ranch. Still, the sense of uneasiness lingered.

Royal Diner was humming with lunchtime activity when Hadley pushed through the glass door in search of a tuna melt and a chance to catch up with Kori. To her relief, her best friend had already snagged one of the booths. Hadley crossed the black-and-white checkerboard floor and slid onto the red faux-leather seat with a grateful sigh.

"I'm so glad you were able to meet me last-minute," Hadley said, settling Maggie's carrier beside her and checking on the sleeping infant.

She'd already fed and changed the baby at Priceless, Raina Patterson's antiques store and craft studio. Hadley had taken a candle-making class there last month and wanted to see what else Raina might be offering.

"Thanks for calling. This time of year is both a blessing and a curse." Kori was a CPA who did a lot of tax work, making January one of her slower months. "I love Scott, but his obsessive need to be busy at all times gets on my nerves." Kori and her husband had started their accounting company two years ago, and despite what she'd just said, the decision had been perfect for them.

"You're the one doing me a favor. I really need your

advice." Hadley trailed off as the waitress brought two Diet Cokes.

They put in their lunch order and when the waitress departed, Kori leaned her forearms on the table and fixed Hadley with an eager stare.

"This is fantastic. You never need my help with anything."

Her friend's statement caught Hadley off guard. "That's not true. I'm always asking for favors."

"Little things, sure, like when you asked me to pick up baby stuff for Miss Maggie or help with your taxes, but when it comes to life stuff you're so self-sufficient." Kori paused. "And I'm always boring you with the stuff that I'm going through."

Hadley considered. "I guess I've been focused on finishing my degree and haven't thought much beyond that. Plus, it's not like I have a social life to speak of."

Kori waved her hands. "Forget all that. Tell me what's going on."

Embarrassment over her early-morning encounter with Liam hadn't faded one bit. Her skin continued to tingle in the aftermath of his touch while other parts of her pulsed with insistent urgency. The only thing that kept her from quitting on the spot was that he'd been asleep when he'd slid his hand beneath her clothes.

"Oh my goodness," Kori exclaimed in awe. "You're blushing."

Hadley clapped her hands over her cheeks. "Am I?"

"What happened?"

"Waldo got out of my room last night when I got up for Maggie's feeding, and when I tracked him down, he was in Liam's room, curled up right here." Hadley indicated where her cat had been on Liam's anatomy.

"You said he isn't a cat person. Was he mad?"

"He was asleep."

Kori began to laugh. "So what happened?"

"I tried to lure him off with a treat, but Waldo being Waldo wouldn't budge. As I was picking him up..." Swept by mortification, Hadley closed her eyes for a span of two heartbeats.

"Yes?" Kori's voice vibrated with anticipation. "You picked him up and what?"

"I was leaning over the bed and Liam was sleeping. And dreaming." Hadley shuddered. "About having sex with some woman, I think."

"And?" Kori's delighted tone prompted Hadley to spill the next part of her tale.

"The next thing I knew, his hand was up my shirt and he—" she mimed a gesture "—my breast." Her voice trailed off in dismay.

"No way. And you're sure he was asleep?"

"Positive. Unfortunately, I was so shocked that I didn't keep a good hold of Waldo and he jumped onto Liam's chest, waking him. I don't think he knew what hit him."

"What did he say?"

"I honestly don't remember. I think I mumbled an apology for waking him. He retrieved his hand from beneath my pajama top and I bolted with Waldo."

"Did you talk to him later?"

"He was gone before Maggie woke up again, and then I took off before he came home for lunch." Hadley glanced at her charge to make sure the baby was sleeping soundly. "What am I supposed to say or do the next time I see him?"

"You could thank him for giving you the best sex you've had in years."

"We didn't have sex." Hadley lowered her voice and hissed the last word, scowling at her friend.

"It's the closest thing you've had to a physical encounter in way too long." Kori fluffed her red hair and gazed in disgust at her friend. "I don't know how you've gone so long without going crazy. If Scott and I go three days without sex we become vile, miserable people."

Hadley rolled her eyes at her friend. "I'm not in a committed, monogamous relationship. You and Scott have been together for seven years. You've forgotten how challenging being single is. And if you recall, the last time I fell in love it didn't work out so well."

"Noah was an ass. He led you on while he was still working through things with his ex-wife."

"She wanted him back," Hadley reminded her friend. "He'd never stopped loving her even after finding out she'd cheated on him. And he was thinking about his kids."

"He still hedged his bets with you. At the very least, he should have told you where things stood between them."

On that, Hadley agreed. Five years earlier, she'd been a blind fool to fall in love with Noah. Not only had he been her employer, but also things had moved too fast between them. Almost immediately he'd made her feel like a part of the family. Because it was her first time being a nanny, she hadn't understood that his behavior had crossed a line. She'd merely felt accepted and loved.

"That was a long time ago." Thinking about Noah made her sad and angry. He'd damaged her ability to trust and opened a hole in her heart that had never healed. "Can we get back to my more immediate problem? Do I quit?"

"Because your boss sleep–felt you up?" Kori shook her head. "Chalk it up to an embarrassing mistake and forget about it."

"You're right." Only she was having a hard time forgetting how much she enjoyed his hands on her skin. In fact, she wanted him to run his hands all over her body and make her come for him over and over.

Kori broke into her thoughts. "You're thinking about him right now, aren't you?"

"What?" Hadley sipped at her cold drink, feeling overly warm. "No. Why would you think that?"

"You've got the hots for him. Good for you."

"No. Not good for me. He's my boss, for one thing. For another, he's a major player. I knew him when I used to race barrels. He had girls chasing after him all the time, and he enjoyed every second of it."

"So he's a playboy. You don't need to fall in love with him, just scratch an itch."

"I can't." Hadley gave her head a vehement shake to dispel the temptation of Kori's matter-of-fact advice. "Besides, I'm not his type. He was asleep during most of what happened this morning."

"Wait. Most?"

Hadley waved to dismiss her friend's query. "It might have taken him a couple extra seconds to move his hand."

Kori began to laugh again. "Oh, he must have really been thrown for a loop. You in his bedroom in the middle of the night with the cat."

The picture Kori painted was funny, and Hadley let herself laugh. "Thank you for putting the whole thing in perspective. I don't know why I was so stressed about it."

"Maybe because despite your best intentions, you like the guy more than you think you should."

Hadley didn't even bother to deny it. "Maybe I do," she said. "But it doesn't matter, because no matter how attractive I may find him, he's my boss, and you know I'm never going there again."

Four

After missing Maggie and Hadley at lunchtime, Liam made sure was home, showered and changed early enough to spend some time with his niece before dinner. She was in her crib and just beginning to wake up when he entered her room. Hadley wasn't there, but he noticed the red light on the baby monitor and suspected she was in her room or downstairs, keeping one ear tuned to the receiver.

Before Maggie could start to fuss, Liam scooped her out of the crib and settled her on the changing table. Already he was becoming an expert with the snaps and Velcro fastenings of Maggie's Onesies and diapers. Before the baby came fully awake, he had her changed and nestled in his arm on the way downstairs.

The domestic life suited him, he decided, entering the kitchen to see what Candace had made for dinner. The large room smelled amazing, and his mouth began to water as soon as he crossed the threshold. He sneaked up behind Candace and gave her a quick hug.

"What's on the menu tonight?"

"I made a roast. There's garlic mashed potatoes, green beans and apple pie for dessert."

"And your wonderful gravy."

"Of course."

"Is Jacob joining us?"

"Actually, we're going to have dinner in town. It's the seventh anniversary of our first date."

Candace and Jacob had been married for the last six years. They'd met when Candace had come to work at Wade Ranch and fell in love almost at first sight. They had the sort of solid relationship that Liam had never had the chance to see as he was growing up.

"You keep track of that sort of thing?" Liam teased, watching as Candace began fixing Maggie's bottle.

"It's keeping track of that sort of thing that keeps our relationship healthy."

Liam accepted the bottle Candace handed him, his thoughts wrapped around what she'd said. "What else keeps your relationship healthy?"

If the seriousness of his tone surprised her, the housekeeper didn't let on. "Trust and honesty. Jacob and I agreed not to let things fester. It's not always easy to talk about what bugs us, especially big issues like his sister's negative attitude toward me and the fact that I hate holding hands in public. Thank goodness we're both morning people and like the same television shows, or we'd never have made it this far."

As Liam watched Maggie suck down the formula, he let Candace's words wash over him. He'd never actually been in a relationship, healthy or otherwise. Oh, he dated a lot of women, some of them for long periods of time, but as he'd realized a year ago, not one of them wanted more than to have a good time.

At first he'd been shocked to discover that he'd let his personal life remain so shallow. Surely a thirty-year-old man should have had at least one serious relationship he could look back on. Liam hadn't been able to point to a single woman who'd impacted his life in any way.

He didn't even have mommy issues, because he'd never gotten to know her. She was a distracted, preoccupied guest at Christmas or when she showed up for his birthday. When she couldn't make it, expensive presents arrived and were dutifully opened. The most up-to-date electronics, gift cards, eventually big checks. For Liam, their mother had been the beautiful young woman in the photo framed by silver that sat on Grandfather's desk. According to him, she'd loved her career more than anything else and wasn't cut out to live on a ranch.

"...and of course, great sex."

The last word caught his attention. Liam grinned. "Of course."

Candace laughed. "I wondered if you were listening to me. Turns out you weren't."

"I was thinking about my past relationships or lack thereof."

"You just haven't found the right girl." Candace patted him on the arm, adopting the persona of wise old aunt. "Once she shows up, you'll have all the relationship you can handle. Just remember to think about her happiness before your own and you'll be all right."

Liam thought about his past girlfriends and knew that advice would have bankrupted him. His former lovers wanted the best things money could buy. Expensive clothes, exotic trips, to be pampered and spoiled. Living such an affluent lifestyle had been fine for short periods of time, but at heart, Liam loved the ranch and his horses. None of his lady friends wanted to live in Royal permanently. It was too far from the rapid pace of city life.

"I'm out of here," Candace said, slipping her coat off the hook near the kitchen door. "You and Hadley should be able to handle things from here. See you tomorrow." She winked. "Probably for lunch. You'll have your choice of cereal or Pop-Tarts for breakfast."

Grimacing, Liam wished her a good night and returned his attention to Maggie. The greedy child had consumed almost the entire bottle while he'd been talking to Candace. Knowing he should have burped her halfway through, he slung a towel over his shoulder and settled her atop it. Hadley's simple ways of handling Maggie's reflux issues had made a huge difference in the baby's manner. She was much less fussy.

Liam walked around the kitchen, swaying with each stride to soothe the infant. He'd been at this for ten minutes when Hadley entered the room. She'd left her hair down tonight, and the pale gold waves cascaded over the shoulders of her earth-tone blanket coat. The weather had turned chilly and wet in the early evening, and Hadley had dressed accordingly in jeans and a dark brown turtleneck sweater.

"Have you already fed her?" Hadley approached and held her hands out for the baby. She avoided meeting his gaze as she said, "I can take her while you eat."

"Maggie and I are doing fine." The baby gave a little burp as if in agreement. "Why don't you fix yourself a plate while I give her the rest of her bottle? I can eat after you're done."

Hadley looked as if she wanted to argue with him, but at last gave a little nod. "Sure."

While he pretended to be absorbed in feeding Maggie, Liam watched Hadley, thinking about their early-morning encounter and wondering if that accounted for her skittishness. Had he done more while asleep than she'd let on? The thought brought with it a rush of heat. He bit back a smile. Obviously his subconscious had been working overtime.

"Look, about this morning—" he began, compelled to clear the air.

"You were sleeping." Hadley's shoulders drooped. "I intruded. I swear I won't let Waldo get out again."

"Maybe it's not good for him to be cooped up all the time."

"My apartment is pretty small. Besides, you don't like cats."

"What makes you say that?" Liam had no real opinion either way.

Hadley crossed her arms over her chest and gave him the sort of stern look he imagined she'd give a disobedient child. "You suggested I put him in the barn."

"My grandfather never wanted animals in the house, so that's what I'm used to."

"The only time Waldo has been outside was after the house where he lived was destroyed by the tornado. He spent a month on his own before someone brought him to Royal Haven, where I adopted him. He gets upset if I leave him alone too long. That's why I couldn't stay here without bringing him."

Talking about her cat had relaxed Hadley. She'd let down her guard as professional caretaker, and Liam found himself charmed by her fond smile and soft eyes. No wonder she had such a magical effect on Maggie. She manifested a serenity that made him long to nestle her body against his and...

Desire flowed through him, brought on by a year of celibacy and Hadley's beauty. But was that all there was to it? Over the last year, he hadn't been a hermit. Promoting the ranch meant he'd attended several horse shows, toured numerous farms. Every public appearance provided opportunities to test his resolve, but not one of the women he'd met had tempted him like Hadley.

Liam cleared his throat, but the tightness remained. "Why don't you bring him down after dinner so he and I can meet properly and then let him have the run of the house?"

"Are you sure?"

He'd made the suggestion impulsively, distracted by

the direction his thoughts had taken, but it was too late to change his mind now. "Absolutely."

The exchange seemed to banish the last of her uneasiness. Unfortunately, his discomfort had only just begun. Maggie had gone still in his arms, and Liam realized she was on the verge of sleep. Knowing her reflux required her to remain upright for half an hour, he shifted her onto his shoulder and followed Hadley to the kitchen table where he ate most of his meals since his grandfather had died.

"Is something the matter?" Hadley asked. She'd carried both their plates to the table.

"No, why?"

"You're frowning." She sat down across from him. "Do you want me to take Maggie?"

"No, she's fine." In less than a week he'd mastered the ability to hold the baby and do other things at the same time. He picked up his fork. "I was just thinking that I haven't used the dining room much since my grandfather died. Every meal he ate in this house was in there. I find it too big and lonely to use by myself."

"You could eat there with Maggie."

"*We* could eat there with Maggie."

Her eyes widened briefly before she gave a reluctant nod. "Of course, I would be there to take care of Maggie."

Liam didn't think they were on the same page. He'd been thinking of her in terms of companionship. She'd obviously assumed he'd want her as Maggie's caretaker. Or was she deliberately reminding him of their different roles in the household?

"I promised I'd bring Maggie down to the barn tomorrow for a visit. I'd like you to come with us." Now that the DNA results had come back indicating that Maggie was Kyle's daughter, he was eager to introduce her to everyone.

"Of course." Hadley didn't sound overly enthusiastic.

"She's a Wade, which means she's going to be spending a lot of time there."

"Or she may take after…my mother. She left the ranch to pursue a career in real estate and rarely visits." He had no idea what had prompted him to share this about his mother.

"Not everyone is cut out for this life, I suppose."

Or for motherhood. She'd left her sons in the care of their grandfather and hadn't returned more than a handful of times during their childhood. Liam knew it had bothered Grandfather that his only child didn't want anything to do with her family's legacy. As for how Kyle felt, Liam and his brother rarely discussed her.

"You mentioned that you're finishing up your degree. What are your plans for after graduation?"

Hadley smiled. "I've submitted my résumé to several school districts in Houston. That's where my parents live."

"You're not planning on staying in Royal then?"

"I like it here. My best friend and her husband run an accounting firm in town. I'm just not sure there are enough job opportunities in the area for someone just starting out in my field. And I'm an only child. My parents hate that I live so far away."

"What sort of a job are you looking for?" Liam found himself wanting to talk her into remaining in the area.

"School counseling. My undergraduate degree is in teaching, but after a couple years, I decided it wasn't my cup of tea and went back for my master's."

"You're certainly good with children," Liam said. "Any school would be lucky to have you."

While they spoke, Hadley had finished eating. She took charge of Maggie, settling her into the nearby infant seat while Liam finished his dinner. He made short work of Candace's excellent cooking and set both of their plates in the sink.

"Can I interest you in a piece of caramel apple pie? Candace makes the best around."

"Sure." Hadley laughed. "I have a weakness for dessert."

Liam heated both pieces in the microwave and added a scoop of ice cream to each. With Maggie sound asleep, she no longer provided any sort of distraction, and Liam was able to focus his full attention on Hadley.

"I took some video of Electric Slide being worked today. Thought you might be interested in seeing him in action." He pulled up the footage he'd taken with his phone and extended it her way. "Even though he's young, I can already tell he has his mother's work ethic and athleticism. I'd love your opinion on him."

"You're the expert," she reminded him, cupping the phone in her hands.

"Yes, but as I was discussing with my head trainer today, I have too many horses, and I need to figure out which ones I should let go."

"You're thinking of selling him?" She looked up from the phone's screen, her expression concerned.

And with that, Liam knew he'd struck the right chord at last.

Knowing she shouldn't care one way or another what Liam did with his horses, Hadley let her gaze be drawn back to the video of the big chestnut colt racing across the arena only to drop his hindquarters and execute a somewhat sloppy sliding stop. His inexperience showed, but she liked his balance and his willingness.

Lolita had been a dream horse. For two years she and Hadley had dominated as barrel racers and scored several championships in the show ring. During that time she'd had several offers to purchase the mare but couldn't imagine being parted from her.

Until Anna's accident, when everything changed.

"He's a nice colt," she said, making an effort to keep her reply noncommittal. She replayed the video, paying close attention to the horse's action. He looked so much like his mother. Same three white socks. Same shoulder and hip. Same nose-out gesture when he moved from a lope into a gallop. How many classes had she lost before that little quirk had been addressed?

"Maybe you can give him a try when you come to the barn tomorrow."

Her stomach tightened as she contemplated how much fun it would be to ride Lolita's son. But Hadley hadn't been on a horse in ten years, not since Anna had ended up in a wheelchair. Remorse over her role in what happened to her friend had burdened Hadley for a decade. The only thing that kept her from being overwhelmed by guilt was her vow never to ride again. And that was a small sacrifice compared with what Anna was living with.

"I'm afraid I don't ride anymore."

"I'm sure you haven't lost any of your skills."

Hadley found dark amusement in his confidence. She was pretty sure any attempt to swing into a saddle would demonstrate just how rusty she was.

"The truth is I don't want to ride." She didn't think Liam would understand her real reason for turning him down.

"But you might enjoy it if only you got back in the saddle."

The man was as stubborn as he was persuasive, and Hadley wasn't sure how to discourage him without being rude. "I assure you I wouldn't. I was pretty crazy about horses when I was young, but it no longer interests me."

"That's a shame. You were a really talented rider."

Her heart gave a little jump. "I really loved it."

"And it showed. Shannon used to complain about you all the time." Liam's intent gaze intensified his allure. "That's when I started watching you ride, and I figured out why all the other girls lost to you."

"Lolita."

"She was a big part of it, but you rode the hell out of her."

Hadley shook her head. "You said it yourself. Shannon won a lot on Lolita."

"Yeah, but her times never matched yours."

The temptation to bask in Liam's warm regard almost derailed Hadley's professionalism. The man had such a knack for making a woman feel attractive and desirable. But was he sincere? She'd labeled him a player, but maybe she'd done that to keep from being sucked in by his charm. The way he cared about Maggie made Hadley want to give him the benefit of the doubt. And yet he hadn't known he'd gotten her mother pregnant. That didn't exactly illustrate his accountability.

"Does Shannon still own her?" Parting with the mare had been one of the hardest things Hadley had ever done.

"No. She sold her after a couple years."

"How did you end up with one of her foals?"

"A client of mine in California had him."

"And Lolita?" For someone who claimed she was no longer interested in anything horse-related, Hadley was asking a lot of questions. But Lolita had been special, and she wanted to hear that the mare had ended up in a good home.

"I don't know." Her disappointment must have shown because Liam offered, "I can find out."

Hadley waved off his concern. "Oh, please don't bother. I was just…curious."

"It's no problem. Jack is a good friend."

"Really, don't trouble yourself. I'm sure she's doing great." A wave of nostalgia swept over Hadley. She wished she could say she hadn't thought about Lolita for years, but that wasn't at all the case.

Hadley didn't realize she was still holding Liam's phone until it began to ring. The image of a stunning brunette appeared on the screen. The name attached to the beautiful face: Andi. She handed Liam back his phone and rose.

"I'll take Maggie upstairs."

Andi looked like the sort of woman he'd want privacy to talk to. Hadley was halfway up the back stairs before she heard him say hello. She didn't notice the disappointment dampening her mood until she reached the nursery and settled into the rocking chair that overlooked the enormous backyard. What did she have to be down about? Of course Liam had a girlfriend. He'd always had a girlfriend, or probably several girls that he kept on ice for when he found himself with a free night.

And yet he hadn't gone out once since she'd moved into the house. He spent his evenings watching sports in the large den, laptop open, pedigrees scattered on the sofa beside him. Back when she'd been a teenager, she'd spent a fair amount of time poring over horse magazines and evaluating one stallion over another. Although it was a hobby, she liked to think her hours of study had been instrumental in how well she'd done in selecting Lolita.

Until coming to Wade Ranch, Hadley hadn't realized how much she missed everything having to do with horses. The familiar scents of the barn that clung to the jacket that Liam hung up in the entry roused emotions she'd suppressed for a long time. She missed riding. Barrel racing was in turns exhilarating and terrifying. Competing in a Western pleasure class might not be an adrenaline rush, but it presented different challenges. And no matter the outcome, a clean ride was its own reward.

Tomorrow when she took Maggie to the barn to visit Liam, she needed to keep a handle on her emotions. Liam was a persuasive salesman. He would have her butt in a saddle before she knew what was happening. Hadley shook her head, bemused and unable to comprehend why he was so determined to revive her interest in horses.

Could it be that his own passion was so strong that he wanted everyone to share in what he enjoyed? Hadley made a mental note to feel Candace out on the subject tomorrow. That settled, she picked up the book she'd been reading and settled back into the story.

A half hour later, Liam appeared in the doorway. He'd donned a warm jacket and was holding his hat.

"I have to head back to the barn. One of the yearlings got cut up in the paddock today and I need to go check on him." Liam's bright green gaze swept over her before settling on Maggie snuggled in her arms. "You two going to be okay in the house by yourselves?"

Hadley had to smile at his earnest concern. "I think we'll be fine."

"It occurs to me that I've been taking advantage of you." His words recalled their early morning encounter, and Hadley's pulse accelerated.

"How so?" she replied, as calmly as her jittery nerves allowed.

"You haven't had any time off since that first night, and I don't think you were gone more than five hours today."

"I don't mind. Maggie isn't a lot of trouble when she's sleeping, and she does a lot of that. I've been catching up on my reading. I don't have a lot of time for that when I'm in school. Although, I do have my last candle-making class at Priceless tomorrow. We're working with molds. I'd like to make it to that."

"Of course."

Almost as soon as Liam left the old Victorian, Hadley wished him back. Swaddled tight in a blanket, Maggie slept contentedly while Hadley paced from parlor to den to library to kitchen and listened to the wind howl outside. The mournful wail made her shiver, but she was too restless to snuggle on the couch in the den and let the television drown out the forlorn sounds.

Although she hadn't shared an apartment in five years, she never thought of herself as lonely. Something about living in town and knowing there was a coffee shop, library or restaurant within walking distance of her apartment was reassuring. Out here, half an hour from town, being on her own in this big old house wasn't the least bit comfortable.

Or maybe she just wanted Liam to come back.

Five

Promptly at ten o'clock the next morning, Hadley parked her SUV in front of the barn's grand entrance and shut off the engine. She'd presumed the Wade Ranch setup would be impressive, but she'd underestimated the cleverness of whoever had designed the entry. During warmer months, the grass on either side of the flagstone walkway would be a welcoming green. Large pots filled with Christmas boughs flanked the glass double doors. If Hadley hadn't been told she was about to enter a barn, she would have mistaken her destination for a showcase mansion.

Icy wind probed beneath the hem of Hadley's warm coat and pinched her cheeks when she emerged from the vehicle's warmth and fetched Maggie from the backseat. Secure in her carrier, a blanket over the retractable hood to protect her from the elements, the infant wouldn't feel the effects of the chilly air, but Hadley rushed to the barn anyway.

Slipping through the door, Hadley found herself in a forty-foot-long rectangular room with windows running the length of the space on both sides. To her right she glimpsed an indoor arena, empty at the moment. On her left, the windows overlooked a stretch of grass broken up into three paddock areas where a half-dozen horses grazed. That side of the room held a wet bar, a refrigerator and a few bar stools.

On the far end of the lounge, a brown leather couch

flanked by two matching chairs formed a seating area in front of the floor-to-ceiling fieldstone fireplace. Beside it was a doorway that Hadley guessed led to the ranch offices.

Her rubber-soled shoes made no sound on the dark wood floor, and she was glad. The room's peaked ceiling magnified even the slightest noise. She imagined when a group gathered here the volume could rattle the windows.

A woman in her early fifties appeared while Hadley was gawking at the wrought iron chandeliers. They had a Western feel without being cliché. In fact, the whole room was masculine, rugged, but at the same time had an expensive vibe that Hadley knew would appeal to a clientele accustomed to the finer things.

"Hello. You must be Hadley." The woman extended her hand and Hadley grasped it. "I'm Ivy. Liam told me you'd be coming today."

"Nice to meet you." Hadley set the baby carrier on the table in the center of the room and swept the blanket away. "And this is Maggie."

"She's beautiful." Ivy peered at the baby, who yawned expansively. "Liam talks about her nonstop."

"I imagine he does. Having her around has been a huge change for him." Hadley unfastened the straps holding the baby in the carrier and lifted her out. Maggie screwed up her face and made the cranky sounds that were a warm-up for all-out wailing. "She didn't eat very well this morning, so she's probably hungry. Would you hold her for me while I get her bottle ready?"

"I'd be happy to." Ivy didn't hesitate to snuggle Maggie despite the infant's increasing distress. "Liam has been worthless since this little one appeared on his doorstep."

Hadley had filled a bottle with premeasured powdered formula and now added warm water from the thermos she carried. "I think discovering he's a father has thrown him for a loop, but he's doing a fantastic job with Maggie."

"You think he's Maggie's father?"

Something about Ivy's neutral voice and the way she asked her question caught Hadley's attention. "Of course. Why else would Maggie's grandmother have brought her here?" She shook Maggie's bottle to mix the formula and water.

"It's not like Liam to be so careless. May I?" Ivy indicated the bottle Hadley held. "With someone as good-looking and wealthy as Liam, if he wasn't careful, a girl would have figured out how to trap him before this."

"You think Kyle is Maggie's father?"

"That would be my guess."

"But I thought he was based on the East Coast and never came home. Candace told me Maggie's mom was from San Antonio."

Hadley was uncomfortable gossiping about her employer, but reminded herself that Ivy was his family and she'd asked a direct question.

Ivy smiled down at the baby. "She's Kyle's daughter. I'm sure of it."

Any further comment Hadley might have made was forestalled by Liam's arrival. His cheeks were reddened by cold, and he carried a chill on his clothes. Hadley's pulse tripped as his penetrating gaze slid over her. The brief look was far from sexual, yet her body awakened as if he'd caressed her.

"Here are my girls," he said, stopping between Ivy and Hadley. After greeting Maggie with a knuckle to her soft cheek, he shifted his attention to Hadley. "Sorry I wasn't here to greet you, but I was delayed on a call. What do you think of the place so far?"

"Impressive." Warmth poured through her at the inconsequential brush of his arm against hers. "I never expected a ranch to have a barn like this." She indicated the stone fireplace and the windows that overlooked the arena. Staring around the large lounge kept her gaze from lingering on Liam's infectious grin and admiring the breadth of his shoulders encased in a rugged brown work jacket.

"It's been a work in progress for a while." He winked at Ivy, who rolled her eyes at him.

The obvious affection between the cousins didn't surprise Hadley. Liam had an easy charisma that tranquilized those around him. She'd wager that Liam had never once had to enforce an order he'd given. Why bully when charm got the job done faster and easier?

"I imagine a setup like this takes years to build."

"And a lot of convincing the old man," Ivy put in. "Calvin was old-school when it came to horses. He bred and sold quality horses for ranch work. And then this one came along with his love of reining and his big ideas about turning Wade Ranch into a breeding farm."

Liam tossed one of Maggie's burp rags on his shoulder and eased the infant out of Ivy's arms. "And it worked out pretty well," he said, setting the baby on his shoulder. "Come on, let's go introduce this little lady around."

With Liam leading the way through the offices, his smile broad, every inch the proud parent, he introduced Hadley to two sales associates, the breeding coordinator, the barn manager and a girl who helped Ivy three mornings a week.

Hadley expected that her role as Maggie's nanny would relegate her to the background, but Liam made her an active part of the conversation. He further startled her by bringing up her former successes at barrel racing and in the show ring. She'd forgotten how small the horse business could be when one of the salespeople, Poppy Gertz, confessed to rejoicing when Hadley had retired.

"Do you still compete?" Hadley questioned, already anticipating what the answer would be.

"Every chance I get." The brunette was in her midthirties with the steady eye and swagger of a winner. "Thinking about getting back into the game?"

At Hadley's head shake, Poppy's posture relaxed.

"We're going to get her into reining," Liam said, shifting Maggie so she faced forward.

Hadley shook her head. "I'm going to finish getting my masters and find a job as a guidance counselor." She reached out for the infant, but Liam turned away.

"Maggie and I are going to check out some horses." His easy smile was meant to lure her after them. "Why don't you join us." It was a command pitched as a suggestion.

Dutifully she did as he wanted. And in truth, it wasn't a hardship. In fact, her heartbeat increased at the opportunity to see what Wade Ranch had to offer. She'd done a little reading up about Liam and the ranch on the internet and wasn't surprised at the quality of the horses coming out of Liam's program.

They started with the stallions, since their barn was right outside the barn lounge. While Liam spoke in depth about each horse, Hadley let her thoughts drift. She'd already done her research and was far more interested in the way her body resonated with the deep, rich tone of Liam's voice. He paused in front of one stall and opened the door.

"This is WR Dakota Blue." Pride shone in Liam's voice and body language.

"He's beautiful," Hadley murmured.

The stallion stepped up to the door and nuzzled Liam's arm, nostrils flaring as he caught Maggie's scent. An infant her age couldn't clearly see objects more than eight to ten inches away, so Hadley had to wonder what Maggie made of the stallion.

"She isn't crying," Liam said as the horse lipped at Maggie's blanket. "I guess that's a good sign."

"I don't think she knows what to make of him."

"He likes her."

The stallion's gentleness and curiosity reminded her a lot of how Liam had first approached Maggie. Watching horse and owner interact with the infant, something unlocked inside Hadley. The abrupt release of the constriction left her reeling. How long had she been binding her emotions? Probably since she'd shouldered a portion of responsibility for Anna's accident.

"Hadley?" Liam's low voice brought her back to the present. He'd closed the door to the stallion's stall and stood regarding her with concern. "Is everything okay?"

"Yes. I was just thinking how lucky Maggie is to grow up in this world of horses." And she meant that with all her heart. As a kid Hadley had been such a nut about horses. She would have moved into the barn if her parents let her.

"I hope she agrees with you. My brother doesn't share my love of horses." Liam turned from the stall, and they continued down the aisle. "You miss it, don't you?"

What was the point in denying it? "I didn't think I did until I came to Wade Ranch. Horses were everything until I went off to college. I was remembering how much I missed riding and what I did to cope."

"What did you do?"

"I focused on the future, on the career I would have once I finished school."

"I'm not sure I could give up what I do."

Hadley shrugged. "You've never had to." She considered his expression as he guided her through the doors that led into the arena and wondered what it would be like to be him, to never give up something because of circumstances. "Have you ever considered what would happen if you lost Wade Ranch?"

His grin was a cocky masterpiece. "I'd start over somewhere else."

And that summed up the differences between them. Hadley let life's disappointments batter her. Liam shrugged off the hits and lived to fight another day. Which is exactly what drew her to him. She admired his confidence. His swagger. What if she hadn't let guilt overwhelm her after Anna's accident? What if she'd stood up to her parents about selling Lolita and changed her major when she realized teaching wasn't her cup of tea?

"I wish I'd gotten to know you better back when I was racing barrels," she said, letting him guide her toward a narrow wooden observation deck that ran the length of the arena.

He handed over Maggie. "You could have if you hadn't disappeared after my advice helped you win the sweepstakes. You were supposed to thank me by taking me to dinner."

"I thought you were kidding about that." Only she hadn't. She'd been thrilled that he'd wanted to go out with her. But Anna's accident had happened before she had the chance to find out if his interest in her was real. "Besides, I wasn't your type."

"What sort of type was that?"

She fussed with Maggie's sweater and didn't look at him. "Experienced."

Liam took the hit without an outward flinch. Inside he raged with frustration. "I'm not sure any woman has a worse opinion of me than you do." It was an effort to keep his voice neutral.

"My opinion isn't bad. It's realistic. And I don't know why you'd care."

Women didn't usually judge him. He was the fun guy to have around. Uncomplicated. Charming. With expensive taste and a willing attitude. But Hadley wanted more than an amiable companion who took her to spendy restaurants and exclusive clubs. Glib phrases and seduction wouldn't work on her. He'd have to demonstrate substance, and Liam wasn't sure how to go about that.

"I care because I like you." He paused a beat before adding, "And I want you to like me."

Without waiting to see her reaction, he strode across the arena toward the horse being led in by one of the grooms. He'd selected four young horses to show Hadley in the hopes of enticing her to get back in the saddle. Why it was so important to see her ride again eluded him. As always he was just going with his gut.

Liam swung up into the saddle and walked the gelding toward the raised viewing deck. "This is a Blue son. Cielo is three. I think he has a great future in reining. At the moment I personally own eight horses and I need to pare that down to five. I'm going to put him and three others through their paces, and I want you to tell me which you think I should keep and which should go."

Hadley looked appalled. "You can't ask me to do that. I'm no judge."

"When I'm done riding all four you will tell me what you think of each." He bared his teeth at her in a challenging smile. "I value your opinion."

He then spent ten minutes working Cielo through his paces all the while staying aware of Hadley's body language and expression. With Maggie asleep in her arms, Hadley had never looked so beautiful, and Liam had a hard time concentrating on his mounts. After he rode all four horses, he had a special one brought out.

"You might recognize Electric Slide from his video."

Hadley's color was high and her eyes were dancing with delight, but her smile dimmed as he approached with the colt her former mare had produced. "I can't get over how much he looks like his mother."

"Want to give him a try?"

She shook her head. "It's been too long since I've ridden, and I'm not dressed for it."

He recognized a lame excuse when he heard one. She'd worn jeans and boots to the barn and didn't want to admit the real reason for her reluctance.

"Next time." Liam swung into the saddle and pivoted the colt away.

Disappointment roared through him, unfamiliar and unpleasant. He couldn't recall the last time he'd invested so much in a project only to have it fall flat. Was that because he didn't throw himself wholly into anything, or because he rarely failed at things he did? His grandfather would say that if he was consistently successful, he wasn't challenging himself.

Isn't that why he'd quit dating a year ago and refocused on Wade Ranch? He'd grown complacent. The horse business was growing at a steady pace. He enjoyed the companionship of several beautiful women. And he was bored.

Liam's mind was only half on what he was doing as he rode Electric Slide. The pleasure had gone out of the exhibition after Hadley turned down a chance to ride. After a little while, he handed the colt off and strode across the arena toward her.

"It's almost noon," he said. "Let's go back to the house and you can tell me which horses I should keep over lunch."

"Sure."

As they ate bowls of beef stew and crusty French bread, Hadley spelled out her take on each of the horses he'd shown her.

"Cielo is a keeper. But I don't think you'd part with him no matter what anyone said to you."

"You're probably right." He missed talking horses with someone. Since his grandfather died, Liam hadn't had anyone to share his passion with. "What did you think of the bay filly?"

"Nice, but the roan mare is better, and bred to Blue you'd get a really nice foal." Hadley's gaze turned thoughtful as she stirred the stew with her spoon. "I also think you'd be fine letting the buckskin go. He's terrific, but Cielo will be a better reining horse." Her lips curved. "But I'm not telling you anything you hadn't already decided."

"I appreciate your feedback. And you're right. Of the four I showed you, I'd selected three to sell. But your suggestion that I breed Tilda to Blue was something I hadn't considered."

Her smile warmed up the already-cozy kitchen. "Glad I could help. It was fun talking horses. It was something my friends and I did all the time when I was younger. I always imagined myself living on a ranch after I finished school, breeding and training horses."

Liam's chest tightened. Hadley possessed the qualities he'd spent the last year deciding his perfect woman must have. Beautiful, loving, maternal and passionate about horses.

"Of course, that wasn't a practical dream," Hadley continued. "My parents were right to insist I put my education first. I figured that out not long after I started college."

"But what if you could have figured out a way to make it work? Start small, build something."

"Maybe ten years ago I could have." Her voice held a hint of wistfulness. A moment later, all nostalgia vanished. "These days it's no longer what I want."

Her declaration put an end to the topic. Liam held his gaze steady on her for a moment longer, wondering if he'd imagined her overselling her point. Or was he simply wishing she'd consider giving up her future plans and sticking around Royal? He'd grown attached to her in a very short period of time and wanted to see more of her. And not as his niece's nanny.

Liam pushed back from the table. "I have a meeting late this afternoon at the Texas Cattleman's Club, but I'll be back in time for you to make your class at seven."

"Thank you. I really enjoy the class as much for the company as the candle making." She carried their bowls to the sink and began rinsing them. "When I'm in school, I don't have a lot of free time."

"Sounds like you don't make enough time for fun," he said.

"I keep telling myself that I'll have plenty of time to enjoy myself once I'm done with school. In the meantime, I make the most of the free hours I have."

Liam was mulling Hadley's attitude as he strode into the Texas Cattleman's Club later that day. Originally built as a men's club around 1910, the club opened its doors to women members as well a few years ago. Liam and his grandfather had been all for the change and had even supported the addition of a child care center. For the most part, though, the decor of the original building had been left intact. The wood floors, paneled walls and hunting trophies created a decidedly masculine atmosphere.

As Liam entered the lounge and approached the bar, he overheard one table discussing the Samson Oil land purchases. This had been going on for months. Several ranchers had gone bankrupt on the heels of the destructive tornado that had swept through Royal and the surrounding ranches. Many of those who'd survived near financial ruin had then had to face the challenge of the drought that reduced lakes and creeks and made sustaining even limited herds difficult. Some without established systems of watering tanks and pumps had been forced to sell early on. Others were holding out for a miracle that wouldn't come.

"I guess I know what's on the agenda for the meeting

today," Liam mentioned as he slid into the space between his best friend, David "Mac" McCallum, and Case Baxter, current president of the Texas Cattleman's Club. "Has anybody heard what's up with all the purchases?"

Mac shook his head. "Maybe they think there are shale deposits."

"Fracking?" The man on the other side of Mac growled. "As if this damned drought isn't bad enough. What sort of poison is that process going to spill into our groundwater? I've got two thousand heads relying on well water."

Liam had heard similar complaints every time he set foot in the clubhouse. The drought was wearing on everyone. Wade Ranch relied on both wells and a spring-fed lake to keep its livestock watered. He couldn't imagine the stress of a situation where he only had one ever-dwindling source to count on.

"Mellie tells me the property lawyer who's been buying up all the land for Samson Oil quit," Case said. His fiancée's family owned several properties the oil company had tried to buy. "She's gotten friendly with one of her tenants, the woman who owns the antiques store in the Courtyard. Apparently she and Nolan Dane are involved."

"Howard Dane's son?"

"Yes, and Nolan's going back to work with him doing family law."

Liam missed who asked the question, but Case's answer got him thinking about Kyle. That his brother was still out of touch reinforced Liam's growing conviction that Maggie deserved a parent who was there for her 24/7. Obviously as long as he was on active duty, Kyle couldn't be counted on. Perhaps Liam should reach out to an attorney familiar with family law and see what his options might be for taking over custody of his niece. He made a mental note to give the man a call the next morning and set up an appointment.

"Maybe we should invite him to join the club," Liam suggested, thinking how their numbers had dwindled over the last year as more and more ranchers sold off their land.

"I think we could use some powerful allies against Samson Oil," Case said. "Nolan might not be able to give us any information on his former client, but he still has a background in property law that could be useful."

The men gathered in the bar began to move toward the boardroom where that night's meeting was to be held.

"How are things going for you at home?" Mac asked. "Is fatherhood all it's cracked up to be?"

"Maggie is not my daughter," Liam replied, wearying of everyone assuming he'd been foolhardy. "But I'm enjoying having her around. She's really quite sweet when she's not crying."

Mac laughed. "I never thought I'd see you settling down."

"A year ago I decided I wanted one good relationship rather than a dozen mediocre ones." Liam was rather impressed with how enlightened he sounded.

"And yet you've buried yourself at the ranch. How are you any closer to a good relationship when you don't get out and meet women?"

"I've heard that when you're ready, the right one comes along." An image of Hadley flashed through his mind.

Mac's hand settled forcefully on Liam's shoulder. "You're talking like an idiot. Is it sleep deprivation?"

"I have a newborn living with me. What do you think?"

But Liam knew that what was keeping him awake at night wasn't Maggie, but her nanny and the persistent hope that Waldo might sneak into Liam's bedroom and Hadley would be forced to rescue him a second time. Because if that happened, Liam had prepared a very different end to that encounter.

Six

Ivy entered Liam's office with her tablet in hand and sat down. The back of the chair thumped against the wall, and her knees bumped his desk. She growled in annoyance and rubbed her legs. Unbefitting his status as half owner of the ranch, Liam had one of the tiniest offices in the complex. He preferred to spend his days out and about and left paperwork for evenings. When he met with clients, he had an informal way of handling the meetings and usually entertained in the large lounge area or brought them into the barns.

"I'm finalizing your plans for Colorado this weekend," she said, her finger moving across the tablet screen. "The caterer is confirmed. A Suburban will be waiting for you at the airport. Give Hannah Lake a call when you land, and she will meet you at the house."

Ivy kept talking, but Liam had stopped listening. He'd forgotten all about the skiing weekend he was hosting for five of his clients. The tradition had begun several years ago. They looked forward to the event for months, and it was far too late to cancel.

"Liam?" Ivy regarded him with a steady gaze. "You seem worried. I assure you everything is ready."

"It's not that. I forgot that I was supposed to be heading to Colorado in a couple days. What am I going to do about Maggie?"

"Take her along." She jotted a note on the tablet with a stylus. "I'll see if they can set up a crib in one of the rooms."

"Have you forgotten this is supposed to be a guys' weekend? A chance for everyone to get away from their wives and families so they can smoke cigars, drink too much scotch, ski and play poker?"

"Sounds lovely." Ivy rolled her eyes.

Liam pointed at Ivy's expression. "And that is exactly what they want to get away from."

"I don't know what you're worrying about. Bring Hadley along to take care of Maggie. The house is big enough for a dozen people. No one will even know they're there."

Ivy's suggestion made sense, but Liam's instincts rebelled at her assumption that no one would realize they were present. He would know. Just like every other night when she slept down the hall.

"That's true enough, and Maggie is doing better at night. She barely fusses at all before going back to sleep." Liam wondered how much of a fight Hadley would make about flying to Colorado. He got to his feet. It was late enough in the afternoon for him to knock off. He'd been looking forward to spending a little time with Maggie before dinner. "I'd better give Hadley a heads-up."

"Let me know if she has anything special to arrange for Maggie." With that, Ivy exited the office.

Liam scooped his hat off the desk and settled it on his head. As he drove the ten minutes between barns and house, Liam considered the arguments for and against taking Maggie with him to Colorado. In the ten days since his niece had become a part of his life, he'd grown very attached to her. When his brother contacted him, Liam intended to convince him to give the baby up. With the dangerous line of work his brother was in, Maggie would be better off with the sort of stable home environment found here on Wade Ranch.

Liam entered the house and followed the scent of wood smoke to the den. Hadley looked up from her book as Liam entered. "You're home early."

"I came home to spend some time with Maggie." And with her. Had he imagined the way her eyes had lit up upon seeing him? They'd spent a great deal of time together in the last few days. All under the guise of caring for Maggie, but Liam knew his own motives weren't as pure as he'd let on.

"She had a rough afternoon."

She glanced down at the sleeping infant nestled in her arms. Hadley's fond expression hit Liam in the gut.

"She looks peaceful now."

"I only got her to sleep half an hour ago." Hadley began shifting the baby in her arms. "Do you want to hold her?"

"Not yet. I spent most of the day in the saddle. I'm going to grab a shower first."

He rushed through his cleanup and ran a comb through his damp hair. Dressed in brown corduroy pants and a denim shirt, he headed back to the den. The afternoon light had faded until it was too dark for Hadley to read, but instead of turning on the lamps, she was relying on the flickering glow of the fire. Outside, the wind howled, and she shivered.

"Is it as chilly as it sounds?"

"I suspect the windchill will be below freezing tonight."

He eased down on the couch beside her and took the baby. Their bodies pressed against each other hip to knee during the exchange, and Liam smiled as her scent tickled his nose. They'd become a well-oiled machine in the last few days, trading off Maggie's care like a couple in sync with each other and their child's needs. It had given him a glimpse of what life would be like with a family. Liam enjoyed Hadley's undemanding company. She'd demonstrated an impish sense of humor when sharing stories of her fellow nannies' adventures in caretaking, and he was wearing down her resistance to talking about horses by sharing tales of people she used to compete against.

"I have a business trip scheduled in a couple days," Liam began, eyeing Hadley as he spoke. Her gaze was on the baby in his arms.

"How long will you be gone?"

"I rented a house in Colorado for a week, but usually I'm only gone for four days." He paused, thinking how he'd prefer to stay in this cozy triangle with Hadley and Maggie rather than flying off to entertain a group of men. "It's a ski weekend for five of my best clients."

"Are you worried about leaving Maggie here?"

"Yes. I want to bring her along." He paused a beat before adding, "I want you to come, as well." He saw the arguments building in her blue eyes. He already had the answer to her first one. "Candace has offered to take Waldo, so you don't have to worry about him."

"I've never traveled with a client before." She wasn't demonstrating the resistance he'd expected. "Are you sure there will be room for us?"

"The house is quite large. There are seven bedrooms. Ivy is coordinating the trip and said you should let her know about anything you think Maggie might need. She is already making arrangements for a crib."

"When would we leave?"

"We'll fly up in two days. I like to get in a day early to make sure everything is in place. Is that enough time for you to get what you'll need?"

"Sure." But she was frowning as she said it.

"Is something wrong?"

She laughed self-consciously. "I've never seen snow before. What will I need to buy besides a warm coat?"

"You've never seen snow?" Liam was excited at the

thought of being there when Hadley experienced the beauty of a winter day in the mountains.

"For someone as well traveled as you are, that must seem pretty unsophisticated."

Liam considered her comment. "You said you'd never traveled with your clients. Is that because you didn't want to?"

"It's mostly been due to school and timing. I always figured there'd be plenty of time to travel after I graduated and settled into a job with regular hours and paid vacation time."

Her wistful smile gave him some notion of how long and arduous a journey it had been toward finishing her master's degree.

He felt a little hesitant to ask his next question. "Have you flown in a small plane before?"

"No." She drew the word out, her gaze finding and holding his. Anxiety and eagerness pulled at the corners of her mouth. "How small is small?"

Small turned out to be forty feet in length with a forty-three-foot wingspan. Hadley's heart gave a little bump as she approached the elegant six-seat jet with three tiny oval windows. She didn't know what she'd been expecting, maybe a single-prop plane with fixed wheels like the ones used by desperate movie heroes to escape or chase bad guys.

"This doesn't look so scary, does it?" She whispered the question to a sleepy Maggie.

Hadley stopped at the steps leading up to the plane. Liam had gone ahead with her luggage and overnight bag carrying all of Maggie's things. Now he emerged from the plane and reached down to take Maggie's carrier.

"Come on in." Liam's irresistible grin pulled Hadley forward.

She almost floated up the stairs. His charm banished her nervousness, allowing her to focus only on the excitement of visiting Colorado for the first time. Not that she'd see much of it. Her job was to take care of Maggie. But even to glimpse the town of Vail covered in snow as they drove past would be thrill enough.

The plane's interior was luxurious, with room enough for a pilot and five passengers. There were six beige leather seats, two facing forward and two backward as well as the two in the cockpit. She knew nothing about aviation equipment, but the instrument panel placed in front of the pilot and copilot seats had three large screens filled with data as well as an abundance of switches and buttons and looked very sophisticated.

"I set up Maggie's car seat here because I thought you'd prefer to face forward. You'll find bottles of water and ice over there." He pointed to the narrow cabinet behind the cockpit. "There's also a thermos of hot water to make Maggie's bottle."

"Thank you. I made one before we left because it helps babies to adjust to altitudes if they're sucking on something."

"Great. We should be set then."

Hadley settled into her seat and buckled herself in. She looked up in time to see Liam closing the airplane's door.

"Wait," she called. "What about the pilot?"

The grin he turned on her was wolfish. "I am the pilot." With a wink, he slid into the left cockpit seat and began going through a preflight check.

Surprise held her immobile for several minutes before her skin heated and her breath rushed out. For almost two weeks now his actions and the things he'd revealed about himself kept knocking askew her preconceived notions about him. It was distracting. And dangerous.

To avoid fretting over her deepening attraction to Liam,

Hadley pulled out Maggie's bottle and a bib. As the plane taxied she had a hard time ignoring the man at the controls, and surrendered to the anxiety rising in her.

What was she doing? Falling for Liam was a stupid thing to do. The man charmed everyone without even trying.

As the plane lifted off, her stomach dipped and her adrenaline surged. Hadley offered Maggie the bottle and the infant sucked greedily at it. Out the window, land fell away, and the small craft bounced a little on the air currents. To keep her nervousness at bay, Hadley focused all her attention on Maggie. The baby was not the least bit disturbed by the plane's movements. In fact, her eyes were wide and staring as if it was one big adventure.

After what felt like an endless climb, the plane leveled off. Hadley freed Maggie from her car seat so she could burp her. Peering out the window, she saw nothing but clouds below them. With Liam occupied in the cockpit and Maggie falling asleep in her arms, Hadley let her thoughts roam free.

Several hours later, after Liam landed the plane at a small airport outside Vail, their rental car sped toward their destination. When she'd stepped off the plane, Hadley had been disappointed to discover that very little snow covered the ground. She'd imagined that in the middle of January there would be piles and piles of the white stuff everywhere she looked. But now, as they neared the mountains, her excitement began to build once more.

Framed against an ice-blue sky, the snow-covered peaks surrounding the town of Vail seemed impossibly high. But she could see the ski runs that started near the summit and carved through the pine-covered face of each mountain. Liam drove the winding roads without checking the navigation, obviously knowing where he was headed.

"What do you think?"

"It's beautiful."

"Wait until you see the views from the house. They're incredible."

"Do you rent this house every year?"

"A longtime friend of my grandfather owns it."

"I didn't realize you like to ski."

"I had a lot more free time when I was younger, but these days I try to get out a couple times a year. I go to New Mexico when I can get away for a weekend because it's close."

"It must be nice having your own plane so you can take off whenever you want."

"I'm afraid it's been pretty idle lately. I've spent almost ninety percent of my time at the ranch this year."

And the other ten percent meeting Maggie's mother and spending the night with her. Hadley glanced into the backseat where the baby was batting at one of the toys clipped to her car seat.

"You said that's been good for your business," Hadley said, "but don't you miss showing?"

"All the time."

"So why'd you give it up?" From the way Liam's expression turned to stone, she could tell her question had touched on something distasteful. "I'm sorry. I didn't mean to pry. Forget I said anything."

"No, it's okay. A lot of people have asked me that question. I'll tell you what I tell them. After my grandfather died, I discovered how much time it takes to run Wade Ranch."

She suspected that was only half of the reason, but she didn't pry anymore. "Any chance your brother, Kyle, will come back to Texas to help you?"

"No." Liam's answer was a clipped single syllable and discouraged further questions. "I'm finding a balance between ranch business as a whole and the horse side that I love. Last summer I hired a sales manager for the cattle division. I think you met Emma Jane. She's been a terrific asset."

She *had* terrific assets, Hadley thought wryly. The beautiful blonde was memorable for many reasons, not the least of which was the way her eyes and her body language communicated her interest in Liam. That he'd seemed oblivious had surprised Hadley. Since when did a man who enjoyed having beautiful women around not notice one right beneath his nose?

Maybe becoming a father had affected him more than Hadley had given him credit for.

Liam continued, "But it's not like having someone I could put in charge of the entire operation."

Obviously Liam was stretched thin. Maybe that's why he'd been looking so lighthearted these last few days. The break from responsibility would do him good.

Forty minutes after they'd left the airport, Liam drove up a steep driveway and approached a sprawling home right at the base of the mountain.

"We're staying here?" Hadley gawked at the enormous house.

"I told you there was enough room for you and Maggie." He stopped the SUV beside a truck and shot her a broad smile. "Let's get settled in and then head into town for dinner. It's a quarter mile walk if you think Maggie would be okay."

"We can bundle her up. The fresh air sounds lovely." The temperature hovered just above freezing, but it was sunny and there wasn't any wind, so Hadley was comfortable in her brand-new ski jacket and winter boots.

A tall man in his midsixties with an athletic bounce to his stride emerged from the house and headed straight for Liam. "Mr. Wade, how good to have you with us again."

"Hello, Ben." The two men shook hands, and Liam turned to gesture to Hadley, who'd unfastened Maggie from her car seat and now walked around to the driver's side. "This is Ms. Stratton and Maggie."

"Ivy mentioned you were bringing family with you this year. How nice."

The vague reference to family disturbed Hadley. Why couldn't Liam just admit that he had a daughter? He obviously loved Maggie. What blocked him from acknowledging her as his? This flaw in his character bothered Hadley more than it should. But it was none of her business. And it wasn't fair that she expected more of him. Liam was her employer. She had no right to judge.

"Nice to meet you, Ben," she said.

While Liam and Ben emptied the SUV of luggage and ski equipment, Hadley carried Maggie inside and passed through the two-story foyer to the large living room. The whole front of the house that faced the mountain was made up of tall windows.

"There's a nice room upstairs for you and Maggie." Liam came over to where she stood staring at the mountain range. "Ben said he was able to get a crib set up in there."

Hadley followed Liam up a broad staircase. At the top he turned right. The home sprawled across the hillside, providing each bedroom with a fantastic view. The room Hadley and Maggie were to share was at the back of the house and looked west, offering views of both mountains and the town. At four in the afternoon, the sun was sliding toward the horizon, gilding the snow.

"Is this okay?"

"It's amazing." The room was large by Hadley's standards, but she guessed it was probably the smallest the house offered. Still, it boasted a queen-size bed, plush seating for two before the enormous picture window and a stone fireplace that took up most of the wall the bed faced. The crib had been set up in the corner nearest to the door that led to the hall.

"I'm next door in case you need me."

Her nerves trumpeted a warning at his proximity. Not that there was any cause for alarm. She and Liam had been sleeping down the hall from each other for almost two weeks.

Plus, it wasn't as though they would be alone. Tomorrow, five others would be joining them, and from the way Liam described past years, the men would be occupied with cards, drinking and conversation late into the night.

"What time should I be ready to leave for dinner?"

"I think we won't want to have Maggie out late. What if we leave here in an hour?"

"I'll have both of us ready."

With Maggie snug in her new winter clothes and Hadley dressed for the cold night air in a turtleneck sweater and black cords, they came downstairs to find Liam waiting in the entry. He held Hadley's insulated jacket while she slid her feet into warm boots and then helped her into the coat. The brush of his knuckles against her shoulders caused butterflies to dance in her stomach. The longing to lean backward against his strong chest was so poignant, Hadley stopped breathing.

Because she'd had her back to him, Liam had no idea how the simple act of chivalry had rocked her equilibrium. Thank goodness she'd learned to master her facial expressions during her last five years of being a nanny. By the time Liam picked up Maggie's carrier, set his hand on the front door latch and turned an expectant gaze upon her, she was ready to offer him a polite smile.

Liam closed and locked the door behind them and then offered his arm to help Hadley negotiate the driveway's steep slope.

"You have Maggie," she told him, considering how lovely it would be to snuggle against his side during the half-mile walk. "Don't worry about me." She might have convinced him if her boots hadn't picked that second to skid on an icy patch.

"I think I can handle a girl on each arm," he said, his voice rich with laughter.

Hadley slipped her arm through Liam's and let him draw her close. The supporting strength of his muscular arm was supposed to steady her, not weaken her knees, but Hadley couldn't prevent her body from reveling in her escort's irresistible masculinity.

At the bottom of the driveway, Hadley expected Liam to release her, but he showed no inclination to set her free. Their boots crunched against the snow-covered pavement as they headed toward town. Sunset was still a little ways off, but clouds had moved in to blanket the sky and speed up the shift to evening. With her heart hammering a distracting tattoo against Hadley's breastbone, she was at a loss for conversation. Liam seemed okay with the silence as he walked beside her.

The restaurant Liam chose was a cute bistro in the heart of Vail Village. "It's my favorite place to eat when I come here," he explained, holding open the door and gesturing her inside.

The early hour meant the tables were only a third full. The hostess led them to a cozy corner table beside the windows that ran along the street front and offered a wonderful view of the trees adorned with white lights. Above their heads, small halogen lights hung from a rustic beam ceiling. A double-sided stone fireplace split the large room into two cozy spaces. White table linens, candlelight and crystal goblets etched with the restaurant's logo added to the romantic ambience.

"I hope the food is half as good as the decor," Hadley commented, bending over Maggie's carrier to remove the infant from her warm nest before she overheated.

"I assure you it's much better. Chef Mongillo is a culinary genius."

Since becoming Maggie's nanny, Hadley had grown accustomed to the rugged rancher Liam was at home and forgot that his alter ego was sophisticated and well traveled. And by extension, his preferred choice of female companionship was worldly and stylish. This abrupt return to reality jarred her out of her dreamy mood, and she chastised herself for forgetting her role in Liam's life.

Taking refuge behind the tall menu, she scanned the delicious selection of entrees and settled on an ahi tuna dish with artichoke, black radish and egg confit potato. The description made her mouth water. Liam suggested the blue crab appetizer and ordered a bottle of sauvignon blanc to accompany it.

She considered the wisdom of drinking while on duty, but deliberated only a few seconds before her first sip. The crisp white burst on her taste buds and her gaze sought Liam. The glint lighting his eyes was a cross between amusement and appreciation. Heat collected in her cheeks and spread downward.

She spoke to distract herself from the longing his scrutiny awakened. "This is delicious."

"Glad you like it." His deep voice pierced her chest and spurred her heart to race. "I'm really glad you were willing to come along this weekend."

This is not a date.

"Are you kidding? You had me at snow." She tried to sound lighthearted and casual, but ended up coming across breathless and silly. Embarrassed, she glanced away. The view out the window seemed the best place for her attention. What she saw made her catch her breath. "And speaking of snow..."

Enormous white flakes drifted past the window. It was

so thick that it was almost impossible to see the storefronts across the cobblestoned street.

"It's really beautiful. I can see why you come here."

"I arranged the weather just for you." As lines went, it wasn't original, but it made her laugh.

Hadley slanted a wry glance his way. "That was very nice of you."

"And I'm sure the guys will be happy to have fresh powder to ski."

When the waiter brought their appetizer, Liam asked about the weather. "How many inches are you expecting?"

"I've heard anywhere from eight to twelve inches here. More elsewhere. It's a pretty huge system moving across the Midwest."

"That's not going to be good for people trying to get in or out of here."

"No. From what I've heard, the Denver airport is expecting to cancel most if not all of their flights tomorrow. I don't know about Eagle County." Which was where they'd landed a few hours earlier.

"Sounds like we're going to be snowed in," Liam said, not appearing particularly concerned.

Hadley didn't share his nonchalance. "What does that mean for your guests?"

"I'll have to check in with them tonight. They might be delayed for a couple days or decide to cancel altogether depending on how long the storm persists."

"But…" What did she plan to say? If the storm moving in made inbound travel impossible, they certainly couldn't fly out. Which meant she, Maggie and Liam were going to be stuck in Vail for the foreseeable future. Alone.

Hadley focused on the food in front of her, annoyed by her heart's irregular beat. What did she think was going to happen in the next few days? Obviously her hormones thought she and Liam would engage in some sort of passionate affair.

The idiocy of the notion made her smile.

Seven

Liam knew he'd concealed his delight at being snowed in with Hadley, so why was she so distracted all of a sudden? And what was with the smile that curved her luscious lips?

He cleared his throat to alleviate the sudden tightness. "I take it you like blue crab?"

Hadley glanced up, and her eyes widened as she met his gaze. "Yes. It's delicious." Her attention strayed toward the window and the swiftly falling flakes. "It's really magical."

Her dreamy expression startled him. He'd become accustomed to her practicality and was excited that her professional mask might be slipping.

With the snow piling up outside, they didn't linger over dinner. As much as Liam would have enjoyed several more hours of gazing into her eyes and telling stories that made her laugh, they needed to get Maggie home and tucked in for the night. His disappointment faded as he considered that they could continue the conversation side by side on the living room sofa. Without the barrier of a table between them, things could get interesting.

"Ready?" he asked, as he settled the check and stood.

"Sure."

Helping her into her coat gave him the excuse to move close enough to inhale her scent and give her shoulders a friendly squeeze. He hoped he hadn't imagined the slight hitch of her breath as he touched her.

Liam gestured for Hadley to go ahead of him out of the restaurant. They retraced their steps through town, navigating the slippery sidewalk past trees strung with white lights and shop windows displaying their wares. Liam insisted Hadley take his arm. He'd enjoyed the feel of her snuggled against him during the walk into town.

Once the commercial center of the town was behind them, the mountain once again dominated the view. As they strolled along, boots sinking into an inch of fresh snow, Liam was convinced he couldn't have planned a more romantic walk home. The gently falling snow captured them in a world all their own, isolating them from obligations and interruptions.

Hadley laughed in delight as fat flakes melted on her cheeks and eyelashes. He wanted to kiss each one away and had a hard time resisting the urge to take her in his arms to do just that. If not for the weight of Maggie's carrier in his hand, he doubted if he could have resisted.

The strength of his desire for Hadley gave him pause. It wasn't just sexual attraction, although heaven knew his lust flared every time she came within arm's reach. No, it was something more profound that made him want her. The way she took care of Maggie, not as if she was being paid to look after her but with affection and genuine concern for her welfare.

He could picture them as partners in the ranch. She had a great eye when it came to seeing the potential in horses, and he had no doubt if she would just remember how much she enjoyed her days of showing that she would relish being involved with the ranch's future.

Yet she'd demonstrated complete disinterest in the horses, and he had yet to figure out why, when it was obviously something she'd been passionate about ten years earlier. Maybe he should accept that she was planning to leave Royal after she graduated. Plus, she'd invested five years getting a graduate degree in guidance counseling. Would she be willing to put that aside?

"You're awfully quiet all of a sudden," Hadley commented. "Cat got your tongue?"

He snorted at her. "I was just thinking about the girl I met ten years ago."

"Which one? There must have been hundreds." An undercurrent of insecurity ran beneath her teasing.

Liam decided to play it straight. "The only one that got away."

His declaration was met with silence, and for a moment the companionable mood between them grew taut with anticipation. He walked on, curious how she'd respond.

"You can't really mean me," she said at last. "You must have met dozens of girls who interested you where the circumstances or the timing weren't right."

"Probably. But only one sticks out in my mind. You. I truly regret never getting a chance to know you better."

While she absorbed this, they reached the driveway of the house where they were staying and began to climb. In minutes he was going to lose her to Maggie's bedtime ritual.

"Why did you sell Lolita and disappear?"

She tensed at his question. "You asked me before why I was no longer interested in horses. It's the same reason I stopped showing. At that sweepstakes show, my best friend fell during her run. She wanted really badly to beat me, so she pushed too hard and her horse lost his footing. He went down with her under him. She broke her back and was paralyzed."

"I remember hearing that someone had been hurt, but I didn't realize how serious it was."

"After that I just couldn't race anymore. It was my fault that she rode the way she did. If I hadn't... She really wanted to beat me." Hadley let out a shaky sigh. "After it happened she refused to talk to me or see me."

Liam sensed there was more to the story he wasn't getting, but didn't want to push deeper into a sensitive issue. "I don't want to downplay your guilt over what was obviously a tragedy, but don't you think it's time you forgave yourself for what happened?"

Hadley gave a bitter laugh. "My best friend is constantly getting on my case for not letting go of mistakes I've made in the past. She's more of a learn-something-and-move-on sort of a girl."

"Maybe if you start riding again you could put it behind you?"

"I'll think about it."

Which sounded like a big fat *no* to Liam's ears. As soon as they entered the front door, Hadley took Maggie's carrier.

"Thank you for dinner."

"You're welcome."

"I'd better get this one into bed." She paused as if having more to say.

"It's still early. I'm going to bet there's some seriously decadent desserts in the kitchen. Ivy knows my guest John Barr has quite a sweet tooth, and she always makes sure it's satisfied."

"It's been a long day, and I'm dying to finish the mystery I started on the plane. I'll see you in the morning."

Liam watched her ascend the stairs and considered following, but decided if she refused to have dessert with him, she was probably not in the mood for his company. He'd ruined what had been a promising evening by asking about matters that were still painful to her. Well, he'd wanted to get to know her better, and he'd succeeded in that.

Pouring himself a scotch, Liam sat down in front of the enormous television and turned on a hockey game. As he watched the players move about the rink, his thoughts ran to the woman upstairs. Getting to know her was not going to be without its ups and downs. She was complicated and enigmatic.

But Liam hadn't won all his reining titles because he lacked finesse and patience. He thrived on the challenge of figuring out what each horse needed to excel. No reason he couldn't put those same talents to use with Hadley.

He intended to figure out what this filly was all about, and if he was lucky—the news reports were already talking about airport shutdowns all over the Midwest—it looked as though he'd have four uninterrupted days and nights to do so.

After a restless night pondering how some inexplicable thing had changed in her interaction with Liam, Hadley got up early and went to explore the gourmet kitchen. Up until last night she'd characterized her relationship with him as boss and employee. Maybe it had grown to friendship of a sort. They enjoyed each other's company, but except for that time she'd gone to retrieve Waldo from his bedroom— which didn't count—he'd never given her any indication that the physical desire she felt for him was reciprocal.

Because of that, Hadley had been confident she could come on this trip and keep Liam from seeing her growing attraction for him. That was before they'd had a romantic dinner together and then walked home in the snow. Now a major storm system had stalled over the Midwest, stranding them alone in this snowy paradise, and she was in trouble.

"I'm sorry your clients won't make the skiing weekend," she said, her gaze glued to the pan of bacon she was fixing. Nearby a carton of eggs sat on the granite counter; she was making omelets.

"I'm not." Liam's deep voice sounded far too close behind her for comfort. "I'm actually looking forward to spending the time with you."

She should ignore the lure of his words and the invitation she'd glimpsed in his eyes the night before. Hadn't she learned her lesson with Noah? Getting emotionally involved with clients was never smart. She couldn't lie to herself and pretend the only thing she felt for Liam was sexual attraction. Granted, there was a great deal of lust interfering with her clear thinking, but she wasn't the type to lose her mind over a hot guy.

What Liam inspired in her was a complicated mixture of physical desire, admiration and wariness. The last was due to how she wanted to trust his word when he claimed he wasn't Maggie's father. Obviously the man had a knack for making women come around to his point of view. She was back to pondering his apparent sincerity and her susceptibility. What other outrageous lie could he tell her that she would believe?

Liam had propped his hip against the counter beside her and was watching her through narrowed eyes. "What can I help you with?"

"You never offer to help Candace." The statement came out sounding like an accusation.

"I've given up trying. Haven't you noticed she doesn't like anyone interfering in her kitchen?" He reached across her to snag a piece of cooked bacon off the plate where it cooled. His gaze snagged hers as he broke the piece in half and offered part to her. "I'm completely at your disposal. What would you like me to do?"

Hadley told herself there was no subtext beneath his question, but her body had a completely different interpretation. She wanted to turn off the stove and find a use for the kitchen that had nothing to do with cooking.

"I'm going to make omelets. Can you get the ingredients you want in yours from the fridge?"

Liam's lazy smile suggested that he'd heard the unevenness of her tone and had an idea he'd put it there. But he didn't push his advantage. Instead, he did as she asked, and Hadley was left with space to breathe and a moment to cool off. Almost immediately she discovered how this had backfired. The gap between them didn't bring relief from her cravings, but increased her longing for him. She was in a great deal of trouble.

Without asking, he pulled out a cutting board and began chopping onion and tomatoes. Engrossed in the task, he didn't notice her stare. Or that's what she thought until he spoke.

"Candace doesn't work 24/7," he commented, setting a second pan on the six-burner stove and adding olive oil. "I have been known to cook for myself from time to time."

"Sorry for misjudging you."

"You do that a lot."

"Apologize?"

"Jump to negative conclusions about me."

"That's not true."

"Isn't it?" He dumped the diced onions into the pan and stirred them. "From the moment you walked into my house you pegged me as a womanizing jerk who slept with some random woman, got her pregnant and never contacted her again."

She couldn't deny his statement. "I don't think you're a jerk."

"But you think I treat women like playthings."

"It's none of my business what you do."

Liam's breath gusted out. "For the rest of this trip I give you a pass to speak your mind with me. I'm not going to dance around topics while you keep the truth bottled up."

"Fine." Hadley couldn't understand why she was so annoyed all of a sudden. "Back when I used to show, you had a reputation for going through girls like chewing gum."

"Sure, I dated a lot, and I know that not every girl was happy when I broke things off, but I never treated any of them like they were disposable."

"What do you call sleeping with them once and then never calling again?"

"I never did that. Who said I did?"

"A friend of mine knew someone..." Hadley trailed off. Why hadn't she ever questioned whether what Anna had said about him was true?

Anger faded from Liam's green eyes. "And because she was your friend, you believed her."

Liam shook his head and went back to stirring the onions. While Hadley searched for answers in his expression, he added raw spinach to the pan and set a lid on it.

"We have cheddar and Cojack cheese," Liam said. "Which would you prefer?"

"Cojack." Hadley had finished with the bacon while they'd been talking and began cracking eggs for their omelets. She moved mechanically, burdened by the notion that she'd done Liam a great injustice. "I'll pour some orange juice. Do you want toast? There's some honey wheat that looks good."

"That's fine. I'll finish up the omelets." His neutral tone gave away none of his thoughts, but Hadley moved around the large kitchen with the sense that she was in the wrong.

Instead of eating in the formal dining room, Hadley set the small kitchen table. She paused to stare out the window at the new blanket of snow covering the mountains and gave a small thank-you to the weather gods for giving her and Liam this weekend alone. He was a far more complicated man than she'd given him credit for, and she welcomed the opportunity to get inside his head between now and when they returned to Royal.

A few minutes later, Hadley carried Maggie's carrier to the table and Liam followed her with plates of omelets and the bacon. Awkward silence had replaced their companionable chatter from the previous evening. It was her fault. She'd wounded him with Anna's tale. But whom was she supposed to believe? Her best friend at the time or a man who admitted to *dating* a lot of women?

The delicious omelet was like a mouthful of sand. Hadley washed the bite down with orange juice and wondered what she was supposed to believe. For ten years she'd lived with guilt over the pain her actions had caused Anna. What if none of it had been as her friend said?

"I know you haven't had any reason to believe I've left my playboy ways behind me," Liam began, his own food untouched. "And perhaps I deserve your skepticism, but I'd like to point out that nothing has happened between you and me, despite my strong attraction to you."

"Strong…attraction?" Hadley fumbled out the words, her heart hammering hard against her ribs.

His gaze was direct and intense as he regarded her. "Very. Strong."

What could she say to that? She looked to Maggie for help, but the baby had her attention locked on the string of stuffed bugs strapped to the handle of her carrier and was too content to provide a convenient distraction.

"I wish you weren't," she said at last, the statement allowing her to retreat from a very dangerous precipice.

"That makes two of us. And I have no intention of worsening your opinion of me by doing anything that makes you uncomfortable. I wouldn't bring it up at all except that I wanted to illustrate that I'm done with casual relationships." He picked up his fork and began breaking up his omelet.

"When you say casual relationships…"

"Ones that are primarily sexual in nature." His head bobbed in a decisive nod.

"So you're not..."

"Having sex? No." He gave her a rueful grin. "I haven't been with anyone in a year."

That wasn't possible. "But Maggie..."

"Isn't mine. She's my brother's daughter."

Hadley stared at him, saw that this wasn't a come-on or a ploy. He was completely serious. And she wanted to believe him. Because if he hadn't been with anyone in a year, that meant he might not be the player she'd taken him for. Suddenly, the speed at which she was falling for him was a little less scary than it had been five minutes ago.

"Why haven't you...?"

He took pity on her and answered her half-asked question. "When Grandfather died and I inherited half of Wade Ranch, it suddenly became apparent that the women I'd been involved with saw me as a good time and nothing more."

"And you wanted to be more?" She couldn't imagine Liam being anything less than completely satisfied with who he was, and this glimpse into his doubts made him more interesting than ever.

"Not to be taken seriously bothered me a great deal."

Hadley was starting to see his problem. "Maybe it was just the women in your sphere who felt that way. If you found some serious women, maybe then you'd be taken seriously."

"You're a serious woman." His green eyes hardened. "And you've been giving me back-off vibes from the moment we met."

"But that's because I work for you and what sort of professional would I be if I let myself get involved with my employer?" *Again.* She clung to the final thought. This conversation had strayed too deep into personal territory.

"You won't be working for me forever. What happens then? Does a serious girl like you give me a chance?"

* * *

Liam watched Hadley's face for some sign of her thoughts. Sharing the details of his recent personal crisis had been a risk. She could decide he was playing her. Building up sympathy to wear down her defenses. Or she might write him off as a sentimental fool in desperate need of a strong woman. The thought of that amused him.

"I...don't know."

He refused to be disappointed by her answer. "Then obviously I have my work cut out for me."

"What does that mean?"

"You need to be convinced I'm sincere. I'm up for the challenge."

"Is that what you think? That I need to be convinced I'm wrong about you?" She shook her head in disgust. "I can make up my own mind, thank you."

Torn between admiration and frustration, Liam debated his next words. "I seem to be saying everything wrong today." To his amazement, she smiled.

"I might be harder on you than you deserve. It's really not for me to offer an opinion on your past behavior or judge the decisions you've made." She glanced at Maggie and then fastened serious blue eyes on him. "You're wonderful with Maggie, and that's the man I'd like to get to know better."

In business and horses, this would be the sort of breakthrough he'd capitalize on. But her next words deflated his optimism.

"Unfortunately, you are also my boss, and that's a line I can't cross."

But she wanted to. He recognized regret in her downcast eyes and the tight line of her lips. With the snow still falling, he would have plenty of time to turn her to his way of thinking. The chemistry between them was worth exploring. As were the emotions she roused in him. She wouldn't react well to being rushed, but it appeared he'd have several days with which to nudge her along.

"Any idea how you'd like to spend the day?" he asked. "It's unlikely we'll be dug out any time soon,"

She gestured to the mountain. "I thought you'd be dying to go skiing. Isn't all this new powder a skier's dream?"

How to explain his reluctance to leave her behind? "It's not as much fun alone."

"That makes sense." But her expression didn't match her words.

"You don't look convinced."

"You've never struck me as a man who sits still for long. I can't imagine you'll be happier here than out on the slopes."

"Are you trying to get rid of me for some reason?"

"No. Nothing like that."

"I don't want to leave you and Maggie alone."

"We'd have been alone if your guests showed up. No reason anything has to be different."

Except that it was. This was no longer a business trip. It had morphed into a vacation. And Liam had very different expectations for how he'd like to spend his time.

That night's dinner had been arranged for six, but since it was beef medallions in a red wine sauce with mushrooms, herb-roasted potatoes and creamed spinach, it had been a simple matter for the chef to make only two portions.

With the chandelier lights dimmed and flickering candlelight setting a romantic scene, the tension kept rising between them. Liam had dated enough women to recognize when a woman was attracted to him, but he'd never known one as miserable about it as Hadley.

"You are obviously uncomfortable about something," he commented, breaking the silence that had grown heavier since the chef had presented them with dessert and left for the night.

"Why would you say that?"

"Because you are as jumpy as a filly being stalked by a mountain lion."

Her brows drew together. "That's ridiculous."

"What's on your mind?" he persisted, ignoring her protest. When she pressed her lips together and shook her head, he decided to talk for her. "Let me guess. Since you started acting all skittish shortly after learning we were going to be snowed in alone together, you think I'm going to seduce you." Liam sipped his wine and observed her reaction.

"I don't think that."

He could see that was true. So what gave her cause for concern? "Oh," he drew the word out, "then you're worried you're going to try to seduce me."

One corner of her mouth lifted in a self-deprecating grin. "As if I could do that." She had visibly relaxed thanks to his bluntness.

"You aren't giving yourself enough credit."

She rolled her eyes, but refrained from arguing. "I thought you'd given up casual sex."

"I have. Which should make you feel more relaxed about our circumstances." He set his elbows on the table and leaned forward.

"Okay, maybe I'm a little on edge."

"What can I do to put you at ease?"

"Nothing. It's my problem."

"But I don't want there to be a problem."

"You really aren't going to let this go, are you?"

He shook his head. "What if I promise that whatever you say will not be held against you after we leave here?" He spread his arms wide. "Go ahead, give me your best shot."

"It's awkward and embarrassing."

She paused as if hoping he'd jump in and reassure her again. Liam held his tongue and tapped his chest to remind her he could take whatever she had to dish out.

"I'm attracted to you, and that's making me uncomfortable, because you're my boss and I shouldn't be having those sorts of feelings for you."

He'd been expecting something along those lines and wished she wasn't so damned miserable about feeling that way. "See, that wasn't so hard. I like you. You like me."

"And nothing can happen between us."

"If that's what you really want." If that was the case, he would respect her decision. But nothing would convince him to like it.

"It is." Her expression closed down. "I made a mistake once, and I promised myself I'd never do anything like that ever again."

"You are too hard on yourself. Everyone screws up. You shouldn't beat yourself up about it."

"That's what my best friend tells me."

"Sounds like a smart friend." Liam dropped the subject. Asking her to confide in him would only cause her to shut down, and he didn't want that to happen. "What should we do after dinner? We could watch a movie. Or there's board games stored in the front closet if you think you can best me at Monopoly or backgammon."

"You don't really want to play either of those, do you?"

"Not really."

"I suppose if you were entertaining clients, you'd go out to a bar, or if you didn't have the energy for that after a full day of skiing, you'd sit around drinking scotch and smoking cigars."

"Something like that." Neither of those activities sounded like much fun while his thoughts were filled with Hadley's soft lips yielding beneath his and the wonders of her generous curves pressed against his body. Gripped by a fit of restlessness, Liam pushed back from the table. "You know, I think I'll head into town and grab a drink. Don't wait up. It'll probably be a late night. I'll see you tomorrow."

Eight

Hadley sat in miserable silence for several minutes after the front door closed behind Liam, cursing her decision to push him away. Was it fair that doing the right thing made her unhappy? Shouldn't she be feeling wretched only after acting against her principles?

With a disgusted snort, Hadley cleared the dessert dishes from the table and set them in the sink. With a lonely evening stretched out before her, she puttered in the kitchen, washing the plates and wineglasses, wiping down the already-immaculate counters and unloading the dishwasher.

None of these tasks kept her thoughts occupied, and she ran her conversation with Liam over and over in her head, wishing she'd explained about Noah so Liam would understand why it was so important that she maintain a professional distance.

After half an hour she'd run out of tasks to occupy her in the kitchen and carried Maggie upstairs. The baby was almost half-asleep and showed no signs of rousing as Hadley settled her into the crib. For a long time she stared down at the motherless child, her heart aching as she contemplated how fond she'd become of the baby and realized that the end of January was fast approaching.

Soon she wouldn't have to worry over Maggie's welfare. Liam would find another nanny. It shouldn't make her heart ache, and yet it did. Hadley began to pace the comfortable guest room. Once again she'd let her heart lead instead of her head. Nor was it only her charge who had slipped beneath her skin. Liam had skirted her defenses as well. Earlier that day she'd accepted that Liam wasn't Maggie's father, but yet he'd demonstrated a willingness to step up and raise his niece, and that said a lot about his character.

Hadley stopped to peer out the window but could see nothing but fat white flakes falling past the glass. The day she'd driven up the driveway to the ranch house, she'd never dreamed that the crush she'd developed on him a decade earlier might have been lying dormant all these years. Born of hero worship and adolescent fantasies, it shouldn't have survived all the life lessons Hadley had learned. Her guilt over the role she'd played in Anna's accident, her poor judgment with Noah, the financial consequences of choosing the wrong career. All of these should have made her incapable of acting foolishly.

So far they had.

But that was before Liam Wade reentered her life. Before, she couldn't think about the man without longing to fall into bed with him, ignoring all consequences for the chance to be wildly happy for a few hours.

The baby made a sound, and Hadley went to make sure she was still asleep. Over the past week, Maggie had grown more vocal as she slept.

Hadley settled a light blanket over the baby, knowing she was fussing for no good reason. She still couldn't calm the agitation that zinged along her nerves in the aftermath of turning aside Liam's advances during dinner.

"I should have just slept with him," she murmured, the declaration sounding unbearably loud in the silent house. Then at least she'd have a good reason to regret her actions.

"It's not too late to change your mind," a low male voice said from the doorway.

Startled, Hadley whirled in Liam's direction. Heat seared her cheeks as she spotted him lounging against the door jam, an intense gleam in his half-lidded eyes. "I thought you went out."

"I did, but it wasn't any fun without you." He advanced toward her, his intent all too clear.

When his arms went around her, pulling her tight against his strong body, Hadley stopped resisting. This is what she wanted. Why fight against something that felt this right?

"Kiss me quick before I change my mind," she told him, her head falling back so she could meet his gaze. "And don't stop."

She laced her fingers through his hair as his mouth seized hers. Nerve endings writhing like live electric wires, she lost all concept of gravity. Up. Down. Left. Right. Without Liam's arms anchoring her to him, she would have shot into space like an overheated bottle rocket.

After the first hard press of his lips to hers, Liam's kiss gentled and slowed. He took his time ravishing her mouth with a bit of pressure here and a flick of his tongue there. Hadley panted in a mix of excitement and frustration. He'd been so greedy for that first kiss. She'd expected what followed would be equally fast and demanding.

"Your lips are amazing," he murmured, nipping at her lower lip. "Soft. Pliant. I could spend all night just kissing you."

Pleasure speared downward as his tongue dipped into the shallow indents left behind by his tender bite. "Other parts of me are just as interesting." She arched her back and rubbed her breasts against his chest, hoping he'd take the hint and relieve their ache.

"I imagine you will provide an unlimited source of fascination." He nuzzled his lips against her neck and bracketed her hips with his long fingers, pulling her against his erection. "Shall we go to my room and see?"

"Oh yes."

He surprised her by scooping her into his arms and carrying her next door. He set her on her feet in the middle of the dark room and pushed her to arm's length.

"I'm going to turn on the fireplace so we have some light. Then I'm going to take off your clothes and spend the rest of the night pleasuring every inch of your body."

His words left her breathless and giddy. "That sounds great," she replied, reaching out to the footboard for balance. "But I demand equal time to get to know you."

White teeth flashed in the darkness as he shot her a wolfish smile. "I love a woman who knows what she wants."

While he crossed to the enormous stone fireplace, Hadley took advantage of his back being turned to strip off her sweater and shimmy out of her black stretch pants. Clad only in a pale blue camisole and bikini briefs, she shivered in anticipation. The gas fireplace lit with a *whoosh*, and Liam turned back to her as flames began to cast flickering shadows around the room. In the dimness, his eyes seemed impossibly bright as his gaze traveled over her.

"You are gorgeous."

Although his tone gave the words a sincerity she appreciated, Hadley doubted she measured up to the women he'd been with in the past. "So are you." A sudden rush of shyness made her sound flip, but Liam didn't seem to notice.

He held out his hand. "Come here."

She couldn't have resisted his command even if her feet had been glued to the floor. More than anything she wanted his hands on her.

Together they stripped off his sweater and the long-sleeve shirt beneath. Firelight highlighted the perfection of his arms, shoulders and abs as her fingers trailed along his hot, silky skin.

"You have such an amazing body," she murmured, marveling at the perfection of every hard muscle. "I'm a little worried that you'll be disappointed in me."

He chuckled. "You have nothing to fear. You are beautiful in every way."

As if to demonstrate that, his hands began to slide upward, catching the hem of her camisole and riding it from her hips to her ribs. Hadley closed her eyes to better savor the magic of his palms gliding over her skin and threw her head back as he reached her breasts, cupping them briefly before sweeping the camisole over her head.

"I was right," he murmured, dropping to his knees to press a kiss to her abdomen.

Hadley quaked as his mouth opened and he laved her skin from belly button to hip. With his head cupped in her hands, she fought to maintain her balance as his fingers hooked in her panties and rode them down her legs. With one knee he nudged her feet apart, and she shut her eyes as his fingers trailed upward, skimming the sensitive inside of her thighs until he reached the spot where she burned.

As his fingers brushed against her pubic hair, she cried out in surprise. He'd barely touched her, and her insides were tense and primed to explode.

"You like that." He wasn't asking a question. "What about this?"

With one finger he opened her and slipped into her wetness. Hadley gasped as pleasure hammered her. Her knees began to shake, threatening to topple her.

"I can't...stand."

He cupped her butt in his hands and steadied her. "I've got you, baby. Just let go."

Her knees buckled, and Liam guided her downward and just a little forward so she ended up straddling his thighs, her breasts flattened against his hard chest. He cupped her head in his hand and brought their lips together once more. This kiss, deep and hungry, held none of the gentle restraint he'd shown earlier. It was a demonstration of his passion for her, and she was enthralled by his need.

"You need to get naked," she gasped as he rolled her beneath him on the thick, fluffy throw rug.

"Soon."

His mouth trailed moisture down her neck and over the upper curve of her breast. As delicious as it was to be slowly devoured by him, the desire clawing at her was building to a painful crescendo. She writhed beneath him, her sensitive inner thighs rasping against his soft corduroy pants as she lifted her knees to shift him deeper into the cradle of her hips.

"Oh, Liam. That's so good."

He'd taken one nipple into his mouth, and the erotic tug sharpened her longing. She ached to feel him buried inside her. Her nails bit into his sides, breath coming in shallow pants as he rocked his hips and drove his erection against her.

When she slipped her hands between them and went for the button that held his trousers closed, he caught her wrists and raised her arms over her head.

"Patience," he murmured before turning his attention to her other breast.

She thrashed her head from side to side as sensation overwhelmed her. Trapped as she was beneath him, Hadley was still able to rotate her hips and grind herself against his hard length. Liam groaned and his lips trailed down her body.

It had never been this good before. Fire consumed her at Liam's every kiss. His hot breath skated across her sensitive flesh. Suddenly her hands were free. Liam continued to slide lower; his shoulders shifted between her thighs, spreading her wide. He grazed his fingertips across her nipples, ripping a moan from her.

Before she'd even registered the pleasure of his large hands cupping her breasts, he dipped his tongue into her hot wet core and sent her spiraling into orbit. Anticipation had been gnawing on her all day, and Liam's expert loving drove her fast and hard into her first orgasm. As it ripped through her, Hadley panted his name. His fingers dug into her backside, holding her tight against his mouth as she shuddered and came in what felt like endless waves of pleasure.

"Nice," she murmured. "Very, very, very nice."

Once her body lay lifeless in the aftermath of her climax, Liam dropped a light kiss on her abdomen and left her to strip off the rest of his clothes. Despite the lack of strength in her limbs, Hadley struggled up onto her elbows to better watch his gorgeous body emerge.

She was awed by his broad shoulders, bulging biceps, washboard abs, but when he stripped off his trousers and she got a glimpse of his strong thighs and the spectacular chiseling of his firm butt, she forgot how to breathe. His erection sprang out as he peeled off his underwear, and her gaze locked on its rigid length.

She licked her lips.

"Do that again and this won't last long," Liam growled as he withdrew a condom from his wallet and made quick work of sliding it on.

She raised an eyebrow. "You're prepared?"

"I've been prepared since the day you walked into my house."

His impassioned declaration made her smile. She held out her arms to him and he lowered himself onto her. Almost immediately the tip of him found where she needed him most, but he held back and framed her face with his hands.

"I don't take this next step lightly," he told her, showing way more restraint than Hadley could manage at the moment.

As much as she appreciated what he was trying to communicate about the depth of his desire for her, she shied away from letting his affirmation into her heart. If this wasn't about two people enjoying an enormous amount of sexual chemistry, she might lose herself to the fantasy that they had a future. Where Liam was concerned, she had to maintain her head.

But all perspective was lost as he kissed her. Not waiting for him to take charge, she drove her tongue into his mouth and let him taste her passion and longing. Something in her soul clicked into place as she fisted her hands in his hair and felt him slide into her in one smooth stroke.

They moaned together and broke off the kiss to pant in agitated gasps.

"Like that," she murmured, losing herself in Liam's intense gaze. She tipped her hips and urged him deeper. "Just like that."

"There's more," he promised, beginning to move, sliding out of her with delicious deliberation before thrusting home.

"That's…" She lost the words as he found the perfect rhythm.

And then it was all heat and friction and a rapidly building pressure in her loins that demanded every bit of her attention. Being crushed beneath Liam's powerful body as he surged inside her was perhaps the most amazing experience of Hadley's life. She'd never known such delirious joy. He was passionate, yet sensitive to her body in a way no one had ever been before.

The beginnings of a second orgasm caught her in its grip. Liam continued his movements, driving her further and further toward fulfillment without taking his own. In a blurry part of her mind, she recognized that and dug her fingers into his back.

"Come with me," she urged, closer now.

"Yes."

At his growl she began to break apart. "Now."

His thrusts grew more frantic. She clung to him as wave after wave of pleasure broke over her. Liam began to shudder as he reached his own climax. She thought she heard her name on his lips as a thousand pinpoints of light exploded inside her. He was everything to her, and for a long, satisfying moment, nothing else mattered.

The weather cleared after thirty-six hours, but neither Liam nor Hadley looked forward to heading back to Texas when the airports reopened. What had happened between them was too new, its metamorphosis incomplete. Liam dreaded the return to reality. The demands of the ranch were sure to overwhelm him, and he wanted more time alone with Hadley.

The wheels of the Cessna Mustang touched down on the Royal airport runway and a sense of melancholy overwhelmed Liam. He sighed as he came in sight of his hangar. The last four days had been perfect. The solitude was exactly what he'd needed to break through Hadley's shell and reach the warm, wonderful woman beneath.

She was funny and sensual. He'd loved introducing her to new foods and wines. She'd matched his ardor in bed and demonstrated a curiosity that amused him. Once she'd let loose, she'd completely mesmerized him. He hadn't been able to get enough of her. And when they were too exhausted to move, he'd held her in his arms and enjoyed the peaceful sounds of her breathing.

He'd never felt in tune with a woman like this. Part of it was likely due to the year off he'd taken to reevaluate his priorities. Hadley was the package. She captivated him both in and out of bed and let him know pretty fast that his past practices in dealing with women weren't going to work on her. He had to be original. She deserved nothing but his best.

Maggie fussed as he locked up the plane. She hadn't slept much on the way home and was probably overtired. He watched Hadley settle the baby into the car seat and sensed the change in the air. Hadley's expression had grown serious, and her eyes lost their infectious sparkle. Playtime was over. She was back on the job.

"She's going to be fine as soon as she gets home and settled into her crib," Hadley said, coaxing the baby to take her pacifier.

"Maybe you should spend the night in case she doesn't settle down."

Hadley shook her head. "I'll stay until you get back from checking in at the ranch, but I can't stay all night."

"Not even if I need you?"

"You'll do just fine without me."

He wasn't sure if she had missed his meaning or if she was pretending not to understand that he wanted her to spend the night with him. Either way, she'd put enough determination behind her declaration to let him know no amount of persuasion was going to change her mind.

"I'm going to miss you," he said, trying a different approach.

"And I'm going to miss you," she replied, her voice brisk and not the least bit romantic. "But that was Colorado and this is Texas. We had a nice time, but it's over."

To Liam's shock, he realized he was back to square one. "I think it takes two people to decide it's over."

"You're my boss. We just need to get things back to normal."

"Or we need to change what normal is."

She didn't look happy. "I'm not sure what you mean."

"We made a great start getting to know each other these last few days. I'd like to continue."

"I don't feel comfortable in that sort of arrangement."

"Then why don't you quit?" He would not fire her. She needed to choose to be with him. "If it's about the money, I'll pay you until the end of the month."

Her mouth popped open, but before she could speak, Maggie let loose a piercing wail. "Why don't we talk about this later? I really think Maggie needs to get home."

Liam agreed, but hated the idea of postponing the conversation. He wanted to batter her with arguments until she came around to his point of view. Giving her space to think would only give her space to fortify her defenses.

"Fine. But we will talk later."

Only they didn't. By the time Liam returned from the ranch offices, it was close to midnight. Hadley was half-dead on her feet, only just having gotten Maggie to sleep after a rough evening. She was in no condition to listen to his arguments for continuing what they'd begun in Colorado, and he had to watch in frustrated silence as she put Waldo in his carrier and drove away.

With disappointment buzzing in his thoughts like a pesky fly, he expected sleep to elude him. But he'd underestimated his own weariness and shortly after his head hit the pillow, he fell asleep.

When the dream came, it didn't feature Hadley, but his mother. They stood in the ranch house's entry hall and he was desperately afraid. She was leaving. He clung to her hand and begged her not to go. She tugged hard against his grip, her face a mask of disgust.

"Mommy, don't go."

"Why would I want to stay with you? I left because I couldn't bear to be trapped in this prison of a ranch in the middle of nowhere."

"But I need you."

"I never wanted to be a mother. You and your brother were a mistake."

She ripped free and strode through the front door without ever looking back. Liam followed her, but it was as if he moved through mud. His short legs couldn't propel him fast enough, and he reached the broad wraparound porch just in time to see her taillights disappear down the driveway.

Liam woke in a sweat. His throat ached and heart pounded as he recalled his mother's words. As realistic as the exchange had felt, he recalled no such event from his childhood. His subconscious had merely been reacting to Hadley's evasiveness. So why hadn't his dream featured her?

Lingering pain carved up his chest. He felt weak and unsteady. A child's fear pummeled him. Buried deep in his mind was the horror of being rejected by his mother. She was supposed to love him and care for him. Instead, she'd demonstrated no remorse when she'd abandoned her sons to pursue her real estate career.

And it was this defining fact that had caused him to never fully invest himself in romantic relationships. He couldn't bear the idea of giving his heart to a woman only to have her choose something else over him. Deep down, what he craved was lasting love.

His heart had led him to Hadley. And given the timing of his dream, his subconscious was worried that he'd made a huge mistake.

Hadley was in the nursery folding a freshly laundered basket of Maggie's clothes when Liam appeared. He'd been subdued and circumspect around her the last couple days, and she suspected she'd done too good a job convincing him that what had happened between them in Vail had been a singular event never to be repeated.

But that wasn't at all what she wanted. She was pretty

sure she'd fallen in love with him during those four days. And that left her in a quandary.

"I know it's short notice," he said. "But will you be my date for the grand reopening of Royal Memorial's west wing tomorrow night?"

The word *date* caused a spike in Hadley's heartbeat. She told herself to stop being stupid.

"Sure. What time should I have Maggie ready?"

"Not Maggie." His green eyes pierced her facade of professionalism. "You. It's a cocktail party complete with adult beverages, finger food and fancy duds." He kept his voice light, but his expression was stony.

"Of course I'll go with you." She matched his tone, kept her glee hidden. "I've heard wonderful things about the new wing. You and the other members of the Texas Cattleman's Club were instrumental in raising the funds that enabled the restoration to move forward, weren't you?"

"We felt it was important for the community to get the hospital back to one hundred percent as soon as possible." He took her hand, threaded his fingers through hers. "How about I pick you up at seven?"

Her brain short-circuited at the way he was staring at their joined hands. As if the simple contact was at once comforting and a puzzle he couldn't figure out.

"Sure." Before she recognized what she planned to do, Hadley stepped into Liam's space and lifted onto her toes to plant a kiss on his lips.

All day long she'd been thinking about how much she wanted to be in his arms. Not to feel the stirring passion of his lovemaking, but the heart-wrenching bliss of their connection, which consisted of both sexual and spiritual components. The blend was different from anything she'd ever known, and she'd begun to neglect her defenses.

Liam brought their clasped hands to his chest and slid his free hand beneath her hair to cup her head. He explored her lips with tantalizing pressure, giving her the merest taste of passion. Although she'd initiated the kiss, she was happy to let him set the pace.

When at last his lips lifted from hers, they were both breathing unsteadily.

"I've been thinking about kissing you all day," he murmured, lips trailing over her ear, making her shudder. "I can't concentrate anymore. The entire ranch staff thinks I've lost my mind."

His words excited a flurry of goose bumps. "It's that way for me, too. I forgot to put a diaper back on Maggie before I put her back in her Onesie this morning. And then I made her bottle and put it into the cupboard instead of the container of formula."

"Will you stay at the ranch tomorrow night after the party?"

She wanted to very much, but would this interfere with her determination not to get emotionally involved? "If you wish."

"I very much wish."

"Then that's what I'll do."

Nine

Liam wasn't sure how he was going to make it through the grand opening, when all he could think about was what he had to look forward to afterward. He pulled his truck into a visitor space at Hadley's apartment building and stepped out. For tonight's event he'd exchanged denim and plaid in favor of a custom-tailored charcoal suit.

Anticipation zipped along his nerve endings as he pushed the button in the entry vestibule that would let Hadley know he'd arrived. Her voice sounded distorted as she told him to come up. Her apartment was on the second floor. He stepped into the elevator, feeling the give of the cables as it adjusted to his weight. The building had obviously seen a lot of tenants, because it showed wear and tear in the carpets, layers of paint and light fixtures.

Standing before Hadley's door, Liam paused to assess his state of agitation. Had he ever been nervous going to pick up a woman for a date? Yet here he stood, palms sweating, heart thundering, mouth dry.

The door opened before he lifted his hand to knock. Hadley looked surprised to see him standing in the hallway. Waldo rushed forward to wind himself around Liam's legs.

"Hi." She gestured him in. "I thought maybe the elevator had decided to be fussy again."

He picked up the cat without taking his eyes from Hadley and stepped into her apartment. "You look beautiful."

She wore a figure-skimming sleeveless black dress with a round neckline and a half-circle cutout that bared her cleavage. Despite there being nothing overtly provocative about the style, Liam thought she looked incredibly sexy. She'd pinned her blond waves up in a complicated hairstyle that looked as if it could tumble onto her shoulders at any second. And he badly wanted to make that happen. Body alive with cravings better reserved for later that evening, he shifted his gaze to her only jewelry, a pair of long crystal earrings that swung in sassy rhythm as she tipped her head and regarded him curiously.

"Thank you." Her half smile captivated him. "You look nice, as well. I'll grab my purse and we can get going." She picked up a small black clutch and a sheer red scarf sparkling with clusters of sequins that she draped over her shoulders. It added a flamboyant touch to her otherwise monochrome black ensemble.

Realizing he was staring at her like a smitten teenager, Liam cleared his throat. His brain was having trouble summoning words. "All set?"

"Are you expecting a large crowd tonight?" she asked as she fit her key into the lock and set the dead bolt.

"About a hundred. Those responsible for coordinating the fund-raising efforts and the largest contributors."

"What a wonderful thing you've done."

Her glowing praise lightened his step. He laced his fingers through hers and lifted her hand to brush a kiss across her knuckles. "It was a group effort," he said, feeling unusually humble. "But thank you."

In truth, he was proud of the work he and the other members of the Texas Cattleman's Club had done in the aftermath of the tornado. As leaders in the community, they'd banded together during the time of crisis and although progress had been slow, they'd restored the town to its former state.

The drive from Hadley's apartment to the hospital took ten minutes. Liam filled the time with a description about an outfit his cousin Ivy had bought for Maggie that featured a chambray Onesie with three tiers of ruffles and a crocheted cowboy hat and boots.

"Complete with yarn spurs." Liam shook his head in mock dismay.

"How adorable." Hadley regarded his expression with a wry smile. "You are just going to have to get used to the fact that girls love to dress up and look pretty."

"I know," he grumbled, knowing she loved to scold him. "But is it really going to be all frilly stuff and hair bows?"

"Yes."

Liam pulled to a stop in front of the hospital's new west wing entrance, and the look he gave Hadley made her laugh. A year ago he never would have imagined himself discussing an infant's wardrobe, much less with a beautiful woman.

A valet opened the passenger door and helped Hadley out of the truck. Liam was grinning as he accepted the ticket from the uniformed attendant and caught up with Hadley, sliding his hand over her hip in a not-so-subtle show of ownership. She sent him an unguarded smile of such delight, his chest hurt. If this was heartache, bring it on.

"This is amazing," Hadley murmured as they entered the spacious lobby of the redesigned west wing, taking in the patterned marble floors and triangular glass ceiling over the entrance. In the center of the room, a bronze statue of a cowboy roping a running cow had the names of all those who'd lost their lives during the tornado etched around the base. "A wonderful tribute."

Spying Case Baxter, Liam drew Hadley toward the rancher, who had eyes only for the redhead beside him.

"Case," Liam called to gain his attention.

The president of the Cattleman's Club looked away from his fiancée and blinked as if to reorient himself. At last his gaze focused on Liam.

"Hey, Liam." His teeth flashed as he extended his hand to meet Liam's. "Mellie, you've met Liam Wade."

"Of course." A friendly smile curved her lips. Her green eyes darted toward Hadley before settling back on Liam. "At the reception when Case was elected president."

"And this is Hadley Stratton." Liam didn't explain how they knew each other. Why introduce her as Maggie's nanny when she'd become so much more? "Mellie Winslow and Case Baxter, our club president."

The two couples finished exchanging greetings and Case spoke. "Gotta hand it to you, Liam." He gestured around, his grin wide, posture relaxed. "This is one hell of a facility."

"Have you toured the neonatal unit?" Mellie asked.

"We just arrived," Hadley admitted, completely at ease tucked into the half circle of Liam's left arm. After their conversation in Vail, he'd half expected her to balk at going public with their developing relationship.

"The whole wing is really terrific," Mellie was saying, "but that unit in particular is very impressive."

Liam agreed. He'd seen the neonatal facility during his many trips to the hospital in his role as chairman of the fund-raising committee, but he was looking forward to showing it to Hadley.

"Why don't we head up now," he suggested, seeing Hadley's interest. There would be plenty of time later to catch up with Mac, Jeff Hartley and other members of the Texas Cattleman's Club. "We'll catch up with you later," he told Case.

"They seem like a nice couple," Hadley commented as they waited for the elevator that would take them to the maternity ward on the fourth floor.

"I don't know Mellie all that well, but Case is a great guy and they appear happy."

The elevator doors opened, and Liam gestured Hadley ahead of him.

Despite the crowd gathered to party in the lobby, they had the elevator to themselves. As soon as the car began to move, Liam tugged Hadley into his arms and dropped his lips to hers.

The instant Liam kissed her, Hadley wrapped her arms around his neck and yielded to his demand. Frantic to enjoy the few seconds of isolation, they feasted on each other. But all too soon, a *ding* announced that they'd reached their floor, cutting short their impassioned embrace.

"Damn these modern elevators," Liam muttered, his hands sliding off her body.

Hadley, her cheeks hot in the aftermath of the kiss, smiled foolishly. She surveyed his chiseled lips, searching for any sign that her red lipstick had rubbed off. Taking the hand Liam offered her, she stepped past a tour group that was waiting to head downstairs.

"Let's see if we can catch that tour," he said, tugging her down the hallway toward a group of well-dressed guests listening to a tall, handsome man in his late thirties.

"Next is our neonatal unit," the man said, gesturing down the hall as he started forward.

"That's Dr. Parker Reese," Liam explained, tucking Hadley's hand into the crook of his arm. "He's a neonatal specialist. Brilliant guy. We're lucky to have him."

It was hard to focus on Dr. Reese's description of the neonatal unit's state-of-the-art equipment and dedicated staff while her senses were filled with the scent, sight and feel of Liam so close beside her.

He stiffened, dragging Hadley out of her musings. She returned her attention to the speaker only to discover Dr.

Reese had passed off the tour to a slender nurse with blond hair pulled back into a bun and a brisk way of speaking.

"We call her Janey Doe," the nurse said, a hint of sadness clouding her direct green gaze. "She is holding her own, but each day is a struggle. However, thanks to Dr. Reese…" The nurse glanced up at the tall doctor, and Hadley got the impression that equal parts personal and professional admiration curved her lips.

The crowd began to follow Dr. Reese toward the birthing suites, but Liam showed no interest in continuing on. He made a beeline straight for the nurse and introduced himself.

"Hello, I'm Liam Ward. And this is Hadley Stratton."

"Clare Connelly." The nurse shook their hands. "Thank you for all your hard work on the restoration of this wing. It's such an amazing facility to work in."

"It was an important project for our town." Although his words were courteous, his tone was strained. "I was wondering if you could tell me a little bit more about Janey Doe."

Knowing that she had missed a big chunk of the story, Hadley scanned Liam's expression, noticed his tight lips, the muscle jumping in his jaw and wondered at his interest.

"She was found on the floor of a truck stop thirty miles from here…"

"No sign of her mother?" Liam's question reverberated with disgust.

Clare shook her head slowly. "None, I'm afraid."

"You mean she just left her there?" Hadley's chest tightened. "How could she do something like that?"

"She was probably young and scared. Janey was very small and obviously premature. It's possible the mother thought she was dead and freaked out."

Hadley appreciated how Clare stuck up for Baby Janey's mother but could see that none of her assumptions had eased Liam's displeasure. He was staring into the neonatal unit, his attention laser focused on the middle incubator. Was Maggie on his mind? Without knowing for certain that Maggie was related to Liam, Diane Garner had left her granddaughter in his care. Or was he thinking how his own mother had left him to be raised by his grandfather?

"What will happen to her?" Hadley asked, her own gaze drawn toward the incubator and the precious bundle. The baby was hooked up to a feeding tube, oxygen and monitors, making it impossible to get a clear look at her face.

"She'll go into foster care and eventually be adopted." Although the words were hopeful, the nurse's smile was strained.

Hadley recognized that look. She'd seen it on the faces of plenty of her fellow nannies who'd grown too attached to their charges.

"Thank you for your time." Liam glanced down at Hadley, his expression unreadable. "Shall we rejoin the party?"

All warmth had been leeched from his manner by the story of Baby Janey. Hadley nodded and strolled back toward the elevator at Liam's side. Although her hand remained tucked in his arm, the emotional distance between them was as wide as an ocean. She recognized that this had nothing to do with her. Liam had retreated behind walls she couldn't penetrate, defenses a young boy had erected to deal with his mother's abandonment.

"Why don't we get out of here," Hadley suggested as they descended in the elevator. "I don't think you're in the mood for a party anymore."

"You're right." One side of his lips kicked up. His gaze warmed as he bent down to brush a kiss across her lips. "But I should at least spend an hour here. If for no other reason than to show off my gorgeous date."

Hadley blushed at the compliment. It didn't matter what

anyone else thought of her looks; as long as she could bask in Liam's sizzling admiration, she felt flawless.

By the time the elevator doors opened, Liam seemed to have gotten past whatever had affected him in the neonatal unit. Once again the charming rascal she adored, he worked his way around the room, collecting smiles and promises of funds for several pieces of equipment the hospital still needed.

Watching him work, Hadley reveled in his charisma and marveled at his ability to strike just the right chord with everyone he met. This is what made him an astute businessman and a masterful horseman. He didn't approach every situation with the same tactic.

"I'm ready to get out of here if you are," he murmured in her ear an hour later.

"Absolutely," she replied, anticipating what awaited them back at the ranch house.

On the ride home, Liam lapsed back into silence, his public persona put aside once more. Hadley stared at his profile in concern. Her hopes for a romantic evening fled. Liam's troubled thoughts preoccupied him.

As Liam unlocked the front door, Hadley set aside her disappointment and decided to see if she could get him to open up. "How about I make some coffee and we talk about what's bothering you?"

Liam's chin dipped in ascent. "I'll get a fire started in the den."

Once she got the coffee brewing, Hadley ran upstairs to check on Maggie. She found the baby sleeping and Candace in the rocking chair, reading on her tablet. The housekeeper looked up in surprise as Hadley crossed to the crib.

"You're home early. Did you have fun?"

"It was a nice party. The facilities are wonderful." Hadley knew she hadn't directly answered Candace's question. While she'd enjoyed the company and the conversation,

Liam's mood after learning about Janey Doe had unsettled her. "Thanks for watching Maggie. Any problems?"

Candace got to her feet. "She went to sleep at eight and hasn't made a peep since."

"Good." Maggie's hair was soft beneath Hadley's fingers as she brushed a strand off the baby's forehead. "I made some coffee if you're interested in joining us for a cup."

"No, thanks. I'm almost done with this book. I'm going to head back to the carriage house and finish it."

The two women headed downstairs. Liam was in the kitchen and gave Candace a cheerful thank-you as she left. By the time the housekeeper pulled the back door shut behind her, icy air filled the space. Hadley shivered and filled the mugs Liam had fetched from the cupboard. Cradling the warm ceramic in her hands, she led the way into the den and settled on the sofa.

Liam set his mug on the mantel and chose to stand, staring into the fire. "I'm sorry I was such bad company tonight."

"You weren't bad company." Hadley was careful not to let her disappointment show. "Obviously something is bothering you. Do you feel like talking about it?"

"It was hearing about Janey Doe."

"That was a very upsetting story." She refrained from adding her own opinion on the subject, wanting Liam to share his thoughts.

"Her mother just leaving her like that. On the floor of a public bathroom. She could have died."

Hadley kept her voice neutral. "She was fortunate that someone found her."

"I thought it was bad that Maggie's grandmother left her with us. This is so much worse. How could any mother abandon her child like that?"

"Not every woman is cut out for motherhood." Hadley

thought about all the families she'd worked for in the last five years and all the stories shared by her fellow nannies. "Sometimes the responsibility is more than they can handle."

"You mean they wish they'd never given birth."

Trying her best to hide a wince, Hadley responded, "I mean that parenting can be challenging, and sometimes if a woman has to do it alone, she might not feel capable."

"Perhaps if she's young and without financial means, I could understand, but what can you say about a woman who has family and fortune and turns her back on her children so she can pursue her career?"

Not wanting to sound as if she were picking sides, Hadley chose her next words carefully. "That she acted in her best interest and not in the best interest of her children."

Liam crossed to the sofa and joined Hadley. A huge gust of air escaped his lungs as he picked up her hand and squeezed her fingers. "Maggie must never know that her grandmother left her with us the way she did. I won't have her wondering why she didn't want to keep her."

This was the true source of Liam's disquiet, Hadley realized. Whether he acknowledged it or not, being abandoned by his mother had sabotaged his ability to trust women. And where did that leave Hadley?

Liam could feel the concern rolling off Hadley as he spoke. He'd grown attuned to her moods since their days in Vail and didn't have to see her expression to know her thoughts.

Hadley covered their clasped hands with her free one and squeezed. "It's okay to be angry with your mother for not being there for you."

The knot of emotions in his chest tightened at her words. Not once as a child had he seen his grandfather demonstrate anything but understanding toward the daughter

who'd run out on her children. Liam had grown up thinking that what his mother had done was acceptable, while
inside him was a howling banshee of anger and hurt that
was never given a voice.

"You might feel better if you talked through how it
made you feel."

"I don't know how to begin." The words, long bottled
up inside him, were poised to explode. "I grew up thinking
it was okay that she chose to leave us with Grandfather."

"Why?"

"She had a career that she loved, and like you said earlier, she really wasn't cut out to be a mom. She got pregnant when she was seventeen. Our father was on the rodeo
circuit and had no interest in settling down to raise a family. Mother felt the same way. Grandfather always said she
had big dreams." Liam offered up a bitter laugh. "I guess
Kyle and I are lucky she decided to have us at all."

Hadley's shocked intake of breath left Liam regretting
the venomous statement.

"You don't mean that."

"No," he agreed. "Although I've thought it a hundred
times, I don't think she ever considered terminating her
pregnancy. In that respect, she didn't take the easy way
out."

"Getting back to what you said earlier, growing up did
you really think that it was okay she left you with your
grandfather, or was that just a coping mechanism?"

"In my mind, I understood her decision. I can't explain
to you why that made sense. Maybe because it happened
when we were babies and I never knew any different. But
recently I started realizing that deep down inside, I hated
her for leaving us."

He'd coped by becoming a champion rider. Throwing
himself into competition had preoccupied him in his teenage years. The closer he'd gotten to manhood, the less he

thought about his mother's absence. The day he'd kissed a girl for the first time, he'd stopped caring.

"Grandfather wasn't exactly the most affectionate guy in the world, but he loved us in his tough-guy way. It might have been different if we were girls, but growing up on the ranch, we had more father figures than anyone could ever want."

"You sound very well adjusted." Her tone said otherwise. "Do you think not having a mother affected your relationships with women?"

"You mean because I never got married?"

"You have a well-earned reputation for being a playboy. I can't imagine you trusted your heart after what your mother did."

"I'll admit to having a wandering eye when it came to women, but that's changed."

"Just because you think you're ready to settle down doesn't mean you've learned to trust." She smiled to take the sting out of the words, but her eyes reflected wariness.

"You're the first woman I've been with in a year," he reminded her, voice rasping as frustration overcame him. "I think that proves I'm already settled down. And I trust you."

Doubt continued to shadow her eyes. He shifted on the couch, angling his body toward her. Gripped by the urgent need to kiss her, Liam dipped his head, shortening the distance between them. He would demonstrate that he was serious about her.

Before he could kiss her, Hadley set her fingertips on his lips. "Thank you for sharing how you felt about your mother not being around. I know that couldn't have been easy."

"It wasn't." And yet it had been a relief to share his anger and sense of betrayal with her. "Thank you for listening."

A moment earlier he'd had something to prove, but the mood was no longer right for seduction. Instead, he planted a friendly kiss on her cheek and held her in a tight hug.

"Let's go upstairs," she murmured, her hands sliding beneath his suit coat, fingers splaying over his back. "I want to make love to you."

At her declaration Liam took a massive hit to his solar plexus. Pulse quickening, he caught her by the hand and drew her toward the stairs. They climbed together in a breathless rush. By the time they reached his bedroom, he was light-headed and more than a little frantic to get them both naked.

Once they crossed the threshold, Hadley plucked the pins from her hair, and it tumbled around her shoulders. Liam came to stand behind her, pushing the thick mass of blond hair away from her neck so he could kiss the slender column and make her shiver. He stripped off his jacket and shirt before turning his attention to the zipper of her dress. With more urgency than finesse, he stroked the dress down her body. When it pooled at her feet, he skimmed his palms back upward, hesitating over the ticklish spot beside her hip bones and investigating each bump of her ribs. The rise and fall of her chest grew less rhythmic as he unfastened her strapless bra and tossed the scrap of fabric on to a nearby chair.

Her hand came up to the back of his head as he cupped her breasts in his palms, thumbs flicking over her tight nipples. She shuddered, her head falling back against his chest, eyes closed as she surrendered to his touch. Although the tightness in his groin demanded that he stop all the foreplay and get down to business, Liam had no intention of rushing. He'd rather savor the silken heat of her skin and bring her body as much pleasure as it could take before seeking his own release.

She turned in his arms, her soft breasts flattening

against his chest as she lifted on tiptoe and sought his mouth with hers. She cupped his face in her hands to hold him still while her tongue darted forward to toy with his. Liam crushed her to him, his fingers dipping below her black lace panties to swallow one butt cheek and lift her against his erection.

They both groaned as he rocked against her. She lifted her foot and wrapped her leg around his hips, angling the bulge behind his zipper into the warm, wet cleft between her thighs. The move unraveled all of Liam's good intentions. He plucked her off her feet and moved toward the bed. She set the soles of her feet against his calves to keep him anchored between her thighs and impatiently removed his belt. It was torture to let her undress him. Every time her fingers glanced off his erection, he ground his teeth and bit back a groan. Only by watching the play of emotions race across her beautiful features was he able to maintain his control. By the time she'd slid open his zipper and pushed the pants down his thighs, his nerves screamed with impatience.

Liam stripped off pants, shoes, socks and underwear without ever taking his eyes off Hadley. With a sensual smile she moved backward, making room for him on the mattress. He stalked onto the bed, fitting between her spread thighs, covering her torso with his before claiming her lips in a hard kiss and her body with a single deep thrust.

He loved the way her hips lifted to meet his. How she arched her back and took him all the way in. Her chest vibrated with a moan. A matching sound gathered in his lungs. For a long moment they lay without moving, lips and tongues engaged.

Framing her face in his hands, Liam lifted his lips from hers and stared into her eyes. "Thank you for being my date tonight." It wasn't what he'd intended to say, but nevertheless his words pleased her.

"Thank you for asking. I had a lovely time."

"Lovely?" He grinned. "Let's see if we can't upgrade that to fantastic."

Her eyebrows lifted, daring him to try, while her fingers stroked down his sides. "We're off to a wonderful start."

Liam nuzzled his face into her throat and began to move inside her. "We certainly are."

Ten

The night after the party at the hospital, Hadley was back on the neonatal floor she and Liam had toured. After receiving Maggie's blood work back, Dr. Stringer had determined she should undergo phototherapy treatments for her jaundice. Despite being overwhelmed with ranch business, Liam had accompanied them, wearing his concern openly, but once he discerned how straightforward the process was, he'd relaxed.

Maggie had been stripped down to her diaper and placed in an incubator equipped with a light box that directed blue fluorescent light onto her skin. The light was meant to change the bilirubin into a form that Maggie could more easily expel through her urine. While the procedure was simple, it also took time to work. Maggie would be in the hospital for a couple days while undergoing the treatment. Hadley had agreed to stay with her to let Liam focus on the ranch.

Hadley caught herself humming as she fed Maggie her late-afternoon bottle. After the party at the hospital and the night spent in Liam's arms, she'd stopped resisting what her heart wanted and let herself enjoy every moment of her time with Liam. Why fight against the inevitable? She'd fallen deeply in love with the man.

While a part of her couldn't help but compare what was between her and Liam to what she'd had with Noah, deep down, Hadley recognized the vast difference between the two relationships. With Noah she'd never enjoyed any sort of emotional security. As much as he'd gone on and on about how much he wanted her, how his kids adored her, she always got the sense that he was looking over her shoulder for someone else. It turned out that someone else had been his ex-wife.

Liam never once let her think she was second best. His focus was always completely on her, and Hadley found that both comforting and wildly exciting. For the first time in a long time, she'd stopped focusing on the future and lived quite happily in the moment. School would start when it started. Her time with Maggie would grow shorter. Already arrangements had been made for the new nanny to start at the end of the month. This freed Hadley from her professional responsibilities, and she was eager to see where her relationship with Liam led.

Maggie's eyelids started to droop before the bottle was finished. Hadley set it aside, lifted the infant onto her shoulder and patted her back to encourage a burp. A nurse stood by to test Maggie's bilirubin levels. The staff members were monitoring her every hour or so. Hadley was calling Liam with the results.

His concern for Maggie's welfare had warmed her when she thought the baby was his daughter. Now that she knew Maggie was his brother's child, Liam's commitment was just another reason Hadley found him so attractive.

She was tired of restraining her emotions. Liam made her happy, and she thought he felt the same way about her. When Maggie left the hospital, Hadley promised herself she would stop holding back.

Several days after the hospital party, Liam had an appointment with former Samson Oil lawyer Nolan Dane, who'd joined his father's family law practice. Recently,

Nolan had been accepted for membership in the Texas Cattleman's Club, and the more Liam got to know the man, the more he liked him. The idea that had begun percolating in his mind took on a whole new urgency on the trip back from Colorado. With Maggie in the hospital and Hadley staying with her, the notion had solidified into a plan that required a savvy lawyer.

Liam stepped into Nolan's office. "Looks like you're all settled in."

Nolan grinned. "It's taken longer than I figured on. I didn't expect to be so busy this early in my start-up."

"That must mean you're good. Looks like I've come to the right place."

"Can I offer you coffee or water before we get started?" Nolan gestured Liam into a chair at the round conference table.

"Thanks, but I'm good." While Nolan took a seat, Liam pulled out the paternity test as well as Maggie's birth certificate and her mother's death certificate that Diane Garner had sent at his request.

Nolan found a blank page on his yellow legal pad and met Liam's gaze. "What can I help you with?"

"I have a situation with my twin brother's baby." Liam explained how Maggie had come to Wade Ranch and showed Nolan the DNA results. "Maggie is definitely Kyle's daughter. As soon as I received the test back, I left messages for him on his cell and with the navy."

"How long ago was this?"

"About two weeks."

"And you haven't heard back?"

"Only that the message was delivered. He's a SEAL, which probably means he's on a mission overseas." Liam leaned forward. "And that's where my concerns lie. I don't know a lot about Kyle's domestic situation, but based on his past track record, I'm guessing he's not in a long-term relationship and certainly isn't in a position to take care of a baby."

"You're not in regular contact?"

"Not since he left Royal and joined the navy." Liam wasn't proud of the way he and Kyle had drifted apart, but growing up they'd been uniquely dissimilar in temperament and interests for identical twins.

"And it sounds like the child's grandmother, Diane Garner, is reluctant to be responsible for Maggie."

"She has serious medical issues that prevent her from taking care of Maggie. Which leaves Kyle." Liam paused to give his next words weight. "Or me."

"You want custody?"

While Liam's first instinct was to say yes, he intended to do what was best for Maggie. "I'd like to evaluate all the options."

One corner of Nolan's lips twitched. "You don't have to be diplomatic with me, Liam. I'm here to help you out. Now, what do you want?"

"I'd like custody, but what is most important is to do right by Maggie." Liam gathered his thoughts for a long moment. "I have concerns that while Kyle is off on missions, he'll have to rely on others to take care of her for extended periods of time. And what happens if he's hurt..." Or killed. But Liam couldn't go there. Most days he didn't give Kyle a thought, but sometimes a news report would catch his attention and Liam would wonder what his brother was up to.

"Do you know if Kyle and Margaret were in touch before she drove to Wade Ranch?" Nolan continued to jot down items on his legal pad. "I'm trying to get a sense of their relationship."

"I don't know, but I have to think if Kyle had any idea he was going to be a father that he would have let me know." Liam wanted to believe his brother would step up and do the right thing by his daughter. Yet the fact that Kyle hadn't been in contact disturbed Liam. "That leads me to believe that he didn't know. Either because she hadn't told him or she had the same trouble getting a hold of him I'm having."

Liam didn't add that it was possible Margaret had been nothing more than a weeklong fling for Kyle and he'd had no intention of keeping in touch.

"Because Margaret died in childbirth and she and Kyle weren't married, only her name appears on Maggie's birth certificate. Normally what would happen in this sort of case is that both parties would fill out an AOP. That's an Acknowledgment of Paternity. This form would normally be filled out and signed at the hospital. Or through a certified entity that would then file it with the Vital Statistics Unit. Unfortunately, without Margaret alive to concede that your brother is the child's father, this case will have to go to court. Of course, DNA evidence will prove Kyle's the father. But with you two being identical twins and no way of proving which one of you is the father..." After a long silence, broken only by the scratch of his pen across the legal pad, Nolan glanced up. His eyes gleamed. "I can see why you came to me. This situation is by no means clear-cut."

"No, it's not." But at least Liam had a clearer picture of what he wanted. Tension he didn't realize he'd been holding unwound from his shoulder muscles. "How do you suggest we proceed?"

"Let's find out what we can about Margaret and her time with Kyle in San Antonio. I have an investigator I've worked with there. If you give me the go-ahead, I'll contact him."

"Do you think I have a case for retaining custody of Maggie?" Before he let Kyle take Maggie away, Liam intended to make sure his brother was willing to fight for her. And fight hard.

"A lot will depend on how determined your brother is

to be a father. You and your brother aren't in contact. We should probably check on Kyle's current financial status and personal life as well and see what sort of environment Maggie would be going into. I think you're right that between the two situations, Wade Ranch promises the most stability for a baby. But a judge might reason that you're both single men and that Maggie should be with her father."

Her *single* father who might be activated at a moment's notice and be out of the country who knew how long.

"What if I were engaged?" Liam suggested, voicing what had been running through his head since his trip to Colorado. "Or married?"

Nolan nodded. "Might sway a judge. Are you?"

"Not yet." For a year Liam had pondered the benefits of settling down. All he'd been waiting for was the right woman. Hadley fit the bill in every way. She was smart, beautiful and great with Maggie. After Colorado he'd decided he'd be a complete idiot not to lock her down as soon as possible before she finished school and headed off to pursue a career elsewhere. "But I plan to pop the question to a special lady in the very near future."

Hadley rocked a sleepy Maggie as she checked out the photos of Liam's family on the walls of the ranch office.

"Thanks for bringing lunch," Liam said. "The day has been crazy."

With calving time a couple weeks away and a whole host of unexpected issues popping up, Liam and Ivy had decided to work through lunch. The weather had turned warmer and Hadley was feeling restless, so she'd offered to bring their meal to the barn.

As if Liam's words had the power to summon trouble, one of the hands appeared in the doorway. "Dean told me to stop by and see if you had an hour or so free. Sam is out sick," the hand said. "Barry is off visiting his kid in Tulsa. We could use some help cutting the cows who aren't pregnant."

"Sure." Liam shifted his weight in the direction of the door, but glanced at Hadley before taking a step. "Ever cut cattle?"

She shook her head, sensing what was coming and wondering why Liam, knowing what he did, would ask her to ride with him.

"Like to try?"

Hadley was surprised by her strong desire to say yes. "What about Maggie?"

"I'd be happy to watch her until you get back," Ivy offered, cooing at the infant. "You'd like to hang out with Cousin Ivy until they get back, wouldn't you?" Maggie waved her arms as if in agreement. "Or I can drive her back to the house if it gets too late."

"See?" Liam's eyes held a hard glint of challenge. "All settled. Let's go find you a mount."

While her gut clenched in happy anticipation of getting on a horse again, Hadley rationalized her agreement by telling herself it was work, not pleasure. She was doing something her employer requested. Never mind that he'd been trying to figure out a way to get her back in the saddle since she'd stepped into his home two and a half weeks ago.

Excitement built as he led her outside to the paddocks where they turned out the horses during the day. Twelve horses occupied four enclosures.

Liam nodded toward a palomino mare in the farthest right paddock. The only horse in the fenced-in area, she stood in the middle, tearing at the winter grass with strong white teeth. "Daisy could use some exercise. I don't think she's been ridden much in the last year. I'll get one of the guys to saddle her for you."

"I can saddle my own horse," Hadley retorted, insulted. "Besides, I'd like to get to know her a little before I get on."

"Okay. She's a nice mare. You shouldn't have any trouble with her on the ground."

As Liam's last three words registered, she glanced over at him, but discovered nothing in his expression to arouse her suspicions. Surely he wouldn't put her on a green horse after such a long absence from the saddle. Once upon a time her skills might have been first-rate, but a decade had passed since she'd used those particular muscles. Riding a horse wasn't the same as riding a bike.

"You said she hasn't been ridden much in the last year?" Hadley decided a little clarification might be in order. "But she has been ridden, right?"

"Oh, sure." Liam walked over to the fence and picked up the halter and lead rope hung on the gate. "We were going to breed her last year, but that didn't work out. So she's just been hanging around, waiting to become a mother." He opened the gate and handed Hadley the halter. "She's easy to catch. I'll meet you in that barn over there." He indicated the building that housed the horses in training. "You might want to do a couple circles in the indoor ring before we head out."

Sensing something was up despite Liam's neutral expression and bland tone, Hadley slipped the halter onto the mare and led her to the building Liam had indicated. He hadn't yet arrived, so Hadley got busy with currycomb and brush. She smiled as the mare leaned into the grooming. Obviously Daisy appreciated Hadley's efforts.

She would have preferred to take more time with the mare, but Liam showed up, leading a gorgeous bay stallion that was already saddled and ready to go. Hadley returned his nod before tossing the saddle onto Daisy's back, settling it in just the right spot and tightening the cinch as if she'd done it last week instead of ten years earlier. Working just as efficiently, she slipped the bit into the mare's mouth and fitted the headstall into place.

"Ready?"

All at once she became aware of Liam's attention and grew self-conscious. "I think so."

"Come on. I'll work the kinks out of Buzzard while you try out Daisy."

Leading Daisy, Hadley followed Liam and the bay into the arena. What if she made a complete hash of it and ended up getting dumped? While Hadley fussed with Daisy's girth and grappled with her nerves, Liam swung up onto the stallion's back. Buzzard took several steps sideways as Liam settled his weight, but quickly relaxed beneath the pressure of his rider's legs and the steadiness of Liam's hands on the reins.

The guy was an amazing rider, and Hadley felt a fangirl moment coming on. Embarrassed at her gawking, she set her foot in the stirrup. Daisy was a little shorter than Lolita, but she felt her muscles protest as she threw her leg up and over the mare's back. Before she'd completely found her balance, Daisy's muscles bunched beneath her and the mare crow-hopped a half dozen times while Hadley clung to the saddle horn, laughter puffing out of her with each jolt of Daisy's four hoofs hitting the ground.

At last the mare got her silliness out of her system and stood still while Hadley retrieved her breath.

"You okay?"

"Fine." Hadley could feel the broad smile on her face. "Is she going to be like this the whole time?"

"No. She just wanted to make sure you were going to stay on. You passed."

"She was testing me?" The notion struck Hadley as ludicrous. What sort of horse had Liam put her on?

"She's a smart horse." His lips kicked up. "Needs a smart rider."

Apparently Daisy wasn't the only one doing the testing. Hadley keyed the mare into a walk and then took

five minutes to work through all her gaits. Whoever had
trained the palomino had done a fabulous job. She was a
dream to ride.

"Let's go cut some cattle," Hadley said, all too aware
how closely Liam had been observing her.

Liam didn't think a woman's pleasure had ever been as
important to him as Hadley's. Between their lovemaking
in Vail and the joy she'd demonstrated cutting cattle today,
especially when Daisy had kept a heifer from returning to
the herd, he was convinced he would know true happiness
only if he continued delighting Hadley.

Would he have felt the same a year ago? Remaining
celibate for twelve months had given him a greater appreciation of companionship. Being with Hadley had enabled
him to understand the difference between what he'd had
with his former girlfriends and true intimacy. Granted,
he'd only barely scratched the surface with her. Instinct
told him she was rich with complex layers she didn't yet
trust him to see. Moving past her defenses wasn't anything
he wanted to rush. Or force.

He had a good thing going. Why make a mistake and
risk losing her?

"That was amazing," Hadley crowed. Cheeks flushed,
eyes dancing with excitement, she was as vibrant as he'd
ever seen her. "You knew I'd love this when you suggested
I ride her."

"She's a natural, boss," one of the ranch hands commented, his gaze lingering on Hadley longer than Liam liked.

"I figured she would be."

The urge to growl at the cowboy was nearly impossible
to repress. Obviously, Liam wasn't the only one dazzled
by the attractive Ms. Hadley Stratton. And since he hadn't
yet staked a public claim, the rest of the male population

assumed she was fair game. That situation was not to his liking. Time he did something to change it.

Liam nudged his stallion forward and cut Hadley off from the admiring cowboys with the ease of someone accustomed to working cattle. "It's late. We should be getting back to Maggie."

Her eyes lost none of their sparkle as she nodded. "I've probably strained enough muscles for one day." She laughed. "I can tell I'm going to be in pain tomorrow, but it was worth it."

"I'm glad you like Daisy." Liam decided to push his luck. "She could probably stand a little work if you felt inclined."

Hadley hesitated but shook her head. He was making progress since the last time he'd tried to persuade her to ride. He wanted her to talk to him, to share how she was feeling. They'd discussed her friend's accident, and Hadley had mulled his suggestion that she move past the guilt that she'd carried for years. Had something about that changed?

"I'm due to go back to school in a week. I don't know how I'd make time."

He'd found a permanent nanny for Maggie. Liam and Hadley had agreed that being together would not work if she was still his employee. But he was realizing that she would no longer be an everyday fixture in his life, and that was a situation he needed to fix.

"I don't mind sharing you with the horses," he said, keeping his voice casual. He'd never had to work so hard to keep from spooking a woman.

"Oh, you don't?" She gave him a wry smile. "What if I don't have enough time for either of you?"

Liam's grip on the reins tightened and Buzzard began trotting in place. If he thought she was flirting, he'd have shot back a provocative retort, but Liam had gotten to know Hadley well enough in the last few weeks to know she had serious concerns.

"Move in with me."

The offer was sudden, but he didn't surprise himself when he made it.

"You already have a full-time nanny moving in."

"Not as a nanny."

Her eyes widened. "Then as what?"

"The woman I'm crazy about." He'd never been in love and had no idea if that's what he felt for Hadley. But he'd been doing a lot of soul-searching these last few days.

"You're crazy about me?" The doubt in her voice wasn't unexpected.

He'd known she wouldn't accept his declaration without some vigorous convincing. Hadley wasn't one to forgive herself easily for past mistakes. She'd fallen for her first employer, only to have her heart torn up when the jerk got back together with his ex-wife. That wasn't a judgment error she would make a second time. And she was already skeptical of Liam's past romantic history.

"If we weren't on these damned horses I'd demonstrate just how crazy."

Liam ground his teeth at her surprise. What kept her from accepting how strong his feelings had become? The mildest of her saucy smiles provoked a befuddling rush of lust. He pondered what her opinion would be on a dozen decisions before lunch. Waking up alone in his big bed had become the most painful part of his day.

"This is happening too fast."

"I'm not going to bail on you."

"I know."

"You don't sound convinced." He was determined to change her mind. "What can I say to reassure you?"

"You don't need to say anything."

After regarding her for a long moment, he shook his head. "I've dated a lot of women."

"This is your way of convincing me to take a chance on you?"

He ignored her interruption. "Enough to recognize that how I feel about you is completely foreign to me." He saw he'd hit the wrong note with the word *foreign*. "And terrific. Scary. Fascinating. I've never been so twisted up by a woman before."

"And somehow you think this is a good thing?"

"You make me better. I feel more alive when I'm with you. Like anything is possible."

She blinked several times. "I think that's the most amazing thing anyone has ever said to me."

"I don't believe that. I do, however, believe that it might be one of the first times you've let yourself hear and trust one of my compliments." He was making progress if she'd stopped perceiving everything he said as a ploy.

"You might be right."

They'd drawn within sight of the ranch buildings, and Liam regretted how fast the ride had gone. He hadn't received an answer from Hadley, and the time to pursue the matter was fast coming to an end.

"I hope that means you're beginning to believe me when I tell you how important you've become to me."

"It's starting to sink in." She watched him from beneath her eyelashes. "But are you ready to have me move in?"

"Absolutely." His conviction rang in his answer. "But it's not the only thing I want."

This was something else he'd thought long and hard about. It wasn't just his feelings for Hadley that were driving him, but also his need to give Maggie a loving home and create for her the sort of stable family denied him and Kyle.

"No?"

"What I really want is for us to get married."

Eleven

While Hadley wondered if she'd heard him correctly, Liam pulled a ring box out of his coat pocket and extended it her way. She stared at it, her heart thundering in her ears. It wasn't the most romantic of proposals, but she had to bite her lower lip to keep from blurting out her acceptance. It took half a minute for her to think rationally.

"I haven't said yes or no to moving in," she reminded him, pleased that she sounded like a sensible adult instead of a giddy teenager.

"I'm afraid I've gone about this in a clumsy fashion." His confident manner belied his words. "I've never asked a woman to marry me before. Especially not one I've known less than a month."

Hadley's brain scrambled to think logically. "And the reason you're rushing into marriage?"

"I'm not rushing into marriage," he corrected her with a wily grin. "I'm rushing into an engagement."

"Semantics." She waved away his explanation. "Are you sure you don't want to live together for a while and see how it goes?"

"I've already lived with you for a while and it's been terrific. I want to keep on living with you. I need you in my life. That's not going to change if we wait to get engaged. Right now your plan is to finish school and move to Houston. I want you to make a life with me in Royal instead."

Hadley clutched her reins in a white-knuckled grip and made no move toward the tempting ring box. "Are you sure this is what you want?"

From the way the light in his eyes dimmed, it wasn't the answer he'd hoped for, but he had to know her well enough to realize she wouldn't jump aboard his runaway freight train without thinking things through. After all, her career goals were designed to carry her far from Royal. And that was something she'd have to reconsider if she married him.

"Are you questioning whether I know my mind?" He lifted the enormous diamond ring from its nest of black velvet and caught her left hand. His eyes mesmerized her as he slid the ring on her finger. "I took a year off dating and spent the time thinking through what I wanted in a woman. I wouldn't have slept with you in Vail if I hadn't already made up my mind that you were special." Liam dismounted and handed off Buzzard's reins to one of the grooms.

"But marriage?" She stared at the ring, mesmerized by the diamond's sparkle.

Here was proof that Liam's proposal wasn't something impulsive and reckless. He'd come prepared to ask her to marry him. And yet he hadn't said anything about love.

"It's been on my mind constantly since we came back from Colorado."

Hearing she hadn't been the only one who'd felt the connection they'd established that snowy weekend eased her mind somewhat. She dismounted and surrendered Daisy to the groom as well. Her feet barely touched the dirt as she walked the short distance to Liam and took the hand he held outstretched.

He tugged her to him and lifted her chin with gentle fingers until their gazes met. "You fill my thoughts when we're apart and make me mad with longing to take you in my arms when we're together."

Liam's assertion awakened a deep, profound thrumming in her heart. "I know the feeling," she said, lifting onto her toes to offer him a single kiss. "I'd better get back to Maggie."

He wrapped a strong arm around her waist and held her snug against his muscular chest. "Will you stay tonight?"

"I can't. I'm having dinner with Kori."

"Afterward?"

She laughed and danced beyond his reach. "I've been neglecting the other guy in my life so I'm going to sleep with him."

"That guy better be Waldo," he growled, but his eyes sparkled with amusement below lowered brows.

"I don't have time for anyone else."

"Bring him with you when you come back. It's time you both settled permanently at the ranch house."

Engagement. Moving in. It was all happening so fast. Her heart hammered against her ribs in a panicked rhythm. All too aware she hadn't actually agreed to marry Liam, despite accepting his ring, she opened her mouth, but her thoughts were too scattered to summon words. He might have been considering this move for a while, but for her this development was brand-new and she needed to think things through.

One of Liam's ranch hands approached, citing a problem with a mare, and Hadley took the opportunity to slip away. As she wove through the connected barns on her way back to the ranch offices, her mood shifted from giddy to concerned. She might not have said yes to marriage, but she'd accepted his ring and kept her doubts to herself.

What had happened to being practical? Falling in love with Liam for starters. How was she supposed to think straight when the man made her feel like it was the Fourth of July, Thanksgiving and Christmas all rolled into one perfect holiday?

Thank goodness she was having dinner with Kori. Talking to her best friend would help sort things out.

Kori held Hadley's engagement ring mere inches from her nose and scrutinized the diamond. "You're not seriously thinking about marrying him, are you?"

"Well, I haven't said no." Hadley wasn't sure why her friend had done such a complete turnaround. "What's changed since last week when you told me to go for it?"

"Sex, yes." Kori regarded her friend as if she'd sprouted a second head as she opened the oven and removed her famous shepherd's pie. The succulent aroma of meat and savory gravy filled the kitchen. "Marriage, no."

Hadley held the plates while Kori filled them. Her friend's unexpected reaction to Liam's proposal was disheartening. "You're right. It's moving too fast."

"For you, yes." Kori and Scott had taken about a month to decide they wanted to be together forever. But they'd spent four years planning and saving money for their wedding.

"What if it feels right?" Hadley set the plates on the table while Kori followed with the salad.

"Did Noah feel right?"

Noah had been about safety. She'd been second-guessing her decision to change careers and had been worried about money. The notion of marrying a stable man had taken that burden off her shoulders.

"At the time." Hadley had no trouble admitting the truth of her failing. In the last five years she'd done a lot of soul-searching to understand why she'd failed to see that Noah was more interested in a mother for his children than a partner for life.

Kori nodded. "You are the most practical person I know until a single guy comes along needing help with his kids and you get all wrapped up in the idea of being a family."

It was her Achilles' heel, and she was wise enough to avoid putting herself in situations like the one with Noah. Like the one with Liam. As much as Hadley needed to hear Kori's blunt summary of her shortcomings, she wanted to protest that things with Liam were different. But were they?

Kori regarded her with a sympathetic expression while she topped off their wineglasses. "I know this isn't what you want to hear."

"You aren't saying anything I haven't thought a hundred times in the last month. I don't know why I do this. It's not like I didn't have a perfectly normal childhood. My parents are happily married, rarely fight and support me in everything I do."

"Don't be so hard on yourself. You are a born caretaker and one of the most nurturing people I know. It's in your nature to get overly invested, which is why you hated teaching a class of thirty kids. You might make a difference with one or two, but it's hard to give each child the sort of attention they need." Kori hit the problem squarely on the head. "Being a guidance counselor suits you so much better."

"I know." Hadley sighed. "But none of this helps me with what to do about Liam's marriage proposal. I really do love him."

"You haven't known him very long."

Hadley couldn't believe Kori of all people would use that argument. "Not directly, but I saw a lot of him ten years ago when I was barrel racing. I had a crush on him then. He was always nice to me. Never made me feel like I was going to be his next conquest." And for Liam, that was saying something.

"Because you weren't that sort of girl," Kori reminded her. "You told me while your friends dated extensively you weren't interested in boys, only horses."

"I was interested in Liam."

"Let me guess. He didn't know you existed?"

"At first, but toward the end of my last show season, that changed. I used to compete with his on-and-off girlfriend, and he'd sometimes show up to watch her. Most of the time I beat her, and he started congratulating me on my rides. At first I thought he was doing it to make her mad, but then I realized he meant it. One thing about Liam, he was always a horseman first and everything else came after."

"So things were warming up between you. What happened?"

"Anna was my best friend at the time, and she had a huge thing for him."

"But he liked you?"

Hadley shrugged. "He was way out of my league."

"What would you have done if he'd made a play for you?"

"Freaked out in true teenage fashion." Hadley trailed off as she recalled how much more intense her emotions had been in those days. Every problem had seemed crippling. Her success had sent her straight into orbit. "I'd never had a crush on anyone before, and Liam was older by a couple years and had a lot of experience. I told myself he couldn't possibly be interested in me that way."

"But you hoped he might be?"

"Sure, but it was complicated."

"Because of Anna?"

"Yes." Hadley hadn't told anyone the story behind Anna's accident. Ashamed that her friend was paralyzed as a result of something Hadley had said in a moment of anger, she'd punished herself all these years by avoiding something she loved: horses. "It bugged her that he'd go out of his way to comment on my rides but didn't notice her at all."

"What did she expect? That you'd tell him to stop being nice to you?" At Hadley's shrug, her friend sighed. "You should've told her to go to hell."

"I did something so much worse, and as a consequence my best friend lost the use of her legs."

Kori's eyes widened. "You need to tell me the whole story."

Haley killed the last of the wine in her glass and refilled from the bottle. "It was July and Wade Ranch was throwing a huge party at their stalls in the show barn to promote one of their stallions. Anna had been flirting with Liam for a month and was convinced he was finally showing interest when he invited her to the celebration. She dragged me along because she didn't want to go alone and then promptly ditched me to go hang with Liam. I lost track of her and spent the night hanging out with some of the other barrel racers.

"It was getting late and Anna didn't want to leave, so I arranged to get a lift with someone else. A little before we took off, I went to check on Lolita for the last time to make sure she had water and because being with her calmed me down. I was mad at Anna for chasing a guy who didn't act like he was into her."

"Because if he had been into her she wouldn't have had to chase him."

"Right." Several girls at the party had poked fun at Anna for thinking Liam could possibly be interested in her. "So, there I was in the stall with Lolita and guess who appears."

"Liam?" Kori said his name with such relish that Hadley had to smile.

"Liam. At first I thought maybe Anna was looking for me and got Liam to help her, but turns out he'd just followed me."

"Where was Anna?"

"I don't know. And really, for a little while, I didn't care. Liam and I talked about my upcoming ride the next day and he offered me advice for how to take a little time off my turns. I was grateful for the feedback and when I told him that, he said that if I won, I could take him out to dinner with my prize money."

"He asked you out?"

"I guess." Even now doubt clouded Hadley's tone. Even with Liam's engagement ring on her finger, she had a hard time believing that he'd been the slightest bit interested in her. She'd been so plain and uninteresting compared with his other girlfriends.

"You guess?" Kori regarded her in bemusement. "Of course he did."

Hadley shrugged. "Like I said, he was nice to a lot of people."

"But you had to suspect he wouldn't have tracked you to Lolita's stall if he wasn't interested in you."

"I could barely hope he liked me. I was excited and terrified. His reputation was something I wasn't sure I could deal with. He dated extensively." She put air quotes around *dated*. "I was eighteen and I'd never really been kissed."

"So did you win and go to dinner with him?"

"I won, but we never went out. Anna rode after I did the next day and had her accident."

"You haven't explained how that was your fault."

"Anna overheard Liam and I talking about dinner and me agreeing to his terms. She interrupted us and told me she was leaving and if I wanted a ride I'd better come with her. Considering I'd been ready to go an hour earlier, her demand seemed pretty unreasonable. I was tempted to tell her I'd already made other arrangements, but she was obviously upset so I agreed to head out."

"She was jealous that Liam had asked you out."

"That's what I figured, but on the way to the car I tried to explain to her that he was just helping me out with my riding."

"And she didn't believe you."

"No. She'd figured out I liked him and accused me of going behind her back. When I denied it, she went ballistic. Said that the only reason he noticed me was because I beat his girlfriend and that I wasn't his type. She insisted I would be the laughingstock of the barn if I kept believing he would ever want to date me."

"Sounds like things she should have been telling herself."

While Hadley agreed with Kori, at the time, each word had struck like a fist. "I wish I hadn't been so surprised by her attack. If I'd been able to stay calm, I might have been able to reason with her. But what she was saying were the same things that had been running through my head. To hear them from my best friend... I was devastated."

"So you didn't tell her she was the one who was acting like an idiot?"

"No." And now they'd arrived at the part of the story Hadley was most ashamed of. "I told her that if Liam only noticed me because of my riding she was out of luck. The way she rode, no wonder he had no idea who she was."

"Ouch."

Hadley winced. "Not my finest moment. And for the last ten years I've regretted those words."

"But it sounds like she was asking to have the truth served up to her."

"Maybe, but she was my best friend. I should have been more understanding. And because of what I said, the next day she pushed too hard and fell badly. So, now you see. If I'd not let my temper get the best of me, Anna never would have tried to prove she was the better rider and wouldn't have fallen and broken her back."

"And you haven't ridden since."

"No." It was a small sacrifice to make for being a bad

friend. "Until today. And now I'm engaged to the guy who came between Anna and me with tragic results."

"And I can tell you still aren't guilt free over moving on. So, as your best friend of seven years, I give you permission to get on with your life and stop beating yourself up over something you said to your friend who was acting like a greedy bitch a decade ago." Kori lifted her wineglass and held it out to Hadley.

Pushing aside all reluctance, Hadley picked up her glass and gently clinked it with Kori's. The crystalline note rang in the dining nook, the sound proclaiming an end to living in the past and the beginning of her bright future.

She'd given enough time and energy to her mistakes. She deserved to be happy, and being Liam's wife, becoming a family with him and Maggie, was the perfect way to spend the rest of her life.

Liam sat on the couch in the den, using one hand to scroll through the report Nolan's investigator had sent him regarding Margaret Garner while cradling a snugly swaddled Maggie in his other arm. She'd been fussy and agitated all day, and her appetite had waned. Hadley had noticed Maggie's temperature was slightly elevated and Liam was glad she was scheduled for a follow-up visit with her pediatrician tomorrow. Maggie continued to show signs of jaundice, and this had both Liam and Hadley concerned.

As a counterpoint to Liam's agitation over Maggie's health issues, Waldo lay on the sofa back directly behind Liam's head, purring. Although he'd grown up believing that cats belonged in barns, keeping the mouse population under control, he'd grown fond of Hadley's fur ball and had to concede that the feline had a knack for reading moods and providing just the right companionship. Just yesterday Liam had been irritated by a particularly demanding client, and Waldo had spent a hilarious ten minutes playing with one of Hadley's ponytail holders, cheering him up.

The only member of his family not sitting on the den's sofa was Hadley. After dinner she'd gone upstairs to call her parents and tell them about the engagement. They'd been on a cruise several days ago when Liam had popped the question and hadn't been immediately available to receive their daughter's news. Hadley was concerned that they'd view the engagement as moving too fast, and Liam had suggested that they take Maggie to Houston this weekend so everyone could meet.

With an effort, Liam brought his attention back to the report. Despite only spending four days on the job, the investigator had built a pretty clear picture of Maggie's mom. Margaret Garner had worked at home as a freelance illustrator and had a pretty limited social life. She'd dated rarely, and her friends had husbands and children who kept them busy. So busy, in fact, that none of them had had a clue that Margaret was pregnant. Nor had there been any contact between her and Kyle after their weeklong affair. The investigator hadn't been able to determine how the two had met, but after digging into Margaret's financials, he'd figured out when the fling had happened.

Margaret's perfectionism and heavy workload explained why she hadn't gone out much, but a couple of her friends had known Margaret since college and confided that they thought Margaret might have had some depression issues. From what the investigator could determine, she'd never sought medical help for that or gone to see a doctor when she'd discovered she was pregnant.

"Well, that's done," Hadley announced, her voice heavy as she crossed the room and settled onto the couch beside him.

"How did it go with your parents?"

"They were surprised." Her head dropped onto his shoulder. She'd been anxious about how the conversation would go all through dinner. Hadley was an only child and from her description of them, Liam got the impression they didn't exactly approve of some of the choices she'd made in the last few years. Especially when she'd quit teaching and moved to Royal in order to get her master's degree.

"What are you working on?"

"I had an investigator look into Margaret Garner's background."

"You hired an investigator? Why?" She peered more closely at the report on his computer screen.

"Nolan suggested it."

"Who is Nolan?"

"Nolan Dane is a family law attorney I hired."

"You hired a lawyer?"

Liam realized he probably should have shared his plans with her regarding Maggie before this, but hadn't anticipated that she'd be surprised. "Because I'm seeking custody of Maggie."

"Have you told your brother?"

"Kyle hasn't responded to my messages about Maggie yet."

Hadley sat up and turned on the cushions to face him. "Don't you think you should talk to him before you make such a big decision regarding his daughter?"

"I think it's obvious from the fact that it's been three weeks and I haven't heard from him that he's not in a place where he can be a father. Either he's overseas and unavailable or he's choosing not to call me back. Whichever it is, Maggie deserves parents who can always be there for her." He studied her expression with a hint of concern. "I thought you'd be on board with this. After all, you love Maggie as much as I do and have to admit we make terrific parents."

Her brows came together. "I guess I thought we'd be great with kids someday. As soon as I accepted that Maggie was your brother's daughter, I guess I thought she'd end up with him."

"Are you trying to tell me you can't see yourself as Maggie's mother?"

"Not at all. I love her…" But it was obvious that Hadley was grappling with something.

"Then what's going on?"

"I was just wondering how long you'd been thinking about this." Her tone had an accusatory edge he didn't understand.

"I've been considering what's best for Maggie since Diane Garner left her on my doorstep."

"And have you thought about what's best for your brother?"

Liam struggled for patience in the face of her growing hostility. "I'm thinking about the fact that he's a navy SEAL and likely to be called to duty at any time. He's not married and lives on the East Coast, far from family. Who is going to take care of Maggie while he's gone for weeks, maybe months at a time?" Liam met Hadley's gaze and didn't care for the indictment he glimpsed in her beautiful blue eyes. "I think Maggie would be better off here with us."

"He's not married." She spoke deliberately as if determined to make a point. "So he's not the best person to raise Maggie."

"He's a career military man with no family support," Liam corrected her, unsure why she wasn't agreeing with him. "How often will he miss a school event? How likely is it he'll be around for her first steps, first words, first… everything."

"You're not married, either," Hadley pointed out, her voice barely audible.

"But I'm engaged."

"Is that why you proposed?"

"What do you mean?"

"Obviously a married couple would be a stronger candidate in a custody battle."

"Sure." Why deny it? She wasn't a fool, and she knew him well enough to suspect he'd want to put forth the strongest case for Maggie.

However, the instant the admission was out, Hadley's whole demeanor transformed. All trace of antagonism vanished. She sagged in defeat.

Liam rushed to defend his rationale. "I'd like to point out that I've never asked any woman to marry me before you," he continued, more determined than ever to convince Hadley how much he needed her. "I want us to spend the rest of our lives together. With Maggie. As a family."

"I am such an idiot."

"I don't understand." He'd missed her jump in logic. "Why do you think you're an idiot?"

"Because it's just like Noah all over again."

"Noah?" The guy who'd broken her heart? "That's absurd. I asked you to marry me. He didn't."

"He said he wanted us to be together, too." Hadley shot to her feet and backed away, but her eyes never left Liam. "Only what he wanted was someone to take care of his kids and his house. Someone to be there when he got home at the end of the day and in his bed at night."

"You don't seriously think I proposed to you simply because I wanted you to fill a role." In order to keep Maggie slumbering peacefully, Liam kept his volume low, but made sure his outrage came through loud and clear.

"Everyone is right. It happened too fast." Hadley covered her mouth with her fingertips as a single tear slid down her cheek.

The sight of it disturbed him. He was fast losing control

of this situation and had no idea how to fix it. "Everyone? You mean your parents?"

"And my best friend, Kori. Not to mention the look on Candace's face when she found out."

"So what if our engagement happened fast?" Marrying Hadley meant both she and Maggie would stay with him at Wade Ranch. "That doesn't mean my motives are anything like you're painting them to be."

She pulled off her engagement ring and extended it to him. "So if I give this back to you and say I want to wait until I'm done with school to discuss our future, you'd be okay with it."

Liam made no move to take the ring back. Gripped by dismay, he stared at her, unable to believe that she was comparing him to some loser who'd used her shamelessly and broken her heart five years earlier.

"You're overreacting."

"Am I?" She crossed her arms over her chest. "When you proposed, you never told me you loved me."

No, he hadn't. He'd known he couldn't live without her, but he'd been consumed with winning custody of Maggie and afraid that Hadley would receive a job offer in Houston that would cement her plans for the future. He hadn't been thinking about romance or love when he'd proposed.

"That was wrong of me and I'm sorry. But I did tell you that I couldn't imagine life without you."

She shook her head. "You said you needed me in your life. That should've warned me that there was more motivating you than love."

"What does it matter what motivated me when it all comes down to how much we want to be together and how committed we are to being a family?"

"I really want that," she said, coming forward to set the engagement ring on the end table. "But I can't be in a relationship with you and know that your reasons for being in it are based on something besides love."

A lifetime of suppressed heartache at his mother's abandonment kept Liam from speaking as Hadley reached past him and disengaged her cat from his snug nest. Waldo's purring hadn't ceased during their argument, and Liam felt a chill race across his skin at the loss of the cat's warmth. It wasn't until she began to leave the room that he realized his mistake.

"Don't leave." He pushed aside his laptop and pursued Hadley into the hallway. "Hadley, wait."

She'd reached the entryway and slipped her coat off the hook. "I think it will be better if Waldo and I move back to my apartment. I'll be back in the morning to take care of Maggie." She didn't point out that the new nanny was set to start work in four days, but Liam was all too aware that he was on the verge of losing her forever.

"Maybe you're right and we moved too fast," he said. "But don't think for one second that I've changed my mind about wanting to spend the rest of my life with you." He extended his hand to catch her arm and stop her from leaving, but she sidestepped him, the unresisting cat clutched to her chest.

"I think it would be better for both of us if we focused on our individual futures. I have to finish school. You have a custody case to win. Once things settle down we can reconnect and see how we feel."

"If you think I'm going to agree to not see you for the next few months you've got it wrong."

"Of course we'll see each other." But her words weren't convincing. She set down the cat. Waldo stretched and wrapped himself around her legs while she donned her coat. Then, picking up her purse and the cat, Hadley opened the front door. "But I'm going to be crazy once classes start again, and you've got a couple hundred cattle set to give birth. Let's give ourselves a couple weeks to see where we're at."

"You're not going to be able to brush me off that easily," he growled as she slipped through the front door and pulled it closed behind her, leaving him and Maggie alone in the enormous, echoing Victorian mansion.

Twelve

Hadley was still reeling from déjà vu as she let herself into her apartment and set Waldo on the floor. The silver tabby's warmth had been a comfort as she'd sped through the early-evening darkness toward her tiny apartment.

How could she have been so stupid as to let herself get blinded by love a second time? So much for being five years older and wiser. She was obviously no less desperate; otherwise she wouldn't have become Liam's convenient solution the way she'd been Noah's. Honestly, what had happened to her common sense?

With her emotions a chaotic mess, Hadley looked for something in her apartment to occupy her, but after straightening a few pillows, dusting and running the vacuum, she ran out of tasks. While water boiled for a cup of tea, she wished her classes had resumed. At least then she'd have a paper to write or a test to study for. Something to occupy her thoughts and keep her mind off Liam.

She could call Kori and pour her heart out. Hadley rejected the idea as soon as it occurred to her. She wasn't ready to tell anyone that she'd screwed up again. The injury to her pride was still too fresh. Not to mention the damage to her confidence. As for the pain in her heart, Hadley could scarcely breathe as she considered all she'd lost tonight. Not just Liam, but Maggie as well.

Would it have been so bad to marry Liam and become

Maggie's mom? The whole time she'd been falling in love with Liam, she'd thought he and Maggie were a package deal. And then came their trip to Colorado. When she'd decided to believe him about his brother being Maggie's dad, letting her heart lead for a change hadn't felt one bit scary. She'd assumed Kyle would eventually come to Wade Ranch and take responsibility for Maggie. It never occurred to her that Liam intended to fight his brother for custody and that he might propose in order to appear to be the better candidate.

Desperate for a distraction from her turbulent thoughts, Hadley carried the hot tea to her small desk and turned on the computer. Before she'd considered her actions, she cued up the internet and impulsively ventured on to a popular social media site. Her fingers tapped out Noah's name and she pushed Enter before she could change her mind.

In seconds his page appeared and her heart gave a little jump as she stared at the photo of him and his kids that he used as his profile picture. Five years had gone by. Peter and Nikki were eight and seven now. They looked happy in their father's arms. Noah's wife wasn't in the shot, and Hadley searched through some of his other photos to see if she showed up anywhere. There were pictures of her with both kids, but none of her with Noah. Were they still married? Nothing in his profile information gave her a clue.

Feeling more than a little stalkerish, Hadley searched for Anna, but found no sign of her onetime friend. She almost left the website, inclined to switch to something with less potential for heartache, when she decided to search for Anna's sister, Char. And there she found Anna. Only she wasn't Anna Johnson any more. She was Anna Bradley now. A happily married woman with two beautiful girls.

Hadley stared at the photos in numb disbelief. This is the woman she'd been feeling guilty about for ten years? Anna hadn't wallowed in her misfortune. She hadn't sat around letting life pass her by. She'd gone to college in Dallas, become an engineer, gotten married and was busy raising a two- and a four-year-old.

It was as if the universe had reached out a hand and smacked Hadley on the back of the head and yelled, *snap out of it.* Noah had moved forward with his life. He had his kids and seemed to be in a good place with his wife or ex-wife. Anna was thriving with a career and family. Apparently Hadley was the only one stuck in limbo.

With revelations pouring over her like ice water, Hadley shut down the computer and picked up a notebook and a pen. It was time for her to stop dwelling on what had happened in the past and to consider how she envisioned her future. What was her idea of a perfect career? Where did she want to live? Was the love in her heart strong enough to overcome her doubts and fears?

Liam entered the pediatrician's office and spotted Hadley seated by the wall, Maggie's carrier on the chair beside her. Overnight the baby's temperature had risen, and the concern radiating from Hadley caused a spike in his anxiety.

"How is she?" he asked as he sat beside Maggie and peered in her carrier.

"A little bit worse than she was when I arrived this morning. She wouldn't eat and seems listless. I'm glad we had this appointment scheduled today."

Hadley was obviously distraught, and Liam badly wanted to offer her the comfort of his embrace, but yesterday she hadn't believed him when he'd told her there was more to his proposal than his determination to seek custody of Maggie. What made him think that a miracle had occurred overnight to change her mind?

"Do you think the jaundice is causing this?"

"More likely the jaundice is a symptom of something more serious."

"Damn it." The curse vibrated in his chest as anxiety flared. He stared down at the sleeping baby. "I can't lose her."

"Liam, you're not going to lose her." Hadley reached across Maggie's carrier and set her fingers on his upper arm.

The light contact burned through him like a wildfire, igniting his hope for a future with her. She loved him. The proof was in her supportive tone and her desire to reassure him. But as he reached to cover her hand with his, she withdrew. When she spoke again, her voice had a professional crispness.

"She's going to be fine."

He hated the distance between them. He'd been wrong to propose to her as part of a scheme to win custody of Maggie. Even though it hadn't been his only reason for asking her to marry him, she'd been right to feel as if he'd treated her no better than Noah.

But how could he convince her to give him another chance when she'd rejected everything he'd already said and done? As with the subject of Maggie's paternity, she was either going to believe him or she wasn't. She'd been burned before, and her lack of trust demonstrated that she hadn't yet moved on. He'd have to be patient and persistent. Two things he was known for when it came to horses, but not in his personal life.

"Hadley, about what happened last night—"

A nurse appeared in the waiting room and called Maggie's name before Hadley could respond. Liam ground his teeth as he and Hadley followed the nurse into an exam room. He refocused his attention on Maggie as the nurse weighed and measured her. After it was determined that her temperature had climbed to 102, the nurse left to fetch Dr. Stringer.

Liam's tension ratcheted upward during the wait. Hadley sat beside him with Maggie cradled in her arms. She'd fixed her gaze on the door to the hall as if she could summon the doctor by sheer will.

After a wait that felt like hours but was less than ten minutes, Maggie's doctor appeared. Dr. Stringer made a quick but thorough examination of his patient, returned her to Hadley's arms and sat down, his expression solemn.

"I'm concerned that she's running a temperature and that the jaundice hasn't gone away after the phototherapy treatments," Dr. Stringer said. "I'd like to draw blood and recheck her bilirubin levels. If they continue to remain high we may want to look at the possibility of doing a blood transfusion."

Liam felt rather than heard Hadley's sharp intake of breath. She had leaned her shoulder against his as the doctor had spoken. The seriousness of Maggie's medical condition was a weight Liam was glad not to have to bear alone.

"Maggie is a rare blood type," Liam said. "AB negative. Is that going to pose a problem finding donors?"

The doctor shook his head. "Not at all. In fact, where O is the universal donor blood type, AB is the universal recipient. But let's not get ahead of ourselves. I'm going to have the nurse draw some blood and then we'll see where we're at."

Maggie's reaction to the blood draw was not as vigorous as Liam expected it to be, and he took that as a sign that she was even sicker than she appeared. This time as they sat alone in the exam room, Liam reached for Hadley's hand. Her fingers were ice cold, but they curved to hold fast to his.

Their second wait was longer, but no less silent. Liam's

heart thumped impatiently, spreading unease through every vein. Beside him, Hadley, locked in her own battle with worry, gripped his hand and stared down at Maggie. Both of them had run out of reassuring things to say.

The door opened again and Dr. Stringer entered. "Looks like it's not her bilirubin levels that are causing the problem," he said, nothing about his manner suggesting this was good news.

"Then what's going on?" Liam asked.

"We're seeing a high level of white blood cells that points to infection. Because of the jaundice and the fact that she's a preemie, I'd like you to take Maggie to the hospital for further testing. I've already contacted my partner, Dr. Davison. He's on call at the hospital today and will be waiting for you."

"The hospital?" Hadley sounded stunned. "It's that serious?"

"At this point we don't know, but I would rather err on the side of caution."

Liam nodded. "Then we'll head right over."

Hadley sat in the passenger side of Liam's Range Rover as he drove to the hospital and silently berated herself for being a terrible caregiver.

"This isn't your fault," Liam said, demonstrating an uncanny knack for knowing what she was thinking.

"You don't know that."

"She only just recently started showing signs of an infection."

"But we don't know how long this has been brewing. You heard the doctor. He said it could have been coming on slowly for a long time. What if she was sick before we went to Colorado and then we walked to town and back? Maybe that's when things started."

"We can't know for sure and you'll make yourself crazy if you keep guessing."

"I should never have…" She trailed off, biting her lip to stifle the rest of the sentence.

"Should never have what?" Liam demanded, taking his eyes off the road to glance her way.

She answered in a rush. "Slept with you."

"Why? Because by doing that you stopped being a good nanny?" He snorted derisively.

Hadley shifted away from his irritation and leaned her head against the cool window. "Maggie was my responsibility. I got distracted."

"She's my responsibility, too," he reminded her. "I'm just as much at fault if something happens to her. You know, one of these days you should stop blaming yourself for every little thing that goes wrong."

With a shock, Hadley realized that Liam was right. She'd taken responsibility for other people's decisions, believing if she'd been a better friend, Anna wouldn't have gotten hurt, and if she'd been more affectionate with Noah or acted more like a parent to his children instead of their nanny, he might not have gone back to his ex-wife.

"It's a habit I should break," she said, her annoyance diminished. "It's really not anyone's fault she's sick. Like the doctor said, her birth wasn't routine. The infection could have been caused by any number of things."

Neither spoke again, but the silence was no longer charged by antagonism. Hadley cast several glances in Liam's direction, wishing she hadn't overreacted last night after finding out Liam intended to seek custody of Maggie. But she'd gone home and filled two sheets of paper with a list of everything that made her happy. It had taken her half a page before she'd begun to break free of the mental patterns she'd fallen into. But it was the last two items that told the real story.

Horses.

Liam.

That it had taken her so long to admit what she needed in her life to be truly happy was telling.

Liam dropped her and Maggie off at the emergency entrance and went to park. Hadley checked in at reception and was directed to the waiting room. She was told someone would come down from pediatrics to get them soon.

To Hadley's relief they only had to wait ten minutes. Liam never even had a chance to sit down before they were on their way to a private room in Royal Memorial's brand-new west wing.

A nurse entered the room while Hadley lifted Maggie from her carrier. "Hello, my name is Agnes and I'll be taking care of Maggie while she's here."

"It's nice to meet you." Hadley followed Agnes's directions and placed Maggie in the bassinet. It was hard to step away from the baby and let the nurse take over, but Hadley forced herself to join Liam by the window.

Liam gave her a tight smile. "She's in good hands."

"I know." Hadley was consumed by the need for Liam's arms around her. But she'd relinquished all rights to his reassurances last night when she'd given back his engagement ring.

The nurse took Maggie's vitals and hooked her up to an IV.

"Because she's not yet four weeks," Agnes began, "we're going to start her on antibiotics right away. It may take twenty-four to forty-eight hours to get the lab results back, so we'd like to take this precaution. The good news is that it hasn't seemed to affect her lungs. That's always a concern with a premature baby." Agnes offered a reassuring smile before continuing. "Dr. Davison will be by in a little while to talk to you."

"Thank you," Liam said while Hadley crossed to Maggie.

"She looks even tinier hooked up to the IV."

Liam came to stand beside her and stared down at Maggie. A muscle jumped in his jaw. His eyes had developed a haunted look. Suddenly it was Hadley's turn to offer comfort.

"She's going to be fine."

"Thank you for being here," he said. "It's…"

She'd never know what he intended to say because a man in a white lab coat entered the room with Agnes at his heels.

"Good morning, I'm Dr. Davison. I've spoken with Dr. Stringer and he filled me in on what's been going on. I'm sure you're anxious to hear about the tests we ran on Maggie," The doctor met each of their gazes in turn before shifting his attention to the infant. "What we're looking at is a blood infection. That's what's causing the fever, her jaundice and her listlessness."

A knot formed in Hadley's chest. She gripped Liam's forearm for stability. "Is it serious?"

"It can be. But Maggie is in good hands with us here at Royal Memorial. I'm sure she'll make a full recovery. The sooner she gets treatment the better the outcome. We've already started her on antibiotics, and we're going to monitor her for the next couple days while we run a battery of tests to determine what's causing the infection."

"How long will she be here?" Liam gave Hadley's fingers a gentle squeeze.

"Probably not more than three days. If there's bacteria in her blood, she'll be on antibiotics for three weeks and you'll be bringing her in for periodic checkups."

"Thank you, Dr. Davison." Liam extended his hand to the pediatrician and appeared less overwhelmed than he had before the doctor's arrival.

"Yes, thank you." Hadley summoned a smile.

Dr. Davison turned to the nurse. "Agnes, would you prepare Maggie for a lumbar puncture?"

"Certainly, Dr. Davison." She smiled at Liam and Hadley. "We have some paperwork at the nurses' station for you to fill out," she said. "We'll need just a few minutes for the spinal tap and then you can come back and be with Maggie."

Hadley tensed, intending to resist being evicted for the procedure, but then she remembered that she was the nanny, nothing more. She'd given up her rights when she'd given Liam back his ring.

When they stepped into the hallway, Hadley turned to Liam. "I should go."

"Go?" he echoed, his expression blank, eyes unfocused. "Go where?"

"I don't really belong here." As much as that was true in a practical sense, she couldn't shake a feeling of responsibility to Maggie and to him.

Foolishness. If anyone besides Liam had hired her, she wouldn't have let herself get personally involved. She'd never slept with any of her other clients, either. Even with Noah she hadn't stepped across that line. They'd been close, but something about sleeping with him with his children down the hall hadn't sat well with her. And right before the weekend they were supposed to go away and be together for the first time was when Noah decided to go back to his ex-wife.

"Maggie needs you," Liam countered. "You can't leave her now."

"I'm her nanny." It hurt to admit it, but Hadley knew that after what had happened between her and Liam, she needed to start pulling back. "What she needs is her family. Why don't you call her grandmother?"

"You mean the woman who left her with me and hasn't demonstrated any grandmotherly concern since?"

Hadley was torn. Her presence wasn't needed while Maggie was at the hospital. The nurses would see to it that the baby was well tended. Liam could give her all the love and snuggling she required.

"I'm sorry that Maggie's mother died and her grandmother is so far away, but I can't be here for you and for her in this way. She's in good hands with the nurses and with you. I've already gotten too involved. I can't keep pretending like nothing has changed." Hadley turned in the direction of the elevator so Liam wouldn't see her tears.

He caught her arm before she could take a step. "I'm sorry, too," he murmured in her ear, his breath warm against her temple. "I never meant for any of this to hurt you."

And then he set her free. Gutted and empty, she walked away without glancing back.

Liam sat on the couch in Maggie's hospital room. A nurse had appeared half an hour ago to take Maggie's temperature and change her diaper. When she'd completed her tasks, she'd dimmed the lights and left Liam in semidarkness. It was a little past six. He'd skipped both lunch and dinner but couldn't bring himself to leave the room. He felt empty, but it wasn't because he was hungry. The hollowness was centralized in his chest. Loneliness engulfed him unlike anything he'd known before.

He hadn't felt this lost when Kyle left for the navy or when his grandfather had died. The ranch had provided abundant distractions to occupy him, and he'd thrown himself into building the business. That wasn't going to work this time.

He rarely felt sorry for himself, but in the eight hours since Hadley had taken off, he'd begun to realize the wrong turn his life had taken. The arrival of Maggie and Hadley had been the best thing that had ever happened to him. Acting as Maggie's caretaker had taught him the true meaning of the word *responsibility*. Up until now, he'd had people who did things for him. Staff, his grandfather, even the women he dated. While he didn't think of himself as selfish, he'd never had to put anyone's needs above his own.

But even as he'd patted himself on the back for championing Maggie's welfare, hadn't he ignored his brother's needs when he'd decided to seek custody of his niece? And Hadley's? How had he believed that being married to him was any sort of reward for her love and the sacrifice to her career that staying in Royal would require?

He'd played it safe, offered her an expensive ring and explained that he needed her and wanted her in his life. But he'd never once told her he was madly, passionately in love with her and that if she didn't marry him, he'd be heartbroken. Of course she'd felt underappreciated.

Liam thought about the nightmare he'd had after returning from Colorado. Sleeping alone for the first time in three nights had dragged powerful emotions from his subconscious. He could still recall the sharp pain in his chest left over by the dream, a child's hysterical panic as he'd chased his mother out of the house, pleading with her not to go.

By the time he'd awakened the next morning, there'd been nothing left of the disturbing dream but a lingering sense of uneasiness. He'd shoved the genie back into the bottle. Craving love only to have it denied him was not something he ever wanted to experience again. And so he'd only shown Hadley physical desire and made a superficial commitment without risking his heart.

She'd been right to leave him. He'd pushed her to ride again, knowing how devastated she'd been by her friend's accident. He'd badgered her to forgive herself for mistakes she'd made in the past without truly understanding how difficult that was for her. But worst of all, he'd taken her love and given nothing back.

Liam reached into his pocket and drew out the engagement ring. The diamonds winked in the dim artificial light. How many of his former girlfriends would have given it back? Probably none. But they would've been more interested in the expensive jewelry than the man who gifted it. Which explained why he'd chosen them in the first place. With women who wanted nothing more from him than pretty things and a good time, he never had to give of himself.

What an idiot he'd been. He'd stopped dating so his head would be clear when the right girl came along. And when she had, he'd thought to impress her with a trip to Vail and a big engagement ring. But Hadley was smart as well as stubborn. She was going to hold out for what really mattered: a man who loved her with all his heart and convinced her with words as well as deeds just how important she was to him.

Up until now, he hadn't been that man. And he'd lost her. But while she remained in Royal, he had a chance to show her how he truly felt. And that's exactly what he was going to do.

Thirteen

After abandoning Liam and Maggie at the hospital, Hadley took a cab home and spent the rest of the day on the couch watching a reality TV marathon. The ridiculous drama of overindulged, pampered women was a poor distraction from the guilt clawing at her for leaving Liam alone to cope with Maggie. Worry ate at her and she chided herself for not staying, but offering Liam comfort was a slippery slope. Already her emotions were far too invested.

At seven she sent Kori a text about getting a ride to Wade Ranch in the morning to pick up her car. She probably should have gone tonight, but felt too lethargic and even had a hard time getting off the couch to answer the door for the pizza delivery guy.

It took her friend an hour to respond to the text. Hadley forgot she hadn't told Kori yet about her broken engagement. Leave it to her to have the world's shortest engagement. It hadn't even lasted three days. With a resigned sigh, Hadley dialed Kori's number.

"So, what's going on that you left your car at Liam's?"

Kori's question unleashed the floodgates. Hadley began to sob. She rambled incoherently about Maggie being in the hospital and how she'd turned her back on Liam right when he needed her the most.

"I'm coming over."

"No. It's okay." Hadley blew her nose and dabbed at her eyes. "I'm fine."

"You are so not fine. Why didn't you tell me about this last night?"

"Because I wasn't ready to admit that I'd screwed up and fallen in love with the wrong man again. Honestly, why do I keep doing this to myself?"

"You didn't know he was the wrong guy until too late."

"It's because I jump in too fast. I get all caught up in his life and fall in love with the idea of being a family."

"I thought you said Liam hadn't told you that he planned to fight for custody of Maggie."

"Well…no."

"Then technically, you weren't planning on being a family with Liam and Maggie, but a couple with Liam."

"And eventually a family."

"Since eventually is in the future, I don't think that counts." Kori's voice was gentle but firm. "You love Liam. You told me you had a crush on him when you were a teenager. Isn't it possible that what you feel for him has nothing to do with seeing yourself as part of a family and everything to do with the fact that you're in love with him?"

"Sure." Did that make things better or worse? "But what about the fact that he asked me to marry him because he thought he would have a better chance to get custody if he was engaged?"

"I'm not really sure it's that straightforward," Kori said. "Liam Wade is a major catch. He's probably got dozens of women on speed dial that he's known a lot longer than you. Don't you wonder why he didn't ask one of them to marry him? I think he fell for you and is too afraid to admit it."

As tempting as it was to believe her friend's interpretation, Hadley knew it would just lead to more heartache. She couldn't spend the rest of her life wondering what if.

Kori's sigh filled Hadley's ear. "I can tell from your

silence that you don't agree. I'm sorry all this happened. You are such a wonderful person. You deserve the best guy in the world."

"And he's out there somewhere," Hadley said with what she hoped was a convincing amount of enthusiasm.

"What time do you want me to come get you tomorrow?"

"It doesn't matter." She figured Liam would stay at the hospital with Maggie until she was ready to go home, and that would give Hadley a chance to collect her things from the house without the risk of running into him.

"I'm meeting a client at eight. We can either go before or after."

"I guess I'd rather go early." The sooner she collected all her things, the sooner she could put all her mistakes behind her.

Maggie's new nanny was set to start the day after tomorrow, and Hadley doubted Dr. Davison would release her before that, so she didn't have to worry about seeing Liam ever again. The thought sent a stabbing pain through her.

"How about seven?"

"That would be perfect," Hadley said and then switched to the less emotionally charged topic of their upcoming girls' night out.

After a few more minutes, Hadley hung up. It took about ten seconds to go back to thinking about Liam. How was Maggie doing? Had her test results come back yet? Liam must be frantic waiting to hear something.

She brought up the messaging app on her phone, but stopped as she realized what she was doing. Contacting Liam would undo what little peace she'd found during the afternoon. It might be agonizing to cut ties with Liam and Maggie, but in the long run it would be better for all of them.

Yet no matter how many times she reminded herself of that fact as the evening dragged on, she wasn't able to put the baby or Liam out of her mind. Finally, she broke down and sent Liam a text around ten thirty, then shut off her phone and went to bed. But sleep eluded her. Despite having reached out to Liam, she couldn't put concern aside.

Around six, Hadley awoke. Feeling sluggish, her thoughts a jittery mess, she dragged herself out of bed and climbed into the shower. The closer it got to Kori's arrival, the more out of sorts Hadley became. Despite how unlikely it was that she'd run into Liam, she couldn't stop the anxiety that crept up her spine and sent a rush of goose bumps down her arm. By the time Hadley eased into Kori's passenger seat, she was a ball of nerves.

"You okay?" Kori asked, steering the car away from Hadley's apartment building.

"Fine. I didn't sleep very well. I couldn't stop thinking about Maggie and wondering how she's doing."

"You should call or text Liam and find out. I don't think he would have a problem with you letting him know you're worried."

"I did last night. He never got back to me." Hadley sounded as deflated as she felt. What had she expected? That Liam would fall all over himself telling her how much he missed her and that he regretted letting her go?

"Oh," Kori said, obviously stumped for an answer. "Well, then to hell with him."

That made Hadley smile. "Yeah," she agreed with fake bravado. "To hell with him."

But she didn't really mean it. She didn't even know if Liam had received her text. His focus was 100 percent fixed on Maggie, as was right. He'd answer in due time.

Twenty minutes later, Kori dropped her off at Wade Ranch. Hadley was relieved that her car was the only one in the driveway. She wouldn't have to run into Liam and make awkward conversation.

As soon as Hadley opened the front door she was assailed by the mouthwatering scent of cinnamon and sugar. She followed her nose to the kitchen and found Candace putting caramel rolls into a plastic container. Forgetting her intention had been to pack her suitcase with the few belongings she'd brought to the ranch house and get out as soon as possible, Hadley succumbed to the lure of Candace's incomparable pastries and sat down on one of the stools next to the island, fixing the housekeeper with a hopeful gaze.

"Those smell incredible."

"I thought I'd take them over to Liam at the hospital and give him a break so he could come home and clean up."

"That's really nice of you."

"But now that you're here, maybe you could take them to him instead." Candace caught Hadley's grimace and frowned. "What's wrong?"

"I don't know that Liam is going to want to see me." At Candace's puzzled expression, Hadley explained, "We broke off our engagement and I left him all alone at the hospital yesterday." *After freaking out on him*, she finished silently.

"I don't understand. Did you have a fight?"

"Not exactly. It's more that we rushed into things. I mean, we've only known each other a short time, and who gets engaged after three weeks?"

"But you two were so much in love. And it is an engagement, after all. You'll have plenty of time to get to know each other while you plan your wedding."

Hadley couldn't bring herself to explain to Candace that Liam didn't love her and only proposed so he could improve his chances of gaining custody of Maggie. "It was all just too fast," she murmured.

"But what about Maggie? I'm sure that Liam would appreciate your support with her being in the hospital."

Nothing Hadley could say would be good enough to rationalize abandoning a sick baby, so she merely hung her head and stared at the veins of silver glinting in the granite countertop. "I'll take the caramel rolls to Liam," she said at last. "And maybe some coffee as well. He's sure to be exhausted."

Candace nodded in approval. "He'll like that."

While Candace sealed up the rolls, Hadley poured coffee into a thermos, wondering how she'd let herself get talked into returning to the hospital. Then she sighed. It hadn't taken much prompting from Candace. In fact, Hadley was happy for an excuse to visit.

"If you're afraid because things between you have happened too fast," Candace began, turning away to carry the empty caramel roll pan to the sink, "I think you should know that I've never seen Liam as happy as he is with you."

"He makes me happy, as well." Had she let a past hurt blind her to everything that was true and loving about Liam?

"Whatever stands between you two can't possibly be insurmountable if you choose to work together to beat it."

What if fear of being hurt again had led to her overreacting to Liam's desire to seek custody of Maggie? Was it possible that she'd misjudged him? Attributed motives to him that didn't exist, all because she couldn't trust her own judgment?

"You're probably right."

"Then maybe you two should consider being open with each other about what it is you want and how you can achieve it."

Hadley offered Candace a wry smile. "It sounds so easy when you say it."

"Being in love isn't always easy, but in my experience, it's totally worth the ride."

"And Liam is totally worth taking that ride with," Hadley agreed. "Perhaps it's time I stopped being afraid of telling him that."

"Perhaps it is."

* * *

Liam hovered over Maggie's bassinet as the nurse took her temperature. "Her appetite was better this morning," he said.

The nurse hadn't missed his anxious tone and gave him a reassuring smile. "Her temperature is down a couple degrees. Looks like the antibiotics are doing what they're supposed to."

While it wasn't a clean bill of health, at least Maggie's situation was trending in the right direction. "That's great news." He wished he could share the update with Hadley, but she'd made it clear yesterday that she needed distance. It cut deep that he'd driven her away.

"She's sleeping now," the nurse said. "Why don't you take the opportunity to get something to eat? From what I hear, you skipped dinner last night."

"I wasn't hungry."

"Well, you're not going to do your little girl any good if you get run-down and can't take care of her once she's ready to go home." The nurse gave him a stern look.

"Sure, you're right." But he couldn't bring himself to leave Maggie alone. "I'll go down to the cafeteria in a little while."

Once the nurse left, Liam brushed a hand through his hair, suddenly aware he was practically asleep on his feet. He hadn't been able to do more than snatch a couple naps during the night and could really use a cup of coffee. It occurred to him that he wasn't going to be able to keep this pace up for long, but he would never be able to forgive himself if Maggie got worse while he was gone.

A soft female voice spoke from the doorway. "How's she doing?"

Blinking back exhaustion, Liam glanced up and spied Hadley hovering in the hallway. From her apprehensive expression, she obviously expected him to throw her out.

"A little better."

"That's great. I hope it's okay that I came by."

"Sure." After yesterday, he could barely believe she'd come back. "Of course."

"I wasn't sure…" She looked around the room as if in search of somewhere to hide. "You didn't answer my text last night."

He rubbed his face to clear some of the blurriness from his mind. "You sent a text? I didn't get it."

"Oh." She held up a rectangular container and a silver thermos. "I brought you coffee and some of Candace's caramel rolls. She was going to come herself, but I had to pick up my car and was heading back this way…" She trailed off as if unnerved by his silence. "I can just leave them and go. Or I can stay with Maggie while you go home and shower or sleep. You don't look like you got any last night."

She didn't look all that refreshed, either. Of course she'd worried. He imagined her tossing and turning in her bed, plagued by concern for Maggie. It was in her nature to care even when it wasn't in her best interest to do so.

"I'm so sorry," he told her, his voice a dry rasp. "I should never have let you leave yesterday. We should have talked."

"No." She shook her head and took two steps toward him. "I should apologize. The way I acted yesterday was unforgivable. I should never have been thinking of myself when Maggie was so sick."

Liam caught her upper arms and pulled her close. He barely noticed the container of rolls bump against his stomach as he bent his head and kissed her firmly on the lips, letting his emotions overwhelm him. The aching tightness in his chest released as she gave a little moan before yielding her lips to his demand.

He let go of her arms and stroked his palms up her shoulders and beneath her hair, cupping her head so he could feast on her mouth. Time stood still. The hospital room fell away as he showed her the emotions he'd been keeping hidden. His fear, his need, his joy. Everything she made him feel. He gave it all to her.

"Liam." She breathed his name in wonder as he nuzzled his face into her neck.

"I love you." The words came so easily to him now. Gone were his defenses, stripped away by an endless, lonely night and his elation that she'd returned. He wasn't going to let her question his devotion ever again. "No, I adore you. And will do whatever it takes for as long as it takes for you to believe you are the only woman for me."

A smile of happiness transformed her. He gazed down into her overly bright eyes and couldn't believe how close he'd come to losing her.

"I love you, too," she replied, lifting on tiptoe to kiss him lightly on the lips.

"I rushed you because I was afraid your career would take you away, and I couldn't bear to lose you." Suddenly it was easy to share his fears with her, and from the way she regarded him, she understood what he'd been going through. "This time we'll take it slow," he promised. "I'm determined that you won't feel rushed into making up your mind about spending the rest of your life with me."

She gave a light laugh. "I don't need any time. I love you and I want to marry you. Together we are going to be a family. No matter what happens with Kyle, Maggie will always be like a daughter to us and a big sister to our future children."

"In that case." He fished the ring out of his pocket and dropped to one knee. "Hadley Stratton, love of my life, would you do me the honor of becoming my wife?"

She shifted the thermos beneath her arm and held out her left hand. "Liam Wade, loving you is the most wonderful thing that has ever happened to me. I can't wait for us to get married and live happily ever after."

He slipped the ring onto her finger and got to his feet. Bending down, he kissed her reverently on the lips. One kiss turned into half a dozen and both of them were out of breath and smiling foolishly when they drew apart.

"Kissing you is always delightful," she said, handing him the coffee. "And we really must do much more of that later, but right now my mouth has been watering over these caramel rolls for the last hour."

"You're choosing food over kissing me?"

"These are Candace's caramel rolls," she reminded him, popping the top on the container and letting the sugary, cinnamon smell fill the room.

"I get your point." He nodded, his appetite returning in a flash. "Let's eat."

The morning of her wedding dawned clear and mild. The winds that had buffeted the Texas landscape for the last week had calmed, and the weather forecasters were promising nothing but pleasant temperatures for several days to come.

Today at eleven o'clock she was marrying Liam in an intimate ceremony at the Texas Cattleman's Club. Naturally Kori was her matron of honor while Liam's best man would be Mac McCallum. Because the wedding was happening so fast, Hadley had opted for a white tulle skirt and sleeveless white lace top that showed a glimpse of her midriff. Since she was marrying a man she'd reconnected with less than a month earlier, Hadley decided to kick conventional to the curb and wear something trendy rather than a traditional gown.

Kori had lent her the white silk flower and crystal headpiece she'd worn at her wedding. Her something borrowed. She wore a pair of pearl-and-diamond earrings once owned by Liam's grandmother. Her something old. For her something blue and new, Hadley purchased a pair of bright blue cowboy boots.

The shock on her mother's face validated Hadley's choice, but it was the possessive gleam in Liam's eyes as she walked down the aisle at the start of the ceremony that assured her she'd been absolutely right to break the mold and let her true self shine.

"You look gorgeous," he told her as she took the hand he held out to her.

She stepped beside him and tucked her hand into the crook of his arm. "I'm glad you think so. I thought of you when I bought everything."

He led her toward the white arch where the minister waited. A harp played in the corner, the tune something familiar to weddings, but Hadley was conscious only of the tall man at her side and the sense of peace that filled her as the minister began to speak.

Swearing to love, honor and be true to Liam until the day she died was the easiest promise she'd ever had to make. And from the sparkle in his eyes as he slid the wedding ring onto her finger, he appeared just as willing to pledge himself completely to her.

At last the minister introduced them as husband and wife, and they led their guests into the banquet room that had been set up for the reception. Draped with white lights and tulle, the room had a romantic atmosphere that stopped Hadley's breath.

Flowers of every color filled the centerpieces on the tables. Because of the limited time for the preparations, Hadley had told the florist to pull together whatever he had. She'd carried a bouquet of orange roses and pink lilies, and Liam wore a hot-pink rose on his lapel.

"I had no idea it was going to be this gorgeous," she murmured.

"The only gorgeous thing in the room is you."

Hadley lifted onto her toes and kissed him. "And that's why I love you. You always know what makes me smile."

And so ended their last intimate moment as newlyweds for the next three hours as social demands kept them occupied with their guests. At long last they collected Maggie from her circle of admirers and headed back to Wade Ranch. Together they put her to bed and stood beside the crib watching her sleep.

"I meant to give this to you earlier but didn't get the chance." Liam extended a small flat box to her.

"What is it?"

"Open it and see."

Hadley raised the lid and peered down at the engraved heart-shaped pendant in white gold. She read the inscription, "Follow your heart. Mine always leads to the barn." She laughed. "I used to have a T-shirt with that on it."

"I remember." Liam lifted the necklace from the bed of black velvet and slipped it over her head. "You were wearing it the first time I saw you."

"That was more than ten years ago." Hadley was stunned. "How could you possibly remember that?"

"You'd be surprised what I remember about you."

She threaded her fingers through his hair and pulled him down for a kiss. "It's a lovely gift, but it no longer pertains."

"I thought you'd gotten past your guilt about your friend."

"I have." She smiled up at him. "But my heart no longer leads me to the barn. It leads me to you."

He bent down and swept her off her feet. "And that, Mrs. Wade, is the way it should be."

* * * * *

COMING SOON!

We really hope you enjoyed reading this book. If you're looking for more romance, be sure to head to the shops when new books are available on

Thursday 21st February

To see which titles are coming soon, please visit

millsandboon.co.uk/nextmonth

LET'S TALK
Romance

For exclusive extracts, competitions
and special offers, find us online:

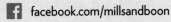 facebook.com/millsandboon

@MillsandBoon

@MillsandBoonUK

Get in touch on 01413 063232